Praise for the novels of Je

'A must read. I've never had a book I felt more like giving more than 5 stars to than this book! . . . The ending will absolutely shake you to your core!' *Stuck in Books*

'A great blend of action, drama, and romance . . . simply amazing from beginning to end.' *The Reading Geek*

'Ramps up the action, suspense, and romance without ever losing a step.' *Dreams in Tandem*

'Oh. My. God. Oh my God. Oh my God! Jennifer Armentrout just keeps getting better and better . . . I am BLOWN AWAY!' *iSoul Reviews*

'Addictive prose, lovable characters, and jaw-dropping twists.' *The Book Basement*

'All the romance anyone could ask for, plus a whole lot of action and suspenseful drama as well.' *The Revolving Bookcase*

'5/5 . . . an A-M-A-Z-I-N-G read from beginning to end.' *Stuck In YA Books*

'One of my favourite reads of the year.' *Book Passion for Life*

About the Author

New York Times #1 bestselling author Jennifer L. Armentrout lives in Martinsburg, West Virginia. Not all the rumours you've heard about her state are true. When she's not hard at work writing, she spends her time reading, working out, watching really bad zombie movies, pretending to write, and hanging out with her husband and her Jack Russell, Loki. Her dream of becoming an author started in algebra class, where she spent most of her time writing short stories . . . which explains her dismal grades in math. Jennifer writes young adult paranormal fiction, science fiction, fantasy, and contemporary romance. She also writes adult and new adult romance under the name J. Lynn. Visit her online at www.jenniferarmentrout.com.

By Jennifer L. Armentrout and available from Hodder:

The *Covenant* series

Half-Blood
Pure
Deity
Apollyon
Sentinel
Daimon (A *Covenant* novella)
Elixir (A *Covenant* novella)

The *Lux* series
Obsidian
Onyx
Opal
Origin
Opposition
Shadows (A *Lux* novella)

Standalone titles

Cursed
Don't Look Back
Unchained

JENNIFER L. ARMENTROUT

Apollyon

HODDER

First published in the United States of America in 2012
by Spencer Hill Press

First published in Great Britain in eBook in 2013
by Hodder & Stoughton
An Hachette UK company

First published in paperback in 2014
2

A CIP catalogue record for this title is available from the British Library

Paperback ISBN 978 1 444 79801 2
eBook ISBN 978 1 444 78146 5

Typeset by Hewer Text UK Ltd, Edinburgh
Printed and bound by Clays Ltd, St Ives plc

Hodder & Stoughton policy is to use papers that are natural, renewable and recyclable products and made from wood grown in sustainable forests. The logging and manufacturing processes are expected to conform to the environmental regulations of the country of origin.

Hodder & Stoughton Ltd
338 Euston Road
London NW1 3BH

www.hodder.co.uk

To my friends who keep me sane
while I'm playing in imaginary worlds.

A NOTE ABOUT ELIXIR

APOLLYON takes place after the events in ELIXIR, which tells the story from Aiden's point of view and picks up from where the nail-biting ending of DEITY left off. APOLLYON returns to Alex's point of view, and it will make sense from her perspective, but if you'd like to know what happened between DEITY and APOLLYON, ELIXIR will reveal all . . .

Pronunciation Guide for *Apollyon*

Aether: EE-ther
Agapi: ah-GAH-pee
Akasha: ah-KAH-sha
Apollyon: ah-POL-ee-on
απόλυτη ηξουψία: ah-POL-ee-tee EX-shoo-shee-ya
αήττητο: EYE-tee-toe
Chlamys: KLIM-is
Daimon: DEE-mun
Eíste pánta mou: EAST-ah PAN-da moo
Hematoi: HEM-a-toy
Iψεύς: ISH-heez
Θάρρος: THA-roesh

I

My blood itched for a fight. Muscles screamed to engage. My thoughts were covered in a heady, amber haze of power. I was the Apollyon. I wielded control over the four elements, and the fifth and the most powerful—*akasha*. I fueled the God Killer. I was his power-up—the ace up his sleeve. I was the beginning and he was the end. And together, we were *everything*.

Yet, all I could do was pace back and forth. Caged and made helpless by the markings etched in the cement above me and by bars crafted by a god.

"Alex."

Of course, I wasn't alone. Oh no. My own personal hell was a party for two. Well, it was really a threesome . . . foursome of sorts. Sounded more fun than it was. Voices . . . there were so many voices in my head.

"Do you remember?"

I tipped my head to the right, feeling the muscles stretch and the bones crack. Then I repeated the movements to the left, my fingers moving—pinky, middle, pointer . . . over and over.

"Alex, I know you can hear me."

I looked over my shoulder, my lip curling at what I saw. Boy, did I have a T-Rex-sized bone to pick with that pure-blood. Aiden St. Delphi stood on the other side of the bars. There, he was an immovable force. But without the protections from Hephaestus or Apollo between us, he would become an inconsequential nothing.

No. No. No.

My hand flew to the crystal rose of its own accord, feeling the smooth and delicate edges. *He* was everything.

Sharp pain sliced between my temples, and I snarled. Sending him a hateful look, I faced the bare cement wall. "You should have kept me on the Elixir."

"I should have never put you on the Elixir," he countered. "That wasn't the way to get to you."

I laughed coldly. "Oh, you got to me all right."

There was a pause. "I know you're still in there, Alex. Underneath that connection, you are still you. The woman I love."

I opened my mouth, but there were no words—only memories of standing by the stream and telling Aiden I loved him, and then an endless stream of thoughts and actions centering on him. Months, if not years, of them cycling over and over again until I couldn't distinguish between the past, present, and what was to become of my future.

As if sensing where my thoughts had gone, he said, "A few days ago you said you loved me."

"And a few days ago I was high as a kite and hiding in closets, thanks to you." I whirled around, just in time to see him flinch. Good. "You put me on the Elixir."

Aiden sucked in a sharp breath, but didn't look away in shame or guilt. He met and held my gaze, locked onto eyes I knew he loathed with every fiber of his being. "I did."

I took a deep, heavy breath. "I will get out of here eventually, Aiden. And I will kill you. Slowly."

"And you'll murder everyone I care for. I know. We've been here before." He leaned against the bars. There wasn't a hint of stubble on his smooth face this time around. He was in his Sentinel uniform—all black. But there were dark shadows under those striking eyes of his.

"I know you won't hurt me if you get out," he continued. "I believe in that."

"Sad."

"What is?"

"That someone as good-looking as you is so incredibly stupid." I smiled as his eyes narrowed. The moment they flashed silver, I knew I'd hit a nerve. That made me all warm and fuzzy for about three seconds, and then I realized I was still in a freaking cage. Pissing Aiden off helped pass the time, but it didn't change anything.

There were better things I could be doing.

I just needed to wait and bide my time. The low-level static was in my head. Constant. All I needed to do was tap into it, but the moment Aiden even thought I was doing that, he started talking.

Going to the mattress on the floor, I sat down and tucked my knees under my chin. I watched Aiden watch me. And I tried to keep the voice that popped up whenever he was around quiet. I didn't like or understand that voice.

Aiden ran a hand through his hair, and then pushed back from the bars. "Do you know what's happening out there, right now?"

I shrugged. Was I supposed to care? All I cared about was getting out of here and connecting with my Seth. Then, if my father was still enslaved in the Catskills, we would free him. My Seth had promised me.

"Do you remember what Poseidon did to Deity Island?"

How in the hell was I supposed to forget that? Poseidon had wiped out the Covenant there.

"Well, it's going to get worse, Alex. Half of the Olympian Twelve want to make war on Seth and Lucian," he continued. "And I'm sure he knows that. Maybe that's what *he* wants, but is that what *you* want? Do you know how many innocent lives will be lost—*have* been lost? Both mortal and half? Is that something you can live with?"

I really wasn't living right now, considering I was *in a cage.*

"Because I know deep down you couldn't live with yourself, knowing you helped cause the death of thousands, if not millions—especially those halfs. You were questioning becoming a Sentinel because of how they were being treated. If Seth goes through with this, they will die." The conviction in his voice was annoying. So was the passion that fueled the words. "Caleb—do you remember how you felt after Caleb—"

"Don't talk about him!"

His dark brows shot up. Shock splashed across his face and then he darted toward those damn bars, grasping them. "Yes, Caleb, Alex! Do you remember how you felt when he died? How you blamed yourself?"

"Shut up, Aiden."

"Do you remember being so torn up that you stayed in bed for five days? Your heart was broken when you lost him. Do you think he'd want to see you do this to yourself? His death was a wrong place at the wrong time thing, but this? There will be thousands of Calebs, but they *will* be your fault."

I pressed my head against my knees and clamped my hands over my ears. But that did nothing to stop the rising tide of emotion beating at me or the ache in my temples that was quickly turning into a sharp, stabbing pain.

And it didn't stop him. "What about your mother, Alex?"

"Shut up!" I screamed.

"This wasn't what she wanted!" The bars shook as he hit them with what I guessed were his fists. *That* had to hurt. "This is what she died to protect you from. How dare you just roll over and let him do this to—"

My entire body snapped like a rubber band pulled too tight. "Shut—"

The buzzing in my ears roared, drowning out Aiden and everything else. In an instant, *he* was there, slipping through my veins like warm, rich honey.

Listen to me. The words were in my thoughts, soothing like balmy summer air. *Listen to me, Alex. Remember what we will do together once we connect. Free the halfs—and your father.*

"Alex," Aiden snapped.

Good gods, doesn't he have anything better to do? Seth's exasperated sigh shuddered through my body. *Close him out. He doesn't matter. We do.*

My fingers tightened in my hair.

"He's in there now, isn't he?" Anger deepened Aiden's voice. The bars shook again. At the rate he was going, his knuckles were going to be mush. Just like my brain. "Don't listen to him, Alex."

Seth's laugh was like chips of ice. *Is he coming in there? Lay him out, Angel. Then make a run for it. No one will be able to stop you.*

I pulled my hair until tiny needles stabbed at my scalp.

"Alex, look at me." The desperate edge in Aiden's voice reached a part of me I wasn't entirely familiar with. My eyes opened and latched onto his. They were silvery, like moonlight. Beautiful eyes. "Together we can break the bond between you and Seth."

Tell him you don't want to break the bond.

Amazing . . . and creepy how much my Seth could see and hear when we were connected. It was like having another person living inside me.

"Alex," Aiden said. "Even if you make it to him, he'll drain you just like a daimon would. Maybe he won't mean to, but he will."

My heart tripped up. I'd been warned before—by my mother, months ago. It was one of the reasons she'd wanted to change me into a daimon. A messed-up reason full of fail logic, but still . . .

I'd never do that to you, Alex. All I want is to keep you safe, to make you happy. Freeing your father is what you want, isn't it? Together we can do that, but only together.

"I'm not going to give up," Aiden said. Blessed silence

stretched out for a few heartbeats. "Do you hear that, Seth? It's not going to ever happen."

He's annoying.

You're both annoying. Then I said out loud, "There's nothing to give up on, Aiden."

His eyes narrowed. "There is everything."

Those words struck me as odd. "Everything" was a ghost of what was and never could be. Everything had changed the moment I'd connected with my Seth. It was hard to explain. Months ago, when I'd had trouble sleeping, and the connection between us had eased my body and mind? Well, this was like that, times a hundred.

There was no *me* in this. Sort of like there'd been no Seth in this before I'd Awakened. I understood that now. How much he'd struggled being around me, fighting to not get sucked into what I had going on. Now there was just us—a single being existing in two separate bodies. One soul split apart. Solaris and the First—

Sharp pain exploded behind my eyes.

Don't. His whisper carried in my veins. *Don't think about them.*

I frowned.

And then my Seth kept chatting. So did Aiden. But he wasn't stupid enough to come into the cell. Even tired and held back by the wards on the walls, I was sure I could take him. Minutes went by, maybe hours, while the two of them slaughtered my brain cells.

When it was all over, I sagged against the mattress. One hell of a headache thumped. Aiden only left because someone—my uncle?—had opened the door from above, which usually meant something was going on. I rolled onto my side, slowly stretching out.

Finally, Seth sighed.

I unfurled my fingers. The joints ached. *He won't stay gone for long.*

We don't need for ever, Angel. We just need to figure out where you are. And then we'll be together.

A faint smile curved my lips up. If I concentrated hard enough, I could feel my Seth at the end of the buzzing cord that was always present. Sometimes he hid himself from me, but not now.

My memory pulled together his image. His golden complexion and slightly arched brows formed in my thoughts. The strong curve of his jaw demanded to be touched, and the smug grin on his full lips spread. Gods, his face was unearthly beautiful—cold and hard as the marble statues that used to line the Covenant building.

But there . . . there were no more statues on Deity Island. There was nothing. Poseidon had ripped it all apart and pulled it back into the ocean. Buildings, statues, sand, and people—all of it gone.

I lost the image of my Seth.

Unease formed in the pit of my stomach. Aiden had been right earlier—sort of. Something about that whole situation bothered me, made me feel helpless, and I wasn't helpless.

I was the Apollyon.

Go back to thinking about how good I look. I liked that.

Some things never changed. My Seth's ego was as big as ever.

But my Seth's image blossomed before me. His hair was curly around his temples and the color of spun gold. He reminded me of the paintings of Adonis. But Adonis wasn't blond. Through the knowledge of the previous Apollyons, I knew his hair had been brown.

Where are you? I asked.

Heading up north, Angel. Are you in the north?

I sighed. *I don't know where I am. There are woods around me. A creek.*

Not helpful. There was a pause, and I imagined the feel of his hand on my cheek, tracing the curve of the bone. I shivered. *I miss you, Angel. Those weeks when you were hidden from me drove me crazy.*

I didn't respond. I hadn't missed my Seth. While I'd been under the influence of the Elixir, I hadn't even known he existed.

Seth chuckled. *You do wonders for my self-esteem. You're supposed to say you missed me, too.*

Rolling onto my back, I tried to work out the kink in my leg. *What will it be like when I transfer my power to you?*

There was a pause and I started to get nervous. *It won't hurt,* his voice whispered. *It will be like when we touched before, when the runes appeared. You liked that.*

I had.

There are a few words spoken, nothing huge, and then I will take your power. I won't drain you, Alex. I'd never do that.

And I believed him, so I relaxed. *What is the plan, Seth?*

You know what the plan is.

He wanted to take out the Olympian Twelve before they found a way to take us out. Legend said we were only vulnerable to another Apollyon, but neither of us was secure in that belief. Loopholes and lesser-known myths were something all the Apollyons had sought to discover. But once the gods were out of the picture, we would rule. Or Lucian would rule. I didn't know or care. All I wanted was to be near my Seth. I was having a mad case of separation anxiety.

No. What's the plan so we can be together?

Seth's approval washed over me like I'd just stepped out into the summer sun. I basked in it, like a good little puppy with a full tummy. *Eventually, they will show a weakness. They always do. Especially St. Delphi. You are his weakness.*

I squirmed. *I am.*

And when you are presented with a chance to escape, take it. Don't hold back, Angel. You're the Apollyon. Once free, they can't stop you. Trust that. And the moment you get an idea of where you are, I'll be there.

I trusted my Seth.

There was that pleasant and heady fog again, invading me. *Have you seen Apollo or any other god recently?*

No. Not since I'd come out of the Elixir high, and that was odd. Apollo had been up my butt from the moment I'd Awakened, but I hadn't felt or seen him—or any god.

I opened my eyes and stared at the bars. Would Hephaestus need to reinforce the bars soon? Gods, I hoped so. If they weakened, then so would the wards. Then I could get out.

Seth said something that caused my toes to curl so I would pay attention to him again. *Where did you go?*

I showed him the bars and my thoughts. He was doubtful. Hephaestus' work rarely weakened, but I was hopeful . . . for a hot second. This . . . this bond wasn't the real deal. Even though my Seth was inside me, he really wasn't here. I was alone—alone in a cell.

He'll never let me out. Aiden will never let me near you. Tears burned my eyes as an endless gulf of hopelessness ripped open. *I'll never see my father.*

Yes, you will. It doesn't matter what he does. I will get to you. The gods say there can only be one of us, but they're wrong. A strange coiling, and then relaxing, filled me. *You're mine, Alex—always have been and always will be. We were created for this.*

Part of me warmed in response. And part of me, the source of the other voice whenever Aiden was around, tucked away and hidden from my Seth, recoiled as I fingered the crystal rose around my neck.

2

Sometime later—I had no idea if it was night, day, or how long I'd slept—I was alone. There was no Aiden sitting in the chair watching me. No Seth at the end of the amber cord. This was a treat.

My head was somewhat clear.

I stood and stalked toward the bars. They looked normal—silvery titanium—but it was the fine mesh circling them that was the problem.

Hephaestus' chain was a real bitch.

Taking a deep breath, I grabbed the bars and squeezed. A flash of blue light volleyed up the bars, billowing along the ceiling and over the mark like smoke full of glitter.

"Dammit," I muttered, backing away.

I tried calling on *akasha*. Nothing stirred inside of me, not even a flicker. Lifting my hand, I opted for something smaller. Well, small to me.

I called upon fire.

Aaaaaand . . . there was nothing.

When I'd Awakened, the power that had broken open and flooded my veins had been a rush—a high so great I could have licked the ceiling, a high of no equal. I got why daimons yearned for aether. I'd had just a taste of it. And I hadn't felt it since Apollo had knocked me into next week with a freaking god bolt.

Jerk.

He was also on my to-kill list.

I went to the bathroom and cleaned up. Freshly showered

and attired, I returned to testing out the bars. The shimmering blue light was sort of pretty. At least it was something to stare at.

I sighed, about ready to put my head through the wall. I searched for my Seth at the end of the cord—still gone. I could call out to him and he would respond, but I was sure he was busy trying to free me. With nothing left to do, I returned to testing sections of the bars.

What seemed like hours later, a door opened upstairs. There were voices. One of them was Aiden's, but the other . . .

"Luke?" I called out.

"Leave," was Aiden's harsh reply.

The door shut, and one heavy set of footsteps came down the stairs. I swear to the gods the sound that came out of my throat was an animalistic growl.

Aiden came into view, holding a plastic plate of eggs and bacon. One eyebrow was arched. "Do you really think I'm going to allow a half-blood near you?"

"A girl can hope." Halfs were more susceptible to compulsions, and I now packed one on steroids.

He held the plate through the space in the bars. The last time I'd done the whole not-eating thing, it hadn't worked. I'd pretty much starved and ended up on the Elixir because of it. Food was my friend this time around.

I reached for the plate.

Aiden's empty hand snaked out and wrapped around my arm. His hand was so large it swallowed my wrist. He said nothing, but his thundercloud eyes willed me to do *something*. What? Remember us together? Remember how much he'd consumed my thoughts? How I'd ached to be with him? Did he want me to remember what it was like when he'd told me about the night the daimons had attacked and massacred his family? And what it felt like being in his arms, being loved by him?

I remembered all those things in detail.

But the emotions that belonged to those events and memories weren't there. They were cut off completely. Gone with the whims of the past . . . Aiden was my past.

No. No. No. That small voice was back again. *Aiden was the future.* For some reason I thought of that damn oracle—Grandma Piperi. *Know the difference between need and love,* she had said. There was no difference. Couldn't she have tried to educate me on how to break out of these bars?

Aiden let go, his eyes as hard as these cement walls. He backed away while I took my food to the mattress. Surprisingly, he let me eat in silence.

Afterward, not so much.

Today Aiden wanted to talk about our first training session and how much I'd apparently annoyed the crap out of him because I hadn't stopped talking. When he got to the part when I'd mimicked his voice, I started to smile. He *had been* irritated and unsure of how to handle me.

Aiden's eyes flared the same moment my lips twitched. "You said I sounded like a father."

I had.

"You also said you were going to have to drop your crack habit when I went over the rules." Aiden smiled.

My lips almost answered in kind. And I didn't like that. Time to change the topic. "I don't want to talk about this."

Aiden leaned back in the metal folding chair. The thing had to be uncomfortable. "What do you want to talk about, Alex?"

"Where has Apollo been? Since he's my great-whatever, I'm feeling unloved."

He folded his arms. "Apollo won't be around."

Oh, interesting development. My little, old ears perked right up. "And why not?"

His stare was level. "And do you really think I'm going to tell you when you'll run right back to tell Seth?"

I put my bare feet on the cold floor and stood. "I won't say a word."

Aiden shot me a bland look. "Call me crazy, but I don't believe you."

Making my way to the bars, I kept an eye on his expression. As I neared, it lost the insipid look. His jaw hardened as if he worked his molars. His eyes turned sharper, lips thinning. When I touched the bars, the flare of light was weak. Somehow it knew the difference between when I was just touching it and when I was trying to escape. Clever chains.

"What are you doing?" Aiden asked.

"If you let me go now, I swear that you and all those you care for will be untouched."

He didn't say anything for a heartbeat. "But I care about you, Alex."

I tilted my head to the side. "But I will be unharmed."

"No. You won't be safe." Sadness crept into his eyes right before his thick lashes swept down.

My stomach shifted in warning. Recalling the bits of information I'd picked up while under the Elixir, I knew there was more to what he said. "What do you know, Aiden?"

"If you leave here still connected to Seth . . . you will die." The last bit came out ragged.

I laughed. "You're lying. Nothing can harm—" Myths and legends, Alex. Duh. What had I thought earlier? There were *always* checks and balances of sorts. That was why the Apollyon had been created in the first place. "What do you know?"

His lashes swept up, revealing startling silver eyes. "It doesn't matter. All you need to know is that it's the truth."

My mouth opened, but I snapped it shut. Aiden was trying to get under my skin. That was it. If Thanatos and his Order hadn't found the Achilles heel of the Apollyons in all their centuries of trying, one pure-blood wouldn't have succeeded. The Order hadn't . . .

Or had they?

But they didn't count. My Seth and his Sentinels had systematically wiped them off Earth.

I lifted my gaze and found Aiden staring at me. The inexplicable urge to stick my tongue out was hard to deny.

"Can I ask you something?"

I shrugged. "If I said no, you would still ask."

"True." There was a tight smile. "When you were with Lucian, before the Council meeting? He took you to his house against your will, didn't he?"

"Yeah," I said slowly, growing uncomfortable already.

"How did that make you feel?"

My hands tightened on the bars. "What are you? A psychologist now?"

"Just answer the question."

Closing my eyes, I leaned against the bars. I could lie, but there really wasn't a point. "I hated it. I tried to kill Lucian with a steak knife." Obviously that hadn't gone as planned. "But I didn't understand then. I do now. I have nothing to be afraid of."

Silence, and then Aiden was right in front of me, his forehead touching mine through the bars. His larger hands were above mine and when he spoke, his breath was warm. I didn't pull back, and I didn't understand why. Being this close to him wasn't right on so many levels.

"Nothing has changed," he said quietly.

"I have."

Aiden sighed. "You haven't."

I opened my eyes. "Will you ever get bored with this? You have to, eventually."

"Never," he said.

"Because you won't give up on me, no matter what I tell you?"

"Exactly."

"You're incredibly stubborn."

Aiden's lips tipped up in a half-smile. "I used to say the same thing about you."

My brows knitted. "And you can't now?"

"Sometimes I don't even know what to say." He reached through the bars and the very tips of his fingers grazed my cheekbone. A moment later, he placed his entire palm against my cheek. I flinched, but he didn't remove his hand. "And there are moments where I doubt everything I do."

He tilted my head back so my eyes met his. "But I don't doubt for one second that what I'm doing right now is the right thing."

Many retorts rose to the surface, but they faded away as the little voice inside me piped up. *I'd give it all up for you . . .*

A knot formed in the back of my throat. Suddenly, this cell was too small. The basement was constricting and the little distance between Aiden and me suffocating. Heart turning over heavily, I searched for the cord—

"Don't," Aiden whispered. "I know what you're about to do. Don't."

I jerked back, breaking the contact between us. "How do you know what I'm doing?"

His hand was outstretched, as if he could still feel my cheek. "I just do."

Anger rose, fueled by frustration and a good mix of what-the-hell. "Well, aren't you special?"

Shaking his head, Aiden lowered his hand. He watched me stomp over to the mattress and plop down. I glared back at him, willing almost every ill thing on him I could think of. And there were things I knew I could say that would hurt him, that would strip away his control and break him down into little pieces. Things that my Seth had whispered and things I'd told him I wanted to do. I could lash out—oh yeah, I could *destroy* Aiden. But when I opened my mouth, all those hurtful, destructive things got stuck around the lump in my throat.

Sitting here, I didn't feel right in my skin, as if I really wasn't a part of it. And the only time I felt comfortable was when I was connected to my Seth. Without him, I wanted to shed that skin, or rip at it until I bled.

I wanted to hit something. Hard.

Drawing in a shallow breath, I focused on the mark on the ceiling. There were two moons drawn, interlocking. Since so many gods were tied to the moon, I didn't know what it represented or how it had the power to strip me of mine.

"What is that?" I asked, pointing at the ceiling.

Part of me didn't expect Aiden to answer, but he did. "It's Phoebe's symbol."

"Phoebe? Obviously you don't mean a *Charmed* one."

He snorted.

Whoa, they'd brought out the big guns. I felt all kinds of special as I squinted at the markings. They held an odd bluish-red tint to them. "So, a Titan . . ."

"Yes."

"And that's a Titan's blood, isn't it?" I tilted my head toward Aiden. "Care to explain how it's possible that a Titan's blood is on this ceiling? Do the Olympians just keep jars of it around?"

Aiden let out a dry laugh. "When the Olympians overthrew the Titans, most were imprisoned in Tartarus. Phoebe wasn't one of them. And she has a fondness for her children."

Racking my brain for who she'd popped out, I came up empty. "Who?"

"Leto," he answered. "Who in turn gave birth to Apollo and Artemis."

I groaned. "Of course. Why not? So Apollo asked his grandma for some blood? Great. But I don't get how it works." I gestured around me. "How is it negating my powers?"

"Titan blood is very powerful. You know that blades dipped in Titan blood can kill an Apollyon." When I sent him a *duh* look, his smile was tight. "Mix that with blood of your own lineage, well, it has the ability to keep you from hurting yourself."

"Or from hurting you," I snapped.

Aiden shrugged.

Anger pumped through my blood like poison; with no way to expel it, I was seriously seconds away from going stir crazy. I stretched my legs, then my arms. In my head, I pictured myself running up and kicking Aiden in the shin.

There was a sigh from the other side of the bars.

Sometimes I wondered if he had the ability to read minds.

"I hate this," Aiden admitted so quietly I wasn't sure I'd heard him. He twisted around, giving me his back. "I *hate* that Seth has done nothing but play you—lie to you—and you trust him. I hate that this connection is more important than everything else going on out there."

I was about to argue, but my Seth *had* lied to me. He'd probably been playing me right from the moment he'd discovered I was the second Apollyon. No doubt Lucian had.

Unease slithered up my spine, leaving cold shivers in its wake. "It . . . it doesn't matter now," I said.

Aiden whirled toward me. "What doesn't?"

I met his stare. "That Seth lied to me. It doesn't matter. Because what he wants, I want. If I—"

"Shut up," Aiden growled.

Surprised, I blinked. I couldn't recall a moment when Aiden had told me to *shut up*. Wow. I so didn't like that for a multitude of reasons.

Aiden's eyes glowed a fierce silver. "*You* do not want what Seth wants because there is *no you* in any of that. There is only him."

Shock rippled through me, stealing any response I could come up with. There was no me. There was only us. That freaking little voice deep inside me roared in fury, then threw itself around.

There was no *me*.

3

When my Seth decided to show up on the other side of the rainbow, I was grumpy and he was . . .well, he was wound up. There were, uh, *things* he said through the connection that just weren't right.

Distracting? Yes.

Acceptable in the mood I was in? No.

I want out of here, I told him, mentally shaking him off. *I can't take it any longer. Aiden . . . he . . .*

Seth's disapproval was like razor blades knocking around in my skull. *Aiden what?*

What could I tell my Seth? That Aiden was making me think? *Aiden talks a lot.*

His laugh tickled the back of my neck. *That he does. Angel, it won't be much longer. Lucian has done us a great favor.*

With who? White Robe of the Month Club?

Another pleasant laugh curled through me. *Let's just say he's given me an endless supply of bait and leverage.*

I gave him a mental eye roll. *Yeah, I don't get it.*

There was a pause, and I could feel what Seth was wanting through the bond. He was in a playful mood, but this conversation was too important for screwing around. Finally, he answered. *The pures that have stood against us have proven to be useful.*

How so?

Do you remember how Telly refused to accept that the daimons could play nice and work together to form a cohesive attack against the Covenants?

Yeah . . . and Marcus didn't believe it was just them working against us.

And neither had I. At the emergency Council meeting Lucian had called before my Seth had leveled the Council members, I'd suspected that Lucian had been behind the daimon attacks somehow, but there hadn't been any real proof. Besides, my hatred for Lucian probably had led to that idea.

Well, Telly was obviously half-right. Without the right motivation—say, an endless supply of aether—they are likely to settle for whatever pure they can get their hands on.

There was another gap, and the intensity of what he was feeling, what he wanted, roared through the connection. For a moment, I really believed I could feel him, and the emotion swamped me, draining my thoughts and filling me with the bliss of the connection.

Alex. His voice was chiding, self-satisfied. *Are you paying attention?*

Yes. Daimon . . . aether . . . stuff . . .

Good. Let me ask you a question, Angel. Do you really think daimons orchestrated those attacks all by their little selves?

Some of the lovely fog my Seth was creating faded as if icy wind had blown down the nape of my neck. *What? What do you mean?*

Even reasonable daimons couldn't pull off what they did in the Catskills. They had to have help, don't you think?

I couldn't think as my pulse kicked up. So I'd been right? A sour taste filled the back of my throat.

Don't be upset, Angel. Lucian needed discord for all of this to happen.

Thinking back to the attack in the Catskills, I tried to remember where Lucian had been in the chaos. I'd assumed that he'd been in the ballroom with the rest of the pures, but I hadn't seen him. All I knew was that my Seth had contacted him . . .

All those dead half-blood servants, the Guards, and Sentinels . . . all innocent . . .

I jerked up, almost losing the connection with my Seth.

Angel, how do you think the daimons got into the Catskills in the first place? You saw the security there. And the ballroom? There were only two entrances, and both were guarded. One of the doors belonged to Lucian's guard.

Suspecting that Lucian had been behind these attacks was one thing—I didn't put anything past that man—but my Seth? He couldn't be okay with that. Believing he was a part of all those innocent people dying was accepting something horrific. What my Seth wanted, I wanted, but the daimons . . . they were and always would be the enemy.

Foes can be allies in war, Angel.

Oh, my gods. A huge, freaking, crater-sized part of me couldn't process what my Seth was saying. I fought the pull of his emotions, resurfacing as if I were drowning, then gulping in air.

There were so many innocent people, I reasoned. Appalling images of the slaughter came one after another—the servants in the hall with their throats ripped open, the Sentinels and Guards who'd been eviscerated and then thrown through windows.

They don't matter, Angel. Only we matter, only what we want matters.

But those people *did* matter. *We could've been killed, Seth. My father could've been killed.*

But he wasn't, and I would never let anything happen to you. Nothing did.

We'd been separated during the attack. And if I'd remembered correctly, I'd come very close to being trampled to death. Not to mention I'd had to fight the furies alone. Not sure how he'd exactly prevented my death in all of that.

Angel, we need this to happen. The daimons will help me get to you. Don't you want that? For us to be together?

Yes, but—

Then trust me. We want the same things, Angel.

Aiden's words came back to me and I squirmed in my own skin. *Seth? You . . . you aren't making me want anything, right? You're not influencing me?*

He didn't respond immediately, which caused my heart to trip over itself. *I could, Angel, if I wanted to. You know that, but I'm not. We just want the same things.*

I bit my lip. We did want the same things, except the thing with the daimons . . . I stopped those thoughts. As if two strong arms were pushing down on my shoulders, I was on my back. And then I was drowning in what Seth was feeling again.

Aiden returned with food, and he brought company with him this time—my Uncle Marcus. The man was actually being sort of decent toward me now. Ironic. I ate and drank my water like a good captive.

And I didn't even yell anything insulting.

I figured I deserved a reward, like time out of the cell or something, but that was asking too much. Instead, Marcus left to go see what the others were up to. As soon as the door closed upstairs, Aiden sat with his back pressed against the bars.

Brave, brave man . . . or really stupid—it was a total toss-up. I could easily fashion the bed sheet into a noose and slip it around his neck before he'd have a chance to react.

But I sat down, my back almost against his. The flare of blue from the chains appeared weaker. Silence stretched out, oddly comforting. Minutes passed and the taut muscles in my back relaxed. Before I knew it, I was leaning against the bars . . . and Aiden's back.

My earlier conversation with my Seth had left a weird taste in my throat and a ball of knots in my stomach. Maybe that's why I wasn't indulging in my murderous intentions with the bed sheet and Aiden's neck? Missed opportunity, I supposed.

Lowering my chin, I sighed. What my Seth wanted, I wanted, but . . . daimons? I rubbed my hands on my bent knees and sighed again—louder, like a petulant child.

Aiden's back twisted as he turned his head. "What, Alex?"

"Nothing," I mumbled.

"There's something." He leaned back, tipping his head against the bars. "You have that tone."

I frowned at the wall. "What tone?"

"The 'I have something I want to say but shouldn't' tone." A little bit of humor seeped into his voice. "I'm well familiar with it."

Well . . . damn. My gaze dropped to my hands. The fingers were okay, I guess. But my nails were chipped and short. Hands of a Sentinel—a Sentinel who killed daimons. I pushed up the sleeve of my sweater. Pale-white bite marks covered my right arm. The crescent-shaped marks were a pain to hide and they were on both arms, as well as my neck. They were so ugly, a vile reminder of being trapped by them.

And no matter how hard I tried, I couldn't wipe the faces of all those slaughtered halfs in the Catskills out of my head . . .or forget the look on Caleb's face when he'd seen the blade embedded in his chest—a blade that had been wielded by a daimon.

Caleb would be so . . . *disappointed* didn't even sum it up, if I didn't say anything.

But my Seth would be pissed. He'd go snooping in my memories, and I wanted him to be happy with me. I wanted—

I didn't want to *work* with daimons. That was a slap in the face to all those who'd died at their hands—my mom, Caleb, those innocent servants—and my scars.

My Seth . . . he'd just have to understand that. He would, because he loved me.

Mind made up, I took a deep breath. "Just so you know, I'm not telling you this because of anything to do with you. Okay?"

He laughed darkly. "I would never think such a crazy thing."

I made a face. "I'm only telling you this because I don't think it's right. It goes against something . . . inherent in me. I have to say something."

"What, Alex?"

Closing my eyes, I drew in a deep breath. "Do you remember how Marcus thought there was more to the daimon attacks, especially the one in the Catskills?"

"Yes."

"I sort of thought it was Lucian, especially at his Council meeting. It made sense. Creating chaos and whatever makes it easier for people to overthrow and take control." I ran a finger over the tag on the fleshy part of my elbow. "Anyway, the daimon attacks have apparently been orchestrated by Lucian and . . . Seth."

Aiden's spine went stiff against mine. No response. He was quiet for so long I scooted around. "Aiden?"

"How many?" His voice was gruff.

"All of them, I think," I said, guilt chewing at my insides. I was betraying my Seth, but I couldn't stay quiet. "They've found a way to control the daimons."

His head lowered and his large shoulders rolled. "How?"

Climbing onto my knees, I grasped the bars and ignored the weak pulse of blue light. "They . . . they are using pures as motivation. The ones who are against them—us, I mean us."

Aiden twisted so fast, I let go of the bars and jerked back. His eyes burned silver. "Do you know where they're keeping these pures?"

I shook my head.

His lashes dipped. "Do you know why they would do something like this?"

The disgust in his voice was understandable. I rubbed my palms over my thighs. Why *were* they doing this? To create discord was obvious. With daimons attacking left and right, the Council had been distracted. The gods had developed doubts about the pures' ability to control the daimon hordes and had sent furies as a result. And now, it would serve as a distraction for me to escape. How they'd work that one out I didn't know. And if the fading blue light was any indication, it wouldn't be necessary.

"No. I don't know."

His eyes met mine and our gazes locked. "Why did you tell me this? I'm sure Seth won't appreciate it."

I looked away. "I told you. It's not right. Those pures . . ."

"Are innocent?"

"Yeah, and Caleb . . . he was killed by a daimon. My mom was turned by one." My breath shuttled through me and I stood. "I want what Seth wants, but I cannot get behind that. He'll understand."

Aiden tipped his head back. "Will he? You know I will forward this information on. It will hinder his plans."

I wrapped my arms around my waist. "He'll understand."

Sadness flowed into his expression and his eyes turned down. "Thank you."

For some reason, anger bubbled up and I wanted to lash out. "I don't want your thanks. It's the last thing I want."

"You have it." He stood in one fluid motion. "And you have my thanks for more than you realize."

Confused, I stared back at him. "I don't understand."

Aiden's smile was tight, tinged with that ever-present sadness whenever he looked at me, as if I was this unfortunate creature who provoked sorrow wherever I went. Behind that sadness though, there was steely determination.

"What?" I said, when he didn't answer.

"You've given me the hope I need."

My Seth wasn't mad that I'd blabbed. I hadn't even tried to hide it from him. As soon as we connected, I told him what I'd done. If anything, he seemed to have expected it. And *that* I didn't understand, but either way, he didn't want to talk about it.

Telling me about his childhood, he was a different Seth—a side of him I'd rarely seen. When he started to talk about his mom, vulnerability seeped through the bond, as if speaking about his mother unnerved him.

What was her name? I asked.

Callista.

Pretty.

She was very beautiful. Tall and blond, regal like a goddess. His words drifted off for a moment. Considering the past tense reference, I assumed she'd died. *But she wasn't kind, Angel. She was cold and unapproachable, and most of all, when she looked upon me, there was always hate in her eyes.*

I flinched as my suspicions were confirmed, and I wanted to make him feel better. *I'm sure she didn't hate you. She—*

She hated me. His sharp reply was like being doused with ice water. *I was a constant reminder of her shame. She'd gotten a taste of the forbidden fruit, and then regretted it.* Halfs and pures were forbidden to mingle. Only recently had I discovered this was because the offspring of a male half and female pure made the Apollyon.

When he spoke again, his voice was soft like a down blanket. *She was nothing like your mother, Angel. There was no great love affair. She used to tell me the only reason why she'd kept me was because a god had visited her after my birth. The most beautiful man she'd ever seen, or so she said. That god told her that she must protect me at all costs, that I would become a great power one day.*

As he talked, I recalled the glimpses of Seth's past that I'd seen when I'd Awakened. Of Seth as a small child, all golden skin and blond curls, playing by a creek or hunched over a toy in a large room stuffed with uncomfortable looking furniture. He was always alone. Nights when he'd awoken crying from a bad dream and no one would come to comfort him. Days when the only person he saw was a nanny who was just as uncaring as his mother. He'd never met his father. To this day, he didn't even know his name.

My heart wept for him.

Then at age eight, he was brought before the Council to determine if he would enter the Covenant. His experience was nothing like mine. There was no poking or pinching. He didn't kick a Minister. They had taken one look at him and seemed to know what he would become.

It was the eyes.

The tawny, amber eyes that held wisdom that belonged to no child—eyes of an Apollyon.

Things got better for him once he was sent to the Covenant in England, and then to the one in Nashville. So odd that we'd been so close to one another for so many years and had never crossed paths.

But something was off. When I'd Awakened, I'd learned all of what the previous Apollyons had discovered during their lifetimes, like being plugged into a computer and booting up. And none of them had been born with the eyes of the Apollyon. All of their eyes had become golden *after* they'd Awakened.

My Seth had been different.

But right now, that raw hurting in his chest was eating at him. *Where were you born?* I asked, hoping to take the topic away from his mother. *You've never told me.*

He laughed and I smiled. Happy Seth was a better Seth. *You won't believe this, but you know how Fate loves to mess with people?*

Boy, did I ever know that.

I was born on the island of Andros.

A shiver danced down my spine. *How . . . ironic.* No large leap of faith to consider that my ancestors had also hailed from that island, since many took the name of where they were born. Or, in some cases, the islands were named after the founding families.

Either way, that was ironic. And something gag-worthy surfaced. Andros was a whopping 147 square miles. *You don't think we're related?*

What? Seth burst into laughter. *No.*

How can you be so sure? Because if we're pulling a Luke and Leia, I'm going to barf.

My family isn't linked to yours in any way. Besides, your lineage is to Apollo.

And who is yours? There was no answer, only a wealth of arrogant silence. *Why do you keep that from me?*

Seth sighed. *I will tell you when we're together. I'll show you everything, Angel. And all the questions you have, you'll have your answers.*

4

After lunch was served the following day, I roamed my cell alone. Something was going on upstairs—doors opening and slamming shut, pounding feet, and happy shouts.

Curious, I went to the bars and strained to hear more. The conversation was too muffled to make head or tail of who it was, but someone had arrived. And it wasn't a god. I would know it if it were. Their essence was strong, something I could feel *inside* me.

Touching the bars, I measured the response. The blue shimmer *was* fading. Take that, Seth. Did that mean the mark above would also fade without a booster? Good gods, I hoped so. I searched for the cord, wanting to tell him about the new development. Seth was there but not talkative. He was with Lucian, at least that much I got. Whatever was being discussed was muted to me.

Immediate dislike rose in response to Lucian's presence. I'd obviously have to get over it, but it was going to be difficult. I would never be a fan of my stepfather.

Unhooking from the connection, I wondered what Aiden was doing. He usually spent a great part of his day sitting in that folding chair, brooding at me.

You've given me the hope I need.

Hope for what? A "happily ever after" for us?

I found myself in the tiny white bathroom, staring into the sucky plastic mirror above the sink. The thing was practically cemented into the wall, lightweight plastic so I couldn't fashion it into some kind of weapon.

Leaning against the sink, I all but plastered my face against the mirror. My reflection was wavy, distorted by the cheap quality, but it was my eyes I was staring at.

They were amber, just like all the other Apollyons after they'd Awakened. It was kind of strange seeing my eyes like that, but it also felt right. Like I'd come into something I was destined to become. Which, duh, I had.

I cocked my head to the side. What would my Seth think when he finally saw me—really saw me—all Apollyoned-out? He would be pleased, so unlike Aiden, who hated my eyes . . .

A sudden sharp feeling speared my chest. *Holy crap* . . . I was lightheaded as I gripped the sink. This wasn't a physical pain, more like the kind when the world drops out from underneath my feet. Or when there's really, sucktastic bad news.

It was the sensation of a heart being annihilated with no possibility of repair.

The breath I sucked in was shrill. The feeling didn't make sense. My heart wasn't broken. It was whole and it belonged to my Seth. And he loved me in return. He'd never told me that he did, but he had to. We were destined for each other, and once together, we would be perfect. We would rule over both Olympus *and* the mortal world.

"We will be gods," I whispered.

"Oh, Alex, even I'm amazed by how inflated your ego has become. Gods, if I was fully corporeal, I'd so kick your ass right now."

I whirled around, fully expecting to find Caleb standing in the bathroom, because that was *his* voice. But no one was there. Heart racing, I peeked into the cell. Empty.

"Caleb?"

No response.

I inched into the cell, willing Caleb to appear if he was really here. Silence stretched out, and just when I was about to admit that I might've lost my damn mind, warmth passed through me.

Did Caleb just . . . walk *through* me?

"Uh . . ."

There was a light chuckle from behind me. Whipping around, I just . . . I could only stare.

Caleb stood there, dark blond brows arched in such a painfully familiar way. He was wearing a tunic-style shirt and white, linen pants. It was Caleb, but . . . not.

I could totally see the bars through him. Freaky. "Caleb?"

He glanced down at himself. "Yeah, it's me, in shade form for your viewing pleasure."

"Are you really here, or have I lost my mind?"

A slow, easy grin pulled at pale lips. "I'm here. Well, as here as I can be."

I drew in a breath, but it got stuck. "Can I touch you?" My legs were moving me forward in jerky motions. No graceful Apollyon here. "Can I hug you?"

His brows lowered. "No, Alex, you can't. You'd go right through me." He grinned. "Though you seemed to enjoy it the first time around."

I laughed, stopping short of touching. "Gods, I want to hug you so badly."

"I know." His grin faded. "But we don't have a lot of time."

We never did. I rocked back on my heels, smiling. "You're here to break me out, aren't you?"

"Ah, no, I'm not here to break you out."

My smile slipped off my face. "Why? I don't understand. I need to get out of here. My Seth needs—"

"I'm here as a last-ditch effort, Alex." He reached out as if to touch me, but stopped. "Apollo sent me."

I folded my arms and scowled. "What does he have to do with this?"

"He hopes that I can reach you, Alex."

"Do you know he hit me with a god bolt?"

Caleb winced. "Yeah, I heard. Everyone in the Underworld

sort of heard, but Alex, you kind of had it coming." When I opened my mouth, he silenced me. "Apollo would be here if he could."

"And why can't he?" I turned away, trying to push down my anger, which was like screwing a lid on a box—it wasn't working. "He's afraid of me, isn't he? He should be. Apollo is totally on my shit list."

"Do you hear yourself? A god afraid of *you*?" He sounded dumbfounded. "Apollo's not here because Aiden, the love of your life, banned him from here."

I spun around, eyes narrowing. "He's not the love of my life."

Caleb shook his head. "He has always been yours, Alex. And you've always been his."

My mouth puckered as if I had tasted something sour. "Is this why you came from the great beyond? To talk about my love life?"

"Well, the love of your life banned Apollo from entering this house because Aiden's afraid Apollo will harm you." Oh, yeah, Caleb got an eyeful of my shock. "And Apollo had one of his nymphs come down to the Underworld, pulled me right out from underneath Hades' nose to help you. Both of them—Aiden and Apollo—are doing crazy things to save you."

"But . . . I don't need anyone to save me."

"Exactly!" Caleb threw his arms up in the air. "That's what I said!"

Okay, I wasn't following this conversation. "Then why aren't you helping me escape? You could go shade yourself right up to wherever the keys are. I'm sure Aiden has them."

He rolled his eyes and they disappeared for an instant. Yikes. "You can save yourself. Only you, and you need to get a-crackin' on it."

My lips pressed together. Here Caleb was, my best friend—my *dead* best friend, but whatever—I hadn't seen in what felt like for ever, and we were arguing. I didn't want to argue with him.

"What are you doing, Alex? This isn't you. None of this is what you ever wanted."

I took a deep breath. "It's what I want now."

Caleb growled low in his throat. He looked like he wanted to strangle me. "What you're doing is going to get you and Seth killed. Yeah, that's right—you aren't invincible. Neither of you are! And there's a war brewing in Olympus and it's going to rain all kinds of holy hell down on Earth. Do you want to be responsible for that?"

Squeezing my hands into fists, I glared up at him. "We want to change things, Caleb! You of all people have to understand that! Together, Seth and I can free the servants—my father! We can overthrow the Council. We can—"

He barked a mad sort of laugh. One that usually meant he was close to pushing me into a corner. "Do you really think that's what's going to happen once you succeed in wiping out all the Councils? That Lucian is going to free the halfs and everyone is going to love one another?"

I opened my mouth, but he kept going. "And let's pretend that's not absurd and we'll all be high on happy pills. The gods are never going to allow it. They will risk exposing themselves to the whole mortal world to stop you. Innocent people will die. *You* will die."

My heart tripped up a little. "So I should do nothing?"

"No. Don't you know? The supreme art of war is to subdue the enemy without fighting."

"And whoever came up with that was a complete and utter idiot. To win the war, the enemy must be stripped down to their bare bones and destroyed."

His eyes narrowed. "You're an idiot."

My lips twitched. "Shut up."

Caleb drifted over to me. "Alex, you have to break the bond with Seth. Break it and you will understand everything."

"No." I backed up, running my hands along my hips. "You told me to not give up on Seth. And now you want me to?"

"I don't want you to give up on him," he said, voice taking on a pleading edge. "There's still hope for him, but only if you can truly reach him. And being the head of Seth's fan club isn't going to do it."

I laughed then. "That was so you when you were . . . you know, around. You totally had a boy crush on him."

"And I still do. He's pretty awesome, but right now he's high on power. Like a meth-head. No. Better yet. A crackhead and a meth-head rolled into one. He's out of control. Good gods, he's working with daimons! And if you get out of here and connect with him—transfer your power to him? It's all over, Alex. He will drain you dry without even meaning to."

I gasped. "He would never do that."

"He wouldn't mean to, Alex. But he would. And once he has, he'll become the God Killer and no one needs you." He shook his head sadly. "That's if you even make it to him. Apollo will stop you. *Every* god will come down here to stop you."

Shaking my head, I refused to believe this. My Seth would never drain me. He needed me, like I needed him. And together, we would be unstoppable. We could change things. As the Apollyon, I wouldn't lose people like I'd lost Caleb and my mom.

I shook my head.

"Alex," he pleaded softly.

"No. No! Because I'm powerful enough now that no one I love will ever die again!"

"Alex—"

Stupid, weak tears burned my eyes. "If I had been the Apollyon when we were attacked, I could've saved you!"

His form flickered. "No, Alex, you couldn't have."

"Don't say that. Don't *ever* say that." My chest was too tight. He faded a little. "What's happening?"

"I have to go." Caleb looked stricken. "Break the connection, Alex. It's the only way to save you both."

I shook my head so fast my hair slapped my cheeks. Before I could utter a word, he flickered out and was gone. I stood there for minutes, maybe hours, staring at the spot where he'd stood, fighting tears and everything he'd said. I didn't—couldn't believe what he'd said.

Caleb didn't get it. He'd never lost people like I had—people like him. While he was in the Underworld playing *Mario Go Kart*, I was up here, knee-deep in the pain and anguish of losing him and my mom. I was dealing with the fact that my father was a damn servant.

He didn't get it!

Being connected with my Seth was the only way to save us. By the time my Seth and I were done, there would be no more pain.

5

I had the distinct impression that Caleb had failed somehow after he'd left, and I hoped he wasn't going to get punished. I didn't think Apollo would do anything to him, but then again, what did I know?

Caleb's visit left me tattered. Keyed up and with no way to expel the nervous energy, I paced the cell. Part of me wanted to rage and scream. A whole other side of me wanted to sit down and cry like a little baby. Seeing Caleb was like a gift, but all we'd done was argue. It left a stone in my stomach that just kept pulling me down, down.

When Aiden appeared with a bag of takeout food, I almost threw it back at him, but I was starving. And I . . . had the strangest urge to tell him about Caleb.

"Who's here?" I asked between mouthfuls of mystery meat and soggy buns.

He didn't answer.

I rolled my eyes, finishing off the burger. Rummaging around in the bag, I pulled out an extra-large order of fries. With all the exercise I was getting, my escape would involve me rolling out of here. "I know someone has shown up."

A handful of fries went into my mouth, and then another. Salt and grease coated my fingertips. Yum. "Are you not going to talk? Just sit there and stare at me like a creeper?"

Aiden cracked a half smile. "You called me that once before."

"Yeah, because you *are* a creeper." I frowned at my almost-empty carton. There were never enough fries.

"Actually, I'd been watching to make sure you didn't sneak off the island."

I remembered. It had been the night of Zarak's house party, back when things had at least seemed simpler. Zarak . . . I wondered what had happened to Zarak. I didn't think he'd been on the island when Poseidon had pitched a fit, but I didn't know.

Finished with the fries, I licked the salt off my finger as I lifted my gaze.

Aiden's eyes flared silver, and something warm unfurled in my stomach. I put my other finger to my lips—

Holy baby daimons everywhere, what the hell was I doing? I grabbed a napkin, wiping furiously at my fingers. Across from me, heat roared off Aiden.

By the time I finally looked at Aiden again, he was all kinds of coolness—the master of impassivity. He even arched his brow at me. Good for him. Whatever. He'd totally checkmated me, but now I knew who was upstairs—Laadan and Olivia. I remembered then that while I'd been on the Elixir, Deacon had told Aiden they were coming. Then I'd hid in the closet because Aiden had raised his voice.

I'd actually hid in *a closet.*

"You look happy," Aiden commented as he unwrapped a chicken sandwich.

Man, who scraped the mayo off and only ate a sandwich on one bun? Aiden. That's who. "Oh, I was just reminiscing about learning how to play chess and hiding in closets."

He'd only taken two bites, but tossed the remainder in his bag. A muscle worked in his jaw. "Alex, I hated seeing you like that. As much as I hate seeing you like this. So if you want me to feel guilty, I do. If you want me to hate myself for making that decision, I do."

I should've been doing a celebratory dance or something, because I'd gotten a nice little jab in there, but my shoulders sagged. Words were on the tip of my tongue, words I shouldn't say. So I said nothing. We spent the rest of whatever time of day it was in silence. When he left, I didn't reach out to Seth. Between Caleb's surprise visit and the thing with Aiden, I was too out of it.

Sometime later, maybe a couple of hours, I heard the door open and shut quickly—way too quickly and quietly to be Aiden, who always came down the stairs like a warrior preparing for battle.

I popped up from the mattress, holding my breath.

Two slender, denim-clad legs came into view, and then a billowy white shirt tucked into the front of the jeans. The knee-high boots gave my visitor away. They were *great* boots.

Olivia.

Opportunity had just come a-knocking.

She came to a halt at the bottom of the stairs, her tight curls pulled back from her face. Olivia's caramel-colored complexion was beautiful, even when it was pale. She looked like she was staring down a horde of daimons right now.

"Alex," she whispered, swallowing.

Slowly, so I wouldn't send her scurrying back up the steps, I approached the bars. I knew the moment she got a good look at my eyes, because she backed up, hitting the bottom step.

"Don't go," I said, gripping the bars. Pale blue light flickered. "Please don't go."

Her throat worked again and she glanced behind her quickly before her gaze swung back to me. "Dear gods, it's true. Your eyes . . ."

I smiled wryly. "They take a little getting used to."

"No doubt." She took a deep breath and stepped closer. "Aiden . . . he's going to kill me if he finds out I'm down here, but I just had to see you for myself. He . . . they're saying you have to stay down here—that you're dangerous."

For once, someone else's impulsivity was a benefit to me. "I'm not dangerous."

"They've said you've threatened to make a crown out of Deacon's ribcage."

Aw, hell . . . "I haven't done anything."

She looked doubtful.

"Okay. You know me. I say mean things when I'm mad."

Her lips twitched. "Yeah, you do. Alex . . ." Her gaze flickered over the bars. "Damn . . ."

I had to proceed with caution, but I had to do it quickly. Who knew how much time we had before Aiden realized Olivia was down here and ruined all my fun? Using a compulsion would be easy and the quickest way to deal with this, but . . . but a part of me, that stupid, *stupid* part of me, wanted to talk to her . . . my friend.

And there was something I hadn't gotten a chance to tell her, something important.

Olivia inched closer to the cell. "You look . . . you look terrible."

I frowned. "I do?"

"Have you been sleeping?" Her gaze drifted over me. "You've lost weight."

Sort of relieved to hear I hadn't packed on the pounds, I shrugged. "You look great."

She touched her cheek. "I don't feel great. You have no idea what's going on out there. Everyone is freaked out, because of . . ."

"Because of us."

"Us?"

"Seth and me." I leaned my head against the bars. "You went to New York, right?"

Olivia shook her head. "We started to, but it's real bad there. They're not letting anyone in. The place is on lockdown, but there's a lot of fighting inside, I hear."

The Elixir had stopped working there, courtesy of Lucian, and my father . . . my father was there.

"The gods, they have these *things* surrounding the Covenants." She shuddered and wrapped her arms around her slender waist.

My interest was piqued. "What things?"

"I don't know. They're like half-bull, half-man—but machines. We ran into them when we were heading to New York. My mother continued on, but she didn't want me there. She sent me here with Laadan."

A foggy memory resurfaced, one of Apollo and Aiden talking about those creatures. I wondered if my Seth knew about them. Probably. I let go of the bars and tucked my tangled hair back. The ends curled halfway down my chest and probably were in need of a cut. Around Olivia, I couldn't help but compare myself.

"Alex, things are going to get worse. You—"

"I saw Caleb."

Her mouth dropped open, and whatever sales pitch she had was forgotten. "What?"

"I've seen Caleb twice since he . . . passed." I needed to get this out, and then I'd do what I had to. My Seth would call this need a weakness and it was, because I was wasting precious time, but Olivia needed to know. I'd promised Caleb I'd tell her, and after I escaped I had no idea if I would see her again. "The Order attacked me while I was still at the Covenant. One of their members killed me. I went to the Underworld—"

"You *died*?"

I winced at the shrill pitch. "Yeah, I was dead, and then I wasn't. Long story. But I saw Caleb."

A hand fluttered to her chest. "Are you messing with me, because I swear to the gods, Alex, I *will* hurt you."

Cute, considering she couldn't touch me, but I grinned. "Caleb's okay. He's really okay. He spends most of his time playing Wii, and he looked great. Nothing like . . ." The back of my throat burned. "He's really good."

Her eyes glistened in the dim light. "You really saw him?"

I nodded. "He wanted me to tell you something. I didn't get a chance, with everything that's going on."

"Understandable." She choked out a laugh. "What . . . what did he tell you?"

Olivia had always had manicured hands, but the nail polish was chipped and old. I kept my eyes on them. "I don't know what this means, but he said to tell you that he would've picked Los Angeles."

There was a sharp inhale, and the silence stretched out so long I eventually had to look, and when I did, I almost wished I hadn't.

Tears streaked down Olivia's cheeks, running over the fingers now pressed to her lips. An answering emotion rose in my throat and I bit down on my lip. Los Angeles must've meant something really important. I wished I were on the other side of these bars, not to escape, but to hug her. But I needed to be on the other side of these bars, and I needed to escape. There was no more time.

"Olivia," I said, and my voice was different, even to my own ears—softer, lyrical. Power hummed.

She stiffened, and then her hands left her mouth as her eyes locked onto mine. Tears clung to her thick lashes, but they weren't what made her eyes glossy now. It was the compulsion in my voice, an ability that had become innate upon Awakening. Part of me abhorred what I was doing. Olivia was my friend. Using a compulsion on her was wrong, but there was no other way. I had to get to my Seth. She would understand eventually.

"Do you know where the keys are, Olivia?"

She nodded slowly.

"Good. That's really good." I reached through the bars, motioning her toward me. When she placed her cool hand in mine, I squeezed gently. "Where are they?"

"With Aiden." Her words were slow.

Dammit. That wasn't good. "And where is Aiden?"

"He's with your uncle and Laadan." A soft sigh leaked from her lips.

Crap. There was no way she could get the keys. My gaze slipped to the cage door and an idea took hold. Letting go of her hand, I gripped the bars and watched the flare of light. It was weak and didn't reach the Titan mark on the ceiling.

"Olivia, will you help me?" I threw as much power as I had into my voice, and her eyes widened. "You'll help me, right?"

"Yes."

"Great." I smiled as I hurried to the door. The weakest point was where the lock was; if both of us worked it at the same time, it might just be enough. "I need you to pull on this door, Olivia, as hard as you can."

She walked to the door in a daze, obediently placing her hands on the handle.

"Put everything into it," I urged softly. "Pull. Pull hard."

And she did. Half-bloods were unbelievably strong, and metal ground as the bars rattled. Olivia bent at the waist, digging in with her boots. I stepped back, wishing I had some shoes, because this was seriously going to hurt.

"Keep pulling," I ordered, and then I took a deep breath.

Turning halfway, I spun and planted my heel into the bars around the lock. Pain splintered into my foot as shimmery blue light flared and faded quickly. An inch-wide gap appeared between the door and the bars.

"Pull really hard, Olivia."

She grunted, bearing down.

Caleb was going to haunt me for this.

Leaning back, I hit the door again. Another gap appeared. With my foot going numb, I gave it one more kick. Metal groaned and gave way. The sudden force sent Olivia to the floor and the door . . . it was open.

Not wasting time, I bolted through the gap, half-expecting to be cut down by some unknown defense, but then I was on the other side of the bars.

I wanted to do a victory dance and shout, but I dropped down and clasped Olivia's cheeks. She stared into my eyes, completely under my control. "Stay here, okay? Stay here until someone comes and gets you."

Olivia nodded.

I started to let go, but paused. "You won't blame yourself for this. You will blame me."

"Okay," came the soft, sleepy reply.

I let go and started for the stairs. A bitter taste was in the back of my mouth as I glanced over my shoulder. Olivia remained on the floor, her eyes fixed on the spot where I'd stood.

"Thank you," I said, not that it mattered. She didn't hear me or understand. She wouldn't do anything until someone came down here, and then it would be like waking from a dream.

I'd see her again. Once my Seth and I changed things, I'd see her again and I'd apologize.

Reassured by that, I slipped up the narrow stairs, pausing at the door. There were no voices on the other side. Taking a second, I tested the bond for Seth. He wasn't there, and I didn't have time to wait around for him to show up. As soon as I was outside and knew where I was, I'd call for him.

Inching the door open, I checked out the hallway. Empty. It was narrow, and paintings hung on the walls. It split two ways. Toward the right, natural light streamed in through a small window, beckoning me. I slid through the door, closing it behind me quietly as I took in my surroundings. I'd been on the Elixir the last time I'd been upstairs—the only time, actually—and I vaguely remembered that this hall led to the kitchen and a living room of sorts. Off the kitchen was the sunroom, which led outside. A strange feeling unfurled inside me, and there was a flash of Aiden and me in that sunroom.

I pushed it out of my head and crept down the hallway. I

seriously wished someone had left a dagger or something lying around. No such luck. Come to think of it, I should've asked Olivia where we were. I rolled my eyes. Gods, I sucked sometimes, but I'd been so concerned with getting free.

As I neared one of the closed doors, I thought I heard Deacon laughing, and then Luke. Biting down on my lip, I slipped around the staircase that led upstairs—

The door swung open and I came face to face with Lea. Crap.

Mouth dropping open, Lea blinked and took a step back, bouncing into the wall.

"Don't—"

Her high-pitched, shrill battle-roar cut me off, and then she swung at me. She actually freaking swung at me. Gods. With no time for a compulsion, I deflected her blow with a brutal swipe that sent her spinning. She caught herself on the wall and grunted. Before she could regain her balance, I swiped her feet out from under her just as Deacon's shocked face appeared in the doorway.

"Oh crap," Deacon said, and he backed up quickly as Luke shot forward.

Luke grabbed for me, but I was quick. "Alex, you don't want to do anything—"

Down the hall, the last door flew up, slamming into the drywall. I caught sight of black pants. *Sentinel.* Without thinking twice, I threw up my arm and the closest one to me took the brunt of the air element.

Luke flew backwards, his eyes wide and stunned. He crashed into Lea, who had moved in front of Deacon as if to protect him. There were several grunts, a yelp of pain, and then someone yelled my name.

Spinning around, I took off for the kitchen. My bare feet slapped off the floor as I skirted the table and entered the sunroom. I reached the door in seconds, tugging then realizing it was locked. Cussing under my breath, I unlocked the damn thing and threw the door open.

Aiden barreled into the kitchen. "Alex! No!"

He was too late. I was out. I was free.

6

The moment sunlight touched my skin, I faltered a step. It felt like years had passed since I had felt the warmth of natural light. My senses came alive. Grass was cold under my feet, and damp. Thick, tall elms blurred as I darted across a small dirt driveway, around a Hummer, and into the heavy woods surrounding the cabin.

Legs and arms pumping, I kept running. My hair streamed out behind me, and I pushed hard, paying attention, looking for any sign of where I was. There was nothing.

A seedling of panic took root. I hurdled a fallen tree, my feet skidding over sharp pine needles. How was I supposed to tell my Seth where I was when I had nothing but freaking trees—

"Alex! Stop!"

My breath hitched and I dared a look back.

It was him—Aiden.

"Crap," I spat, picking up speed.

Up ahead, there was a creek—*the* creek. I remembered that. Thousands of years of Apollyons and their abilities rushed through me. Tapping into that ability was so easy, like slipping into well-worn jeans, which was irritating considering the heinous training I'd gone through in preparation for Awakening, and of course, my Seth would have known that. Punk.

Extending one arm, I summoned the water, willing it to respond to me.

Water stirred, and then a stream jetted into the air, arcing high above me. The wall of water kept coming, draining the shallow creek within seconds. It spun into a funnel, slamming into the earth behind me. A curse was drowned out. That should've bought me some time.

Racing over the creek bed, mud splattered my feet and jeans. Low-hanging branches tore at my hair, snagging strands and my shirt. Cloth ripped, but I kept going. Sunlight peeked through the thick branches as I headed deeper into the forest, away from the cabin . . . away from *him*.

Without warning, the bond snapped alive. *Alex?*

I'm out. I leapt off a boulder over a small gulley and landed in a crouch. Springing up, I took off. *I don't know where I'm at, but I'm out. Seth, I'm—*

I could hear Aiden. He was close and fast, powered by something stronger than aether and I knew, even as fast as I was, I wouldn't have been able to outrun him this long if a wall of water hadn't stopped him. I'd have to fight. But I wouldn't be alone. My Seth was here.

Skidding to a stop, I turned. Wind blew my hair back as I dragged in fresh, mountain air. Aiden cleared the small gulley, landing in a nimble crouch several feet away from me. Water streamed from the dark waves plastered to his head, and his black shirt clung to the hard muscles of his chest and stomach. Under the thin, soaked material, his shoulders tensed.

Our eyes locked.

He rose gracefully, hands open at his sides.

"You don't want to do this," I warned. "Turn away."

Aiden came forward. "I'm not going to leave you. I'll never do that."

There was a flutter in my chest that didn't belong there. I took a step back, feeling heat radiating from my fingers.

My Seth's voice hummed through the bond and I knew what he wanted me to do, therefore I understood why I had to do this.

I took a shallow breath and raised my chin. "Then it's your funeral."

"So be it."

I launched myself at Aiden.

He was prepared for it. He darted to the left, avoiding my attack. He was fast and also very skilled. I knew, because he had trained me, but I was better than him. I was something else.

Moving lightning-fast, I dipped and went for his legs. Aiden jumped, and I shot up, slamming my fist into his stomach. He stumbled back a step, but quickly regained his footing. My next punch was deflected. The third one caught him in the jaw, snapping his head back.

Sunlight reflected off the daggers attached to his thighs, and I went for them.

Aiden spun to the left at the last second, and my fingers only grasped the handle of one. He took a hold of my wrist, twisting only enough that I yelped and let go. My head jerked up at the surprise burst of pain, and it reflected in his gunmetal gray eyes. For some reason, I hadn't expected him to hurt me. I guess . . . I didn't know what I thought.

He pushed me back and as if he could read my thoughts, he said, "I don't want to."

Fury blasted through me like a rocket. "You *can't* hurt me."

Aiden jerked out of the way as I shot forward. I whirled, delivering a spin kick to the kidneys. I moved to deliver another, but Aiden caught my leg and tossed me back. I hit the ground and popped up, throwing my head back.

Energy slammed into me. Akasha simmered beneath the surface, waiting to be called upon, demanding it.

I flew at Aiden and we went at it—brutally. Mostly on my end, because Aiden was more about the defensive instead of the offensive, but bruises were traded, one after another.

Memories of training together surfaced. I wasn't sure if that was a benefit to either of us, because we anticipated each other's moves and neither of us could gain the upper hand. I dropped and he'd be there to deflect. He moved for a submission hold and I escaped before he could lock me down. Blow for blow we went, and in the back of my head, I knew I could've called upon the elements, but I didn't. Maybe it was all the pent-up rage from being caged for so long, and I needed the physicality of fighting. Maybe it was something else.

Blood trickled from Aiden's lip. A red mark bloomed across his jaw. His shirt was torn along the midsection, exposing a row of taut abs, but he didn't show any signs of slowing down.

Frustrated, I pushed off the tree, gained some air and twisted, realizing my mistake an instant after it was too late. As I spun, Aiden stepped into it, catching me around the waist and spinning me around. In training, I'd never been able to get past him this way. I should've known better.

I tipped my weight forward and we both went down on our knees. I tasted blood, but Aiden hadn't hit me. Not once. But my face had connected with his more than a few times.

"Give up," I growled, throwing my head back.

His arms tightened around me. "You should know by now I'm not going to give up on you. You're not that stupid."

"Can't say the same thing about you." I spread my thighs and gathered my strength. "You can't win."

His breath danced over my check. "You want to bet on that?"

I ground my teeth. "You can't have me. I'm not—"

"You're not his, Alex. You don't belong to anyone but yourself!"

He was wrong, so wrong. I belonged to my Seth. I was created for him, only him, and Aiden was in the way.

Rocking forward, I put enough space between us and powered to my feet, breaking his hold. Throwing my arm back, I caught him across the cheek with a closed fist. The impact bruised my knuckles.

Aiden went down on one knee and spat out a mouthful of blood. "*Gods.*"

Spinning around, I started running, ignoring the sharp pebbles digging into the soles of my feet.

I made it about five feet before I was tackled from behind.

Aiden pulled me up so that my back was pinned to his chest. "Leaving so quick? When the fun is just getting started?"

"I hate you!" I struggled wildly, trying to dig into the ground. Loose dirt kicked up as I thrashed, becoming more like an animal caught in a net. Hours of training slipped away. "I hate you!"

"You can hate me all you want, but it doesn't change a thing." He made it to his feet and started dragging me backward, and I knew he'd drag me all the way back to the cabin, to the cage. "I'm not going to let you do this to yourself."

I wriggled and threw myself side to side, but we were back to the cluster of trees within seconds. "You can't stop me! You can't do this!"

"You don't understand, Alex. You can't be out here."

I elbowed him.

He grunted but didn't let go. "They'll kill you. Do you understand?" He shook me. "They'll come to kill you!"

"I don't care!" I screamed myself hoarse. "I need to go. I need to be with him."

Aiden sucked in a sharp breath and his grip loosened a fraction.

Using my core, I pulled my legs up and the combined effort toppled us over. Aiden hit the ground first and rolled before I could break free, shoving his hands into my back, forcing me down. I got a mouthful of mud and grass.

"Stop it!" he hissed in my ear. "This isn't going to work, Alex. You may not care about dying, but I care enough for you."

"I don't care! All that matters is Seth. If I can't be with him, then I'd rather be dead."

"Do you even hear yourself?" His hands pressed into my shoulders. "You'd rather die than not be with him? Do you know how weak that is? The Alex I know would never feel something like that!"

What he said reached deep and broke *something* inside me. Enraged, I planted my hands in the rich soil and felt the earth tremble. A great roar started below, and the ground buckled under us, rolling like stormy seas. We were thrown apart. I smacked into a tree and hit the ground on my hands and knees.

Lightning pierced the sky, blinding me for an instant. Clouds rolled in, blocking the sun, and darkness fell. The skies opened and a torrential downpour pounded us.

I didn't know if it was me or something else. I was beyond caring. A giant ball of messy emotion settled in my stomach, unraveling with dizzying speed. Anger. Frustration. Fear. All of it rushed me.

Air whipped under me and I rose off the ground. Static charged. Sparks flew. The world was colored in amber tones. I wasn't me. I wasn't anything anymore.

Aiden stood a few feet away, his silvery eyes fixed on me. A look of horror and awe marked his striking features.

I was a god, like Seth had said. We were gods.

Do it. Seth's whisper penetrated my blood. *It's time.*

My feet touched the ground and I took a step forward—one, and then another. And Aiden didn't move. He waited. It was in those eyes of his, the finality of this. He wouldn't win, he couldn't and he knew it. Aiden accepted it.

As I reached him, the rain stopped and the clouds parted. The sun followed my footsteps.

"Alex." Aiden's voice was broken.

Like a cobra striking, I took Aiden's legs out from under him and he was on his back before another breath could be taken. Straddling him, I placed my hands on his shoulders. The marks of the Apollyon glowed a vibrant blue and raced over my skin.

I leaned in, placing my lips above his, and the words that came out of my mouth were mine . . . but weren't. "All moments end, St. Delphi. And now yours has." I pressed my lips to the corner of his and he flinched. "You are weak because you love."

Aiden stared up at me, unblinking. "To love is not weak. Love is the strongest thing there is."

My lips curved into a smile. Idiot.

Akasha raced to the surface. My skin was on fire, *I* was on fire. Bright blue light formed over my right arm, circling it as it climbed down to my fingers. Light flared, intense and beautiful as it was destructive.

Sunlight fell over us, and I reared back. Akasha covered my right hand. When I let it go, it would snuff out the life of everything in its path. There was death in that beauty. And Aiden made no move to defend his life.

His eyes fixed on mine and he reached up slowly. The tips of his fingers, calloused over from years of training and fighting, grazed my cheek tenderly. "I love you, Alex. I always will."

I blinked. My heart stuttered. I couldn't wrap my head around how he could say that, touch me so . . . so lovingly, seconds from death.

Do it, Alex, and then we can be together. We'll free the halfs—your father. We'll change the world. You and me, Angel, we'll be together always.

My gaze fell between us. The rose necklace had slipped out, exposed by the torn collar of my shirt. A ray of light caught the deep-red crystal edges of the rose in bloom—such a delicate thing, crafted by the hands of a true warrior.

Air left my lungs and my arm started to shake.

We're in this together, Alex, to the end. Those words weren't Seth's, but this *was* the end. My eyes burned like it was raining acid, but the skies were clear. I was seconds from freedom . . . but so much, so many memories started flipping through my head.

I couldn't stop staring at the rose.

Images of the first time I'd seen Aiden while I'd been training with Caleb, then again when he'd come through the wall of fire and saved me—saved my life. Memories of his patience, his support, even his frustration with me.

Seth called to me, but I swatted him away. These memories were important. They meant something—everything—to me, right? There hadn't been any feelings attached to them before, but now they were soaked in emotion. I focused on them, remembering how he'd cared for me after Gatlinburg, how he'd been there for me when I broke down after Mom . . . *my mom.* The first time he'd held me—kissed me. There was never any judgment in Aiden's eyes, like I was his equal.

I'd always been Aiden's equal.

My chest rose sharply. The day at the zoo washed over me, and then Valentine's Day. The love we had shared. It had to mean something.

I couldn't breathe.

I'd give it all up for you.

Seth called for me again, but I was breaking apart. Shattering. Everything was coming undone. Pieces of who I used to be were repelled by what I'd become. The past and the present couldn't coexist with the future.

I was torn in two.

Seth yelled now, his voice roaring in my head, and there was no escaping him. He was everywhere, in every cell and thought, pulling at me. But I couldn't breathe and *he* was under me, and I couldn't think straight. There were so many voices again. So many different ones, some were my own . . . and I couldn't *think.*

I focused on the mental shields Seth had taught me. I needed a moment, just a second of silence to think this through, to understand why *he* wasn't defending himself and how *he* could love me.

Seth was furious. Pain sliced through my skull as if someone had taken an ice pick and started slamming it into my head, and I knew he hated this, but I needed *time.* He screamed for me, but

I pictured those walls. They were neon-pink, dazzling walls, and they went up, stacked higher and higher. I made them thick and full of titanium, topped them off with barbed wire and threw a nice little electrical fence over them, and all of that was backed by the power of the gods. A film of shimmery blue light draped over the walls.

The cord snapped inside me, recoiling like whiplash, and then it was gone.

Except for a low hum, there was silence, and it was just me now, alone with everything I had done.

Tipping my head back, I screamed.

Unlocked from the depths of my soul, it kept coming and coming. I couldn't stop it. I couldn't comprehend what I'd become—the things I had done. And when I stopped, it was only because my throat was raw.

I scrambled off of Aiden, unable to look at him, because I . . . the things . . . Body trembling, I crawled over the muddy ground and tucked into a ball against a tree. Pressing my face to my knees, I dragged in breaths, but my chest ached and the pressure kept building.

"Alex?" Aiden called out, his voice hoarse and ragged.

I shied away, wanting him to leave. He needed to leave me, to run away as fast as he could.

Strong hands landed on my shoulders and then slid over my arms, gently wrapping around my wrists. He pried my hands away, and even though I couldn't bear to look at him, my eyes opened.

It was like seeing Aiden after months of separation. He was clear to me. The curve of his broad cheekbones, the hint of dimples, and the strong line of his jaw—features I'd committed to memory eons ago. Dark waves curled over his naturally tan skin . . . skin marred by bruises and streaks of crimson. Bruises I'd given him, but he still held that masculine beauty that always undid me.

Aiden shuddered, and then clasped my cheeks. His silver

eyes searched mine. They were covered in a fine sheen—like tears, but Aiden never cried. "Alex . . . oh, gods, Alex, are you here?"

I burst into tears.

7

Yeah, I wasn't going to stop crying anytime soon. These were the big, body-shaking, embarrassing kind of sobs. The ones I really couldn't think or see around—Hell, even breathe around.

Aiden held me through it, his arms a strange and grounding contact. He murmured words in ancient Greek. I picked up *agapi mou* several times, and the rest made as much sense as the words I tried to speak around the sobs. I knew that I'd be able to understand them now if I weren't choking on my tears, but I could barely understand English at the moment.

I soaked Aiden's shirt.

And he still held me against his chest as he leaned against the tree, smoothing back my hair, pressing his cheek against the top of my head. He rocked us. We both needed it, I think.

There were footsteps and voices at some point and I stiffened in his arms. I didn't know who came, but I felt Aiden shake his head, and then the footsteps retreated.

Gods, I could think—really think—after what felt like for ever. But every thought was overshadowed by the pain inside me. The sharp spearing I'd felt in the bathroom—I understood it now. My heart and my soul had been screaming out, trying to reach me. That pain was everywhere now, clamping down on me from all sides.

I couldn't escape all the things I'd said and done since I'd Awakened. From the moment I'd connected with Seth, I'd turned into a living, breathing embodiment of my worst fear and I hadn't even realized it. Seth and what he wanted had consumed me until there had been nothing left, and I'd thought I was stronger than that.

Oh gods, the things I'd said to Aiden horrified and sickened me. The things Seth had said he wanted to do to me—that I'd wanted him to do, back when we'd been connected . . . Now I wanted to crawl out of my skin, to shower for years, and I didn't think I'd ever feel the same again even then.

How Aiden could still hold me was beyond my comprehension. I clearly remembered threatening to kill Deacon about twenty times. My behavior had forced him to do the unthinkable—place me on the Elixir. I knew that had to have killed a part of him.

I remembered all the little things. *My Seth?* Oh, yuck. I wanted to scrub out my brain with detergent. And those things I'd yelled when I fought Aiden—actually fought *Aiden?* Scrub my brain? Add mouth and soul to that laundry list.

"Shh," Aiden murmured, smoothing a hand along my back. "It's okay. Everything is okay, *agapi mou.* You're here now and I have you."

I gripped the collar of his torn shirt with my aching hands. "I'm so sorry. I'm sorry, Aiden. I'm sorry."

"Stop." He leaned back, but I followed him, keeping my face pressed to his chest. "Alex."

I shook my head, my breath catching on another sob.

"Look at me."

Tears streamed down my face, and he carefully cradled my cheeks, forcing me to look up. I wanted to squeeze my eyes shut, but I also needed to see him, even if it was just his blurry face right now.

"How can you look at me?" I asked. "How can you stand to touch me?"

His brows furrowed and he became very serious. "How could I not, Alex? I don't blame you for what happened. The things you did and said weren't you. I know that. I've always known that."

"But it *was* me."

"No." His voice was firm, eyes pure silver. "It was a shell of you, Alex. You were there, in the background, but it wasn't you. It wasn't the Alex I love, but you're here now and that's all that matters. That's it. Nothing else does."

His blind faith in me, his acceptance and forgiveness, brought forth another round of waterworks. I cried so much that I didn't think I could ever cry again, and when it was finally over, I couldn't lift my head from his chest.

The sun was starting to set, and the temperature was dropping when Aiden pressed his lips against the top of my head. "Are you ready?"

No, I wanted to say, because I wasn't sure I'd ever be ready to face everyone. Besides turning into Evil Alex, I'd also been dopey, hiding-in-closets Alex.

But I drew in a breath and it felt okay, good even. "Okay."

"Okay," he repeated, and he stood, keeping me nestled close to his chest, my cheek resting on his shoulder.

Aiden took one step, and a fissure of unnatural energy rolled down my spine—godly energy. The marks of the Apollyon roared to life, whipping over my skin. His arms stiffened around me as he turned, lifting his head to the sky. Gods could shield their presence if they wanted to—Apollo had for months—but we both felt the ripple of power.

"This isn't good," I said, stirring in his arms.

He placed me on my feet, his hands on my hips. One look into his stormy eyes and I knew he was thinking the same thing.

Before he could open his mouth, a high-pitched wail rattled the branches overhead. Air around us stilled, and then the sound of wings beating pulled the breath from my lungs in a painful rush.

Aiden shoved me behind him—actually shoved *me* behind

him. "Go back to the house now, Alex. The wards will keep them out."

What? And leave him? He was insane. Heart leaping into my throat, I shook my head. "No. No—"

Another shriek turned my blood ice-cold. Then a great howl barreled through the trees, blowing my hair back from my face.

The furies arrived, darting down to earth like heat-seeking missiles with "Alex" written all over them. Each hit the ground in a crouch, knocking up plumes of dirt and small pebbles.

They were beautiful—the two furies. All pale and shimmering skin and long, flowing blonde curls as they rose simultaneously, their bodies moving sinuously as one stepped forward, her bare feet sinking deep into the soil.

Thunder cracked the air and a flash of blinding light exploded. Throwing up my arm, I stumbled back and reached out for Aiden. Pulse pounding, my fingers wrapped around his thick forearm.

When the light receded, a god stood between the two furies, and my heart felt like it stopped right then and there. I'd seen him before. Oh, gods, I'd seen him.

Honey-colored hair brushed his shoulders, framing a square, defiant chin and features that were angelic and pure—peaceful, even.

Thanatos.

Electricity sparked from his all-white eyes. "I may not be able to kill you, Apollyon, but I can make sure you cannot reach the First."

"Wait!" Aiden yelled, one hand curling around the hilt of the dagger. "She's broken—"

The furies flew forward, luminous skin shedding away to reveal ghastly gray complexions that resembled corpses that had been floating in the water waaay too long. Long, glowing hair shriveled up and turned into tight coils that snapped at the air with vicious fangs around their skeletal faces. Claws formed—talons that could rip through bone and tissue like they were paper.

They came right at us.

Aiden lurched to the side and twisted toward me. "Alex!" He threw one of the daggers.

Leaping up, I caught the dagger as the first fury reached Aiden, her razor-sharp nails aimed right for his throat. He spun around, whipping out a sickle blade. In one smooth, elegant motion he brought the sharp edge of the blade down, severing the arm of the fury.

She keened a mixture of a baby's scream and a hyena's as she arched up, clutching her bloody stump.

Damn.

With absolutely no time to run over to Aiden and give him a high-five, I pivoted and dipped as the second fury made a grab for my hair. Shooting up at the same moment the fury dive-bombed me, I shoved the blade deep into her sunken stomach.

Her distorted face inches from mine, the fury opened her mouth, revealing a row of serrated teeth, and laughed.

I bit back a gag. "Gods, your breath is kicking." I pulled the blade free, revolted by the sucking sound. "For real."

Cocking her head to the side, she blinked. "Kicking?"

"Yeah." Spinning around, I planted my left foot and kicked out, catching the fury in the stomach. She flew back, smacking into the tree. "See? Kicking."

The other fury was going at Aiden with her one good arm, backing him up while avoiding the dangerous sickle. He glanced over at me and that tiny moment cost him.

She knocked the sickle out of his hand with a cackle. "Pretty pure-blood . . ."

Forgetting about the god and the other fury, forgetting about everything other than Aiden, I raced forward, ignoring the ache building in my legs.

Aiden dipped under the fury's sweeping arm, popping up

behind her, but she turned wicked fast and swung out, hitting Aiden along the chest with the broad side of her arm.

He went down on one knee, staggered by the blow.

Swiping the sickle off the ground, I yelled his name and repaid the favor by tossing the sickle to him. Aiden snapped it out of the air and rolled, narrowly missing the fury. She flew up and flipped over him, reaching down, grabbing a handful of his hair. She yanked his head back.

"No!" My heart stopped—my world stopped.

Akasha surged under my skin and the marks brightened. Each and every one of them burned and tingled with the power of the fifth element.

Something snapped inside me; my vision dimmed, and then brightened. I heard nothing but my own thundering heart and the hum in the back of my head.

Throwing my arm out, a bolt of intense blue light flared from my open palm and arced. My aim was off since I was going for the bitch's head, but the bolt of energy clipped the fury's wing, whirling her around.

Absolute insanity broke out.

Thanatos roared his rage. The fury shot into the air, but sputtered out with one wing and came spinning back down. Aiden darted to the side, but not fast enough. Weary from fighting me just like I was exhausted from our battle, she crashed into him and they rolled in a tangle of arms, blades, and deadly-sharp claws.

Out of the corner of my eye, forms crested the valley—Solos and Marcus bearing sickle blades. *Marcus?* What the . . .?

I shot toward the wrestling forms before me.

Thanatos whipped around and extended an arm. He didn't physically touch Solos, but boy did he fly like he'd been smacked with a cannonball. The half-blood Sentinel hit the tree with a loud grunt and dropped to his knees.

The god turned his creeptastic eyes on my uncle and raised

another hand. "Stand down, pure-blood, or you shall meet an untimely fate."

Marcus lowered his chin. "Sorry, but that's my niece, so that's not going to happen."

Something with sharp claws and rank breath caught hold of my hair and pulled hard. I hit the ground and in a heartbeat, air punched from my lungs. Scrambling to my knees, a second passed and the fury's bare foot connected with my chin, snapping my head back.

A metallic taste flooded my mouth. The dagger flew from my hands as pain radiated down my spine, exploding out over my nerves.

Panic dug in—raw, unbridled panic.

All around me the sounds of fighting escalated. There were grunts and yelps of pain. The fury that had kicked me into next week reared up, her fingers splaying. I stared, numb and unflinching as death . . .

Death? It struck me then. They couldn't kill me. Yeah, they could put a serious hurting on me, but kill me? No. I was the Apollyon. I wielded control over the four elements and the fifth and the most powerful—akasha. I fueled the God Killer. I was his power-up—the ace up his sleeve. I was the beginning and he was the end. And together . . . there was no together.

There was just me.

My eyes locked with the fury's and I smiled.

She hesitated.

I snapped to my feet. "Bitch, please."

The fury's mouth gaped open, and I summoned the air element, letting it go. The hurricane-force winds smacked into the fury and sent her flying back through the trees as if she was connected to a rope and Zeus himself had given a good old pull.

"One down," I said, turning around. "Who's ne—?"

Thanatos tossed Marcus to the ground, deflected Solos' attack, and turned on me in a nanosecond. It was pretty epic.

A bolt of white light flew from Thanatos' hand and there wasn't a single thing in this world that could move fast enough to avoid it. Not even Seth, I was betting.

It hit me just below the chest, and my legs collapsed from underneath me. Red-hot, searing pain sliced through my skin and my face smacked off the ground. I didn't even feel it. There was nothing but the razing pain locking up my muscles.

God bolts *sucked.*

Aiden yelled my name, and then I thought I heard my name called again, but it was inside my head, loud, and so very angry . . . and it sounded like Seth.

Without any warning, the ground trembled under my twitching body. A flash of golden light cascaded through the clearing. Warmth stole over my body. Weakly, I lifted my head.

Two leather-clad legs stood before me.

"That is enough, Thanatos." Apollo's voice was calm, but it was that creepy, deadly calm I never wanted to be on the receiving end of.

"N-n-nice of y-you to s-show up," I gasped.

"Shut up, Alex." Apollo strode forward. A ray of light followed his steps.

Thanatos held his ground. "She must be neutralized if we cannot kill her. Let me take care of this, Apollo. We must do something to prevent war."

"She broke the bond, you idiot."

The other god huffed. "Like that matters. Time will pass and she will connect with him again."

"It does matter!" Apollo roared. "If she is not connected with the First we are not to harm her! You—" Apollo growled at the increasingly close sound of hissing. "Call your two furies off or they will join their sister. I promise you."

"We must—"

Too weak to hold my head up, I rested my forehead against the ground, but I didn't need to see what happened to know that

Apollo had lost his patience. Wind picked up and the ground shook. The two gods collided with a crack.

I closed my eyes and hoped that Apollo had won this round, because there was no way I was fighting anymore. No way at all.

Someone was body-slammed into the ground, followed by a quick succession of pops. The air crackled with electricity, and then silence, blissful silence.

Strong hands gripped my arms and gently rolled me onto my back. I stared up into silver eyes. "Alex?"

"I'm okay. Just . . . just a little twitchy. You?"

Aiden had seen better days. Blood trickled out of the corner of his mouth. A bruise shadowed his jaw and the front of his shirt was torn, but he was alive and he was okay.

His gaze scanned over me and then he lifted me up, not even bothering to put me on my feet. Holding me close, he turned and I surveyed the damage.

Solos and Marcus stood near Apollo, who held one of the Covenant daggers in his hand. Blood dripped from the edge, making me stare.

Apollo glanced down at it and shrugged. "He'll get over it."

I changed focus and stared at him.

"But I'm going to have to answer for that, I think." Apollo handed the dagger to a bruised Solos. "And it may take a few days . . ."

Apollo stalked forward, stopping in front of us, and Aiden placed me down and stepped between us. The god smirked. "I know she's broken the bond. Good to have you back, Alex."

"Yeah," I breathed.

He turned his attention to Aiden. "Keep the wards on the house until I can return. In the meantim e, prepare for battle."

Battle? What the hell did he think we'd just done?

Aiden nodded.

The god took a breath and flexed his hands. "And you were right. I was wrong."

"I know," Aiden said, and I glanced up, confused.

Apollo turned to the other men and nodded. His form started to fade. "Wait," I called out. There were so many questions I had, but all he did was look over his shoulder and smile.

8

I don't remember much of the trek back to the cabin. At some point, I'd wriggled enough to get free and walk, but I was moving so slowly and so pathetically that Aiden had finally stopped grumbling under his breath and picked me back up.

I didn't fight it after that. On my feet, I was more of a hindrance.

The cabin was quiet upon our return. Marcus and Solos had limped off, no doubt to tend to their injuries. Somehow the rest of the occupants knew that right now wasn't time for a welcome back to the world of the sane and logical. Aiden carried me up the stairs and down the narrow hall, toward the bedroom he'd slept in when I'd been on the Elixir. I remembered that, even when I'd been high on the happy drink, I'd sought out his presence and snuggled against him on the couch. My heart tripped up.

Aiden started toward the bed, but I stopped him. "Shower," I said hoarsely. "I need a shower."

"Yeah, you kind of do—we both do." Pivoting around, he headed for the bathroom. There he placed me on my feet, his eyes shadowed with concern when I swayed a little. "Are you okay?"

"Yeah, I'm just tired. There's nothing seriously wrong with me." And that was true. I was bruised and sore, but that was all. And I was lucky, considering we'd just been in a death match with a god of death and two furies. "Are you . . .?"

"I'm fine." He stared a moment, then pressed a kiss on my cheek. "I'll be right back."

"Okay." I was a zombie on my feet.

His eyes searched my face with such stark relief that I gripped the sink. "Don't hog all the hot water, all right?" he said.

That brought a small smile to my lips. As soon as he left, I turned slowly to the shower and twisted the faucets. Pulling off my ruined clothing was a painful experience. Every muscle ached and it took a few minutes. By the time I stepped into the stall, steam filled the bathroom.

I was probably going to use a week's worth of hot water while Aiden most likely was rallying the troops and convincing them that I wasn't a sociopath anymore.

I shivered under the stream, pressing my face to my hands. They shook. I shook. I moved them to the chain around my neck, slid my fingers to the rose. Something so small had been the one thing to break the connection.

But it wasn't the rose itself, but what it symbolized—Aiden's love for me and how I felt for him—something pure and natural, an emotion not forced. Seeing that had broken the bond between Seth and me.

Bringing the crystal to my lips, I pressed a kiss against the rose.

The bond *was* broken, but Seth was still there . . . at the end of the cord slumbering in the pit of my stomach. Gods, he'd been so furious, murderous really, but shock had rippled through our bond the second before it had ended. And then again, when Thanatos had hit me with the god bolt, he had been *there* like a creepy stalker with a one-way ticket to my brain.

Seth hadn't believed I'd be capable of breaking the bond. And how far would this have gone if I hadn't?

They'll come to kill you. And although Thanatos didn't have the juice to carry it out, he sure as hell didn't have a problem putting a hurting on me—or anyone who defended me. People could've died today because of me.

I sucked in a sharp breath.

And why had Aiden blocked Apollo from the cabin? What happened to that love-fest?

Gods, there were so many questions, and I was too weary for this right now. I needed a moment to regroup. I *needed* a bed after this shower.

Water streamed over my body, over skin that was as bruised as my insides, and plastered my hair to my back. Closing my eyes, I lifted my chin and let the showerhead do its thing, erasing the tears that had clung to my lashes with a death grip, clearing my mind of everything.

There would be time to ask those questions, to plan Seth's very painful death, and to find my father, but right now, I just couldn't do it. I couldn't think about anything other than right now, right this moment, because everything was too raw and too fresh to delve into.

I heard the bathroom door close and I kept my eyes screwed shut, but my heart rate skyrocketed into uncharted territories. I folded my arms around me and held my breath.

There was the slightest movement behind me. Skin brushed against mine. A fine shiver rolled up my spine. An infinite spark transferred between us, something that couldn't be replicated or forced. How could I have forgotten that while connected with Seth? My heart turned over heavily.

Aiden brushed the mass of thick hair over one shoulder and his lips met the space between my neck and shoulder. His hands slid down the slick skin of my arms, cupping over my elbows and then to my wrists. Gently, slowly, he eased my arms to my sides.

I bit down on my lip and my legs started trembling. But he was there. Like always, holding me up when I couldn't stand and letting me go when he knew I needed him to. He was more than just a shelter. Aiden *was* my other half, my equal. And he needed no weird Apollyon connection.

Aiden waited, still as a statue, patient as ever, until my muscles unlocked, one by one. Then his hands dropped to my waist and he turned me toward him. A heartbeat passed and he placed his fingers on my chin, tipping my head back.

I opened my eyes, blinking the wetness off my lashes, and the air hitched in my throat. Faint, purplish bruises shadowed his jaw. There was a cut over the bridge of his nose. No doubt injuries I had given him.

"I'm so sorry, Aiden." My voice cracked. "I can't say it enough, I know, but I'm so—"

He dipped his head and his mouth brushed mine, silencing my words. My lips opened to his, as did my heart and everything else. The sweet and tender kiss, well, it lessened the heaviness, eased some of the guilt and shame. My skin—my insides—were scraped and aching, but his touch soothed the frayed edges. I imagined it was the same for Aiden. Gods, it was probably worse for him, considering everything I had done and said. What he'd had to do, to sacrifice, to keep me safe.

The kiss deepened, flipping and twisting my insides into a pleasant mess, and it was like the very first time we'd kissed. Sensations raced over my skin, my heart sang, and the feeling unfurling in the pit of my stomach was better than tapping into akasha, stronger and more addicting. He kissed me like he'd never expected to do so again, as if he could somehow kiss away the weeks.

I placed my hands on his upper arms. His muscles coiled under them as he lifted me up and I wrapped my legs around him. Desire wasn't the only thing between us. There was so much more: forgiveness, acceptance, relief, and most importantly, love.

Not the kind of love that was fueled by need and that destroyed cities and entire civilizations, but the kind that rebuilt them, that much I knew.

Keeping an arm around my waist, his other hand tangled in my wet hair. And we didn't stop kissing, because this was *right* and that was all that mattered. My heart was pounding way too fast, but it was perfect, it was like coming home after never believing I'd be able to.

I don't know how we made it to the bed or if the water was ever turned off in the shower. But we were together, our bodies slippery, our wet hair soaking the sheets we were tangled in. And then *we* were tangled, our legs and arms. His hands were everywhere, paying reverence to the many scars on my body. His lips followed, and I grew reacquainted with the hard muscles of his stomach, the feel of him.

I glanced down at my body, surprised to see the marks of the Apollyon glowing faintly as they swirled across my skin, forming one rare symbol and then another.

"What?" Aiden cupped my cheek, drawing my eyes back to his. "Is this too fast? I should—"

"No. No, it's . . . it's the marks of the Apollyon. They're kind of doing their thing right now."

"Should I be worried?"

I laughed self-consciously, feeling like one of those venomous snakes that warned of its poison in its vibrant colors. "I think they like you."

Aiden's hand slid off my cheek, down my throat, to right below my chest. The marks slid toward his hand, as if drawn to him. Maybe they were. I wasn't sure how the marks worked. The answer probably lay in the thousands of years of memories, but that was like digging for a needle in a pile of needles.

"I saw them," he said, his voice raw and deep and his eyes like pools of liquid silver. "When you Awakened, and when you went on the Elixir." His brows drew tight as he smoothed his hand over my hip. "They were beautiful."

"Really?" I felt beautiful when he looked at me, even all tattooed up.

"Yes. It was the most beautiful thing I'd ever seen."

A long, agonizing moment passed as he hovered above me,

his eyes locked onto mine, his body coiled tight like a rope ready to snap. And when he did, his lips found mine and there was a sound that came from the back of his throat that seared me. Our bodies met and for a few moments, neither of us moved, and then we did, our voices soft whispers in the dark room.

Sometime later, we lay facing each other, his hand wrapped around my smaller one. Our bodies were pressed close. Exhaustion dogged me now, and Aiden, too—had done for weeks. The fighting and everything else had tipped us over the edge. Sleep claimed me first. I only knew this because I could feel Aiden's gaze on my face, and seconds before I slipped away I felt his lips on my forehead.

I heard him whisper, "Eíste pánta mou . . ."

You are my everything.

9

No matter how convoluted my life got, one thing remained consistent—my hair looked like a baby opossum had taken refuge in it, invited some friends over, and thrown a party. That's what I got for sleeping on it wet.

I wrangled it into a thick braid and took a deep breath.

Admittedly, I'd seen better days. Well, my face at least. Most of the damage I'd done to myself. Aiden hadn't raised a hand against me the entire time we'd fought. He'd only defended himself. But we were both lucky to be standing after facing Thanatos and the furies.

My reflection winced.

Aiden was gone by the time I had crawled out of bed. I'd wanted to stay among the covers, inhaling his unique scent of sea and burning leaves, holding the pillow he'd used close to my chest. I'd wanted to wait there until he returned, so I could wrap myself around him, doing a replay of last night.

But reality wasn't going to pause or wait for us. There was way too much to be done and I needed to face everyone. I took a long breath and pushed away from the mirror. Staring at my face for hours wasn't going to fix anything.

I found the bag of clothes I'd brought with me when I'd stayed at Aiden's parents' house and Aiden had the sense to take when we left Deity Island. There were some items in there I hadn't packed or noticed before—one of them being a Sentinel uniform. That brought a smile to my face. I tugged on a pair of jeans, surprised to find how loose they were. Slipping on a pair of boots that were nothing like Olivia's, I went to the doorway and flinched. *Olivia.* Oh, dear gods, I'd used a compulsion on her. I seriously hoped she wasn't still in the basement.

I crept down the silent hall, scrubbing at the itchy bruise on my cheek. I didn't even know what month we were in. It had been cool, but not freezing when I'd been outside yesterday. Hell. I didn't even know where I was.

Grabbing the middle of my braid, I went down the steps, fiddling with the ropey sections. At the bottom of the stairs, I caught sight of a tall Sentinel with brown hair pulled into a low ponytail. Solos. As far as I recalled, I hadn't threatened him with bodily harm—at least, not to his face.

He turned at the waist. "Well, look who's back."

My cheeks flushed and I stopped on the landing, wholly unsure of what to say.

Solos smiled, and it distorted the scar that cut deep into his cheek. "I'm not going to bite, little one."

Heat now swept over my body and I raised my chin. Gods, what was wrong with me? "Good. Because I bite back."

"That's what I hear." His blue eyes glimmered. Now I flushed for a whole new reason. "I'm sure you're hungry. You've slept for almost a whole day. Everyone's in the kitchen now."

My stomach growled at the thought of food, but then soured. "There's not sharp silverware or anything?"

Solos' laugh was deep and rich. "No. It's a takeout night, so you're in luck."

Finding my courage, I followed him down the hallway. He went into the kitchen first and I peeked around the corner. Deacon and Luke sat on one side, several cartons of Chinese spread out in front of them. Laadan was beside them. Marcus, Lea, and Olivia were across the table. I had no idea where Aiden was.

"We have company," Solos announced, grabbing one of those yummy dumplings and popping it into his mouth.

Everyone turned. And everyone stopped eating and stared.

I let go of my braid and gave the group the most awkward wave ever. "Hi."

Luke dropped his chopsticks into his noodles. There was a nasty bruise on the side of his face, disappearing into his hairline.

"Did I do that?" I stepped into the kitchen. "The bruise?"

"Yeah," he said slowly. "When you slammed me into the wall . . . without touching me."

I winced. "I'm really sorry about that."

"Aw, don't worry about it." Deacon smiled as he leaned back in his chair, rocking it up on two legs. "He's okay."

"My ego's not." He shot Aiden's brother a dirty look. "She didn't even touch me."

Deacon shrugged. "Well, she *is* the Apollyon. Duh."

A chair scraped over tile and my head jerked toward the sound. Marcus walked around the table and stopped in front of me. Now, I had threatened him quite a bit to his face, but he'd still come to fight yesterday, as had Solos.

I felt horrid.

Marcus placed his hands on my shoulders. There was a fine tremble to them. "Alexandria . . ."

My uncle had always refused to call me by my nickname, and I'd always called him Dean, due to his position at the Covenant, but things . . . things were different now. "Marcus?"

There was a long, terse moment, and then he gathered me in a fierce hug. For once, it wasn't an awkward, weak one with my arms stuck out at my sides. I hugged him back, just as tightly, and tears burned the back of my throat.

Marcus and I . . . well, we'd come a long, long way.

When he pulled back, I bit back a gasp. Those emerald-colored eyes were normally cool, but they weren't now. They were like staring into my mother's eyes.

He inhaled sharply. "I'm glad to have you back."

I nodded, swallowing thickly. "I'm glad to be back."

"Hell, we all can agree on that." Luke picked up a donut. "There's nothing creepier than having a psychotic Apollyon caged in the basement."

"Ha," I said.

Luke winked and then tossed the donut to me. I caught it. Sugar flew everywhere.

"Or waiting for her to break loose and run amuck," Deacon added as I took a bite. He glanced across the table. "Or waiting for someone, no names mentioned, to not listen to us and go say hi."

Olivia's cheeks reddened as she stood. She approached slowly, waited for me to finish chewing. I started to apologize. "I'm really sorry—"

She socked me in the stomach. *Hard.* I doubled over, gasping for air. "Gods."

Solos and Marcus both stepped forward, but I waved my hand at them. "That's okay. I deserved that."

Then I realized they weren't moving in to protect me, but to guard Olivia. I guessed no one was a hundred percent relaxed around me. Guess I couldn't blame them when I wielded the most powerful weapon on earth, and only a day ago I'd been willing to use it against them.

"You totally deserved that." Olivia's voice shook. "Do you know how terrible I felt when Marcus came down and found me sitting there like a turd? I helped you escape!"

I thought she might hit me again, so I took a step back.

Olivia smoothed her hands over her tight curls. "But I'm better now, especially since I got to hit you." Then she sprang forward and hugged me.

Standing there, I patted her back, hoping she didn't change her mind and snap my spinal cord. "I'm really sorry."

"I know." She pulled back, smiling. Her eyes were misty.

Laadan was next. The raven-haired beauty was as elegant as ever. Dressed in a form-fitting red turtleneck and white slacks, she enveloped me in a warm hug. She smelled of spring roses and when she pulled back, I didn't want to let go.

"We'll talk later. Promise," she said, and I knew she was talking about my father. Taking my hand, she pulled me to the empty spot next to Olivia. "Sit. Eat."

Glancing around the table, I watched as a plastic plate was passed around, each person slopping a helping of food on it. Even Lea, who hadn't said a word to me yet, placed some shrimp on the plate. When it came back to me, my mouth watered, but I had to say something first.

"Guys, I'm really sorry for everything." I glanced down at my plate, but forced my eyes back up. "I know I was a terror and I wish . . . I wish none of you'd had to go through that."

Marcus returned to his seat. "We know you weren't yourself, Alexandria. We understand."

Beside him, Lea cleared her throat. "I actually preferred the crazy Apollyon version to the Elixired up one, to be honest." She glanced at me, thick lashes hiding amethyst eyes. "That was kind of freaky watching you hide behind Aiden."

"You were pretty different," Luke agreed, and then shuddered. "Man, the Elixir is no joke."

"You hid in a closet," Deacon felt the need to inform me.

Poking at my noodles, I frowned as fragments of my time on the Elixir slid into place. "I bet that was amusing to watch."

"I don't know if I would say it was amusing," a new voice added.

My head jerked up and my heart toppled over itself. Aiden stood just inside the kitchen door, dressed as always—as a Sentinel. He stalked toward the table and picked up the carton of brown rice. He leaned against the counter, the curve of his jaw hard, eyes like flint.

They met mine. He gestured at my plate with his carton. "Eat. You need to eat."

Everyone stared at their plates as I picked up the fork I hadn't even realized I'd dropped. I dared a peek at Aiden as I twirled my fork around the noodles. He was watching, always watching.

Deacon offered me a pair of chopsticks. "You shouldn't be using a fork."

I shot him a bland look. "Do I look like I know how to use chopsticks?"

He grinned. "Poser."

"Punk," I retorted.

His eyes rolled. "It's not that hard. Here, let me show you."

Deacon's impromptu chopsticks lesson and my absolute failure at mastering them eased the sudden awkward tension around the table. Laughing, I gave up when Aiden finally ordered his brother to let me eat in peace.

Digging in, I listened to the conversation around me. There was talk of nothing important and I figured they were waiting for me to finish eating before the real, necessary conversations took place.

I finished off everything I'd been given, ate the remaining rice that Aiden had dumped on my plate as he prowled around the table, and then finished off the sugary goodness of the donuts.

Stomach full, I leaned back in my chair and sighed. "That hit the spot and then some."

Olivia patted my stomach. "You need it . . . and probably a couple of Big Macs, too."

My eyes widened. "Mmm, Big Macs . . . please tell me there's a McDonald's around here? Actually, where am I?"

Everyone grew silent, and no one looked at me.

"What? *What*?" I sat up, looking around the table. And then it hit me. "You guys don't trust me, do you?"

Lea was the first to meet my eyes. "Okay. I'll rain on this happy parade. How do we know you're not still connected to Seth?"

"She's not," Aiden said, picking up the empty cartons and tossing them in a black trash bag he carried. "Trust me, she's not connected to him anymore."

Deacon snorted.

I glared at him.

Lea settled back in her chair, folding her arms. "Is there any other concrete proof, other than you telling us to trust you?"

Aiden glanced at me and I quickly looked away. I doubted Lea wanted to hear about that kind of proof. "I'm not connected to Seth. I promise you."

"Promises are weak; you could be faking it," she shot back.

"Lea, dear, she has no reason to fake it." Laadan smiled gently. "If she was connected to the First, she wouldn't be sitting here."

"And my brother wouldn't be cleaning up after us, right?" Deacon slumped back, as if it had just occurred to him that Aiden had been seconds away from death. I wanted to hide under the table as Deacon shook his head, dumbfounded. "Gods, we'd have to get a maid then or something."

Aiden smacked the back of Deacon's head as he passed by. "I feel the love."

His brother tipped his head back, grinning.

Taking a breath, I stood and clenched the back of my chair. "I'm not connected to him and I'm pretty sure he can't get through the shields. But I know he's there. I can feel him."

Aiden stopped and turned to me.

Whoops, better clarify that. "I mean, I can feel him, but he can't reach me, not really. There's just a low-level buzz. Nothing like before. He can't get to me. I'm pretty sure."

"Pretty sure?" Marcus asked, throat working.

I nodded and took another breath. "Look, I can't say that something freaky won't happen. I don't know what he's really capable of, but he's going to have to try really hard to get past these shields."

"You'll be okay," Aiden said. Tying off the garbage bag, muscles popped in his arms. "He won't break through."

Forcing a smile, I knew Aiden believed that. "And you'll

know the second he does. I don't think I have the patience to try to fool anyone."

Luke barked out a short laugh. "Don't I know that."

"Let's take the conversation to a more comfortable place, then." Marcus stood, grasping his glass of what I assumed was wine. I eyed the crystal longingly. "I'm sure all of us have a lot of questions."

The group followed Marcus, but I stayed behind. Picking up the empty cans, I brought them over to the trashcan Aiden was placing a fresh bag in.

"Cleaning up?" he asked, fitting the bag to the can. "This is unexpected."

"I'm a new girl." I dumped the cans. "Are you okay?"

Aiden hooked a finger into the belt of my jeans and led me over to the sink. Then he rolled up my sleeves, turned on the tap and picked up the hand soap.

I rolled my eyes, but shoved my hands under the warm water. "Aiden?"

"What? You're going to have sticky hands and be touching everything." He squirted the apple-scented soap on my hands. "You'll leave little fingerprints all over the place."

I watched my hands disappear under his larger ones and sort of forgot about what I was asking. Who knew washing hands could be so . . . distracting? "Are you concerned about CSI visiting the place?"

"You never know."

I let him finish, because who was I to stop his OCD at the moment, then I dried my hands. "That's not what I meant. Are you okay?"

"Are you?"

I balled my freshly clean hands into fists. "Yes, I'm okay. Answer my question."

He tilted to his head to the side. "What did you mean earlier about being able to feel Seth?"

So was this what had him suddenly uptight? "You know what it's like when you're in a house with a TV on mute? There's that weird frequency you can feel?" When he nodded, I smiled. "It's like that. He's just there, but he can't reach me."

There was a pause. "Have you had any headaches?"

Confused, I shook my head. "No. Why do you ask?"

"Nothing," he said, and he smiled. "And I'm okay, Alex. I'm the last person you should worry about."

"But I do worry." There was so much to worry about. Turning back to the fridge, I stretched up to grab a bottle of water. As I pulled one down, it revealed another bottle, but it was different.

The contents had been emptied out and replaced with vibrant blue liquid.

Aiden's sharp inhale was like a blast of cold air. "Alex—"

Ignoring him, I dropped my bottle and reached for the other one. Hands shaking, I wrapped my fingers around the plastic. I knew what was in the bottle. I knew what harmlessly sloshed around inside would carry a sickeningly sweet aroma and could rob me of who I was in minutes.

Aiden swore under his breath.

Facing him, I held the bottle. "This is the Elixir, isn't it?"

His hand clenched at his side. "It is."

I glanced down at the water bottle. Two fears in life: losing myself to Seth and losing myself to the Elixir. Both had happened, and somehow I'd come back out of those rabbit holes. But holding it in my hands, I couldn't deny the raw taste of fear building in the back of my throat.

It was like holding a bomb—a bomb designed to decay my mind.

Aiden looked like he wanted to rip it from my hands, and I gave a weak smile. "Should we keep it?"

"What?" Tension rolled off him, and something else. Disgust? Bits and pieces of memories of when I'd been under the Elixir weren't pretty.

"What if we need it again?" I asked, fighting that cold lump in my throat. "Isn't that why you . . . you all were keeping it?"

"No. I'd placed it there and forgot about it." Then he did take it out of my hands. Moving stiffly, he brought it back to the sink and unscrewed the lid.

"Aiden?"

Without saying a word, he dumped what was left of the Elixir. Sweetness filled the air, rinsed away when he turned on the tap. I hoped he wasn't making a mistake.

I placed my hand on his arm.

Muscles tensed as he stepped into me, placing the tips of his fingers on my chin, but before he could do anything, someone cleared their throat behind us. I turned, spying Solos in the doorway.

"Just making sure you two are okay," he said, a single eyebrow arched.

A rush of shame and guilt smacked into my stomach. "I'm not going to kill him and stash his body in the fridge."

"That's good to know," Aiden muttered.

"One can never be too safe." Solos pivoted. "Chop, chop, kids; people are getting antsy."

I sighed. "Gods, I kind of miss Apollo. At least he didn't think I wanted to kill you."

"Yeah, well, about that . . ."

I faced Aiden slowly, remembering that he had somehow banned Apollo. "What did you do? You banned him, right? How? Why?"

His brows arched. "I'm not sure you really want to know what provoked that."

Crossing my arms, I waited.

Aiden cocked his head to the side, jaw clenching. "Apollo wasn't completely honest about a lot of things, namely how an Apollyon can be killed."

I had a real bad feeling about this.

"Apollo can kill you, Alex. He was planning to if I took you off the Elixir and you connected with Seth again. And whoever is responsible for Seth can do him in, but it seems like that god may be working with them." He paused, grimacing. "So, I banned Apollo from the house."

My stomach lurched. Yeah, maybe I should've waited on that explanation until after my food had settled.

10

After I forced Aiden to drop that little bomb, we went into the large sitting room. I was numb. Apollo could kill me? Apollo had *wanted* to kill me? Then why had he shown up and put a smack-down on Thanatos? Gods, why was I trying to be logical about this? Apollo was a god. Who knew?

I sat beside Deacon and decided to push the Apollo issue aside for right now. "Okay, can I start small? What is today's date?"

Marcus leaned against a desk. I realized then he was in jeans and I couldn't think of a time when I'd ever seen him so casual. "Today is April 5th."

Blinking a couple of times, I sat back. A month . . . I'd basically lost an entire month. Gods, what was going on in the world outside this cabin? I cleared my throat. "And where am I? If it makes you feel better, you can just tell me the state."

"Apple River," Aiden said, keeping watch by the large picture window.

I folded my arms, which kind of hurt. "Okay, I know you have to be making that name up."

A slight smile formed on Aiden's lips. "It's real. You're in Illinois."

"Illinois?" My brain was stuck on the name Apple River being real.

"And it's about as empty and boring as it sounds," Deacon said, tipping his head at Luke. "And really backwoods. I went out once. Scary. Lumberjacks, enough said."

Solos scuffed. "This is my father's hunting cabin—one of many—and it's not that scary."

I nodded slowly. "Okay. So the gods? How many of them are ticked off right now?"

"All of them." Marcus laughed, swishing the contents of his glass. The smile quickly left his face. "All of them, Alexandria."

"We haven't seen many of the gods, but Hephaestus reinforced the bars," Lea said, studying her nails. "He was kind of scary."

I guessed I'd been out of it when he'd showed. "I can't believe Apollo hit me with a god bolt."

"I can't believe Aiden punched him," Marcus said, downing the rest of his wine.

"What?" My mouth dropped open. "You did not."

The half-grin spread until a dimple appeared in his left cheek. "I did."

"All those times you yelled at me for hitting people, and you hit a *god*?" I couldn't believe it.

That half-grin turned into a full smile. "This was a different situation."

Oh. Okay. Shaking my head, I moved on. "All right, have there been any more attacks like . . . like what happened to the Covenant?"

Laadan stared at me. "He . . . he didn't tell you?"

I figured by "he" she meant Seth. "I'm not sure. He kept me out of a lot of stuff."

"Except for telling you that they were working with daimons," she said, and I nodded. She glanced at Marcus and sighed. "A lot has been happening out there, dear. And very little of it is good."

Steeling myself for the worst, I wrapped my fingers around the crystal rose. "Tell me."

"We really don't have to tell you." Lea picked up a slim remote control and twisted, pointing it at a flatscreen on the wall. "We can just show you."

Lea picked one of the nationwide news stations. I didn't think there'd be anything happening right this instant, but apparently so much had happened, it was always on the news.

An image of destroyed buildings and toppled cars streamed over the screen. It was Los Angeles. Three days ago, there had been a catastrophic earthquake, a magnitude 7.0. A day later, another had hit the Indian Ocean, triggering a destructive tsunami that had wiped out an entire island.

And there was more.

Devastating wildfires plagued the Midwest and portions of South Dakota—near the University. I figured Hephaestus' automatons had something to do with that, considering they breathed balls of fire or whatever. There were various skirmishes in the Middle East. Several countries were on the brink of war.

Scrolling along the bottom of the screen was a breaking news announcement—seismic activity had begun below Mount St. Helens. Fears of a full volcanic eruption had people fleeing nearby towns.

Holy baby daimons . . .

The news anchor was interviewing a doomsday fanatic.

I sat back, soaking it in, horrified by what was happening. All of this because of Seth—and me—and there were so many innocent lives that had been lost, so many more that hung in the balance. There was a good chance I was going to hurl noodles all over the floor.

Lea turned the TV off.

"The gods are responsible for all of that?" I asked.

Laadan nodded.

Man, the gods *were* pissed.

"There is more," she said gently, and a mad laugh bubbled up in my throat. How could there be more? "So many Sentinels have been killed by Lucian's . . . by his army. And many pure-bloods have simply disappeared. Those who have reached the Covenants are holding strong, but no one is safe. Then there are the occurrences with mortals that look like wild animal attacks, but we believe them to be the work of the daimons. It appears that they are trying to provoke the gods."

At some point, Aiden had moved to stand behind the couch. His hands were on the back of the cushion. His presence was comforting, but I was shocked to the core. Apollo could have appeared in front of me and done a naked jig and I wouldn't have blinked an eye. Seth hadn't mentioned any of this, but Aiden *had* tried to tell me while I was in the cage.

And I'd told him I hadn't cared.

I started to stand, but my legs wouldn't cooperate.

"It's a lot to swallow, huh?" Luke said as he stared at his black boots. "The world's gone to shit in about a month."

"It's not too late. The gods are showing us what they want." Lea sounded entirely too mature to be the girl I'd thrown an apple at a couple of months ago. "They want Seth dead."

I knew that wasn't so much the case. They wanted *one of* us dead, preferably before we came within hugging distance. I racked my brain for something useful. After I'd Awakened, I'd learned the history of all the Apollyons, but none of that was useful. None of it except something with Solaris . . .

"It's just not as simple as killing Seth." Solos scratched at the stubble on his chin. "There is the problem of getting close. Dionysus said that Lucian had many Sentinels and Guards, mostly halfs."

Dionysus? How in the world had he come into the picture? Wasn't he the god of drunks or something?

"And if we get too close—if Alex gets too close, then . . ." Marcus trailed off.

Then he would take my power, possibly even drain me, because I now wasn't sure Seth could stop if he wanted to. No matter what he'd said to me while we were connected, I couldn't rely on his promises—his sales pitch—because I really didn't believe Seth knew what he was doing.

I stood then, because I couldn't sit anymore. Walking to the window, I stared at the shadowy landscape as I twisted the necklace between my fingers. Night had fallen and, even with my suped-up eyesight, the trees were dark and ominous. My reflection stared back at me, pale and unfamiliar. It was me—Alex, slightly rounded cheeks and wide lips. With the exception of the freaky amber eyes, I looked the same.

But I felt different.

There was a stillness *in* me that had never been there before. I didn't really know what it meant yet.

"Then what do we do?" Luke asked. "Hide Alex for ever?"

My lips twisted into a grim smile. That wasn't going to work.

"I could get behind that as long as someone brings in a DS or a Wii," Deacon joked, but it fell flat. "Or not . . ."

There was a pause and then Lea said, "Please gods, tell me you're not still against killing Seth."

"Now is probably not the best time to go there," Marcus said.

"What?" I heard her come to her feet, and her anger blasted the room. "Alex, you have to understand, especially after everything he's done to you."

"Lea," Aiden snapped, finally getting involved in the conversation.

"Don't 'Lea' me. Seth has to die, and Alex is the only person who can do it!"

Dropping the necklace, I faced them. "I know . . . he needs to be dealt with. I understand that."

Everyone, including Aiden, stared at me. He started to speak, but closed his mouth. Truth be told, I loathed the idea of killing anything at this point. Didn't mean I wouldn't do it when I faced a daimon again, and even though Seth had been a real bastard about things, I knew that deep down he was nothing more than an unloved little boy who wanted acceptance. And yeah, he had a major akasha addiction, but he was a victim in all of this, too. The only person I'd probably enjoy taking out, just a little bit, was Lucian. Yeah, I could get behind that.

But getting to Lucian wasn't going to happen.

"Alex," Marcus said softly.

I took a breath, unable to put forth the words necessary for what needed to be said. "What do we do?" I glanced at Aiden and then Solos. They were the skilled Sentinels here. Time for some battle strategy, which wasn't my strong suit, because I was more of a "run into things head-first and face-plant a wall" type of fighter. "We have to stop Seth and Lucian, but we can't just walk up to them. We need to be able to get close without them knowing, and we—*I* need to know how to fight Seth without transferring my power to him."

Aiden looked like he didn't like the sound of that, but he turned to Solos and nodded. "Apollo said that it may take a few days for him to come back, but he asked that we don't lift the wards until he can come to us. Those wards prevent them from finding us, and right now they are the *only* thing stopping the gods from finding us."

"How did Thanatos find me?" I asked, curious.

"You went outside, beyond the wards," Aiden said. "Hopefully Apollo can tell us more when he returns."

"So we wait in here until then and do nothing?" Lea slumped against the cushion, crossing her arms. A petulant look crossed her face.

"We don't sit and do nothing," Solos said, eyeing the girl. "What we need to do is train and prepare for what . . . for what's coming. That's what Apollo wanted."

Because something *was* coming, and it was a war.

"Hopefully Apollo can convince the gods to lay off," Aiden said, jaw working. "Right now, we need the gods on our side."

"Agreed," half the room said.

Hope flickered in my chest. "Do you think they'll stop this . . .

zombie-apocalypse-in-the-making if they realize I'm back on Team Not-Insane?"

No one really looked hopeful, but Aiden smiled at me, and I knew he did it to make me feel better, because it was what I wanted to hear. It took everything in me not to cross the room and jump him.

Priorities, Alex, priorities . . .

Everyone agreed on starting training as soon as possible. And it made sense. Fighting was not like riding a bicycle. Muscles weakened, reflexes slowed. Honestly, we had no other choice. Hopefully no other gods would show up, dishing out some good old god wrath.

I sat on the edge of the couch and started fiddling with the rose again. I knew everyone was waiting to hear any plans Seth had shared with me. They were going to be disappointed. "The only thing Seth told me about was the daimons, and he knew I'd told Aiden afterward. I don't think he was too concerned. He really didn't tell me anything else. The plans he . . . the plans we made were about freeing my father."

Laadan's eyes dampened, and I hoped we could talk soon. There was so much I had to ask her.

Solos didn't even try to hide his displeasure. "Well, that's not really helpful."

"It's not her fault," Aiden shot back.

The Sentinel cracked a distorted smile. "Simmer down, Loverboy."

My mouth opened to deny that Aiden was my loverboy. The response was immediate, inherent in nature. I forced my mouth closed before I could say anything. Everyone in this room already knew that Aiden and I were *together* together. Hell, everyone in the world probably guessed, courtesy of Lucian's announcement before Seth blew up the Council, which had made Aiden Public Enemy Number Two.

It was odd being so open about it, though—not odd in a bad

way, but something that would take me a little while to get used to. I wasn't Aiden's dirty little secret.

I'd never been his dirty little secret.

Deacon laughed. "Oh, you're *so* going to be the next person who gets hit. I'm putting money on that."

"You need to add yourself to that list." Aiden looked about seventy-percent serious.

"And I'm putting money on *that*," Luke threw in.

I shot forward, gripping my knees. "I do remember something! It's not major, but Seth was heading north. He's probably heading to the Catskills."

"That's something to go on." Marcus glanced at his glass, as if he couldn't fathom how it was empty. "He won't reach it. Not with the Khalkotauroi surrounding the place."

Olivia shuddered. "You think they can actually stop him?"

"They'll slow him down." Marcus pushed off the desk, heading for the door. "Anyone else in need of refreshments?"

"You sharing?" Deacon perked up.

Surprisingly, Aiden didn't caution him. Perhaps a little underage wine drinking wasn't our biggest concern at the moment. Our group scattered, some following Marcus on the wine run. Only after they left did I realize that the Dean of the Covenant was supplying alcohol to minors.

This really was an alternate universe.

After a few minutes, it was just Aiden and me. He sat beside me, exhaling a long breath. "You doing okay?"

Wondering how many times he was going to ask that in twenty-four hours, I turned to him. "I'm fine, really."

He looked like there was something he wanted to say, but he leaned forward and kissed my forehead instead. "I'm going to go check the grounds."

"I'll come with you."

"Stay here and take it easy, Alex. Just for tonight, okay?"

I felt the urge to pout. "You shouldn't have to do that alone."

"I'm not." He flashed a grin. "Solos will be with me."

"He wasn't with you earlier. That's what you were doing when everyone was eating, right? Checking the grounds, making sure no daimons were sneaking up on us?"

"I doubt there are any daimons out here."

But he was still patrolling, because that's what Sentinels did, and I thought about how he was willing to leave this life . . . leave it for us. I bet, if we lived in some place like Apple River, he'd still check the yard every night. Thinking that brought a smile to my lips.

"I've missed your smiles," he said, standing.

I looked up, wanting to grab his hand and make him stay. "I'll be here waiting."

"I know."

He looked at me strangely and then he left, and I was alone . . . alone except for the low buzz in the back of my head. I tried not to pay attention to it, because it symbolized a whole truckload of potential problems. That damn buzzing meant that Seth was still there, and I didn't know what that really meant in terms of him contacting me.

Glancing at the window, I took a breath but it got stuck. What if Seth could reach me? Would I be able to fight off what he wanted? If I did, could I somehow reason with him? Or would I just lose myself again, and this time there'd be no reaching me? An ache pierced my chest.

Unable to think about that without ending up in the corner rocking, I reached for the remote and turned the TV on. The news still focused on the horrific earthquake in Los Angeles and the developing story coming out the Pacific Northwest.

Taking in the destruction the gods were wreaking, I knew only one thing—and it hurt in a way that shouldn't have, in a way I couldn't really explain. Seth had to die, but I had no idea how to do it . . . or if I really could, when it came down to it.

11

I stayed in front of that TV the entire night, tired but not sleepy. Aiden passed out in the recliner beside the couch around three in the morning. I doubted that he was cool with leaving my side for long stretches of time. I didn't know if he was worried that I'd turn into Evil Alex again, or if he just needed to be near me. Either way, I was comforted by his soft snores. I think he was waiting for me to give up on my morbid fascination with the news, but I didn't.

Every newscaster had something different to add. More pictures streamed in from all around the globe. Mortals poured into the L.A. streets, rioting and looting, but in the Middle East, they dropped to their knees in the streets and prayed.

Clutching the remote until my knuckles ached, I tried—really tried—to imagine what it must be like to be these mortals. To be caught in something so much bigger than them while having no idea that, at any given second, everything could be ripped away from them.

I had more in common with them than I realized.

It really did seem like the end of the world. No mortal could explain the series of catastrophic events that, in their limited knowledge, couldn't be related to each other.

What was happening out there was beyond horrifying, and the destruction was because of Seth and me. Maybe it wouldn't have come to this if Seth hadn't attacked the Council. Maybe the gods would've left us alone to live our lives.

Maybe they would've found a way to kill us anyway.

I didn't know and it really didn't matter. This was where we were now, and things were screwed up. While all the knowledge of the Apollyons was floating around in my head, none of it was useful when it came to fixing this.

Laadan appeared in the doorway, dressed in slacks and a white sweater today. Her hair was perfectly coifed, in spite of the fact the world had donned its crazy pants. The woman was awe-inspiring.

She glanced at Aiden and smiled. "Care to join me for some coffee?"

How could I ever turn down caffeine? Nodding, I started out of the room, but backtracked to where Aiden rested and fixed the quilt I'd draped over him a few hours ago. The man must have been exhausted, because he didn't wake up, which was rare.

I followed Laadan into the kitchen and watched her make quick work of the coffee. With our steaming cups in hand, we went into the sunroom for the privacy it offered. We sat on the window seat, our legs tucked toward each other. Finally, we were going to talk about my father, and I had no idea what was going to come out of her mouth.

I was even a little scared, stupid and weak as that was, and my stomach was flipping all over the place. I knew nothing of my father, having only discovered that he was a half-blood and alive a few months ago.

Laadan took a sip of her coffee and blinked several times. "First, I want to apologize for what happened to you at the Council. I—"

"You don't have to apologize. That wasn't your fault." And it wasn't. Laadan had been compelled to give me the Brew—like a suped-up roofie of the gods—by one of Telly's Guards, probably the one I'd killed . . .

"What they tried to do to you was horrid." Tears filled her eyes, shining like crystals. "I wish—I wish I had known. I am so sorry—"

"Laadan, seriously, you don't have to apologize. I know you would never willingly do something like that. And I know you don't remember who did it. It's okay." And gods, I did not want to talk about that night. Beside the fact that it made me think about the Guard I'd killed, if I hadn't ended up puking my guts out, Seth and I . . . we would've done it, and after everything now, I don't think I'd ever get over that.

I sat my coffee on the small wicker table as my stomach roiled. "I want to know about my dad."

A remarkable change occurred in Laadan. A different kind of sheen misted in her eyes. She took another drink, her pointer finger tapping off the glass. The anticipation was killing me.

"Your father is a . . . an incredible man, Alex. You should know that above all else."

My breath fell short. "I know." I did know, because he had to be to break the rules and love my mother. "The Elixir didn't work on my father, did it?"

Laadan smiled wistfully. "Your father—Alexander—well, he always had a strong will, much like you. The Elixir has taken its toll on him, but he never completely fell to the compulsion. I do not know how, but he resisted it from the beginning."

I clasped my hands together. "I think I saw him on the stairs once, and then toward the end, during the attack. He was fighting . . ."

"You did see him." Her gaze moved to the window behind us. Early-morning sunlight sliced over the frost-covered glass. "He was in the library the night we spoke of your mother and him."

I could only stare. I knew someone had been in there. "The books that fell over—that was him?"

She nodded.

How many times had I been close to the man—to my father—without knowing? A hurricane of disappointment swelled inside me. "And . . . and he knows I'm his daughter?"

"Yes, he knows." She reached out with her free hand, gently

touching the skin of my face, near a bruise that was already starting to heal. "He would recognize you anywhere. You look so much like your mother."

That bite of sadness strengthened and I pulled back. "Then why didn't he talk to me?"

Laadan looked away, her chin lowering.

"I tried talking to him, Laadan. In the stairwell, but he just . . . stared at me. And why didn't he come up to me in the library? I know he couldn't just announce who he was, but why . . ." My throat tightened. "Why didn't he want to talk to me, at least?"

Her head snapped toward me. "Oh, honey, he wanted to talk to you more than anything, but it's not that simple."

"Seems simple to me. You open your mouth and talk." I struggled to sit still. Had he heard of my escapades? Gods know rumors of my problems with authority had traveled far and wide. Had he been embarrassed as a trained Sentinel? Worse yet, as a father? "I just don't understand."

She took a breath. "He was close to you a lot when you were there and you didn't know, but it was also very dangerous for him to be seen around you. The truth of what he is, what your mother was, and what you are, was too much of a risk. You already had too many eyes on you."

The conversation Seth and I had overheard came back to me. *We already have one here.* Anger sparked and was quick to ignite a fire inside me. Marcus . . . Marcus had known, and now that it was all out in the open, we were so going to talk about that.

"What I told you in the library that night? That he would be proud of you because of who you have become and not what you will become?" She clasped my fisted hand in her gentle grip. "That is the truth. From the moment you arrived back at the Covenant last summer, I did my best to keep him up to date on how you were. Your mother . . . she didn't know what had happened to him and Alexander wanted it that way. In a way, death was easier than the truth."

I blinked away sudden tears and wanted to pull my hand free, but like always, Laadan's calming nature was disarming.

"Things are more complicated than you realize, Alex. He couldn't talk to you."

Shaking my head, I tried and failed to understand that. I'd think that a father would've done anything to speak to his daughter just once.

Laadan squeezed my hands and let go. "The Masters always suspected that your father was different, and that perhaps he was influencing other servants. They treated him quite cruelly. He cannot talk to you, Alex. They removed half his tongue."

I balked at what she said. I'd heard her wrong. There were no other options. "No. I saw him talking with another servant in the dining hall."

She shook her head sadly. "If anything, you saw a servant talking *to* him."

Forcing myself to remember the morning after I'd been slipped the Brew more clearly, I tried to see my father and the younger servant. Things had looked tense and his back had been to me most of the time. I'd assumed that he'd been talking by the reaction of the other servant.

I *hadn't* seen him talk.

Shooting to my feet, I heard Laadan's little gasp of surprise. Even I was a little shocked by how fast I moved. The marks of the Apollyon appeared on my skin and tingled as they glided in various directions. She couldn't see them, but some innate sense coaxed her to scoot back.

"They cut out his tongue?" Power surged over my skin.

"Yes."

That was it. I was going to take out the Council and every freaking Master on this planet. Bad, dangerous thoughts, but gods, how could they do something like that?

"How can I be so surprised?" I said out loud, and then laughed madly. "How am I surprised by this, Laadan?"

There was no answer.

Turning away, I struggled to control my fury. Already I could hear the branches slapping along the side of the cabin. Knowing my luck, I'd probably cause an earthquake. Controlling the elements was easy, but I'd learned through the Awakening that my emotions affected them, made them violent and unpredictable.

As did the amount of aether, the essence of the gods, that coursed through my veins.

Our society had always been cruel to the half-bloods. Pures had always taken a role of dominance, and the things that I knew went on behind the closed doors of some of the pures—things no one talked about, things I wanted to rage about—happened every day. And like every other half, I'd been in a subservient role my entire life. I'd grown up being taught to accept these things, because there was no other choice for me, or for any other half. Even after living in the mortal world, I'd come back into the fold, barely missing a step when I'd seen the servants.

And only once had I intervened. I'd received a punch in the jaw for it, but stopping a Master from striking a female servant was nothing compared to what those halfs went through.

In reality, it was more than accepting the Breed Order. I'd grown cold to it, because it hadn't affected me.

And that was inexcusable.

Stepping away, I ran my hands down my outer thighs. The breath I inhaled was harsh. This was bigger than me and my own problems with becoming a Sentinel and continuing on while others of my kind were enslaved. This was more than my father. It was the Breed Order.

"This has to change," I said.

"I agree, but . . ."

But now, right this instant, there was nothing I could do. Believe it or not, we had bigger problems. The Breed Order and how halfs were treated wouldn't matter if we were all dead.

Facing Laadan, I realized something huge—huge to me, at least. Old Alex would've probably stormed off somewhere and kicked a Master in the junk. A huge part of me wanted to do that, but the new Alex—this girl/woman/whatever who came out of nowhere knew that some battles had to be planned.

That new Alex waited.

I sort of struck myself speechless.

Laadan, more observant than I realized, smiled and patted the spot beside her. "You're growing up."

"I am?" Seemed late in the game for that sort of nonsense. I sat, and when she nodded, I sighed and sounded ten years older. "Growing up sucks, then."

"There is a naïveté to young selfishness."

My brows rose. I was itchy, like I had slipped on more responsible and mature skin and a part of me didn't like that. Shaking it off, I went back to my dad. "You talk to him a lot?"

"As much as I can. Communication is one-sided at times, but he can write, obviously. I know he got your letter, but unfortunately with everything happening, I do not know his response or if he had the chance."

I nodded in a jerking motion. "Do you know where he is right now?"

She fingered the lace on the edge of her sweater. "Alexander is at the New York Covenant."

"He's still there?" When she nodded, I wanted to get up and figure out how to get to New York, but logic seeped in. It would be near impossible to get to him. And with Seth out there, looking for us? It would just be plain stupid to go running off.

"When the Elixir stopped working, there was a lot of confusion among the servants. There are very few like him who resisted the compulsions. Those who are going through their own awakening of sorts need a leader, and that is your father. There is a lot of turmoil there, with the recent attack and with what the First is doing."

But I wanted to scream that I needed him here with me. Wasn't I more important? His long-lost daughter? I frowned. Well, good to see some of my *naïve selfishness* was still present.

"Does he still love my mother?" I asked, peeking at her.

Her expression was guarded. "I think a part of him will always love her."

"Do you love him?" I blurted out.

Laadan swallowed and a long pause followed. In the gap, I heard someone moving around in the kitchen.

I started to grin. "You like him."

Looking away, her lips pursed.

I nudged her with my elbow. "You like him *a lot*."

She drew herself up. "Your father—"

"Is the love of your life?"

"Alexandria," she snapped, but there was no real heat to her tone.

I laughed as I leaned back against the cool windowpane. I knew that my parents had this wondrous, forbidden love affair that started long before Stepfather Douchey had come into the picture. And if it hadn't been for the Breed . . . the godsdamn Breed Order, they'd still be together. Gods, so many things would be different. Namely my mother . . . she'd still be alive, because I bet my dad was like Aiden. He would've never allowed anything to happen to my mom.

Laadan's lips curved up at the corners. "You are so much like your father. Your stubbornness and tenacity." Her gaze went to the closed door. The smell of fresh coffee grew. "And just like your father, you dared to love a pure-blood."

My mouth opened. *Touché*. "Well, I kind of walked into that one."

I thought she snickered, but I had to be wrong, because that would be so unladylike of her.

For some odd reason, some of the weight lifted from my shoulders and I went from vengeful, albeit more mature Alex, to girlie-girl in less than two seconds flat. "I do love him. I really do. More than . . . more than I probably should."

She patted my hand. "You can never love someone more than you probably should."

I wasn't sure about that.

"He loves you just as strongly. It was obvious to me from the beginning."

"It was?"

"The Aiden I knew, the one before he went to Atlanta to find you, had always respected and viewed halfs equally, but he never would've taken time away from his Sentinel duties to help any half."

Knowing what had been done to his parents in front of him while he was a small boy, I could see why she would think that. Becoming a Sentinel and avenging his parents had become everything to him.

"And then I saw the way he was around you in New York." Her smiled turned wistful again. "It's all in the way he looked at you—the way he *constantly* looked at you. You were his world, probably before either of you realized that."

"You could tell all that by the way he looked at me?" I may've sounded skeptical, but oh, wow, that girlie-girl was jumping and shrieking inside me.

Laadan laughed then, the sound like wind chimes. "He watched you like a man starved for the only thing that could fulfill his hunger."

My eyes popped out and my body flushed about a thousand shades of red. "Oh, wow . . ."

That was TMI. How come more people hadn't noticed that? And then it hit me. Laadan would know, because it was how she looked at my father . . . and probably had witnessed my father looking at my mother in the same manner.

I was suddenly very sad for her.

Scooting closer to her, I wrapped my arms around her

slender shoulders. It was awkward at first, because I seriously gave the worst hugs. "Thank you."

Tears filled her eyes again. "Talking to you about your father is the least I could do. If you like, there are many stories I can tell you. It will be a . . . joy to speak openly about them."

"I'd like that," I whispered.

Laadan rested her cheek atop my head, and in that moment, she reminded me so much of my mom that it was almost too much to keep the tears at bay, but I couldn't stop the question that formed on the tip of my tongue.

"Do you think I'll ever get to meet him?"

Her embrace tightened. "You will. Both of you are determined enough to make it happen. I have no doubt."

Closing my eyes, I latched on to her words. I wanted to believe them—I needed to—but doubt swelled like bitter wisps of acrid smoke. A lot stood between me and my father—years of rules and secrets existed, an army of half-man/half-bulls, and most importantly, Seth.

12

A few hours later, I stood in the warded-up clearing by the cabin, covered in mud and chilled to the bone. All around me, the sounds of grunts and hard falls echoed through the otherwise silent forest.

I glanced down at my dirty hands and sighed. I was filthy. Maybe I'd get a repeat of that shower later. My gaze found Aiden's lithe form. He was fighting Luke. In other words, he was repeatedly kicking Luke's ass.

I doubted a shower repeat was on the menu.

A sharp pang of dissatisfaction formed in the back of my throat. I'd really thought that, since I was supposed to be training, I'd end up with Aiden and it would be like old times with a lot more touchy-feely stuff going on. Boy, was I wrong.

Solos exhaled loudly. "How long are you going to stare at your hands? I'm not getting any younger over here."

But oh no, the moment we stepped outside, Aiden had paired up with Luke and Olivia, Lea with Marcus. Deacon and Laadan were inside, supposedly making dinner.

Now I was in full internal whine mode.

I moved forward, wincing as my cold jeans chafed my skin. "I don't think this is the kind of training Apollo had in mind."

Solos tucked a loose strand of hair back behind his ear. "When's the last time you trained?"

I honestly couldn't remember. "I was fighting, like, two days ago."

"One day in the span of many means nothing." Broken

branches crunched under his booted feet. "Our muscles need to be used daily."

I caught the tail end of Luke ending up on his butt. "I think they could use your help more. I could be working on using akasha right now. Seth has years of practical experience on me."

"And you will work with that, but not right now." Solos was nowhere near as patient as *some* of my previous trainers had been. He ranked up there with Romvi.

Eyes narrowing, I raised my hand. "I could just use the air element and knock—"

"Alex," Aiden snapped, stopping Luke's vicious kick with one hand. He gently pushed him back as thundercloud eyes sharpened on me. "I also doubt Apollo meant for your mouth to be the only thing getting a workout."

So many inappropriate comments rose to the tip of my tongue and danced around, but I snapped my jaw shut and glared at him.

"He's trying to help you." Aiden swiped up a titanium dagger from where it was implanted deep in the ground. "The least you could do is go along with this without torturing those who are helping you."

Embarrassed and angry, I was two seconds from raining my wrath down on Aiden when I stopped. Aiden *was* right. I was being whiny and bitchy and flat-out annoying.

Our eyes met, and there wasn't much heat behind his words, but he was frustrated with me and I hated that, because I was being a brat. I wasn't sure what was wrong with me. Ever since Laadan and I had spoken, my mood had plummeted. Lack of sleep, maybe?

The sting of Aiden's admonishment forced me back to Solos, who, by the way, had mud splattered on him like gore at a gruesome crime scene. No one in this world could get me to do what I was supposed to be doing as quickly as Aiden.

Part of me hated that. The other part respected and thanked him for it.

Cheeks burning, I dropped into stance. Solos launched at me. We went at it, blow for blow. He dipped. I spun. More times than not, he ended up sprawled on the ground, kicking up dirt and loose grass on me. My muscles were a little out of use, but I was fast—faster than I ever remembered being. When I'd been fighting Aiden the other day, I hadn't been aware of what I was really doing, not the mechanics of it. But now? Whoa, I felt like Superwoman.

Solos picked himself off the ground, exhaling out his nose. We moved on to disarming one another, which usually had been a weak area for me.

I darted under Solos' outstretched arm, caught both of his elbows and pulled back, running my hands down to his wrists as I planted a foot in his back. He released the blades and I caught them.

Waving them in his face, I grinned. "I kind of rock at this."

He turned, brows furrowed. "I don't even know what that move was."

I flipped the dagger in my right hand. "It's called being awesome and it worked."

"There's a difference between skill and speed." He snatched the dagger out of my other hand. "You won't always have speed."

"But I have the elements," I reminded him.

"That you do." He gave a lopsided grin that didn't stretch his scar. He was handsome when he smiled like that. Hell, he was handsome even with the scar—kind of like a pirate. "But correct me if I'm wrong—doesn't using the elements tire you out?"

"That's what I hear." Olivia dropped down on a tree stump and stretched out her long legs slowly. "Well, I heard Seth say that once."

With only one dagger left in hand, I pointed it at Solos. "Using the elements can tire us out, but not as much as akasha.

That's why he doesn't use it all the time. Zaps him—us, I guess."

Aiden threaded his fingers and stretched, bowing his back. My gaze followed the movement quite obsessively. Everything he did looked fluid and graceful. "That's why it's important not to rely solely on those abilities."

As long as I'd known Aiden, I could count on one hand how many times he'd used the fire element. Each pure had an affinity to a certain element, while the Apollyon could wield control over all of them. Aiden liked to fight hand-to-hand.

Or titanium-to-titanium.

Lea was leaning against a large oak, her hair a mess as Marcus retrieved the fallen blades they'd been practicing with. My uncle handled them expertly. Sometimes I forgot that he had trained as a Sentinel, once upon a time.

Our little recess was over, and under the cloudy April skies we continued until the sun began its descent in the west. Only then did we shuffle back into the cabin, and I guessed practicing akasha was on the schedule for tomorrow. The smell of roasted meat teased my taste buds. I was so hungry I could eat a daimon, but a shower came first.

And as I'd expected earlier, I was all by my lonesome in that endeavor.

All of us sat at the kitchen table and dug in. Someone thanked Laadan for the meal and Deacon about had a coronary.

"Who tenderized the meat? Who marinated and watched it dutifully?" His blond brows lowered as he held his fork like Luke held a dagger. "That would be *me*."

Laadan nodded. "I peeled potatoes. That was about it."

"I didn't know you could cook," I said, surprised.

Freshly showered, Aiden dropped into the seat beside his brother. His dark hair was damp and swept back, revealing his broad cheekbones. He clapped his brother on the shoulder. "Deacon is one hell of a cook."

"Hmm." Olivia grinned as she chased a scalloped potato across her plate. "Learn something new every day, right?"

Not even trying to hide his proud smile, Deacon glanced at Luke. "I'm full of surprises."

I arched a brow, but shoved a piece of succulent meat into my mouth rather than saying anything. For a little while, sitting at that table with everyone, things were, well, they were nice and warm.

Aiden remained mostly quiet while everyone traded stories, cracking a grin every once in a while, but still slightly apart from the boisterous group. More than once, our gazes met. Something churned in his gray eyes. I could easily see the sharp slice of sorrow mixing with regret before he looked away.

After dinner, bellies full, the group split into different sections of the house. Lea disappeared with one of the books Laadan had brought with her. Olivia and the boys set up in the living room with a deck of cards. Solos and Marcus went out to check the perimeter with Aiden. It was getting late, and I was trying to stay up for when they came back, but eventually I said good-night to the group and dragged myself upstairs.

I stopped in front of Aiden's bedroom, suddenly unsure of where I was supposed to be sleeping. There was another bedroom adjoining the bathroom, which was supposed to be mine, but I couldn't recall ever sleeping in there. Was I supposed to be in that room? And if I made myself at home in Aiden's, was I overstepping something?

Shifting my weight wearily, I chewed on my bottom lip. Gods, this shouldn't be this complicated. *Come on, Alex, you're being stupid.* And I did feel stupid.

Heading to my room, I discovered I was severely lacking in the nightclothes department. Going back through the bath-room, I found a few of Aiden's longer shirts folded separately from the rest of his clothing, as if they'd been purposefully left aside.

I changed into one of the thin cotton shirts that reached my thighs, and there was no way I wanted to go back to the cool, untouched room that was supposed to be mine. Slipping under the covers, I snuggled down, inhaling the earthy scent that blanketed the bed.

It didn't take long to drift off to sleep. Probably only minutes, and I was floating in a comforting haze, but something made me open my eyes. And when I did, I was staring right into a pair of amber-colored ones.

13

Seth.

Oh gods, I was staring at *Seth*. He was here. Impossible, but he was here with me.

My heart raced in a chaotic rhythm as I pressed away. So afraid, so terrified by his sudden appearance, I couldn't catch my breath.

His arms formed a cage around me. I didn't dare move, for his skin was too close to mine, his lips a fraction of an inch away. His amber eyes glowed under thick, dark-blond eyelashes. Marks of the Apollyon raced up over his neck, spreading over his cheeks in a vibrant wave of blue over his golden complexion. My own marks responded to his proximity, causing my skin to tingle. The cord snapped alive.

The force of Seth's presence was everywhere, invading my body and thoughts, but when I finally breathed in, the scent was all wrong. It was earthy with a hint of sea salt. *Aiden*.

Seth's lips curved into a satisfied smile and he placed his mouth near my ear. "I told you, Alex. I'd find you anywhere."

My mouth opened, but my scream was strangled by the lump of terror in my throat as I twisted to the side and jerked awake . . . *awake*.

Pulse pounding, I sat up and the bedroom slowly came into focus. My frantic gaze traveled the room, searching out the shadows for any sign of Seth. A sliver of moonlight seeped in under the blinds, spreading across the floor, its fingers brushing over the antique dresser. Under the bathroom door, a slit of yellow gleamed. Other than the tingling marks, there was no sign of him.

It was just a dream—a nightmare. Nothing more, but the adrenaline kicking around inside me begged to differ.

The bathroom door opened and Aiden filled the doorway. Lit by the soft glow of the light behind him, he was a study of shadowy contrasts—shirtless and wearing only a pair of pajama bottoms that hung low on his hips.

That didn't help my heart *or* breathing problem.

The light behind him flipped off.

"Alex?" He moved silently to the bed, dipping down beside me. "I didn't wake you, did I?"

I shook my head.

His head tilted to the side and dark hair fell over his forehead. "Are you okay?"

"Yeah," I croaked out, feeling ridiculous now for overreacting to a stupid nightmare.

Aiden reached out, stopping with his hand a hair's breadth from my cheek. He pulled away, settling onto his back. One arm stretched out, beckoning me. Stretching out beside him, I placed my head on his shoulder, my hand on his chest above his thundering heart. His skin was warm, comforting.

Several heartbeats passed in silence while his heart slowed down. Why it had been beating so fast, I didn't know. I snuggled closer, fitting my body to his side, and his arm curled around my waist. I felt his jaw graze the top of my head, and then his lips pressed against my forehead.

I squeezed my eyes shut, wanting to tell him about the dream, but instead, something else came out. "They cut out my father's tongue, Aiden. He can't talk. *They* did that to him."

He seemed to hold his breath for a moment.

"Why would they do something like that?" I asked, and my own voice sounded incredibly small and fragile.

"I don't know." His hand came up, pressing between my

shoulders, moving in a soothing circle. "There isn't any justification for something as horrific as that." There was a pause. "I'm sorry, Alex."

I nodded, squeezing my eyes shut. We needed to do something about the Breed Order, and I knew Aiden would agree, but discussing something so political at two in the morning seemed out of place.

Stretching up, I placed my lips to Aiden's, but the kiss turned out more chaste than the hot and steamy action I was going for. His arm tightened, though, and a fine tremor coursed through his body as if he was fighting the pull between us.

Confused, I ceased my attempt at seducing him, since it really wasn't working, and settled back down, heart racing again. Why hadn't he kissed me back? Was he still upset over my bratty display earlier while training with Solos? If so, then geez, there was nothing I could do to fix that. Or was it something else? Like the regret and sadness that flashed in his gray eyes?

Out of the silence that had fallen in the room once more, Aiden said, "I love you."

There was no missing the heavy thread of emotion in his voice. My breath caught. Even with my failed seduction attempt, hearing him say those three little words was something I'd never get tired of. "I love you, too."

Very little time later, the steady rise and fall of Aiden's chest deepened. I stayed in his embrace, staring through the darkness at the empty wall across the room for what seemed like hours before I carefully disentangled myself from his arms and crept out of the bed.

Unable to sleep or stay put, I found a pair of sweats in the darkness and drew them on, rolling the cuffs at the bottom. My bare feet padded off the wood floors as I slipped out of the door and headed downstairs.

The house was tomb-quiet and chilly. Folding my arms, I piddled around in the kitchen, even though I wasn't hungry or thirsty. Restless and wide awake, with no idea of what to do, I made my way to the sunroom.

It was colder in there, but in a weird way, surrounded by all the plants and windows with nothing but darkness looming outside, it was peaceful.

Sitting at the window seat, I tucked my legs against my chest and stared out one of the windows. Too much was running through my head – my father, training again, the Breed Order, Aiden and his sudden resistance, everything that was happening outside these walls, and . . .

And I was thinking about Seth, courtesy of the nightmarish visit.

A sharp slice of panic pierced my belly. What had happened had to have been a nightmare. Which was completely understandable considering Seth was pulling a Doctor Evil right now. It couldn't be anything else, so I needed to stop freaking over it. But that low buzz in the back of my head—it was still there and it signified that, no matter what I did or how strong I was, I would always be connected to him.

And that he could possibly still reach me.

That anxious pang was back, spreading to my chest. I squeezed my eyes shut. Fear was a sour taste on the roof of my mouth. Could that nightmare really have been Seth reaching out to me?

I checked my mental shields. Almost like running my tongue over my teeth after Jackson had stomped me in the face during class, I poked and prodded at the shield, making sure nothing had been knocked out of place or loose. The shield was sturdy, but the traces of alarm lingered.

When I'd been connected to Seth after I'd Awakened, I could hear his thoughts as clear as my own.

I rocked back a little, squeezing my legs until my arms ached.

Seth had really seemed like he'd been here tonight, leaning over me and whispering his warning. Even my nightmares from what had happened in Gatlinburg hadn't been that real, and they'd been pretty damn visual.

Footsteps neared the sunroom and my head snapped up. "Marcus."

He was still dressed like he'd been at dinner, jeans and a tailored flannel shirt—a sure sign he hadn't gone to bed yet. "Up a little late?" he asked, leaning against the doorframe.

I gave a lopsided shrug and kept my arms locked around my knees. "I'm not sleepy."

"You were dragging all evening. I figured you'd sleep another day away."

It wasn't like I could tell him the truth, so I said nothing.

Marcus hesitated in the doorway and then strode forward, sure and strong. I watched him wearily as he sat beside me, taking the same spot Laadan had when we'd spoken. Several tense, uncomfortable minutes passed, and although Marcus and I had come a long way, we still had mountains to climb before things weren't so epically awkward between us.

He placed his hands in his lap and sighed. "Are you feeling well, Alexandria?"

So formal . . . "Yeah, like I said, just not sleepy. How about you?"

"Was out patrolling and just switched out with Solos." He cast me a quick sidelong glance. "I'm not sleepy, either."

I turned back to the window. "Do you guys think it's necessary to patrol?"

"Some of it may just be out of habit, especially for Aiden and Solos, but stranger things have been known to happen."

Surprised that he answered honestly, I faced him. With my Apollyon sight, I could make out the lines of his face in the shadows. Another shocker came when I found his expression was open. "And even though the gods might not be gunning for us this very second, that could always change," he said. "So we watch . . . and we wait."

I didn't say anything for a long moment. "I hate that."

"What?" Curiosity marked his tone.

My hands curled into themselves, balling next to my thighs. "That people would so willingly give their lives away to protect me. I hate that."

Marcus twisted toward me and then leaned his head back against the window. "Don't take this the wrong way, but it's not just you that we're protecting, Alexandria. There's Lea and Deacon, Olivia and Luke. Three of them are trained to a certain extent, but not against gods or a horde of daimons. Even though a daimon attack out here seems unlikely . . ."

Stranger things had happened. I nodded.

His vibrant eyes slid closed. "It's not always about you."

My mouth worked on a refusal. I didn't think it was always about me, but wait . . . I kind of sort of did by assuming that everyone was throwing themselves in front of a bus for me. My cheeks burned.

"I didn't . . . I didn't mean it like that." I took a breath. "Well, I kind of did, but I know you guys are protecting them, too. And that's . . . that's a good thing."

His shoulders relaxed. "And I didn't mean how that came out."

I laughed and the sound surprised me. It wasn't forced or snarky, just amused. "Yeah, you did, and I get it. I've been riding the Alex-Is-Important train for quite some time."

One eyebrow arched.

The urge to laugh came again, but I stopped it and placed my cheek on my knees. "I've been . . . uh, I've been a handful. I know that. Most of the time it was on purpose."

"I knew," was all he said.

"You did?"

Marcus nodded. "You're like any child—"

"I'm not a child."

His lips curved up at the corners. "You *were* like any child who was seeking a place to fit in. It's especially hard with you half-bloods. Many of you come from unhappy homes, or no homes at all. The environment you're raised in is violent and aggressive. I've seen so many . . ." He shook his head slightly. "Anyway, you were different, though."

I glanced toward the empty question. "Why?"

"For starters, you're my niece."

"Wow." I blinked, loosening my grip on my legs. "I'm surprised that the first thing wasn't that you knew I was the Apollyon."

Marcus's eyes opened and met mine. "That was never first, second, or third. You are my niece. You are my sister's daughter. And you are so much like her . . ." He exhaled through the nose, his jaw locking. "You were so much like her that when you came back to the Covenant . . . and even now, I have a hard time looking at you without seeing my sister."

Something . . . something came unhinged in my chest. Never had Marcus been this open with me. And it'd seemed more likely for me to waltz around the living room with a daimon before Marcus would talk to me about my mother, but here he was.

Holy daimon butt, we were climbing that mountain.

The breath I inhaled was a bit raspy. "You loved my mom a lot."

"Rachelle was my little sister and I . . . I loved her dearly." His eyes closed again. "Rachelle was full of life—vibrant. We were opposites. She drew people to her in droves, and I pretty much repelled them."

My lips quirked at the corners.

"She was probably the only person who could get me to relax." He sat up suddenly, dropping his hands on his knees. "When you were really little, she used to bring you over to my home, and if you behaved, which wasn't always likely, she'd take you for ice cream afterward." A pensive smile formed. "You were such a tiny thing then, but my gods, I knew immediately you would look just like her. Everything except the eyes . . ."

Searching my memories, I found I could recall nothing of him from when I'd been a little girl, only the few visits when I was older, and they had been cold and impersonal. Marcus had been like every other pure.

"She always claimed that your father was a mortal, but that one Sentinel was always with her, always following her . . . and you."

"What?" My head snapped up.

Marcus focused on something I couldn't see. "You were too young, Alexandria, to remember your father."

Hearing Marcus mention my father stopped the world.

"You were just a baby. Your mother couldn't so much as walk outside without Alexander not too far behind her, especially if she had you with her. Looking back, it seemed obvious, but Sentinels and Guards were always around. And they'd attended the Covenant together, two years behind me. I just thought they were friends. But I think I always knew, deep down, and I couldn't see past that. Every time I looked at you, I saw my sister's downfall."

My eyes widened. "Ouch."

"Yeah," he sighed. "Sounds terrible, but you of all people know what happens to halfs and pures that mix. I was so angry with my sister for putting herself into that position and for bringing a child into it." Marcus paused, pensive. "I took it out on you. It was wrong."

Pigs had just officially sprouted wings and were flying alongside airplanes. Instead of jumping around and pointing out what he just admitted and acting like a general douche about it, I focused on something else. Sometimes I amazed myself with my own maturity.

"Did . . . did you know my father personally?"

His lips thinned. "I trained with your father before I decided to go a more political route. He was a damn good Sentinel. Like you."

I stared. Once upon a time, hearing something like that would've have filled me with pleasure, but now it wasn't the compliment that had drawn me in; it was hearing that *my father* had been a damn good Sentinel that did.

"I think your mother hoped she wouldn't be paired. I wasn't. Neither was Laadan. But when your mother was paired with Lucian, Alexander . . . you just knew, if you knew the man behind the uniform."

Again, I had no idea what to say.

"There was nothing he could do but stand back and let the woman he loved marry someone else. And he had to live with that someone else raising his child." Marcus cleared his throat. "And I'm sure Alexander knew that Lucian wasn't kind to you, but there was nothing he could do. Coming forward would have put both your mother and you in danger. He was helpless."

My muscles were tensing and relaxing at the same time. "What happened? How did he end up a servant?"

Marcus faced me. "When you were three years old, Alexander disappeared. It wasn't uncommon. We were told he'd been killed by a daimon."

I shook my head, brows furrowing. "How did you not know where he was? He was in the Catskills, under Telly's thumb."

"I didn't see him there until about a year prior to your return." The sincerity in his words rocked me. "I'd believed that he was dead, and I didn't know that a male half and a female pure made an Apollyon. Even when Rachelle came to me before she took you away, I didn't suspect what that truly meant. Not until I saw Alexander in the Catskills, and then what could I do?"

"You could've helped him!"

"How? How was I to do that? What do you think would've happened if everyone realized that your father was a half-blood?

Halfs and pures have mixed before and have been caught. Those children were not allowed to live."

Sickened, I swallowed. "That's so wrong."

"I don't disagree." He reached over, running his fingers over a nearby leafy plant. "Your father didn't seem to recognize me. Only recently did I learn from Laadan that that must've been an act."

Then it hit me—smacked me right upside my ever-loving head. The conversation that I'd overheard between him and Telly resurfaced. Marcus had been furious with Telly. "Telly wanted you to hand me over, didn't he? He even offered you a seat on the Council."

He looked at me sharply.

I grinned. "I overheard you guys."

Staring at me a moment, he shook his head. "He did."

"And you refused."

"Yes." His look said *how could I do anything else?*

Wow. Things kind of made sense now, after all this time. I reminded him of Mom and he missed her, which probably made him uncomfortable around me. And Marcus wasn't really a people person, anyway. He hadn't known about my father until it was too late. I believed that. *And* he hadn't handed me over to Telly. I remembered how he'd picked me up and carried me after Seth had attacked the Council and I'd been sick.

How, like Aiden, he hadn't given up on me.

Marcus . . . he cared about me. And that meant a lot. Beside my father, who was out of reach to me, Marcus was the last of my family—my blood.

"Thank you," I said. And then, impulsively, even though he wasn't a hugging man, I sprang forward before he knew what was coming and hugged him. It was quick, though—I didn't want to freak the man out.

I settled back in my spot as he stared at me, eyes wide. Guess I *had* freaked him out.

"Why are you thanking me?" he asked slowly.

I shrugged.

"You are a strange girl."

Laughing, I leaned back against the cushions on the window seat. "I bet Mom was a strange girl."

"That she was."

"Will you tell me what you know about my dad? I mean, if you're not tired or anything?"

"There're some stories I could tell you." He mirrored my position. "And I'm not tired. Not at all." His smile was tentative, but real, and I couldn't think of any other time that he had smiled like that.

My lips responded in kind. "That would be really nice."

It wasn't until dawn came and the sun rose, chasing away the murky shadows, that I thought about how happy my mom would be, knowing that Marcus and I had sort of patched things up.

And I couldn't help but believe that she did. And maybe she was smiling upon us now. Just like the sun filtering through the windows, warming our backs.

14

Over the next three days, our little band fell into a rhythm of sorts. Things had settled down in the world. There'd been no more natural disasters, and Mount St. Helens seemed to have quieted. Apollo was still a no-show and the cabin out in the middle of nowhere had become a god-free zone. A good thing, but I figured one would just pop in, most likely in Deacon's bed or something, where we'd least expect them. But even though there'd been no godly interference, it was like watching the countdown clock on a time bomb. We all were just waiting.

Each day had been filled with training, training, and more training. Parts were worse than any days at the Covenant, because *everyone* stopped and watched when it came time for me to break out the akasha.

Marcus and Solos had lined up several large rocks they'd found scattered about, and my job was to make itty, bitty pebbles out of them. And that worked—up close. Say, like a few feet away. But the further away I got, the worse my aim became.

Sweating under Aiden's loose thermal, I grunted as I pulled from where akasha rested just below my ribcage. The power of the gods' mark tingled as the fifth element crackled across my knuckles.

Under the canopy of trees, Aiden and Olivia stopped their sparring to watch.

Focusing on the element, I felt my senses sharpen. Using akasha was like being connected directly with the Earth—like run-and-hug-a-tree connected. I could feel the vibrations of the grass and soil under my feet, as well as the dozens of scents carried on the low moan of the wind, and I could *feel* the air gliding over my skin with ghostly fingers.

Akasha crackled over my right arm as I threw my hand out. A bolt of lightning erupted from my palm, shooting across the ten feet and smacking into the right edge of the boulder. With a loud *crack*, the thing splintered.

Luke darted out of the way, but he was still pelted with rubble. He doubled over, about to kiss the ground.

"Whoops." I winced. "Sorry?"

Rubbing his back, he waved it off and limped toward where Deacon was trying to hide his laughter. "Shut up," he grumbled.

"You should've known better than to be that close," Deacon replied.

I sighed and turned to Solos. "I have terrible aim."

Solos nodded. "It's slightly off."

"Slightly?" My brows lifted.

"You're hitting the target, and I suppose that's all that matters."

Peeking at Aiden, I found that his attention was now on the sparring Lea and Olivia. The two girls were marvelous fighters and equally matched, and Aiden was in full Instructor mode, calling out commands in his deep, oddly musical voice. I found myself missing that one-on-one attention.

Heck, I was missing a lot of attention.

One thing had been certain over the last three days—something was definitely up with Aiden. It wasn't that he avoided me. Every night he joined me in bed, pulled me close, and held me. Nothing progressed further than that, even though I could sense he wanted more. He just didn't make a move, and I had no idea why. I was pretty sure the way I ended up curling all around him was evidence I was down for some happy times.

I bit my lip as I turned to the last boulder, shaking out my shoulders. There hadn't been another nightmare of Seth, thank the gods. Part of me suspected it had something to do with the fact that I didn't go to sleep until after Aiden did. Maybe just knowing that he was there helped, but he didn't go to sleep until late, which usually meant it took another couple of hours for me to drift off, and when he awoke at the crack of freaking dawn, so did I. Since I was tapping into akasha daily, I was drained like a daimon victim.

But I pushed away the fatigue. Like Marcus had once said, I was a lot of things, but not stupid. I knew why Apollo wanted me working with akasha. He was preparing me to fight Seth. And I would need everything in my arsenal to avoid the power transfer that would end everything.

There was an inherent problem with training for a face-off with Seth. How was I supposed to fight him when all it would take from him was a touch and a few whispered words in Greek?

Yeah, we were doomed to failure.

Panic hammered me in the chest as my gaze drifted over those around me. If anything went wrong, which it most likely would, all of them were at risk. Lea could end up like her sister, Olivia like Caleb, Luke and Solos like every Sentinel that had been slaughtered by Lucian and his army. Marcus could end up like my mom.

My eyes settled on Aiden.

Deacon had gotten up and was standing next to his older brother. Under the sunlight, his blond curls were a pale platinum. The brothers shared the same striking eye color, but that was all. They were like yin and yang, night and day, standing side by side.

Deacon's hands were cupped around something, and as he lifted his head, a genuine smile spread across his lips and those gray eyes glittered. Aiden laughed at whatever Deacon had said.

They could end up like their parents.

Fear made my skin tight as it replaced the panic. I rubbed at my temple, forcing my breath to saw in and out evenly. No one was going to die. There would be no more deaths. There couldn't be. *Everyone* had suffered enough already.

But there was Fate. There was no such thing as paying dues when it came to Fate. It simply did not care, or recognize past experience.

Knowing that made me want to plop down in the cold, damp grass and cry like an angry, fat baby.

"Alex?" Solos' soft voice drew me out of my troublesome thoughts.

I nodded and focused on the last rock. What I didn't like about using akasha was the fact that the buzzing in my head was always the strongest then, like tapping into the most powerful element somehow affected the bond. None of the Apollyons had ever thought or discussed that in the past, so I had no idea if that was true.

Calling upon akasha, I let it go. The bolt of blue lightning was incredibly intense, shattering in its power. Silence and then another loud *crack* followed. This time it hit the rock in the middle and the thing didn't explode, but was reduced to a pile of dust.

Solos let out a low whistle as he stared at the dust and the scorched soil below. "Remind me to never piss you off."

I cracked a smile as I backed off, letting the buzz of akasha settle back down. Bending at the waist, I snatched up my water. Over the rim, I watched Olivia deliver a spin kick that knocked Lea back several feet.

Aiden clapped. "Perfect, Olivia." And then to Lea, "You hesitated. If you hadn't, you would've blocked that kick."

Nodding, Lea stood up and dusted herself off. She quickly fell back into stance and went at it again.

A low, annoying ache blossomed in my temple, making my right eye all twitchy. I tossed the bottle back down and turned to Solos. Out of rocks to destroy, I was handed off to Marcus to work on elements.

Off a little from the main group, he raised his hands. A gust of wind picked up. Branches rattled, and fresh, tiny leaves swirled in the air as the wind barreled toward me.

I raised my hands, and unlike before I'd Awakened, I met the air element with my own. His sputtered out weakly under the force of mine. Amazing how the air element had been my greatest enemy before, but now was only a mild annoyance.

Deacon and Laadan even got involved in the later part of the day. Laadan worked with the air element and Deacon set about creating small fires and controlling them. I couldn't picture those two fighting, but at this point, everyone had become a warrior.

Aiden watched his brother with narrowed eyes and a tight jaw, so tight I wondered if he had any molars left. Finally, he left the halfs and stalked over to where Deacon had several piles of twigs burning.

"What are you doing?" Aiden demanded.

Deacon looked up from under the mop of curls. "I'm becoming a fire bug."

The humor was lost on Aiden. "I know what you're thinking."

"Ah, hell, well if that's the case, then that's embarrassing."

Aiden's back went rigid. "Unless you're practicing starting campfires, you're wasting your time."

"But—"

"You don't need to do this." Aiden waved his hand over the piles of burning twigs and the flames fizzled out. "I don't want you involved in any of this."

Deacon drew himself up to his full height, which meant he only came to Aiden's shoulders. "You can't stop me, Aiden."

Ah, wrong thing to say.

"You want to bet on that?" Aiden growled, his head dropping so that he was eye level with his brother.

Undaunted, Deacon held his ground but dropped his voice.

"Do you expect me to sit back and play card games while everyone else is doing something important?"

"Yes, I do, actually."

Deacon laughed humorlessly. "I can help."

"You're not trained." His hands formed into fists at his sides. "And before you say it, you're not everyone else."

"I know I'm not trained, but I'm not freaking useless, Aiden. I *can* help." They were in an epic staredown I hadn't seen before, especially not from easy-going Deacon. "And asking me to sit back and watch everyone else—people that I care about, people like *you*—prepare to risk their lives while I do nothing isn't fair."

Aiden opened his mouth, but his brother rushed on. "I know your over-controlling behavior comes from a good place, bro, but you can't protect me for ever and you can't continue babying me. It's a waste of time, because even if you forbid me to get involved, it won't matter. You can't stop me." Deacon took a deep breath. "I need to help, Aiden."

Something in what Deacon said caused Aiden to string together an atrocity of f-bombs. My brows flew up. Aiden rarely cussed or lost his cool, but boy, he was a grenade whose pin had just been pulled.

He took a step back, placing his hands on his hips. I almost expected him to drag Deacon into the cabin and lock him in there, but instead, he jerked his head in a curt nod. "Okay. If this is what you . . . need, then okay."

I was stunned into silence. So was Deacon. Without another word, Aiden returned to where the halfs waited.

Deacon's eyes met mine and he shrugged.

Shocked that Aiden had given in—and somewhat pleased that he was seeing Deacon as something more than his little brother who partied too much—I followed Marcus over to the rest of the group.

We practiced at that for the rest of the day and even went as far as to use the air element against the rest of the halfs, forcing them to break my hold. I hated doing that, because I knew how helpless I'd felt when the air element used to pin me down, but air users were the most common, which meant over half of the daimons used air. It was one of the reasons so many halfs died in battle against them.

So we had to deal with it.

Fire and earth were rare among pures. Aiden and Deacon were the only two I knew who wielded fire, and I hadn't met a pure who controlled earth, although I'd seen it used once, in the New York Covenant. The water element came in handy if the user was near water or in the rain. Some thought they had gotten the crappy element, but I knew it wasn't true. They could pull water from pipes—from *anything*.

I was squared off against Lea. Not that long ago, I would've experienced a twisted sort of satisfaction at taking her down, but things . . . things were so different now.

We stared at each other for a few seconds, and then she nodded.

Slowly, reluctantly, I raised my hands and drew the air around me. A vicious stream of wind formed just behind my fingers, and then slid through them. Like with akasha, my aim wasn't great, but it struck Lea below the chest, knocking her right on her back.

I moved forward, my arms shaking as I forced the element on her. It was hard to look at her, hard to not see myself struggling and thrashing on the ground, unable to gain footing.

Aiden crouched behind her, barking out orders in his own soft way, but the best she could do was draw her legs up and that was all.

Her body trembled as her lips pulled back in a snarl. She fought to just sit up, and I wanted her to, because from there, it was easier to break the hold, but the element pinned her shoulders down to the grass.

Wave after wave of air beat down on her, and she threw her

head back and screamed as she raised one hand, her fingers clawing at the invisible enemy.

"Lea, come on. Use your core muscles," Aiden said, lifting his lashes to pierce me with concrete eyes. "Push through it . . ."

I hated this, hated this so much. My entire body shook.

Another scream as she slammed her hands down into the short blades of grass. Her fingers dug in, tearing through dirt. Clumps came up as she pushed up into a sitting position. I started to smile, but Lea powered up quickly and rushed me.

She cut through the element, arms wrapping around my waist as she smashed into me. We went down, a tangle of arms and legs. The back of my head smacked off the ground. Starbursts exploded behind my eyelids. Air rushed from my lungs in a painful grasp.

The sound of applause was thundering, and I think Deacon yelled, "Girl fight!"

And then there was silence. No one moved. I like to think everyone was preparing for a massive Apollyon bitch-smack from my end.

"Damn," I grunted, blinking several times. Through Lea's coppery hair, the sky was a light color of blue.

Using her arms, Lea lifted up and grinned at me. "Let's just call that a little bit of payback." She rolled off and sprang to her feet, still grinning broadly. "Well, that was fun."

I remained sprawled on the ground, the throbbing in my right temple now spreading to the back of my skull. Quite possibly she'd knocked something loose—hopefully nothing important.

A strong, tan-colored hand appeared in my vision. "Up?"

Placing my hand in Aiden's, I let him haul me to my feet and stood there while he brushed clumps of dirt off my aching shoulders. On second thought, my whole body ached. A small smile played over his full lips. Our eyes met, and while everyone milled around about us, in that moment, it was just him and me.

Aiden leaned over me, his breath warm against the curve of my neck. A fine shiver scuttled over my skin, and the ache in my right temple eased off. I inhaled deeply, surrounding myself in his masculine, earthy scent. Everyone around us disappeared.

"I know what you did," he whispered.

I jerked back, eyes narrowing. Not the sweet nothings I'd been hoping he'd whisper. "What?"

Arching a brow, he then turned and swaggered off to join the congratulatory group forming around Lea. I popped my hands on my hips, shaking my head. There was no way he could know. No way at all.

15

Later that night, I was on the hunt and Aiden was my prey. After training, he'd disappeared. After dinner, he'd disappeared again, and hours had gone by since then. It was a few minutes past midnight, and I knew he wasn't on rounds. Solos was, and the niggling suspicion that Aiden was avoiding me was turning into full-blown paranoia.

Prowling through the lower floor, I hoped to burn off most of the nervous energy and stave off the beginnings of a headache. Right now, it was just a dull ache behind my eyes, but I had a feeling it was going to turn into a head-splitter.

There was another long night ahead, made worse by where my thoughts were. Of all things I should've been worried about at the moment, I knew this wasn't it, but I hated that there was this wall that had come out of nowhere. And it was a weird wall that . . .

I weathered a sudden, terrible memory of Aiden staring at the bottle of Elixir I'd held in the kitchen after my first dinner back in the land of the sane. Had seeing that Elixir reminded him of what he'd taken part in? He couldn't be . . . feeling guilty over placing me on the Elixir, could he? I'm pretty sure everyone in the world would agree that had been necessary.

"You look pissy." Lea's voice rattled me out of my thoughts.

I stood outside a small study that held only a couch and a desk. Bookcases lined the wall, but most of the shelves were empty. The only light came from the little lamp peeking over the back of the couch.

"I'm not pissy." I was confused, frustrated and paranoid, tired and . . . okay, I was a tiny bit pissy.

She tucked a stray strand of hair back. A moment of silence passed and then, "I know what you did."

That was the second time someone had said that to me in a few hours, and honestly, neither of them could really know. Could they? Wasn't like I wore a sign on my forehead.

I stared at Lea blankly. "I have no idea what you're talking about."

She made a show of slowly closing her book and putting it aside. Biting back a groan, I walked into the room and leaned against the desk. "What?" I demanded, folding my arms.

My arch-nemesis stared back at me unflinchingly. Whatever I'd dished out at her over the years, she'd always returned. In some ways, we were a lot alike. We were two alpha females, constantly at one another's throats.

But it was more than that.

In a flash of disturbing insight, I knew why we'd become sandbox enemies so very long ago. When I was younger, before Mom had yanked my butt out of the Covenant, before Lea and I hated each other, we used to be decent. That is, until one day, I'd said something terrible to her.

Even at the age of ten, Lea had loved her pure-blooded stepmother and half-sister—to the point that the rest of us halfs thought something was wrong with her. Most of the pures ignored their half-blood children, especially the ones who hadn't birthed or sired the half-bloods. Step-parents in our world were truly step-monsters. But in Lea's world, her pure-blooded stepmother must've loved her dearly. Every Monday, after spending the weekend with her stepmother, Lea would talk about all the wonderful things they'd done together—shopping, watching movies, and getting ice cream. None of us had that with our step-monsters. Lucian used to lock me in my bedroom when Mom wasn't home.

So naturally, we'd been jealous.

We'd dogged her constantly about her love of her stepmother. Destroyed the dress she had bought Lea by spilling cranberry juice on it. Hid the tiny photo album Lea carried with her all the time. It had been polka-dotted with pink stripes, full of these pictures of her and Dawn, her pure-blooded half-sister. Once I'd found a card Lea's stepmother had written to Lea, tucked away in one of her textbooks.

I had ripped it to shreds in front of Lea, laughing as she cried.

Then one day, while we were all running laps, Lea had stopped to stare at a visiting pure-blood Council member. Her face had taken on this glow that none of us understood. It looked like respect and wonder. But that couldn't be right. Because, as halfs, we didn't stare at pures in open admiration, like we'd cut off our left arm to be like them.

After class, I had found Lea sitting in the courtyard with her friends. Followed by Caleb and a few others, I'd stormed their circle and stood in the middle. And I'd said the biggest, meanest thing I could ever say to another half-blood.

"You have more pure-blood in you than half."

The same thing Seth had said to me once before.

Come to think of it, I think I may have spit on her, too.

Lea pretty much hated me after that, and honestly, I don't know how I had forgotten that. Then again, I probably chose to forget what'd started our sandbox hate. I always chalked Lea's animosity toward me up to her general bitchiness, when in reality I had been nothing more than a bully.

It seemed too late to apologize now, and knowing Lea, it wouldn't change anything, not that I expected it would.

Lea watched me now, head tilted to the side as if she knew where my thoughts had gone. She smiled tightly. "You let up on the air element while we were fighting."

My mouth dropped open, but she rushed on.

"I wouldn't have broken your hold if you hadn't let up. I felt it lessen—the pressure—and I didn't realize right away that you did it, but I figured it out," she said, as if she wanted to prove that she'd been smart enough to see through it. "What I don't get is why you did it. You could've pushed me straight through the ground. Gods know you never had a problem coming after me before. What's so different now?"

Unfolding my arms, I gripped the edge of the desk. I had no idea what to say. Lea was right. I *had* let up on the air element, and that wasn't the only thing she called me out on. A few months ago, if I'd had control over the element then, I would've tossed her around the forest for the fun of it, maybe even thrown another apple at her face. Anything was possible.

I tugged on my hair, pulling the thick braid over one shoulder. Lea waited for my explanation and I felt my cheeks redden.

Her amethyst eyes narrowed.

Blowing out a low breath, I rolled my eyes and tossed my hair back over my shoulder. "Okay. You got me. I did let up, and I did it because I remember how much it sucked to be held down like that and be helpless. I *hated* it when Seth did it to me."

She paled under her ever-present tan. "He . . . he did that to you?"

"In training," I said, dismissing where her mind was obviously going with that. "Anyway, I just couldn't do that to someone else, even if that person *is* a stuck-up, tan-as-leather hooch."

Lea watched me a moment, then cracked a smile. "And that's coming from Alex, Covenant dropout extraordinaire and psycho Apollyon."

My lips twitched. "Ow. Burn."

Turning her head, she hid her grin but quickly sobered as she faced me. "You've changed so much, Alex."

Part of me wanted to deny it, but it was true. As I stared back at the copper-haired girl, I realized we'd both irrevocably changed. There was no going back to the girls we'd been over the past summer.

Lea sighed and her nose wrinkled. "So . . . this is awkward."

I laughed. "Yeah, it is. I feel like I need to insult you some more."

She leaned back in an arrogant sprawl as she raised her hands. "Do your best."

"It's too easy," I said, letting go of the desk, feeling the blood rush back into my fingertips. "I'll just wait for you to do something to tick me off. I'm sure it won't take long."

"Probably not," she replied. "I'm surprised you're not all up Olivia's butt."

I arched a brow. "Trying to tick me off so soon? I'm surprised."

Lea shrugged and then there was a pause. "Olivia told me that you saw Caleb twice. Was that . . . was that true?"

I nodded. "I saw him when I went to the Underworld, and he visited me right before I escaped."

Her thick lashes swept down. "Was he okay?"

And then it hit me. It wasn't concern for Caleb or anything—the reason she was asking had to do with her half-sister. "Yeah, he was more than okay. He was happier than he was before he passed." A lump formed in my throat and I focused on the empty bookshelves. "He said my mom was there, too, so I'm sure your parents and Dawn are there . . . and they're okay."

She drew in a choked breath, and like me, she suddenly became focused on the frayed edges of the couch arm. All half-bloods had been trained to show no pain, and gods forbid we cried. The whole show-no-weakness mantra was hard to leave behind.

I dropped down on the cushion beside Lea and picked up the book she'd been reading. Turning the book over, my brows flew up as I got an eyeful of the hottie on the cover. "Wait. Is this book about aliens?"

She snatched it back from me. "Yes."

"Really?"

"But they're hot aliens." She tapped on the guy's face with one thin finger. "And he can be my ET any day."

I laughed outright, and it did feel a little odd to be laughing with Lea of all people, but she smiled a little. Lea and I would never be BFF's, but I wondered if, one day, we'd actually consider each other friends.

A sharp slice of pain shot from behind my eyes and across my temples. Wincing, I stood and took a deep breath. "Do we have any Tylenol around?" Another shot of pain, like fire streaking through the vessels in my brain, caused nausea to rise in my throat. "Or a sledgehammer? Something?"

"I'm sure there's something—hey—*hey*—are you okay?" Lea's voice suddenly sounded so, so far away, but her hand was on my arm.

"Yeah, I'm . . . okay." I took a step and felt a tremble in my legs. Muscles twitched, gave way.

An explosion flashed white in the dimly lit room, blinding me temporarily. I thought I screamed a warning. I thought I turned to move in front of Lea, but when the intense white light receded, I wasn't in the little room anymore.

The circular chamber was made of sandstone and lined with marble pillars. Strange glyphs covered the walls, runes that matched the ones gliding over my skin. There was nothing in the room—no couch or bookshelves or Lea—but I wasn't alone.

"What the hell?" I demanded.

Standing before me was a god, one who looked like he wasn't much older than me. The winged cap he wore hid most of his hair, but light brown wisps poked out from underneath. He wore a white chlamys cloak.

The god gave a little smile. "Don't kill the messenger."

And then he blinked out.

"What the fu—"

Then I saw him. He leaned against one of the pillars, his back to me. The familiar black garb, the wave of blond hair—now slightly longer . . . Recognition sent a terrible, icy Shockwave of disbelief through me.

"Seth?" I whispered.

A heartbeat passed and he turned his head to the side. "I am not very happy with you, Alex."

Horror rose quickly and I took an involuntary step back. Before, I never would've feared him—would've laughed at the thought. But now I was terrified—not of him, but what he could do.

Seth turned to me and his face was as I remembered—strong jaw and expressive lips, eyes like liquid amber and a beauty that was too perfect. It always reminded me of sculptures done in the images of the gods.

He arched a mocking brow. "What? Are you struck speechless? That would be a first."

"How?" I croaked, heart racing painfully.

"We're still connected, and I've been waiting for the right moment to . . . how should I say this? 'Make a long-distance call via our bond'?" He smiled that smug half-grin. "Shield or not, I can still reach you . . . with a little help from friends in high places."

The god . . . "Hermes?"

Seth nodded. "He's always been a fan of mine. Bringing you to me will surely piss off some of the other gods, which was all it took to convince Hermes to do it. And before you jump to the wrong conclusion, Hermes is not the god responsible for me."

The fact that Seth had gotten Hermes to swoop in ticked me off, but it didn't make sense. How had Hermes found me? Confusion swamped me, but there was something that tasted like blood behind it. "I don't understand. Where am I?"

"You're where I want you to be." He took a calculated step forward.

I inched backward. "That's not much of an answer."

Seth cocked his head to the side, eyes narrowing as he kept coming forward. "Do you think you deserve an answer?"

Now I knew what tasted like metal in the back of my throat. Anger. "Am I dreaming, Seth?"

He laughed; while we'd been connected, he had laughed a lot, but now I realized there was a difference between real Seth and the ghost version of him. His presence was potent; his voice held a husky, musical quality to it with the slightest accent. And his laugh . . . his laugh was deep and smug.

"You're not dreaming, Alex. Like I said, I used our connection, and Hermes helped. This . . ." He spread his arms out, and the golden skin was covered in moving symbols. "This is in here." He tapped a finger off his skull. "It's like Skyping."

My hand itched to knock that smile off his face. "So this isn't real?"

"Oh, it's real to a certain extent."

I found that I'd kept backing up and now my back was against the warm sandstone wall. "This can't be real."

Seth stopped in front of me and leaned in, coming so close that I turned my head, my fingers curling helplessly at my sides. His breath danced over my cheek. "If you're worried that I can transfer your power in this state, I can't. Neither can I really get anything out of our bond. Your shields—" he rolled his eyes "—are still intact. I probably shouldn't have taught you how to do that, but anyway, you're not really here. Hermes rode our connection to your subconscious and pulled you into mine."

Gods, that sounded so entirely messed up.

"I missed you. So relax."

Relax? I was supposed to relax when I was here, wherever here was, with crazy-pants Seth? My head jerked toward him. Our faces were mere inches apart. "You missed me?"

"I miss the Alex who lived to make me happy." He laughed at what I was sure was an *I'm going to murder you* look that crossed my face. "Okay. I wanted to see if this would work and it did."

"So if I touch you, then nothing will happen?"

"Correct." His amber eyes flared. "Wait. You want to touch me? I like where this is going."

I smiled, and then a second later I planted my fist in his stomach with everything I had in me. Doubling over, Seth grunted and let out a low curse. Moving forward, I brought my knee up, slamming into the same spot my fist had connected with seconds before.

"Dammit, Alex, I can *feel* that." Seth straightened, rubbing his stomach.

Sweet satisfaction tasted like sugar on my tongue. "Good! Because there's more where that came from, you psychotic douchebag!" I swung again.

Seth reacted quickly, capturing my hand in his. He pushed back, snatching my other wrist, which was heading for his face. Less than a second later, he had both my wrists pinned above my head.

Smiling like I hadn't just kicked the air out of his stomach, which totally ticked me off, he pressed in. "How many times have I told you, Alex? Hitting isn't nice."

I pushed off the wall, but all that succeeded in doing was bringing our bodies flush. Anger deepened the hue of his eyes, as did something else—interest and lust. And even though that made my skin crawl, I realized something important. The cord wasn't snapping alive like it usually did when I was around him, especially when he was practically on top of me. It rested dormant in the pit of my stomach.

This was real . . . but it wasn't real. Still, I wasn't thrilled with what was happening.

"You're in my personal space." My jaw ached from how hard I was grinding my molars. "Let go."

"No." His eyes widened. "You might hit me again."

"You can count on it!" Rage boiled inside me, swallowing the confusion and terror that had held such a tight grip on me. "How could you do that to me?" I kicked off the wall, but Seth pushed back. "You promised you wouldn't use our bond against me, and you did! You turned me into the president of the Seth Fan Club."

His lips twitched. "I see nothing wrong with that."

I seethed. "I referred to you as *my* Seth!"

"Again, I see nothing wrong with that."

Hands curling into fists, I glared at him. "It was wrong, Seth! What you're doing is wrong! Don't you understand that? Dammit!" Throwing my hand back, it cracked against the wall. Very real pain exploded up my arm. "Shit!"

"Now, calm down. You're just going to hurt yourself." Mischief sparkled in his golden eyes, and for an instant, I was reminded of Seth—Seth before he went crazy on aether power, who ticked me off just as much as he made me laugh—the boy who had stolen a piece of my heart.

I stared into his eyes, feeling some of the rage seep away. "What happened to you?"

He blinked. "What?"

Slumping against the wall, I lowered my gaze. "You've always been arrogant as hell and crazy, but . . ."

"Thanks," he said dryly, but the grip around my wrists loosened.

"But you never would've done this to me—used the bond against me." I lifted my gaze. "You never would've attacked the Council or sided with Lucian. *What* happened to you?"

A muscle popped out in Seth's jaw. "I got smart, Alex. What happened to *you* is the better question. The girl I met would've gone against the Council without a second thought. She would've still hated Lucian, but she would've seen that what he was trying to do was the right thing."

"No." I turned my head, swallowing hard.

"Yes!" Moving my wrists to one hand, he caught my chin in his other, forcing me to look at him, and I hated the near-feverish gleam to his eyes. "He wants to change the world."

"He wants to rule it, Seth! There's a big difference. And you're nothing but a pawn." I dug into that fury in me, clinging to it. "He's *using* you, Seth. You used to be stronger than that, but you're weak—weak on power."

Anger flashed across his face like lightning as his grip tightened on my chin. "I am not weak."

"You are! You're so weak that you can't even see what Lucian is doing to you! Don't you ever care about what's happening to the world? Innocent people are dying, Seth." Meeting his furious gaze, I willed him to understand, to see where everything went wrong. "How can you be okay with that? You have to stop this."

His silence was stony.

"Do you understand what I'm going to have to do?" Tears welled in my eyes at the same moment I heard the whisper of my name being called from what sounded like miles away.

Seth heard it too, and he recognized the voice. His lips pulled back in a snarl.

"I'm going to have to kill you, Seth." My voice gave out.

He jerked back, letting go of me so quickly that I nearly fell. Something a lot like disbelief flickered across his features and there was more. A look I couldn't figure out, and then his expression went cold. "You can't kill me."

The sound of Aiden's voice calling for me tugged at every cell in my body. "I will find a way, because I can't let you do this."

Seth folded his arms. "You'll fail."

My heart tripped over itself. "What do I have to do to make you stop? Tell me!"

His lips twisted in a cruel smile. "There is nothing you can do, Alex. You need to accept what's happening—accept our Fate. You were made for me, and I *will* find you. And if anyone stands in my way, I won't think twice about taking them down."

I gasped, sickened, saddened, and a whole lot disturbed to hear him say that. He'd done so many hideous things, but to hear that, to see how truly far gone he was, cut deep into me. "Seth . . ."

He shot forward, clasping the sides of my head. "So go ahead and shield me out all you want. As you can see, I can still get to you." Pressing his forehead against mine, he dragged in a deep breath. "We'll be seeing each other again real soon."

Seth shifted again and I felt his lips brush my forehead a second before light exploded in and around me.

16

Lungs burning as if I'd been underwater, I sucked in a deep breath and jerked. When the light receded this time, gunmetal gray eyes stared into mine.

"Alex?" Relief tinged Aiden's tone, making his voice deep and tight. His eyes were shadowed by concern, but there was a twinge of anger way in the back of them. "Gods, Alex, I thought . . ."

I blinked a couple of times as the small den came into focus around me. It was the one Lea and I had been in. Aiden's arms were around me, and I was half on the floor, half in his lap. I started to sit up, but he placed his hand on my cheek, pressing my head against his own.

"Hold on there for a few minutes," he said, shifting so that his back was against the lower part of the couch. "Are you okay?"

"Yeah." I cleared my throat, willing the pounding of my heart to slow. "That . . . that was trippy. Where's Lea?"

"Outside the room with everyone else." His thumb traced a soothing circle over my cheekbone. "She came and found me when you passed out. She said you complained about a headache before you dropped. It . . . it freaked her out. Are you sure you're okay?"

I dropped? Geez, not only could Seth just reach out and touch me, but he could cause me to faint like a wuss? "Yeah, the headache is gone. I just feel a little out of it."

Pushing into a sitting position, I twisted to face Aiden in his embrace. "How long have I been out?"

"A few minutes." His eyes searched mine. "Alex, you . . . you said Seth's name. I thought . . ." He shook his head and his lashes swept down, hiding his eyes.

"What?" I placed my hand on his smooth cheek, and then it hit me. My breath hitched in my throat. "You thought I connected with Seth again?"

He didn't immediately respond. "I thought it—yes, especially when I heard you say his name. I got everyone out of the room." Aiden looked up, his gaze meeting mine. "I didn't know what I was going to do . . ."

Elixir wouldn't have been an option. He'd tossed the last of that down the drain. What would he have done? The look in his eyes shattered me.

I leaned in, pressing my forehead against his. The act reminded me of Seth, but it was so much different, meant so much more. "I did see Seth, but I didn't connect with him."

Aiden reached with both hands, placing them on either side of my face. There was a faint tremble in his powerful arms. Neither of us spoke for a long second. My heart raced in a different kind of pounding. "What happened?" he asked finally.

"Hermes—freaking Hermes," I said. "I really don't understand how he did it, but he followed the connection between Seth and me and pulled me into Seth's subconscious, or some kind of junk like that."

I was sure Aiden was quiet because he was so angry he couldn't form words.

Taking a deep breath, I wrapped my hands around his wrists and told him everything. With each word, Aiden's fury increased until it became a tangible thing in the room, thick like smoke.

I ended up lowering his hands, keeping mine wrapped around his. "It was real . . . but not real. I don't know if he'll be able to do it again, or if Hermes will help him again. Or if there was something I was doing or not doing that made it easier."

"You got a headache before it happened?" When I nodded, his eyes turned as cool as steel. "When you were on the Elixir, do you remember getting headaches?"

I shook my head.

He let out a low curse. "You would get a headache when the Elixir was starting to wear off. You would also start to hear Seth's voice. It was him trying to connect with you. I think the same kind of thing is happening here with Hermes."

"Crap," I said, stunned. Then I thought of the nightmare. Moving faster than Aiden could track, I stood and backed away. "I had a nightmare a few nights ago."

He rose fluidly. "I remember."

"I dreamt that Seth was in the room, but maybe it wasn't a nightmare. Maybe it was him testing out our freaking long-distance calling feature with Hermes?" I cursed, fighting the urge to pick up and throw something. "Well, the good thing is he couldn't get anything through the bond. He can't pick at my thoughts or take control."

"There's nothing good about this," Aiden all but growled.

"Well, I *was* trying to be Positive Polly."

His hands clenched at his sides. "You could hit him, so that means he can hit back, Alex. Yeah, he may not find out where you are, but that is a huge violation."

I nodded numbly. Aiden was right. There was no telling if Seth could do it again.

"And there's nothing I can do if he does this again. I swear to the gods . . ." Spinning quickly, Aiden picked up a small figurine and threw it across the room. It shattered off the wall, an explosion of plaster and glass.

The door to the room swung open and Solos peeked in, brows raised. "Is—"

"Leave us!" Aiden ordered sharply, then he took a shuddering breath. "Alex is fine. We're both fine."

Solos looked like he was about to disagree, but he took

another look at Aiden and decided against it. He shut the door.

I slid Aiden a look. "Did that make you feel better?"

"No," he shot back, taking a deep breath as he gestured at the dent in the wall. "I wish that was Seth's head."

Seeing Aiden lose his control was something I always found nothing short of awe-inducing, mainly because he *never* lost control, but sometimes I forgot that he was far from perfect or saintly. He had a temper—nothing as crazy as Seth's or mine, but fire hummed in his blood.

I crossed my arms, suddenly feeling chilled. "But there has to be a reason why he was only able to do this now. And—*and*—he heard you calling my name." Hope sparked inside me. "His hold on me wasn't that strong."

"I bet he was thrilled about that."

Recalling the way Seth had appeared when he heard Aiden's voice, I was sure he'd been damn near murderous. "There has to be something, Aiden. We just need to figure it out."

Aiden cut me a dark look as he stalked across the room, stopping before the window.

I bit my lip. "We will. We always do."

He said nothing, his back unnaturally stiff. "Are you sure you're fine?"

"Yes," I said, exasperated. "Can you stop asking me that? I'm fine. I'm okay. Tonight was a small setback, but—"

"I know." He looked over his shoulder, his voice measurably lower and even. "I know, Alex. I'm sorry."

"You don't have anything to apologize for."

He let out a short laugh. "I have a lot to apologize for, Alex."

I stared at him. This was about something more than what had just happened with Seth. Yeah, he was ticked off, mostly for my benefit and I appreciated that, but this was more. I thought of the weird gap between us in the last few days.

Irritation pricked my skin. "What is your deal?"

"I have no idea what you're talking about."

"You don't?" I stalked up to him and reached up to place my hand on his face. He flinched away, and I felt that in the pang in my chest. "That! That's what I'm talking about."

He scowled.

Like with any other situation in my life, when I was annoyed or frightened by one thing, I pretty much turned all that energy on something else. "You've been acting weird for days and practically hiding from me."

"I haven't been hiding from you, Alex." A muscle worked in his jaw as he stared out the window. "Do you really think this is the time to be talking about this?"

I took a deep breath and felt my famous temper rise to the occasion. "Is there a better time?"

"Maybe when you haven't just been sucked into gods-know-where by Seth and we're not planning on going out there and coming face-to-face with gods-know-what." He glanced over his shoulder, eyes a cool gray. "Maybe then."

Oh, I was two seconds from jumping on his back and strangling him from behind . . . with love, of course.

"Do you think we're going to get a better time to talk about this? That sometime in the near future everything is just going to pause for us to have a heart-to-heart?" Aiden had turned back to the window, but I didn't need to see his face to know he wasn't a happy camper. "Okay. I don't get this. You were fine when we came back. We—"

"We shouldn't have done that."

Pain sliced into my chest like he'd socked me. At once, I felt the marks respond, bleeding across my skin.

Aiden's head tipped down and he cursed. "I didn't mean it like that. That night—it was the best night of my life. I don't regret it, but I should've waited until you'd had time to come to grips with everything. I lost . . . I lost control."

I stepped forward. "I like when you lose control."

He shook his head mutely.

"I was okay, Aiden. I wasn't damaged. I'm not damaged now. So why are you hiding from me?"

"I'm not hiding from you."

"Bull! You avoid spending any time alone with me, except at night."

Aiden faced me, thrusting his fingers through his hair. "At night, when I'm sleeping, is the only time I don't think about it—what I did. You . . . don't understand. What I did to you—putting you on the Elixir? I don't deserve anything else."

"You—"

"I didn't have to, Alex. It was weak of me. I didn't trust that eventually you'd break the bond. And seeing what it did to you? I can't forgive myself for that."

My mouth dropped open. "You can't blame yourself for that! You did what was right."

Anger flashed in his eyes. "It wasn't right."

"Aiden—"

"The Elixir was one of your greatest fears, Alex! And I did that to you!"

Surprised, I took a step back. Rarely did Aiden ever raise his voice, but I knew his anger and frustration weren't directed at me. It was his own guilt—guilt he shouldn't be carrying around with him.

"How . . ." He came forward, lowering his voice as his eyes locked with mine. "How is what I did any different than what Seth did to you—is still doing to you?"

I gaped. "Putting me on the Elixir isn't the same thing as Seth twisting me into a psychotic Apollyon!"

"But I stripped you of *who* you are, Alex. It's the same." Heat rolled off him in waves, intensifying as the seconds passed. Most people would've been terrified of him like this.

I was mostly annoyed—and saddened.

"I held you down and forced your mouth open as Marcus gave you the Elixir." He shook his head a little, as if he was dumbfounded by his own actions. "You begged for me to stop and I didn't. I watched the Elixir take hold, and it was *me* who became your Master. I can't . . ." He cut off and turned away.

Tears filled my eyes. Wanting nothing more than to take that guilt away, I was at a loss as to how I could. I stepped behind him, wanting to just hug him until he understood I didn't blame him. If there was anyone else more stubborn than me in this world, it was Aiden. If the tables were turned, Aiden would've had something ridiculously supportive to say. He would use an eloquent mash-up of words that meant something, and when that didn't work, he would just tell me how it was.

I didn't have pretty words, so I settled on second—er, third best. "Look, I hate to cut through your self-pity with a big dose of grow-up."

Turning around, Aiden's brows shot up and he opened his mouth.

"No." I placed my hand over his lips—his warm, warm lips. My entire arm tingled from the contact. "You had to make a tough decision. All of you did. I was Evil Alex. And I remember threatening to pull out Deacon's ribcage. I can understand why you did it."

He wrapped his fingers around my wrist and gently removed my hand, though he didn't let go. Score! "Alex, this isn't about you forgiving me."

"Then what's it about?" I moved closer, my thighs knocking into his locked knees. "I forgive you. Hell, there's nothing to forgive. And if anything, I should be thanking you."

Dropping my hand, he looked away and shook his head as he moved to the couch, sitting heavily. "Don't *ever* thank me for putting you on the Elixir."

"Ugh!" I threw up my hand. I was *this close* to knocking him off the couch. "I wasn't thanking you for that. I was thanking you for not giving up on me. For still being there for me when I was acting like a psycho."

He stared up at me, stony as ever.

"I want to strangle you."

Aiden arched a brow.

I let out a long breath. "We've all done things that we regret. I'm living with the fact that I threatened everyone that I care about. You have no idea the things I thought—the things I believed in—when I was connected with Seth. Or maybe you do, but it's not the same. And if I can get over it, then by gods, you need to get over it."

His mouth opened, but I wasn't done. "I need you right now, more than ever. And I don't need you to just hold me at night." I paused, frowning. "Even though that's really nice and all, I need you to really be here."

Hurt flashed in his silvery eyes. "I am here for you."

"You're not." I shook my head. "You can't be when you're sulking around here, blaming yourself for something you had to do. I need you to man up, Aiden."

"Man up?" He sat back in a lazy, arrogant sprawl, but the coiled tension was in every muscle in his body. "It's a good thing I love you or I'd find that particularly insulting."

"If you love me, you'd get over this. You'd deal with it, accept that you had to do it, and get past it." My breath got caught. "Because I'm scared out of my mind, Aiden, and I don't know how any of us are going to survive what's happening. Right now, I need you—*all* of you. We—*we*—are more important than your guilt, or at least I thought so, but apparently I'm wasting my breath."

I was really close to tipping the couch back and dumping him off of it, but he shot up and was in front of me before I could blink an eye. He wrapped an arm around my waist and our eyes locked. Everywhere our bodies touched, heat rushed to the surface. It wasn't like I had forgotten what it was like to be in his arms, I just wasn't prepared for it.

I could never be prepared for it.

Neither was Aiden. His eyes were burning a liquid silver and his arm tightened around me. "I would *never* give up on you, Alex. Never."

"Then why are you being such a—"

"What?" His voice dropped low. "I'm being what?"

Infuriating. Stubborn. Thick-skulled. Freaking sexy. "Good gods, can we stop arguing and just, I don't know, make out?"

A deep, husky laugh rumbled through his body and teased mine. "Is that what you want?"

More than the air I breathed. "What do you think?"

He moved forward, backing me up until I was pressed against the closed door. "That I'm seriously in love with your one-track mind."

I opened my mouth to point out that my multitasking skills had drastically improved, but Aiden took advantage. His mouth was on mine, and the kiss—oh, the kiss killed that freshly acquired skill. Blew it right out the window.

When he lifted his head, just by the slightest, I gasped.

"Okay. You may have a point," he said.

"A point?" I thought I'd made several.

"It's hard, Alex, remembering how you were," Aiden admitted quietly. He slid a hand through the mess of hair at the nape of my neck, sending shivers dancing over my skin. "I hated it. Hated every moment of it."

I placed my hand on his cheek. "I know."

"And all I could think about was getting you back." He pressed his lips to my temple and then the hollow of my cheek. "But you're right. I haven't been *here* completely."

"You're not going to feel guilty over that, too?"

He grinned against the side of my neck, his lips moving

against my wildly pounding pulse. "You always have to be such a smart-ass."

Looping my arm around his neck, I smiled. "Maybe . . ." Hope dared to spark. "Are you okay, now? Are we okay?"

"We're okay." Aiden kissed me softly and kept on kissing me as he lifted me just by one arm and turned me around. Within seconds, my back was pressing into the cushion and he was over me, fully clothed and covered with weapons. "I'm okay."

"You are?"

He smiled and it revealed those dimples. "I will be."

I started to say something, but his hand drifted down my side, tracing the line of my ribcage and then higher, and I totally forgot what I was going to say. I felt dizzy with expectation, of want and need, and a hundred other things as my heart pounded and my breath grew short.

"Thank you," he whispered, and then brought his lips to mine again, pressing me closer, until our hips fitted together tightly. Crazy-insane sensations rushed over my body. "Thank you."

I wasn't sure how we went from arguing to this, or what he was really thanking me for, but I wasn't complaining, and in a really twisted way it seemed normal. Aiden worshipped me as if I'd been born worthy of such a beautiful, complicated man, and over the course of that night, he truly showed me that *we* were okay, that *he* was okay, and, for now, that was what I needed to face tomorrow.

17

I had a stupid grin on my face for the most of the next day. Even though I was chilly, covered in mud from training in the warded area, and tired from using akasha and the elements, I looked like I'd been smacked with a silly stick.

Only a few times did it slip, and that was when I thought about Seth and the stunt he'd managed to pull yesterday. After Aiden and I . . . well, when we'd started actually using our mouths for words again, we agreed to keep what had happened between us and Marcus. There was no reason to freak everyone else out, and going by the way Marcus had reacted, it'd been a smart decision.

Marcus hadn't thrown anything, but he'd been as angry as Aiden.

And I knew that was why Marcus had switched out with Solos when it came to training today. But it was weird beating up my uncle.

Whenever our ragtag group took a break, Aiden was by my side. There were moments when he'd become unbearably quiet and Broody McBroodsters, and I knew he was thinking about what he had done with the Elixir. He was trying though, and that was what mattered.

We ended the day and hobbled back inside, greeted by the scent of the stew Laadan had cooked up. I went upstairs to wash the day's worth of grime off, and Aiden followed.

Once inside the room, I tossed him a coy look over my shoulder. At least, I thought it was coy, but I probably looked like I had something in my eye.

Aiden grinned nonetheless.

"Are you following me?" I asked, kicking off my boots.

He prowled forward, moving like one of those caged panthers we'd seen at the zoo. "I'm just being here for you, and I think you really need me right now."

"Ha. Ha." Out of my shoes, Aiden towered over me; I felt like a hobbit standing in front of him.

Aiden's grin spread and a dimple appeared in his left cheek. He tucked a strand of my hair back, then his hands dropped and he tugged the shirt out of my cargos. "I think you called it 'manning up'."

This wasn't the kind of manning up I'd been talking about the night before, because even with my limited knowledge of such things, he excelled in that department. But I said nothing as I stared up at him.

Lowering his head, his lips brushed over mine. I was sure I tasted of dirt and sour apple, courtesy of the Blow Pop I'd been nursing earlier, but he made this sound against my mouth, part growl and part something deeper. As the kiss deepened, like he could just devour the taste and feel, I melted against him.

"I really like your idea of manning up," I murmured, clutching at the front of his shirt.

Aiden chuckled as the tips of his fingers skimmed over my stomach. Heat followed, chasing away the chill in my skin. I reached up, wanting more, always needing more—

"Don't stop on my account."

I shrieked at the sound of Apollo's voice and jerked back, tripping over my feet. Aiden caught my arm, steadying me before I face-planted the floor.

"Gods," I muttered, placing a hand over my pounding heart. I'd been so caught up in Aiden I hadn't even sensed Apollo's presence.

Apollo sat on the edge of the bed, head cocked to the side, one leg crossed over the other. His blond hair was loose, framing a face that was eerily perfect. Vibrant blue eyes stared back at me instead of the creepy all-white eyes of a god. I was surprised that he remembered how much they freaked me out.

Aiden recovered first, moving to stand in front of me. He stiffened at the sound of Apollo's amused chuckle. "How did you get in here?"

"The wards on the house faded about three hours ago. Luckily, none of the other gods have realized that and, for the most part, they don't want Alex dead." And then he tacked on, ". . . right at this moment."

I looked at him blandly. "Good to know."

"Maybe next time you'd want to knock?" Aiden suggested, relaxing a fraction of an inch.

Apollo's shoulders lifted. "Where is the fun in that?" But he stood, his head inclining to the side. "We need to talk, but both of you look like you've been wrestling in mud."

"We've been training," I pointed out. "Like you suggested."

If he was grateful that we'd actually followed instructions, it didn't show. "I will be waiting downstairs. Try not to take ten years."

With that, he simply blinked out of existence. A moment later, I heard a startled yelp downstairs. Glad we weren't the only ones he liked to do that to.

I slumped against the wall. "I think he took a few years off my life."

Aiden's brow arched. "I still think we need to put a bell on him."

My lips twitched. "And I still think that's a good idea."

He glanced at the door and then took my hand, tugging me toward the bathroom. "We only have a few minutes. Let's make them worth our while."

More than a few minutes later, Aiden and I stood in the large living room with everyone else. Apollo was busying himself with a bowl of the stew Laadan and Deacon had made.

"Hungry?" I asked, after several moments of awkward silence stretched out.

He looked up. "Not really, but this is delicious."

Laadan all but beamed from the couch. "Thank you."

"We wouldn't know," Aiden said. He was leaning against the wall, arms crossed.

Apollo's lips spread into a smile. "Sorry. I'll try to come after dinner next time." The bowl disappeared from his hands, and I wondered where it went. "Well, it's good to see the Scooby gang all in one piece. Warms my heart and all that jazz, but let's get to the point."

"Let's do that," I murmured as I hopped up on the desk, letting my feet dangle off the edge. "You said we needed to talk."

"We do." Apollo drifted toward where Olivia and Deacon sat primly beside Laadan. He looked at them a long moment, as if he could see something beyond what our eyes were capable of, and then turned around. "First, I need you to fill me in on everything the First has shared with you."

Kicking my legs off the side of the desk, I gave him the quick and dirty version of events. There wasn't much to tell, and Apollo didn't pass over that fact.

"That's it?" He didn't even attempt to hide his irritation and disappointment. "You guys have this unbreakable bond that nearly destroyed the entire world, and all you can tell me is that you *think* he's heading north, which is something I already know?"

My lips pursed. Way to make me feel like an epic failure of an Apollyon.

"It's not her fault," Aiden snapped, eyes flashing like quicksilver. "He kept most of his plans to himself."

"Probably because he feared that she might eventually break the bond," Marcus said. "So the question remains—what do we do with the knowledge that we have?"

"And hopefully you have some knowledge to bring to the

table?" I fixed an innocent look on my face. "That would be a nice change of pace."

His eyes narrowed.

"Can you tell us how Thanatos was able to discover us?" Marcus asked.

"Yes, that's rather easy. Alex's little display of akasha while fighting Aiden drew Thanatos to her."

I frowned at the reminder. "But I've been practicing with it since then."

"Practicing with akasha is one thing, Alex. It doesn't even register on our scale, especially if you stayed within the wards I sensed outside." His eyes slid toward Aiden. "Using it to try to kill someone is like throwing up a homing beacon."

Flinching, I looked away. "So you're saying not to use akasha then?"

"I have a work around for that." Apollo held out his hand and the air around it shimmered an electric blue. A second later, a small medallion appeared in his palm, connected to a chain that dangled from his fingers. A smug, satisfied grin stretched Apollo's lips. "I took Hermes' helmet, melted the mother down, and here you go. An invisibility charm just for you."

Apollo dropped the necklace into my palm. It was a reddish-gold color, and a crudely shaped wing was etched into it. "Ha," I said. "It's like Harry Potter and the invisibility cloak."

Everyone stared at me.

I rolled my eyes. "Whatever. So I'm invisible if I wear this?"

Apollo laughed like I'd asked the stupidest question ever. "No. Your energy will just be hidden from the gods—all except me—even if you use akasha."

"Oh," I said, holding up the necklace. "Handy."

As Aiden came over and helped clasp the necklace, he asked, "What else have you been able to find out?"

"Oh, you know, I've been doing nothing." Apollo glared at us. "I've managed to convince my brothers and sisters to stop their destruction long enough to give us a chance to make this right, but they will not be held back for long. With every moment, Lucian and the First draw closer to overthrowing the Council. And with daimons attacking humans in droves, they will risk millions of innocent lives to put a stop to it."

"Not because they're actually concerned about the mortals." I tucked the necklace under my shirt, ignoring how oddly warm the metal was. It hung about an inch below the crystal rose. "But because if Lucian and Seth overthrow the Council in the Catskills, then they'll be one step away from overthrowing the gods, right? Because whoever controls those seats are the rulers."

Apollo said nothing.

"You know, that's what I don't get." Deacon stretched out his long legs from the chair, wiggling his toes. "I know that, if Seth and Lucian overthrow the Council, it's a big deal for the Hematoi, but the gods can't be that frightened."

Without saying a word, Apollo faced Aiden's brother. I knew that he was probably giving the boy one of his Leon/Apollo looks that said *do I really need to explain this*?

Deacon fidgeted. "I mean, you guys can just hide in Olympus and call it a day."

"He has a point," Luke said carefully. "Not like Seth can storm Olympus—not really."

I rifled through the memories of the other Apollyons, and nervousness moved through me, quick and slithery like a snake.

"Well . . ." Apollo sighed. "There *is* a way to get to Olympus."

My jaw smacked off my knee. "Portals?"

He nodded. "They are headed there. It's how we move between Olympus and the mortal world."

"You know," Aiden said. "This kind of information would've been helpful weeks ago. We could have had Sentinels we trust guarding these portals."

"And what Sentinels can you truly trust?" Apollo asked evenly. "Lucian's offer is enticing enough to sway them to his side. Most of the Sentinels have turned on the Council, turned on the gods. Besides, it wasn't necessary for any of you to know that."

Aiden looked like he wanted to say more, but wisely remained quiet.

"And luckily we've kept their locations secret, even from the previous Apollyons." Apollo's gaze flickered to me. "What have you learned from the Awakening?"

I was sort of surprised by Apollo's faith in my ability to block Seth. I doubted that faith would remain if I told him about Seth and Hermes.

Still kicking my legs, I shrugged. "A lot of it is about their lives, and there are so many. It's like watching every episode of a TV series that has been on for a millennium. It's hard to sort through all of it. Sometimes something is said and it wiggles a memory free."

An unsympathetic look crossed Apollo's features.

Well, wasn't like I was expecting a hug from him. "Most of it is how to use the elements and akasha. And Greek—I can read Greek now."

Most of the room looked unimpressed by that, but Aiden caught my eye and smiled reassuringly. I grinned back. Reading Greek was a pretty big damn deal to me.

"Well, that's all fine and dandy," Apollo said, letting out an exaggerated sigh.

I kicked off the desk extra hard, my leg bouncing.

Aiden slid me a look. "What do we do from here? Obviously the gods expect us to do something."

"The gods expect *her* to do something." Apollo jerked his chin at me.

"But how can she fight him without touching him?" Aiden pushed off the wall and strode to the middle of the room. "The gods have to understand that."

"They do." Apollo's eyes narrowed on me. "But I was hoping

there was something knocking around in her brain that held the answer to that little problem. But—"

Apollo smacked a hand down on my leg. "Must you always be moving some part of your body?"

I glared at him as I not-so-gently removed his hand. The contact of his flesh on mine brought the marks of Apollyon out like nothing else. And I knew he saw them by the way his eyes darted over my face. "It's not hurting you," I said.

"It's annoying."

"*You're* annoying," I shot back.

To our left, Aiden rolled his eyes. "All right, children, back to the important stuff."

"Think, Alex, there has to be something that can help us—possibly with Solaris." Apollo leaned in, planting his hands on either side of my now-still legs. Over his shoulder, I saw Aiden move toward us, but then Apollo moved his head so that he blocked him. "Alex."

"What?" I gripped the edge of the table. "Look, it's not like I'm being stubborn or stupid. If I could remember something useful, I would. It's not like I'm stopping myself—" *Stopping myself from seeing or remembering something very important*—that was what I was going to say, but like it was with other things, that wave of familiarity washed over me again, raising the hairs on the back of my neck.

When I'd been connected to Seth, there had been something that he hadn't wanted me to think about, and it had to do with Solaris—probably just the whole morbid ending of the two Apollyons. But going back further, there was something that I'd seen, something that Solaris had done, or . . . tried to do.

In the moments before I'd connected with Seth, I had seen her turn on the First.

"Alexandria?" Apollo said.

I held up my hand, resisting the urge to shush him. "There's something with Solaris, but it's weird. Almost like I wasn't meant to know, but I can't . . ."

Slipping off the desk, I brushed past Apollo. Without realizing what I'd done, I had moved toward the shelter of Aiden's body. Completely at ease, he slipped an arm over my shoulders, the look on his face daring anyone to say a word.

I looked up at him, remembering how much Solaris had cared for the First. The love I saw in Aiden's silvery eyes had been reflected in the First. And I felt—remembered feeling—the terrible decision Solaris had made—protecting others by destroying the First. Piece by piece, it came together.

"Solaris tried to stop the First, and there was something she did . . . or was trying to do. Something that would've worked, but the Order of Thanatos made their move before she could complete it." I let out a frustrated sigh. "She knew how to stop the First—kill him, somehow—but I don't know what it was. It's like that information was shielded or erased somehow." Frustrated, I bit out a groan. "Too bad I can't talk to Solaris."

Laadan cleared her throat. "But that is something, dear. At least we know there is something out there."

"Wait," Marcus said. "Solaris would be in the Underworld, right?"

Apollo's eyes were suddenly sharp. "She would be, but I can't travel to the Underworld. Hades still has his panties in a bunch."

Solos smirked as he leaned over the back of the couch. "Well, that's another dead end."

"Not really," Apollo said.

I suddenly got a real bad feeling about this.

"What do you mean 'not really'?" Aiden asked, his arm tightening around my shoulders.

Apollo moved to stand in front of the window. Pale moonlight cast a strange glow around him. "Well, if Alex thinks Solaris can help us, then it's an avenue we want to check out. And who better than Alex?"

Aiden stiffened. "What?"

"She could have some Apollyon girl-talk," Apollo said, his blue eyes dancing with amusement. "Actually, I'm not really suggesting that Alex—"

"Wait." I slipped out from under Aiden's arm. "There's a possibility that we could reach Solaris?"

When Apollo nodded, optimism took hold. The rush was like getting buzzed off of wine coolers—harmless at first, but packing a hell of a downer the morning after. "And I could get to the Underworld?"

Apollo's gaze flickered beyond me, settling on Aiden for a moment, and I knew that, if I went down there, Aiden would come, too. An old part of me would've protested, but now I understood why he wouldn't allow me to do something like that alone, and I wasn't insane enough to try it. I'd need help.

"You could," Apollo answered.

I could barely contain my excitement. Little Alex wanted to do cartwheels across the living room. I knew in my marrow that Solaris knew how to stop the First. That she held the knowledge to stop this, because she'd planned on doing it before.

But then the one big problem surrounding going to the Underworld surfaced.

"Do I have to die again?" I added quickly, because I was pretty sure Apollo might be thrilled with the idea of killing me at this moment. "Because the whole dying part of going to the Underworld sucked butt last time."

Apollo's eyes rolled. "Dying isn't the only way into the Underworld, but it's the safest."

Well, that sounded like an oxymoron if I'd ever heard one.

"There are several entrances to the Underworld in the mortal realm," Apollo continued. "The closest to our location would be the one in Kansas."

"If you say Stull Cemetery, I'll probably hug you," Luke said, and then he shrank back when the Sun God turned to him. "Or not—no hugging necessary."

"Stull Cemetery?" I asked, glancing around the room. Something about the name did sound familiar. "I cannot be the only person who has no idea what that is . . . other than a cemetery."

Aiden shook his head. "I'm right with you."

"How cute," Apollo murmured.

I ignored him. "So?"

"Go ahead," Apollo said to Luke. "Tell them what it is, since it's obviously hugging material."

Crimson stained Luke's cheeks. "Legend goes that one of the gates to hell is in Stull Cemetery in Kansas."

"Oh, gods," I muttered, remembering where I'd heard this before. "Wasn't that a season finale on *Supernatural*?" When the boys nodded, my eyes rolled. "Seriously? Are Sam and Dean going to be there?"

Luke and Deacon looked way too happy about that idea, and then Deacon threw out, "Luke has a theory."

"I do." Luke flashed a grin. "Stull Cemetery is a freaky place with a lot of unexplained things happening, just like other places labeled 'gates to hell'. I think that the gates to hell are actually gates to the Underworld."

"You're correct." A ball of golden light appeared above Apollo's hand and he started tossing it up in the air, over and over, reminding me of Seth. "The gateway was actually inside a church there, but Hades came through one night on Halloween and everyone thought the idiot was the devil. Kind of blew our cover—we tore the church down."

"Nice," I said, watching the ball. He was inches from smacking it into the light fixture.

"But the gateway is still where the church stood." Up went the ball of golden light. "And we've taken some precautions, after a few mortals accidentally stumbled upon it."

My brows rose.

"So, what happens to mortals when they find one of the gates?" Aiden asked.

Apollo caught the ball of light. "Oh, you know. They tend to become one of Hades' dogs' chew toys. Anyway, the gates only show now to someone of godly descent."

"Pures?" Marcus asked.

"Ah . . . no." The ball vanished and Apollo looked straight at me. "They'll appear to gods, original demigods, those created by taking ambrosia, or the Apollyon."

I elbowed Aiden. "I feel so special."

"That you are." He grinned when I shot him a look. "So, we find the gate and go through it. Sounds easy."

Apollo laughed. "It's not that easy. The gate is guarded now, even to those it appears to."

My stomach sank. "Do I even want to know?"

He flashed a smile, and my tummy hit my toes. I so did not like when Apollo smiled like that. "There are hellhounds and guards."

"Oh, goodie."

"And then there are spirits—most don't get past the spirits." Apollo stepped back. "But if you do, the gate appears and you're in the Underworld, but going into the Underworld without a guide is not only dangerous, but stupid."

So I needed to play with some dogs, beat up a company of guards, *and* call the Ghostbusters? And I needed a guide? Okay. This didn't sound too bad.

I smiled. "I know just the person."

18

"Caleb," Olivia whispered, speaking for the first time. When I nodded, she shot to her feet. "I want to go."

Apollo arched a brow. "Two people sneaking into the Underworld trying to find one soul among millions is insane and dangerous. No one else can go."

Olivia turned her wide, pleading eyes on me. "I have to go then. It has to be me. I need to—"

"And that's why it cannot be you," Apollo said before I could respond. "You will be focused on finding Caleb instead of the mission at hand."

Her hands curled into fists at her side. "How is that any different than Aiden? He'll be focused on Alex!"

I slid the person in question a look, but Aiden had the same expression that Apollo did. There might be a lot of tears and pleading, but there would be no debate.

"And that's what we need," Apollo said, almost gently. For a moment, I was almost convinced that he pitied her. Not in a bad way, but like he could sympathize with her, which would be amazing since gods were really lacking in the empathy department. "There's no guarantee that they will even find Caleb, but either way, we need Alex to come back out of the Underworld with the information we need. Alive."

Some of the other gods probably didn't feel that way.

Apollo's gaze settled on Aiden again. "You would give your life for her?"

I didn't like that question at all and I opened my mouth, but Aiden answered without hesitation. "Yes."

The god nodded. "I know you would too, Marcus, but Aiden would . . ."

Marcus looked less than pleased but nodded. "I know what you mean."

A bitter taste crawled up my throat as my heart turned over heavily. Going into the Underworld would be insanely dangerous, and the idea of Aiden risking his life scared the crap out of me, but as my gaze fell over the room, I knew that out of everyone there he was the most skilled.

Realizing that she wouldn't be able to change anyone's mind, Olivia said nothing as she walked out of the room, head high. Sorrow panged in my chest, as potent as the fear. It wasn't fair. I wished that Caleb and Olivia could have had one more moment together before all their future moments were stolen from them.

After Olivia's exit, plans were quickly made for our departure. The group would stay behind, as was safest for them, and Aiden and I would leave in the morning for . . . Kansas. Other than an apparent Underworld gate, I had no idea what was in Kansas. Hay bales? Dorothy?

"There's something else," I said to Apollo after the group scattered. Aiden remained behind, closing the door, seeming to know what I intended to tell Apollo.

"I can't wait to hear," Apollo said dryly.

I took a deep breath. "I saw Seth yesterday."

Apollo's brows slammed down as he opened his mouth, but no words came out. Maybe I should have clarified. "What I mean is," I said quickly, "kind of."

"Kind of?"

I nodded. "He was able to pull me . . . inside my own head. It looked and felt real, and it was like I was dreaming . . . but I wasn't."

His eyebrows began to lift. "That makes no sense, Alex."

"She was talking with Lea and started to get a headache right before it happened, like before, when she was on the Elixir," Aiden explained, since obviously I couldn't form a coherent sentence. "Alex fainted—"

"I didn't faint," I grumbled, feeling my cheeks flush.

Aiden's lip curved up on one side. "Okay. She was suddenly not walking or talking anymore. During that time, she saw Seth. Apparently, he used Hermes to pull her in."

"Hermes?" Apollo hissed—actually hissed like an angry lion. "That little, punk-ass bitch."

My brows rose.

"I actually felt somewhat bad about stealing his helmet and melting it down." Apollo sounded indignant. "Hermes won't be helping Seth anymore."

It was hard not to laugh when Apollo got all butt sore, but somehow I managed. "By the way, when did you steal his helmet?"

Apollo shrugged. "A couple of days ago."

"Do you think that's why he might have helped Seth?"

"Hmm . . ." Apollo's face screwed up. "Good point. Anyway, did Seth tell you anything?"

Geez. "He didn't really say anything important. I have this feeling he was really just testing it out, but if you can stop Hermes from helping, then it shouldn't be a problem."

A muscle flexed in Apollo's jaw. "Can he transfer power in this state?"

"No. And he can't read my thoughts." I leaned against the wall, smothering a yawn. "It seems more like an annoyance than anything else."

"It's more than an annoyance." Aiden's eyes flashed silver.

"He sees it as a 'violation'," I explained, upon seeing Apollo's puzzled look. "But it could be worse."

"As in him doing something like that when you're in the middle of a battle or in the Underworld?" Apollo asked.

"Well . . ." I frowned.

"I've been thinking," Aiden continued. "We know Hermes helped, but it has to be more than that or Seth would have done this the moment you broke the connection. When you were on the Elixir, he seemed to be able to reach you when it started to wear off, and when it wore off, you were exhausted. Maybe that has something to do with it—how tired you are."

"Makes sense. I guess I just need to get my beauty sleep."

Aiden looked unimpressed. "That's the best theory I can come up with."

"It does make sense." Apollo stretched his head to the side, his striking face tense with annoyance. "You two are still connected, and even though you've shielded out the bulk of that connection, he may be able to get to you when you're weakened, with or without Hermes."

"Like a crappy two-way radio," I muttered.

"Exactly. And especially if Hermes created a path to you."

I so did not like the sound of that.

Apollo smiled at Aiden then. "Needless to say, I think you know how important it is to stay close to Alex."

"Like you even have to point that out," Aiden responded.

Apollo smirked. "The trip to the Underworld isn't going to be easy, and that's not even taking into consideration Alex's newly-acquired narcoleptic tendencies."

I rolled my eyes. What part of "wasn't asleep" did they not understand?

"And if this happens again, you may not believe he can glean any important information, but you need to be careful that you do not let on what you are doing, especially your new mission."

"I know," I said, staring at the worn chair next to the god. "I'm pretty sure he doesn't know what Solaris was planning to do with the First, but he knew there was *something*. And maybe we'll get lucky. Seth may not be able to pull it off again."

Neither of them looked convinced.

"Okay, back to the bigger problem at hand. The one I can sort of help you with." Apollo strode over to the desk, finding a piece of paper and pen. "The Stull portal should place you beyond the entrance to the Underworld, at the beginning of Asphodel Fields. They might not really be fields, or they could be." He paused, glanced over his shoulders. "They have changed every time I've been there. Sometimes they are vacant. Other times they are not. Souls that you encounter there will be . . . relatively harmless."

I crept closer, peering over his shoulder. He was drawing a map. I recognized "Styx." The rest I figured I'd have recognized if I'd paid attention in class.

"There will be tunnels you will enter. You should be able to find a place to rest there for a few hours since the souls are unable to travel through them. Get there before night falls and stay there until the sky is golden. If you don't make it there before night, you'll find out why souls don't travel there."

I waited for him to elaborate and when he didn't, I exchanged a look with Aiden.

"You do not want to be roaming *any* part of the Underworld at night." Apollo's pen swept over the paper. "From there, you will cross into the Vale of Mourning."

"Oh, that sounds fun," I said.

Apollo smirked. "You will eventually come to a crossroads. One way will lead you to Tartarus, and the other will lead you to the Elysian Fields—this will be the Plain of Judgment. You'll want to make yourself as invisible as possible. And I don't mean necklace-invisible."

He set the pen down and handed the map over to Aiden. "I can call in a favor and get word to Caleb, have him meet you there. But from that point . . ."

"We're on our own." When Apollo nodded, I bit on my lip. "Okay."

"Wait," Aiden said, eyes narrowing on the map. "Isn't the Plain of Judgment near Hades' Palace?"

"As I said, you two will want to make yourselves as invisible as possible. I have it on good faith that Hades will be at Olympus, but he has many eyes guarding the palace." Apollo's folded arms were the size of tree trunks. "I need you both to understand that the Underworld will be dangerous. Caleb could be anywhere, and it won't be like the last time, when your arrival was noted. You will see things you cannot understand. Things that you will want to intervene in, but you won't be able to."

I swallowed at the seriousness in his tone. "I understand."

"Do you? You have shown very little impulse control in the past, Alex. You will be unwelcome there. And it's just not the Underworld." His cold, steely gaze moved to Aiden. "The gates are well-protected."

"We understand," Aiden responded calmly.

Keen knowledge flared in the god's eyes. "Be careful. Most who enter the Underworld do not leave, and those who do are irrevocably changed by what they experience."

Apollo started to fade out as we stared at him, our expressions no doubt mirroring the seriousness of what he'd said. Just before his body was enveloped in shimmery blue dust, he said, "I'll owe you two for this, and everything else."

It was way too early to be up moving around, but here I was, standing beside one of the Hummers, glaring up at the morning sun.

Aiden was saying goodbye to his brother, and I was trying to give them some space while maintaining my balance on one foot. It was the only thing keeping me from falling over on my face. Last night, Aiden had called an "early night" and literally forced me to bed like he was my babysitter.

"You need to be well-rested," he had argued, and then sat watch until I went to sleep. And even after about eight hours of shut-eye, I still didn't want to get up at the crack of dawn. We had a long drive ahead of us—about nine hours and nearly five hundred miles. A plane would've been quicker, but there was no way we were getting the weapon stash past mortal security without using compulsion on half the TSA. And it would've been harder to explain why Aiden was painting runes in Titan blood inside a 747. With that and the talisman Apollo had given me, at least it should be a relatively uneventful road trip.

"Alexandria?"

I turned at the sound of my uncle's voice and headed toward where he stood just off the porch. "Hey."

He tried to smile, but it was forced. "I know you'll be careful, but really—be careful. Okay?"

"I'm always careful."

Marcus' expression turned bland.

Unable to help myself, I grinned. "I'll be careful. I promise."

At the sound of Aiden's approaching footsteps, he stepped back and pinned the other pure with a dark look. "If anything happens to her, it's your ass."

My mouth dropped. "Did you just cuss? I've never heard you cuss before. Wow."

Instead of responding, Marcus hugged me. He let go quickly and looked away, swallowing hard. Within seconds, we'd said our goodbyes to the rest of the group.

"Try not to let any souls free," Luke said, grinning.

"Unless it's Sam or Dean's souls, right?" When they laughed, I gave them each a quick hug and then trotted over to where Aiden was packing the Hummer.

Once I got a load of the heavy sack of weapons and provisions, I said, "Not it."

Aiden chuckled. "I got it." He lifted it with one arm—impressive—and tossed it in the back. "I've already stashed a few daggers in front. You ready?"

"Yeah." I glanced over my shoulder, taking in those waiting on the porch. An odd ache filled my chest. For a moment, everything was peaceful, though. Birds called. Rays of bright light sliced through the thick trees. It was almost like Aiden and I were going on a vacation or something.

Not going to the Underworld.

Aiden placed a hand on my arm. "We'll see them again."

"I know." I smiled, but it felt all kinds of wrong. "It's just . . ."

"What?" He closed the trunk.

Shaking my head, I tore my gaze from my friends—my family. As I turned to Aiden, a flash of movement caught my attention. Near the edge of the oak trees stood a doe on thin, elegant legs, and I'd swear our eyes met. There was something intelligent in the gaze—something foreign. Then it shot off, disappearing into the abundant foliage.

"Do you think they'll be okay?" I asked, meeting Aiden's eyes.

"I wouldn't leave my brother behind if I didn't think so."

There was truth in those words. Nodding, I headed to the passenger side, my gaze drifting to where the doe had stood. I thought of Artemis. The gods shouldn't be able to find us, but it took no stretch of the imagination to assume that Apollo would've told his twin where we were.

A small smile played at my lips as I climbed in. They would be okay. Over half of them were trained and damn good with a dagger. Not to mention that all of Deacon's playing around with fire was paying off. With Laadan and Marcus capable of controlling air, they could protect themselves. And if Artemis was really hanging around, they had one badass goddess on their side.

Belting myself in, I then placed my hands in my lap. They balled into fists. I glanced over at Aiden as he started the engine. The Hummer rumbled to life. "You know I suck at long car rides, right?"

A half-grin appeared. "I remember."

"You'll need to entertain me. A lot."

He laughed as he coaxed the massive vehicle down the narrow, one-lane dirt road that was all new to me. "By the way,"

Aiden said, casting me a long look that had me totally forgetting about the seriousness of our mission. "You look damn good in a Sentinel uniform."

A hot flush that had nothing to do with embarrassment spread over me. "So do you."

"I know."

I laughed outright. "Wow. Healthy ego there."

Aiden's eyes were light, a heather gray, as they focused on the rural road. "Check out the glovebox."

Curious, I leaned forward and threw the latch. Inside were two black, shiny objects. I pulled one out carefully, turning the heavy thing over. It was a specially designed Glock. Feeling like a badass, I checked the clip—titanium bullets.

The gun felt weird in my hands, though. "I've only held one of these once outside the Covenant."

Aiden was quiet as he waited for me to continue. Of course, he knew when. "I didn't use it. I hesitated."

"You were facing down your own mother, Alex. It's understandable."

I nodded, ignoring the lump in my throat as I placed the gun back in the glovebox. "What else is stashed away?"

"Look under the seats," he murmured as the Hummer's tires evened out on pavement.

Under the seat were two daggers and a sickle blade. "The same under yours?"

He nodded.

"What are you expecting? A daimon siege?"

"Safe than sorry, Alex. We have no idea what or who we're going to run into out here."

I straightened. "Seth's nowhere near here and we're protected." I tapped a finger off the talisman I wore, and then gestured at the mark above our heads.

Aiden grunted something unintelligible.

My brows rose, but I dropped it. Not like I was bothered by

the things designed to stab, shoot, and otherwise kill. "Man, I wish we had coffee."

"Like you need more caffeine."

"Ha. Ha." I stared out the window, nibbling on my lower lip. "Caffeine is my friend."

"And red meat—can't forget red meat."

I grinned at his teasing tone. "Whatever. Eat your bland chicken breast, but soon . . . very soon, I shall sway you to the dark side of red meat."

We went back and forth for a while, distracting ourselves, and it worked. My muscles relaxed with each passing mile and we weren't bombarded by daimons dropping from the sky from the moment we hit civilization, otherwise known as the interstate. When we took a detour to grab a quick lunch from the drive-through, I ordered a hamburger . . .

Aiden got a grilled chicken sandwich . . . and took one of the buns off.

Rolling up the wrapper, I laughed. "Why do you do that? It's like you have something against two-bun sandwiches."

"One bun is enough." He glanced down at his lap, one hand on the steering wheel and the other covered with specks of seasoning. Looking up, he sighed. "Did you take all the napkins?"

I looked at him sheepishly. "Maybe, but I saved you . . . half of one." Digging into my bag, I pulled out a napkin and tore it into two. Then I dabbed at his hand, not as graceful as he'd been when he'd washed my hands the night in the kitchen.

I think I may have rubbed his skin raw.

Snatching the bag out of his lap, I pulled out the other bun, wiggling it near his mouth.

"Alex . . ." He leaned toward the window, avoiding the dangerous second bun. "Come on."

"Eat it," I ordered, holding it with two hands now, making it dance in the air. "It's begging you. 'Eat me'."

He arched a brow.

"Perv," I muttered.

Aiden pressed his lips together, but when he glanced at me and my dancing bun, he burst into laughter. "All right, give me the bun."

Grinning, I watched him eat the bun, and then pulled out the small order of fries. "Want some?"

Surprisingly, he didn't turn them down. But after the food was gone and neither of us could find anything remotely worth listening to on the radio, I started to get twitchy. Four hours in, we hit a convenience store a few miles beyond Des Moines, refilling the tank and stocking up on what looked like gerbil food. Mindful of considering my run-in with Hades last time I was in a convenience store, I stayed in the car and asked for some Doritos, but apparently nacho cheese wasn't appropriate Underworld food.

"Want to drive?"

I shook my head as I buckled in. "If I was driving this, I'd take out a family of four."

"What?" he laughed.

"I've only driven a car, like, once. And it was a bug compared to this thing. I mean, I know how to drive, but I don't think you want me on the interstate."

Aiden reached over, wrapping his hand around mine. "When all of this is over, I'll get you up to speed. You'll be driving one of those trucks over there."

I laughed as I eyed the eighteen-wheeler. "You might want to add 'small town' to the list of casualties."

"You'll do okay—more than okay." He slid the Hummer between two trucks. "Anything you set your mind to, you succeed at it. So no worries."

Tipping my head back against the leather seat, I smiled. "You always say the right things."

Aiden's brows furrowed. "Nah, I don't think so."

"You do," I said quietly, holding his hand tighter. "I don't think you even try. It just comes natural to you."

Two points on his cheeks flushed, and I found it terribly cute. So I leaned over the center console and kissed one of those flaming cheeks. I settled back, grinning at the bemused look he sent my way.

The rest of the trip was uneventful, and I actually dozed off about an hour or so from Stull. At first I didn't realize I was dreaming. Everything was foggy, like I was staring down a narrow tube filled with mist. As it cleared and the glimpse of images settled into place, I thought the circular chamber and its sandstone walls looked vaguely familiar. But it wasn't the place that caught my attention.

It was what was on the floor.

Apollo was on his knees, his hands outstretched, and he wasn't alone. Aiden was there, his back to me as he held something—*someone*—to his chest, his body bowed over the still form as he rocked back and forth, his broad shoulders trembling. There was another person in the room, but their form and image was too hazy to make out.

Unease slithered through me like murky fog as I focused on Aiden, wanting to reach out to him. I called his name, but I had no voice. The anxiety grew and I felt cold—too cold. Something wasn't right. I felt like I was there but detached, as if I was watching what was happening from a great distance.

Aiden was saying something, but it was too low for me to make out. All I heard was Apollo's response.

"I'm sorry."

Without warning, Aiden straightened and threw his head back, letting loose a roar full of pain and fury.

I jerked awake to the low sound of Aiden singing along to The Maine's "Saving Grace," slamming my knee into the dashboard.

"You okay?" he asked.

Dragging in a deep breath, I nodded as I pushed loose strands of hair out of my face. My heart pounded in my chest. I'd seen the lifeless body Aiden had been holding and I'd understood that scream that tore from the depths of his soul.

It had been me in his arms.

I slumped back against the seat, staring out the window. It was just a dream—only a dream. And could I be surprised that I was having messed-up dreams like that? All the stress and crazy stuff going on had to foster some whacked-out nightmares, but . . .

There had been something to the dream that made it hard to shake, that had left behind a chill deep in my bones. It took a lot to push the dream out of my thoughts. I settled back against the seat, watching Aiden from behind my lashes, picturing us going somewhere else—anywhere other than a freaking cemetery. Like maybe if we were driving to Disney World. Okay, maybe not. Maybe a beach for a sunny, romantic weekend, and I could almost see it. I could *taste* it.

Us being normal, living among mortals like we'd talked about, having a future where we weren't doing crazy stuff like this, where I wasn't connected to a psychotic Seth. We'd have a house, because I couldn't picture Aiden in an apartment or a townhouse. He'd want space—a yard—and even though a dog was out of the question because of the power daimons had over animals, it was my perfect future, so we had a Labrador that ran along the fence.

And I'd have a cat that curled up in my lap, a fat tabby that ate Aiden's leftover sandwich buns. We'd have a deck where we'd sit out on the evenings. Aiden would be reading a comic or some boring historical text written in Latin, and I'd be doing everything in my power to distract him.

I could get behind a future like that.

"What are you thinking?" Aiden's quiet voice startled me.

"How did you know I was awake?"

There was a pause. "I just did. So tell me . . .?"

Feeling a bit foolish, I told him about my fantasy future.

Aiden didn't laugh. He didn't poke fun at it or ask why a cat would be eating sandwich buns. He looked at me—looked at me so long I started to worry about crashing. Then he looked away, a muscle popping along his jaw.

"What?" I asked, squirming in the seat. "Did I divulge a little TMI?"

"No." That single word was hoarse.

"Then what?"

Aiden's eyes were so bright and luminous when they met mine again—shiny and strong like the titanium daggers we wore. "Only that I love you."

19

Kansas was . . . flat and grassy.

As far as the eye could see, was nothing more than flat fields with yellowish grass and tall reeds. In the distance, the horizon seemed to meet the land, a dark and ominous blue-gray as night neared, bleeding onto the brownish tall grass and white wildflowers.

"Prairie land", according to Aiden's impromptu history lesson, but what I picked up was that we were driving straight into Tornado Alley. All things considered, probably not the best place to be, especially when I got an eyeful of some of the most recent destruction caused by the bipolar gods.

Entire towns leveled. Debris-strewn fields and streets. The aftermath of so many lives uprooted, and knowing that it had something to do with me—the response to my initial inability to fight Seth's influence.

It was hard to look past that, but I knew I couldn't drown in the guilt right now or analyze the dream I'd just had like I was rocking a mad case of OCD. I needed my A-game. We were too close to Stull Cemetery.

Nervous energy hummed through both of us. Even with Apollo's insight on the gates and the Underworld, neither of us really knew what we were going to face.

About ten miles west of Lawrence, we came upon the small, unincorporated town of Stull. I sat up straighter, eyes glued to the window.

At dusk, the main street, which appeared to be the only street, was completely abandoned. None of the businesses were open. People didn't stroll down the sidewalks. There was nothing. Man, we were definitely in rural Kansas.

"So creepy," I whispered.

"What?"

"There's not a single soul on the street." I shivered in full heebie-jeebies mode.

"Maybe they're all in the cemetery." When I shot him a dirty look, he laughed. "Alex, we're about to go to the Underworld. A seemingly empty town can't scare you that much."

We came to a three-way stop and Aiden hung a right. "You know, Luke was saying that there's only like twenty people who live here and that it's believed they aren't from Earth," I said, glancing at Aiden. "Do you think they're gods?"

"Could be. Maybe Stull is their summer home."

I took another look at the squat, ancient-looking houses. "Pretty odd vacation spot, but hey, the gods are weird."

"That they are." Aiden leaned toward the steering wheel, eyes squinting. "There it is."

Following his gaze, I sucked in a soft gasp. A dozen or so feet down the road, up on the right hand side, was Stull Cemetery. Not a gateway to hell, but one to the Underworld.

And in the fading sun and gathering darkness, it was creepy as hell.

"I hope no one tries to kick us out," I murmured as Aiden coaxed the Hummer through the narrow entrance in the chain link fence. We were planning to leave the Hummer inside the cemetery. It wouldn't be there very long; time in the Underworld moved differently. Hours there were half-seconds here. Days would be minutes. Weeks would be hours.

"For some reason, I don't think we'll have a problem." Aiden pulled the vehicle to the side and killed the engine. Off went the lights.

Staring at the tombstones, I shuddered.

"Are you going to get out?" Aiden already had his door open.

A tumbleweed rolled down a walkway that had seen better days and my eyes widened as I followed it until it came to rest against the fence. "Do I have to?"

Aiden chuckled as he closed the door, disappearing around the back of the Hummer. Not wanting to re-enact a scene from *Night of the Living Dead*, I hopped out and quickly followed him. I found him sliding his arms through the straps of the heavy backpack.

By the time he closed the Hummer and hit the security system—who in the hell was going to steal the car here?—the cemetery had been plunged into dark shadows. Thick, dark-as-oil clouds blocked the moon, but my eyes adjusted quickly and I almost wished they hadn't.

Thrusting out of the swaying weeds and overgrown prairie grass were fewer than a hundred gravestones. Scattered among the newer tombstones were ancient ones whose inscriptions had faded long ago. Some were square; others reminded me of mini-Washington Monuments, and a few were old crosses that tipped heavily to one side or another.

At the very cusp of the cemetery was a crumbled stone foundation edged by a few trees. Two mounds of sandy brick marked where the church had once stood, before the gods had burned it down due to Hades' untimely midnight showing.

The pathway was nothing more than a dirt track about a foot wide, and I was almost a hundred percent positive I was strolling on unmarked graves.

"Gods, I hate cemeteries."

Aiden placed a hand on my back. "Dead people can't hurt you."

"Unless they're zombies."

"I doubt there are any zombies around here."

I huffed, hitting the button on the sickle blade. It extended, one end forming a sharp point, the other a nasty, reaper-looking scythe. "One can never be too safe."

Aiden shook his head, but kept on trekking up the narrow path. Eventually the walkway faded, overgrown by brush weeds and itchy grass that clung to my cargos. A prickly feeling skated across my neck and down my spine as we neared the foundation of the church. I wanted to look behind me, but I seriously expected to find a horde of brain-eating zombies standing there.

I edged around one lonely-looking tombstone and stepped beside Aiden. We were no more than a foot away from the crushed stone.

Aiden straightened the straps on the bag as he cocked his head to the side. "So, you see anything—?"

Suddenly, the wind stopped. Like, completely.

An unnatural stillness permeated the air, raising the tiny hairs at the nape of my neck. Under the black thermal, tiny bumps stole across my flesh. A stale, musky scent seeped in from nowhere. I let out a ragged breath and a small, frothy white cloud formed.

"Okay," I whispered, tightening my hold on the blade. "Not normal."

Aiden's breath lingered in the air, too. Holding a hand between us, he nodded toward the thick stand of trees crowding the remains of the church. Two darker shadows stood a few feet in, almost indistinguishable among the foliage.

My muscles tensed. Guards? Ghosts? I wasn't sure which was worse.

"Showtime," Aiden said, silently slipping off the backpack. He placed it near a rickety stone cross.

I nodded. "Yeppers peppers."

The two figures drifted forward. They were hooded and shapeless, and I realized that their feet—if they had feet, which was up in the air—didn't touch the ground. Their dark-red robes trailed an inch above the grass.

Slowly, their arms rose and the material slipped back. A weird creaking noise followed the motion. Slender, pale-white fingers reached for the hoods, drawing them back.

Oh . . . oh, wow.

Under the hoods were nothing but bones. Pale white bones and empty, vast blackness where eye sockets and nostrils would've been. The mouths . . . the jaws hinged on loose joints, so the mouths gaped open. There was no skin, no meat or hair. They were skeletons—floating, freaking skeletons.

Not as frightening or dangerous as zombies, but still, they were creepy.

I stared at them, wanting to look away but unable. It was eerie . . . their eyes. They were just holes, but the longer I stared at them, something . . . something moved deep inside them, teeny, tiny dots of flickering light.

My fingers loosened around the sickle blade. "I could just . . . blast them with akasha."

"Your idea has been noted and discarded."

"Oh, come on."

"Using akasha tires you out, right?" Aiden said evenly, keeping his eyes on the things. "Why not use it for something other than a bag of bones?"

"Oh. Good point."

Those "bags of bones" reached into their robes at the same moment.

I arched a brow. "I hope they don't flash us. Really don't want to see a skeleton pe—"

And then they withdrew two thick and shiny handles. Wondering if they were going to chuck the handles at us, I admit I was quite disappointed by the guards. No wonder mortals had discovered the gateway when all that stood between them and the portal were two walking Halloween decorations.

"Alex," Aiden murmured.

My chin jerked up, just as sparks flew from the handles, bright and intense in the darkness. Fire spread rapidly, fiery red and powerful, each forming the shape of a long, deadly blade.

"What the . . .?" My eyes widened.

They flew at us, bones rattling and knocking in a gruesome chorus. Aiden ducked under the first burning blade. Pivoting around cleanly, he planted a foot in the back of one skeleton.

The other lurched toward me, swiping the blade so close to my neck that I felt the heat. Darting to the side, I swung the sickle in a wide arc. The deadly sharp blade sliced through the robe and bone.

In a flash of light, the sword fizzled out and the bones collapsed into a smoldering heap. Taking a step back, I caught the sight of the same thing happening with Aiden's opponent. The fire-sword disappeared, and then nothing remained but bone and wisps of smoke.

I waited for them to get back up and do something, maybe even an entertaining jig, but nothing. Lowering the sickle, I frowned. "That was way, way too easy."

Aiden stalked toward me, his eyes darting over the landscape. "You're telling me. Stay close, because I have a feeling they were just meant to distract us."

A low growl rippled through the silent cemetery, and my stomach dropped all the way to my toes. Together, Aiden and I turned. I don't know who reacted first. Whether it was Aiden's explosive curse or my groan, it didn't matter.

Crouched in the ruined remains of the church was one big, mean, ticked-off-looking hellhound.

Stone crumbled under meaty paws the size of Aiden's hands. Claws, as sharp as the blades we held, gleamed like onyx. The body was huge, about the size of one of those energy-efficient deathtrap cars, but the heads—those were three of the biggest, ugliest things I'd ever seen. It was like taking a mutant sewer rat and mixing it with a pit bull. And the teeth . . . they belonged in a shark's mouth—white, wet and very, very sharp. Drool foamed under pink gums and dripped onto the ground, where the soil burned as if splashed with acid.

Six ghoulish yellow eyes settled on us.

"Damn," I muttered, falling into a crouch. "Don't cut the heads off. It's the hearts that we need to hit."

"Got it." Aiden flipped the dagger in his hand, like a total badass.

"Show-off."

Aiden smirked. "Wonder what this one is called?"

The hellhound's ears twitched as the massive body lowered, preparing for attack. I slid my hand to the middle of the blade, feeling my heart pound and the adrenaline kick my system into overdrive. In the pit of my stomach, the cord started to unravel.

I swallowed. "Let's call this one . . . Toto."

Three mouths opened in a growl that sent a cold chill down my spine, and a wave of hot, fetid breath smacked into us. Bile burned the back of my throat.

"I guess it doesn't like the name," I said, moving slowly to the right.

Aiden's powerful body tensed. "Here, Toto . . ." One head snapped in his direction. "That's a good Toto."

I slipped around the ancient cross, creeping up on the hellhound from the right. The middle and left head focused on me, snapping and growling.

Aiden clucked his tongue. "Come on, Toto, I'm pretty tasty."

I almost laughed, but the damn thing lurched from the pile of rubble, landing between us. The ground shook from the impact. Behind us, a few tombstones shuddered loose and toppled over. For a brief moment, it looked like Toto was coming straight for me, but at the last second, it lunged at Aiden.

Caught off-guard, Aiden stumbled back a step, his foot snagging on a fragment of stone. My heart leapt into my throat as I spun toward them, throwing out my free hand. There was a spark, a strong scent of burnt ozone, and then a ball of fire shot forward, more violet then red, unnatural and consuming. It smacked into the belly of the hellhound.

Toto reared back, shaking his three heads, about as affected if a bee had stung his paw.

Well, apparently the fire element didn't hurt it. Good to know.

Then Toto powered off the ground, launching into the air. There was only a second, if that, before he came crashing down on me. I hit the ground, inwardly cringing because I was sure I was atop a grave, and rolled, shoving the pointed end of the sickle up.

I hit the gut, missing the heart by a mile.

"Dammit." Pulling the blade free, I scrambled back. Toto's claws dug into the earth between my spread legs, twisting around so fast it left my head spinning. I jerked back, but the hellhound was huge. Rotten breath blew my hair back. Acid drool dripped, splattering off my shoulder. Clothing burned, and red-hot pain seared my skin. Panic was an icy wind in my veins.

Aiden's hoarse shout of my name was warning enough.

Screw this.

Tapping into the cord, I felt it come alive, sparking into a low, steady hum that rushed through me. Marks of the Apollyon bled through my skin, churning into glyphs. Something flared in the hellhound's eyes, as if it could see the marks and understood them for what they were.

Toto snarled. All three heads snapped down on me with the precision and deadliness of a king cobra. Thrusting my hand up, dug my fingers into the matted, coarse hair. Supreme power rushed down my arm. Blue light crackled.

Without any warning, Toto's heads whipped back in a yelp. The big body tensed, and then shuddered. It flopped to the side, legs twitching. The sharp end of the sickle jutted out from its chest, coated in slick darkness. A moment later, Toto was nothing more than a pile of shimmery, blue dust.

Stunned, I looked up as akasha settled back into the cord, unused.

Aiden stood above me, legs spread wide and shoulders back, dark hair falling in messy disarray, eyes the color of steel and just as hard. Power—natural, trained power that came from years of dedication—radiated from him. He was a tall, looming force to be reckoned with, and here I was, the Apollyon, laid flat out on my rear while he stood.

He was a warrior, and I was awed.

Aiden extended his arm. "Are you okay?"

"Yes," I croaked, placing my hand in his. He carefully hauled me to my feet. "Thank you."

"Don't—"

Clasping the sides of his face, I kissed him. Long. Deep. Hard. When I pulled back, his eyes were pools of silver. "Just say you're welcome. It isn't hard. Say it."

For the longest moment, Aiden said nothing and then, "You're welcome."

My lips split into a wide smile. "That wasn't hard, was it?"

Aiden's gaze drifted over my face and then lower. He sucked in a sharp breath. "You're hurt."

"It's nothing." I dodged the hand that reached for my shoulder. The burn had already dulled. "I'm fine. It's just doggy slobber. Don't come too close; I smell like wet hellhound. I'm really—"

"Lexie."

The name—the sound of the voice—wasn't Aiden's, but I recognized it in my heart and soul. It couldn't be, but it was. My breath stalled in my lungs. My legs felt suddenly weak as I turned from a shell-shocked Aiden. My heart—*my heart* already knew the source of that wonderful, soft, and beautiful voice.

I stumbled back a step, suddenly swamped in emotion that tightened my chest and stole my breath. Confusion followed as I shook my head in a daze. Tears sprung to my eyes. My chest cracked wide open, because this couldn't be real.

"Mom?"

20

She didn't look like I remembered.

When I'd seen her last—when I'd killed her—she had been a daimon, with black holes where her eyes should've been and a mouth full of razor-sharp teeth, set in skin so pale and translucent that inky veins had shown through.

That image had tarnished my memory of her. Something I'd been too ashamed to really delve into. The fact I couldn't recall how beautiful she'd been horrified me, but she . . .

She was beautiful now.

Dark brown hair fell past her shoulders, framing her oval face. Her skin was slightly darker than mine, more olive in nature. She looked like me, but better—more refined and beautiful—and her eyes were a bright, emerald-gem color. Even in the darkness, I could see them, was drawn to the warmth in them.

I staggered a step forward, pulling free of Aiden's grasp. "Mom?"

"Baby," she said, and a little of my world shattered in response to her voice. "You shouldn't be here. You can't be here."

I didn't care about "here" or whatever. All that mattered was that it was my mom, and I *needed* her—needed to feel one of her hugs, because they made everything so much better and I'd been needing one for so, so long.

I stumbled up the incline, dropping the sickle in the prickly weeds. "Mom. *Mommy* . . ."

"Alex," Aiden called out, his voice pained, and I couldn't understand why.

He should've been happy for me. To get to see my mom again was something I'd secretly hoped would occur while we were in the Underworld, so to see her so soon, before we'd even made it through the gates, was so . . .

Then I remembered Apollo's warning. There would be spirits, but my mom? I drew up short, standing a few feet from her. That . . . that was too cruel, even for the gods.

She cocked her head to the side, a small and very sad smile forming on her lips. "You shouldn't be here. Turn away before it's too late."

I blinked, unable to move. Was it really her? Or was it some kind of ploy? Heart racing, I opened my suddenly dry mouth, but then her form flickered, much like Caleb's had in the cell. She was a shade—so there'd be no hugs—but was it her?

Aiden came up the hill behind me, stopping short of standing by my side. "Alex, it's . . ."

"Don't say it." I shook my head, because I couldn't deal with this right now. I tried and was failing to see this objectively. "*Please* don't."

My mom's form flickered again. "You must turn away. Leave this place before it's too late. You can't go there. You'll never come back."

My throat worked to let a sob loose. Lowering my chin, I squeezed my eyes shut. It was her, but it . . . it wasn't. *Déjà vu*, I thought bitterly. I could almost see it—Mom and me standing there, me holding the gun pointed directly at her, my arm trembling, unable to do what needed to be done.

And we could've died right then or over the course of the time in Gatlinburg. Caleb could've died then, instead of months later, within the false safety of the Covenant. I had failed then and was on the verge of failing again. And this time, would it be Aiden who died because of my inability to see past what was the truth?

This wasn't my mom. This was just an *it*—a ward to keep us

from reaching the gates. Chest constricting, I lifted my damp lashes.

"You're not my mom," I said, voice hoarse.

Her delicate brows furrowed and she shook her head a little. "Baby, don't do this. Whatever reason why you think you have to do this, you don't. Turn away, before you lose everything."

It sort of felt like I'd already lost everything.

Aiden placed his hand on my back and I drew strength from the simple gesture. I sucked in a deep breath and let it out slowly. "This isn't going to work. You're not my mom. So . . . I don't know. Go do whatever you're supposed to do."

An exasperated sigh, so much like my mom, came from her. For a moment, I doubted myself. Maybe this was her and I was making a terrible ass out of myself. But then she changed.

Face fish-pale, veins slithered under her papery skin like baby snakes. Her eyes were sunken, black pits, and when her mouth opened, razor-sharp teeth filled them. "Is this better?" she asked in that sweet voice of hers.

"Gods," I whispered, horrified. "That's so wrong."

Her lips formed a twisted smile. "You're going to have to go through me, and baby, we know you don't have it in you to do it again."

My stomach sank with understanding. "Crap . . ."

Aiden moved to stand in front of me. I saw him raise the dagger and I knew that he was going to do this—take care of this for me. As much as I appreciated that and really wanted him to do it, I couldn't.

I placed my hand on his arm, stilling him. "I . . . I have this."

My mother's cold laugh was like a shockwave.

"Are you sure?" Aiden asked.

The grim set to his jaw told me he didn't want to listen, but when I nodded, he stepped back and handed me the sickle blade I had dropped. I felt cold as my fingers wrapped around the handle. I hated the fine tremble in my arm and the heavy weight of the weapon.

Most of all, I hated what I had to do.

Mom watched me curiously. "Aw, baby, you really want to do this?" She took a step straight *through* the rubble, stopping in front of me. She laughed again. "Kill your mother twice? Wait. It's actually three times."

"Shut up," Aiden growled.

But this thing—whatever it was—was on a roll. "She died—at least in all ways that mattered—in Miami. And that was to keep you safe. So, that was also your fault. Three's a charm, eh? And you think you can do it? So what? Doesn't mean anything. You haven't seen anything yet."

The back of my throat burned as I took a wobbly step forward, lifting my arm.

"You bring nothing but death to those around you," she continued. "You should've never been born, because you will kill the ones you love, one way or another."

Those words dug in deep, shattering in the depths of my heart. Without saying a word, because I knew it wouldn't matter, I brought the blade down.

It swept clean through her. There was a dull flash of light, and then her form faded away as if she was nothing more than smoke and mirrors. Within seconds, it was like she'd never been there, and only the cruel, punishing words lingered.

"Well," I said a bit unsteadily. "Can't get any worse than that."

And it did . . . within a heartbeat.

Two forms appeared beyond the broken foundation, quickly taking shape. Having no idea what or who the gate was going to throw at us now, I stood by Aiden and waited as the ghostly shadows became two people.

Aiden sucked in a breath and went ramrod straight. I didn't realize the significance at first. The two shades were strangers to me, a male and a female. Both were tall and elegant-looking, carrying the air of pure-bloods. The woman had springy, curly hair the color of spun corn silk, and the man was dark-haired, with shockingly familiar silver . . .

I *had* seen them before . . . in a photo frame back in the room in Aiden's home—his parents' home.

The man and woman were his father and mother.

"Oh, gods," I whispered, lowering the sickle blade.

Seeing Aiden's parents—the appearance of our deceased loved ones—suddenly made sense. It wasn't a physical fight that guarded the gates, not like with the guards and hellhound. This was on an emotional and mental stage—a different tactic to get us to turn away, because if we didn't, we had to face the unthinkable.

Aiden said nothing as he stared at them. I'd never seen him so still—not even after the first time he'd seen me cleaned up, after I'd punched him in the face, and then kissed him. Or even when the furies attacked the Council, or after he realized I'd killed a pure-blood. Not even when he stood above my bed, waiting for me to wake up after Linard had stabbed me.

I'd never seen Aiden like this—his face utterly devoid of emotion, but his eyes churning in gray and silver. Tension radiated from every locked limb. After witnessing what I had just gone through, he knew this wasn't going to be good.

And I wanted to stop it before it even got started—spare him the pain of brutal, hurtful words that would lance open old wounds. But when I stepped forward, he snapped alive.

"Don't," he said, his voice thick. "I want to hear this."

I stared at him like he was crazy.

"Of course he does," Aiden's father said. "My son is no coward. Foolish, but no coward."

I jerked toward the sound of his voice. I couldn't get over how much he sounded like Aiden.

His mother's smile seemed warm enough. "My son, you do

not want to do this. The answers you seek do not exist where you wish to tread."

"I have to," Aiden replied stonily.

The father tipped his chin up. "No. What you have to do—the right thing to do—is turn around and leave this place." When Aiden didn't respond, his father drifted closer and his voice was stern, relentless. "You must do the right thing, Aiden. We raised you to always do the right thing."

Aiden nodded stiffly. "You have, and that is why I have to do this."

The man's eyes narrowed, and I knew I was about to witness some epic family drama. "The right thing would've been to take your place among the Council, as you were raised to do."

Oh no . . .

A muscle popped in Aiden's jaw.

"Do you think you can accomplish anything as a Sentinel?" his father asked, and I wondered if he'd been this way in real life. Cold. Disciplined. Was that where Aiden's near-rigid control came from? But Aiden had never let on that was the case.

His father wasn't done. "You're wasting your life, and for what? A sense of revenge? Justice? You shirk your duties while our family's seat remains empty?"

"You don't understand," Aiden said. "And . . . none of that matters right now."

The change that came over his mother was nothing short of dramatic. Gone was the warmth and elegance. "You shame us, Aiden. You *shame* us."

I blinked. "Wait a second—"

"You have no control." Disgust dripped from his father's voice. "We taught you to never take advantage of those who are under your charge. Look at what you have done."

The mother clucked her tongue. "You risk her, knowing she could be harmed because of your lack of control. How could you be so reckless? How could you do this to someone you claim to love?"

My mouth dropped open. "Oh, now that's not—"

"You can't protect her." His father gestured toward me. "You couldn't protect us. You're a failure. You just don't see it yet, but you will just keep on plowing forward until you can't go any more."

His mother nodded. "I'm surprised that Deacon has made it this far. But then again, look at my baby boy—a drunk and an addict, all before eighteen. I'm so proud."

I whipped toward Aiden and pleaded, "You don't need to listen to this! You can stop this."

She smiled coldly, continuing as if I hadn't even spoken. "And her—look at what you did to her. Placed her on the Elixir, stripped her of her will. You're less than a man."

"You *bitch*," I spat, readying to throw my blade at her, ninja-style.

"Go now," his father said. "Leave this place. Or her blood will be on your hands."

Never in my life did I want to exorcise some ghosts more than I did right then. Anger hummed like venom through me. "Aiden, don't listen to them. They aren't real. What they're saying is bull. You—"

"What they are saying is real." Aiden swallowed hard, sparing me a brief glance. "But it's not them saying it."

I didn't get it at first, because I so doubted his parents were such big douchebags in life, but then it sank in.

"What my mom had said . . . it's us." I turned to him slowly. "What they are saying? It's what you really think?"

When Aiden said nothing, I think I was more horrified by that than anything else that'd happened so far. He thought those terrible, horrific things about himself? And how long had he been carrying that with him? Years?

"And your brother?" his father said, shaking his head as concern pinched his face.

I was going to gut both of his parents.

"He is unprotected right now," added the mother. "You should be there, not here, chasing a fool's errand. He will die, too, like us, and it will be your—"

"Enough!" Aiden roared, shooting forward.

I hadn't even seen or felt him take the sickle blade from my fingers, but he had. The blade arced through the dark sky.

"You'll be sorry," his mother said, a second before the blade sliced through both his parents.

Like my mother, they broke apart into thin, wispy strands of color and smoke and then vanished, scattered into the air around them. And like with my mother, their words lingered.

Aiden stood with his back to me. Wordlessly, he hit the release on the sickle blade and with a soft, sucking noise it disappeared into the tube of the handle. There was no danger now. Three wards had come to pass—guards, hellhounds, and spirits.

But I couldn't control my pounding heart. "Aiden . . .?"

His shoulders tensed and he turned his head to the side. His profile was grim, the line of his jaw hard. "I have thought those things for a long time. Becoming a Sentinel was the right thing for me, what I wanted and needed, but was it really the right thing?"

I didn't know how to answer that. "But you're not shirking your duties or whatever. You are still doing something so important, Aiden. And one day, if you wanted to take your seat . . . you could." The words hurt to say more than they should've, and for a purely selfish reason. If Aiden took his seat, there'd be no chance of us ever being together. No future with the house, the dog, and the cat.

But I wouldn't stop Aiden if he felt he needed to take his seat. And his parents or inner voice could be right in some sense. With a seat on the Council, he could do more in regards to changing things, but . . .

Hell, nothing mattered if Seth was successful.

"I could," he said almost to himself, and I winced. "My brother—"

"Isn't an addict." I paused. "Okay. He was a bit of a drunk and stoner, but he's not an addict. Seth's an addict. A daimon is an addict. Deacon is at the cabin making marinated steaks."

That brought a faint half-smile to his face. "He's safe."

"Yes."

He faced me and exhaled roughly. "I really don't think I'll get you killed."

"That's a relief to hear."

Aiden closed his eyes briefly. When they reopened, they were a soft gray. "I have to say, it was kind of nice to shut those damn voices up, if just for once."

Stepping forward, I placed my hand on his arm and squeezed. "Are you okay?"

"I am." He bent his head, placing his lips on my forehead. "Let me grab the bag and then we'll enter the church together. Okay?"

I nodded, waiting outside the foundation. Aiden returned with the bag and knelt. Reaching in, he pulled out a dark, shapeless material and offered it to me. Another followed as I took mine.

"A cloak?" I slipped it over my head. "Where you'd get two of these?"

Aiden stood, throwing the backpack onto his back. "You'd be surprised by what Solos' father has stashed away in his cabins. I actually picked these up when we were in Athens. Figured we might need them."

"You're so smart and organized."

Laughing, he pulled his on and then reached over, grasping the edges of my hood. He tugged it up. "We have to hide that pretty face of yours."

I flushed. "Same for you."

"I have a pretty face?" Aiden pulled up his own hood, which cast his face in shadows. "I'd like to go with handsome instead of pretty."

"Handsome" wasn't a strong enough word, but I nodded. He extended his hand, and I took it, comforted by the steady, warm grasp.

"Are you ready?" he asked.

"Yeah."

Together, we moved down the line of the fallen stones and found the opening. Together, we stepped through where a door had once stood. There were no more warnings or wards. We moved through the patches of crumbling cement and overgrown weeds.

We waited.

After about ten seconds, a fissure of energy coursed down my spine. Aiden felt it too, for his hand tightened around mine. Anxious energy built in my stomach, forming tight balls of dread and even a little bit of excitement.

Hopefully, my visit to the Underworld would be different this time.

Toward the back of the foundation, the air rippled, reminding me of heat rolling off of hot pavement in the summer. The veil that separated the truth from the mortal world simply slipped away.

"Do you see it?" I asked.

Aiden squeezed my hand. "Yes."

The wrought-iron gate encased in titanium was huge, latching into something neither of us could see. Instead of bars, there were two-pronged spears decorated with images of black bulls and ewes. Where the two gates joined, a replica of the invisible helmet was engraved into the iron. The musty scent grew stronger.

With his free hand, Aiden pushed the gate open. It swung backward, making no sound, revealing nothing but darkness—not the kind associated with night, but a black void. A portal. And together, hand in hand, we stepped through the gates to the Underworld.

21

I almost expected that, when we stepped into the void, we'd fall flat on our faces. But the ground remained under our feet as we continued into the darkness, which eventually gave way to fog as thick as soup.

Glancing over my shoulder, I sought to find the gate before the fog swallowed us whole, but it was gone and the fog was even heavier. I gripped Aiden's hand as tendrils seeped between us, wrapping a different kind of cloak around us. I couldn't even see Aiden . . . or two feet in front of me. A pang of panic unfurled in my chest.

"I'm right here." Aiden's deep voice parted the veil and he squeezed my hand. "Just keep hold."

I briefly considered using the air element to dispel some of the fog, but if the fog was supposed to be here, that could be potentially bad news if it suddenly up and disappeared.

The further we moved into the fog, the more unnerving it became to be so blind. And then there was a sound other than my own pounding heart—a shuffling type of sound, like feet and cloth dragging all around us, and a low hum, like a soft, never-ending gasp of a moan, and I didn't even want to know what it was. Following the path of Aiden's arm, I stepped closer to him, so close that I was surprised I didn't trip him up.

After several minutes of nothing but blindly walking through fog and that terrible dragging and moaning sound, the fog started to break apart until the path was revealed before us.

I sucked in a breath, unable to stop from clutching his arm.

What little part of the Underworld I'd seen before hadn't prepared me.

The fog gave way to a sky that was the color of the fading sun, a cross between red and orange. But from what I could tell, there was no sun. And all around us were people, moving about aimlessly. Dressed in bland, tattered clothing, they shuffled to and fro. Many stayed silent; some moaned quietly, while others muttered under their breath from behind their own cloaks, but all had their gazes trained on the ground. They were young and old, from the smallest child to the most aged crone.

This . . . this holding place continued as far as the eye could see, to the cusp of the hills Apollo had spoken of. I didn't understand what this place really was. It wasn't limbo—that much I knew—as I had been there before.

None of the souls looked up as we navigated around them. There were no guards on horses, like I'd seen in limbo. It appeared as if these people had been placed here, left alone to their own devices and boredom.

"Why?" I asked in a hushed voice.

Aiden knew what I was asking. "The majority of the dead reside here." He led me around a group of three huddled together on the dirt. "Those who have been buried, but haven't gone on to face their judgment. Some of them may have done something in their lives to make them fear their judgment. Others are . . ."

A woman moved in front of us, her gaze glued to the ground as she wrung her hands. She muttered under her breath, "Where's my baby?" over and over again.

"Some are confused," I answered. "They don't know they're dead."

Aiden nodded solemnly.

And then the sad woman simply vanished, as if she had walked through an invisible portal—there one moment and gone the next.

I halted. "What the . . .?"

"I'll explain, but we must keep moving." Aiden tugged me forward. "Legend says that some of these souls leave limbo and have turned shade. They go back to the mortal world, and then return here again. I don't think they can even control it."

I swallowed. "They're ghosts."

"Thought you didn't believe in ghosts." Humor laced his tone.

Now was a pretty good time to change my mind. As I peered out from beneath my hood, there was something ghastly to some of the souls. Many of them looked solid and from how they'd brushed against me, I knew they had mass, but others had that wonky fuzziness to them. And the more I paid attention, the more others simply vanished.

This place was creepy, like walking through a maze of the hopeless and forgotten. And we hadn't even reached the Vale of Mourning yet. Yee haw, this was going to be fun.

A sudden damp coldness clung to the air around us. I lifted my head, eyeing the burnt orange sky. One drop of water fell, splashing off my cheek. Then the sky opened up, drenching us in cold rain within seconds.

I sighed. "Really, it has to rain?"

"At least it's not acid."

That was Aiden, always looking on the bright side of things.

Tugging my hood down closer, I trudged forward. The souls paid no heed to the heavy rainfall. Perhaps they'd grown used to it. I wanted to stop and yell at them to go to judgment, because whatever waited for them couldn't be worse than this.

Especially for the little ones who were all alone—there was nothing they could have done to earn them eternity in Tartarus.

One small boy sat alone in a large puddle the rain had already created. The child couldn't have been more than four or five. He moved his chubby fingers in the mud, drawing a circle and then wiggly lines all around it.

The sun—he was drawing the sun.

I started toward him, not sure what I'd do, but I had to do something—maybe convince him to go to judgment. Gods knew how long he'd been here. His family could already be in Elysian Fields.

"No," Aiden said softly.

"But—"

"Remember what Apollo said. We cannot intervene."

I stared at the little boy, fighting the urge to break free. "It's wrong."

Aiden's grip on my hand tightened. "I know, but there's nothing we can do."

My heart ached as I watched the little boy carve a moon beside the sun, heedless of the rain or the other souls practically trampling him. I wanted to be angry and I was—even at Aiden, because he was right. There was nothing we could do. And there would be more like this little boy—more forgotten souls.

Fighting back the sting of tears, I pulled my hand free from Aiden's but didn't run off. I fell in step beside him as we passed beyond the poor child, navigating the endless field of souls that had been either left behind or cast aside.

It took hours to pass through the Asphodel Fields. By the time we left the ankle-deep mud and our boots touched scattered patches of grass, we were drenched and cold, our cloaks weighted down and heavy. Rain had somehow snuck into my boot and, with each step, my foot sloshed back and forth. Exhaustion dogged me, and probably Aiden too, but neither of us complained. Traveling through the field of all those souls had served as a reminder that things could always be worse.

The rain had let up a little, turning to a constant, steady drizzle. The sky was now a darker orange, signaling that night was close at hand. Ahead, the rolling green hills led up to a thick, nearly impenetrable slate wall. It was going to be a steep climb.

"Do you want to take a breather?" Aiden asked from behind his cloak as he surveyed the hills. "It looks relatively safe. We could take a—"

"No. I'm fine." I stepped around him, slowly climbing the first hill, ignoring the dull ache taking up residency in my temples. "Besides, the faster we can get into the tunnels, the sooner we can rest, right? We'll be safe there at night."

"Yes." Aiden was beside me in a second. His hand came out from the cloak and slipped inside my hood. His palm was warm against my cheek. The gesture was brief, and gone all too quickly.

We traveled on in silence, but worry nagged at me. The headache wasn't severe, nothing like what I'd experienced before Seth had paid a call, but I had no idea how long it would take for it to progress. The only hope was that we reached somewhere safe—preferably dry—where we could bunk down for the night. Sleep was what I needed, and the sooner the better.

The odd sky darkened with each hill we crested, forcing us to pick up our pace. We crossed a field of narcissus that rose to our knees, petals a luminous white and carrying an incredibly sweet scent. The slate wall drew closer as the flowers gave way to trees.

At least that's what I thought they were.

They rose into the sky, their branches bare for the most part, like slender fingers reaching for the ever-increasing darkness. Around the lower branches, ruby-red fruit hung in the air. Pomegranates.

Curious as to how they tasted, I reached for one.

Aiden's hand snatched mine in a near painful grasp. I let out a startled gasp.

"No," he said harshly. From behind the cloak, his eyes shone a bright silver. "Do you know nothing of Persephone?"

I glared at him. "Uh, she's the Queen of the Underworld. I'm not stupid."

"I didn't say you were stupid." His grip loosened as he led me through the trees, toward the last mound. "Though, I'm really starting to think you should've spent less time in class sleeping or doing whatever you were doing."

"Ha. Ha."

"Persephone ate from the pomegranate trees here. If you eat anything from this world, you can never leave."

All my smart-ass responses faded away. Boy, did I feel like an idiot for not recalling that. "Okay. Maybe I should've paid attention in class."

He chuckled.

But all humor left him when he got a good look at the hill. "Gods . . ."

It was steep, covered with grassy patches, exposed roots, trees with enormous black, teardrop-shaped fruit hanging from their branches, and what I seriously hoped were fragments of pale rock—not bones, like they appeared. At the very top, a ledge butted up to the thick gray wall.

Sighing, I sidled past Aiden. "We better get going."

We climbed the hill, using the roots to gain purchase and to keep climbing. I don't know how Aiden did it, carrying the heavy pack on his back, but he moved a hell of a lot quicker than me.

Halfway to the top, a twittering sound rose above the canopy of odd fruit. I stopped, lifting my head. The heavy hood slipped back as I stared through the drizzle, beyond the trees, to the now dark-blue sky.

Night had fallen, and I recalled Apollo's warning.

"Come on," Aiden called. "We need to hurry."

Grabbing a root, I hauled myself up. "That noise—do you hear it?"

Aiden said nothing, just kept on climbing.

The branches above us began to shudder, rocking the giant fruit. The twittering grew louder. "I . . . I think . . . it's coming from the fruit."

Above me, a black teardrop the size of a beanbag chair

shook—and then it spread open, one . . . one long, black and hairy *leg* at a time. The center of the mass twitched—and then a row of ruby-red eyes peered down at me.

"Oh, my gods . . . they're not fruit." And I *so* got why the souls didn't travel near the tunnels now.

The giant spider dropped from the tree, hitting the ground on six of its eight legs. Its squeal turned my blood to ice. Another smacked onto the grass . . . and then another and another. Their sick chorus drowned out the sound of everything else.

Aiden slid down the hill, kicking up loose pebbles and bones as he came to my side. He grabbed my hand as one dropped beside us, fangs gleaming, raised two of its legs and made a fingers-on-a-chalkboard screech.

Shrieking, I jumped back, knocking into Aiden as the huge spider scuttled over the ground. Aiden shoved me to the side and whipped out a dagger. Jerking up, he slammed the blade up to the hilt into the center of the spider.

I rolled to my knees and scrambled up, catching the sight of thousands of black legs scurrying across the ground.

Weight slammed into my back, pushing me face-first into the loose dirt and wet grass. Sharp pain sliced across my lip and I tasted blood in my mouth, but that was a non-issue when I felt the heavy, hairy weight of the spider on my back.

Its legs dug through the cloak as it hissed in my ear. Summoning the power that rested inside me, I felt . . . felt nothing.

Crap.

Digging my knees in, I powered off the ground and threw the spider. It landed on its back a few feet away, legs thrashing in the air as it hissed.

"Gods, I hate—I *hate* spiders."

Aiden leaned down, hooking his hand around my arm. He hauled me to my feet and pushed forward. "This would be a good time to use akasha."

Hundreds of beady red eyes stared at us. "I can't. I don't think it works down here."

With his hands on my back he pushed me up the hill, swearing under his breath. "I can still feel the fire element. Can you?"

Lifting my muddy hand, I was surprised and relieved to find a tiny spark. "Yes."

"Good. At the count of three, we'll clear a path to the rocks ahead—" He cut off, swiping the sickle blade at a spider that ventured too close. Legs flew in every direction. "See the break in the rock there?"

I saw it. I also saw about a hundred spiders between us and the slim crack. "Uh-uh."

"On the count of three, light it up and run. Do not stop. Okay?"

"Yeah."

"One . . . two . . . *three*!"

Concentrating on the fire element, I extended my hand, as did Aiden. Balls of violet-colored flame hit the ground on both sides, spreading rapidly as they formed a wall.

"Go!" Aiden ordered, pushing me upward.

I scrambled over the ground, not surprised when I saw some of the hairy bastards leaping over the fire. Others rammed straight into it, but they fell to the side, hissing in pain. Aiden grabbed hold of my arm as we climbed the last of the rain-slick hill. Behind us, the spiders overtook the flames. The sound of their legs scuttling across the ground would haunt me right into group therapy. Reaching the top of the ledge, my fingers smacked off rock and I almost cried out in joy.

One of the quicker monsters lurched from below, latching on to my leg. My grip slipped and my heart leapt into my throat as the weight of the spider and the heavy cloak dragged me right back over the edge.

I let out a hoarse shout as my fingers continued to slip, but then Aiden was suddenly there, threading his arms under mine.

He threw himself back, powerful muscles tensing and popping under the cloak as he pulled me over the ledge, spider and all. Pulling my free leg up, I twisted and rolled, slamming the heel of my boot into one of the spider's eyes. Letting out a hiss, the spider slipped off my leg and tumbled down the hill, taking out a few of its friends with it.

Staggering to our feet, we slipped through the narrow crevice just as the mass of spiders breached the ledge and hit the wall.

22

We traveled for what felt like hours through a cramped tunnel so dark that even my eyes were having a hard time adjusting to it. Aiden sent out a tiny ball of flame every few minutes, but neither of us wanted to risk the light for long—who knew what might be down here? Those spiders couldn't fit into the narrow crack, but, knowing our luck, they probably had babies that would be more than eager to find us in the labyrinth of tunnel work.

Exhausted and soaked to the bone, we stopped as the tunnel widened into what appeared to be an entrance to a cavern. Aiden inched toward it, peering into the blackness. He held up a hand as I moved forward to check it out.

"Let me see what we got first, okay?" he asked.

I checked my urge to push him aside and help out. "Be my guest. If there's an Underworld bear inside, let him gnaw on you first."

Shooting me a wry grin, he shook his head and crept forward, dagger in hand. The tiny ball of flame he sent out was swallowed by the dark. Staying outside the cavern literally took all my self-control.

I leaned against the unseen but probably slimy rock, numb in my soaked clothing. I wasn't even sure I still had all my fingers. It was a good thing that Aiden loved me and could look past my appearance. I didn't doubt I looked like last week's prom queen after a hellish night.

Aiden returned, his daggers sheathed for now. "All clear. We should be good for the night."

Pushing off the rock, I followed him inside. It was a narrow fit for a few steps, and then it opened into a circular chamber—definitely drier inside, so that was a plus. Rain pelted the rock bed from a few relatively small holes in one part of the ceiling, but the rest was dry and suitable.

There was also something else inside . . .

Toward the left of the chamber was some kind of natural spring. Well, down here, I wasn't sure what it was. For all we knew, it could be a vat of acid, but it smelled like . . .

"Jasmine," I said.

"I know." Aiden appeared at my side. He eased the hood back on my cloak and gently smoothed his thumb under my lip that no longer throbbed. "Strange, huh?"

"Everything is strange down here." Moving closer to the pool of scented water, I held my hand out. Warmth tickled my palm. "It's heated, but doesn't seem too hot."

Aiden had removed his hood. "I doubt we'd get lucky enough for a bath—Alex, don't!"

Too late. I'd already knelt down and gingerly placed a finger into the water, figuring I could spare one. Water fizzled.

Air stirred around me as Aiden shot forward, grasping my shoulders.

"It's okay." I told him. Other than the sudden frothy bubbling, the water actually felt pleasant. It was so clear I could see the floor of the rock pool.

"Gods, Alex, you don't just stick your finger into things."

I arched a brow.

He rolled his eyes. "Your mind scares me."

I grinned. "You like how my mind works."

Instant heat darkened his eyes to silver. "Most of the time, yes." He relaxed, letting go of my shoulders. "I'm not sure if we should start a fire."

Straightening, I glared at my itchy, wet clothing. Damn.

His lips twitched. "It may draw unwanted attention."

"Spiders," I whispered.

Aiden nodded.

I shuddered.

"You're so fierce." He came to stand before me, cocking his head to the side as he placed the tips of his fingers on my chin. "And so brave, but spiders send you into a fit."

"Those spiders were twice the size of Rottweilers, Aiden. They were not normal spiders."

"Still, spiders," he murmured, lowering his head. His lips brushed mine. The gentle sweep was all too quick, but powerful. "But if you take off your clothes, I'm sure I can get them dry."

My eyes went wide. "Wow. Are you trying to get me naked?"

His silvery gaze met mine. "Do you really need me to answer that?"

A hot, sweet flush stole across my cheeks. When he was like this—open, flirty, and downright sexy—I was at my lamest. I wasn't used to this side of him. I didn't think I ever would be, and there was something thrilling in that. But I stared at him, caught between the images playing out in my head and the very real *man* standing before me.

Aiden chuckled. "You should see yourself right now."

Snapping out of it, I hoped my expression now looked like Alex the Sex Goddess and not Alex the Spaz. "What do I look like?"

His grin was small and secretive. "Cute."

"Cute?"

"Mmm hmm." He prowled toward the edges of the cavern, searching the shadows for gods knew what. "But seriously, if you get out of those clothes, I can dry them."

But I'd be totally naked. There was no need for me to be shy around him, but something about that, here . . .

He took off the cloak and shrugged off the backpack. As if he read my mind, he raised his brow. "I packed two blankets. They're not much, but they're big enough to cover you."

My lips spread into a smile. Yep, Aiden thought of everything. "You're awesome."

The look he cast over his shoulder said he knew. "I know the clothes are bothering you."

"Are not." The last thing I wanted was to be whiny and weak in front of Aiden.

His gaze dropped. "They're not?"

"Yeah . . ." My gaze followed his to where I was scratching at my hip. I stilled. "Okay. They are bothering me."

"Delicate skin?" He stalked over, then knelt and unzipped the bag.

I stared at his wet, dark curls as he rummaged through the bag. "Yep, I have sensitive skin. Did you pack any lotion?"

"No," he laughed. "But we have some trail mix."

"Yum."

"Also some mixed nuts . . ."

"Double yum."

"And some water." He tipped his chin up, eyes dancing. "Sorry. I couldn't pack a McDonald's for you."

"Well, no one's perfect."

Aiden laughed again. Gods, I loved that deep, husky sound, and I'd never grow tired of hearing it. Not too long ago, Aiden hadn't laughed enough. So every time he did, I cherished it like a most prized possession.

He placed the blanket on a dry spot and then stood. "I'll go check the entrance just to make sure we're okay for the night."

I nodded, and he turned without a word, disappearing back into the crack in the wall.

Feeling oddly giddy, considering where I was, I turned to the pool. Just thinking about slipping into the warm water had my chilled, dirty skin begging.

But Aiden so wouldn't approve.

Tugging off the cloak, I kicked off my boots, eyeing the water like it was a slab of filet. If the water was dangerous, it surely would've peeled the skin off my finger by now or have me running around, squawking like a chicken. Mind made up, I quickly stripped down and slipped my toes into the water. I sighed as the pool frothed and bubbled, and carefully made my way down the natural steps. Water lapped and fizzled at my hips as I moved further out. Warmth, heady and pleasant, seeped through my skin, into my muscles. It didn't sting the numerous bruises or cuts—if anything, the water seemed to soothe them. The soft, seductive scent appeared to soothe the dull ache in my temples, too.

In the middle of the spring, the water reached just below my chest, but my presence stirred the water and the white-tipped foam reached my collarbone, bubbling around the talisman.

Closing my eyes, I let out a low breath. The water felt too good. I could stay in here all night, feeling the little bubbles teasing my toes, sliding up my legs.

It was heaven in the Underworld.

I smiled, thinking Hades had the good stuff when it came to spas and relaxation.

"Alex . . ."

Aiden's voice pulled me out of my musings. I glanced over my shoulder, smiling sheepishly. "I couldn't resist. Sorry."

He didn't look angry. Surprisingly, he didn't look exasperated either. I couldn't say he looked thrilled either, but . . .

Oh . . .

Aiden looked hungry.

My breath hitched in my throat, and it took me a few tries to find my voice. "Is everything clear outside the cave?"

Eyes hooded, he nodded.

I bit my lip. Of course it was fine. We were safe for the night, but resting wasn't on my mind. What *was* was wholly inappropriate and I seriously had my priorities mixed up, but we were facing the unknown. This trip was dangerous and both of us could be hurt. Worse yet, Aiden could die.

Raw panic punched through my chest at the thought of losing him. I simply could not bear his loss. And because of that, I wanted to press pause. I wanted to live, to really live in the moment, and with Aiden, that was always possible. It was magical, actually.

I took a deep, long breath. "You . . . you should join me."

Part of me expected that I would have to do a decent amount of begging. Aiden was "on the job," and I was prepared to deploy every technique I knew, including whining.

So when he stepped back and slid off his boots, I was pretty damn surprised. Shock splashed over me as he quietly tugged his shirt out of the waistband of his tactical pants and pulled the wet cloth over his head.

I bit back a gasp.

His stomach was some serious perfection, a product of years of rigorous training. It looked like someone had placed paint rollers under his taut skin. And his chest . . .

Yeah, I couldn't stop staring.

And the whole time he watched me with an intense gaze like heated silver. I felt the flush return to my cheeks as my breath quickened.

When his hands moved to the top of his pants, I did turn away. Only because I was sure I'd pass out and drown if I kept staring, and well, that would so kill the moment.

Clothing hit the rock bed and there was a second, too long, of silence, and then the water stirred in the pool, bubbling even more. Pulse pounding everywhere, I twisted toward him and lost my breath and my heart all over again.

Aiden stood there like a god.

So much taller than me, water grazed his navel. White foam lapped at the ribbed planes of his stomach, and I was struck by the image of Poseidon rising from the ocean.

Poseidon had nothing on him.

He glided through the fizzing water, hands out to his sides. I had to tip my head back to meet his gaze. "Hey," I said.

One side of his lips curved up. "This probably isn't a good idea."

"Why?"

"I have a feeling I'm going to be very distracted here in a few seconds." He reached out though, finding the band that kept most of my hair up. "Actually, I'm already distracted."

My heart was trying to come out of my chest. "But we're safe here. Apollo said so."

"We are, but . . ." He gently pulled the band out and then set about rearranging the thick strands around my shoulders. A great deal of it sank below the surface. "But we should be careful. I should be paying attention."

I stepped into the loose circle his arms created as he played with my hair. Placing my hand on his chest, I was thrilled by the way he jerked and sucked in a breath. "Can't you multitask? I can."

Aiden lazily tossed a damp strand over my shoulder and moved to another. "You're such a liar. Your multitasking skills suck."

"Do not. And we're not talking about *my* multitasking skills." My hand slid down, having a mind of its own. "I think you can handle doing two things at once."

He'd gathered all my hair now, twisting it around his fist. "You do?" He placed a finger on my bottom lip, slowly tracing the curve. His lashes lowered even more, and only the thinnest sliver of silvery eyes shone. "You should be resting."

"I will." I took the last step forward. The bubbles fizzled and gave way. Stretching up, I looped an arm around his neck. "But you should rest, too."

Aiden's free hand drifted down my neck, over my shoulder, and then his arm was around my waist, holding me tight against him, our bodies touching length to length. It was maddening, and when his lips brushed over the curve of my jaw, my eyes fluttered shut. Every muscle in my body tensed, and then I felt the marks gliding over my skin.

"We can take shifts," Aiden said against my chin, and then on the other jaw. "You sleep first. Get a couple of hours in and I'll wake you up." He paused, pressing a kiss to the sensitive spot below my ear. I shivered. "Okay?"

I'd have agreed to anything at that point, so I did.

"Then we head out first thing." Aiden lowered the hand wrapped tightly in my hair, arching my back. The chilled air of the cavern spread goosebumps over my exposed skin. I sucked in a breath when I felt his lips return to where my pulse pounded and then lower, over the rise of my collarbone, and still lower.

Then he pulled back, letting go, his chest rising and falling unsteadily as he moved toward the edge of the pool. "And you should be resting right now. This—"

"Stop talking." I pushed through the water, well aware that as I moved closer to him, the cloak of water slowly receded.

Aiden was well aware too. A muscle flexed in his jaw as his gaze dropped. "Did you just tell me to shut up?"

"No." I followed him as he kept backing up, until he had no other place to run to, until his back was against the edge of the rock pool and he was trapped. Placing my hands on either side of him, I looked up. "Okay. I did tell you to shut up, but I did so nicely."

He took a deep, long breath. "I may be able to overlook it."

I floated in, letting my legs tangle with his. "For someone who doesn't talk a lot, you sure do talk a lot when I'd rather you not be talking."

Aiden's laugh sounded choked. "That makes very little sense, Alex."

Grinning, I leaned in and pressed my lips to the strong curve of his jaw, repeating what he had done until my pulse thundered in every part of me. "Making sense is overrated."

"I think you believe a lot of things are overrated." Aiden's head fell back, the thick cords of his muscles in his neck and shoulders tensing as his hands dug into the edge of the pool.

For a moment, I froze in awe of him. It wasn't often that anyone got to see Aiden like this, completely vulnerable to someone else. I touched his cheek, wanting to remember this moment. The enormity of what lay ahead was a cold draft on my skin and deeper, on my soul. There was no telling what my future held—what Aiden's would end up being. So many things were still so uncertain.

Apollo's words intruded. *There can only be one.*

I shuddered, understanding what that meant more than I wanted to. Even Seth had understood it. I thought about the damn dream I'd had on the way here.

There might not be years for Aiden and me—maybe not even months or weeks. There might not even be days. And what time we had left, we'd be spending in constant danger. The next hour wasn't even guaranteed, and I didn't want to spend every moment racing toward the end time.

Aiden's eyes opened. "Alex?"

I blinked back the sudden tears. "I love you." It was all I could say.

His head lifted, eyes searching mine, and maybe he saw what I was thinking. Maybe he too knew that, in the end, there would be more lives lost—ones that would be nearly impossible to overcome and move on from, losses that would steal a part of us. That this moment together, we might never have again.

He was done talking.

Aiden came off the wall so fast the water reacted in a frenzy of bubbling. He—*we*—were in a frenzy. His arms crushed me to him, his mouth demanding, saying those three little words over and over again without speaking them. Aiden lifted me up, one hand burying deep in my hair, the other pressing into my lower back, fitting us together. He turned and my back was against the edge and he was everywhere all at once, stealing my breath, my heart, my soul. There was no coming up for air, no control or limits. There was no tottering on the edge. We both fell headfirst.

In his arms, in the way the water bubbled and moved with our bodies, I may've lost track of time, but I gained a little part of me. I gained a part of *him* that I would hold close for the rest of my days, no matter how long or short that turned out to be.

23

While I'd slept, Aiden had managed to dry our clothes without turning them crispy. If it'd been left to me, I probably would've turned them into torches. I slept for a little over four hours, waking before he told me to. I changed, and then settled back down beside him on one of the two thin blankets. Both of us smelled of jasmine, which was better than the dank smell of the Underworld.

Aiden lay on his side, one heavy arm over my waist. "You could've slept longer."

I idly played with the hand that rested on my stomach. "I'm fine. It's your turn. I'll keep an eye on things, make sure no spiders run off with you."

He pressed his lips to my cheek and let out a little chuckle. "I'm worried if it comes down between me and a spider, I might be screwed."

"I'd face down a horde of spiders for you, baby." I grinned at the sound of his laugh again. "For real."

"That's true love there. Some serious stuff," he teased.

"It is."

There was a pause and then he said, "While you were sleeping, I was thinking about what Apollo said about there being another god involved."

Curiosity piqued, I tipped my head back so I could see his face. "Yeah?"

"I know Seth hasn't let on to who it could be, but Marcus has his bets on Hermes, and since he did help Seth . . ."

"It's always Hermes. He's like the gods' punching bag. The big joke."

"Exactly." Aiden brushed a damp strand of hair off my forehead. "It seems too obvious that it would be him. And even though Hermes has been known to pull some stunts, his actions are usually relatively harmless. This—what has been done to the whole world, Olympus included—is bigger than him, almost like it's personal."

He had a point. "I bet being the butt of Olympus's jokes could make things personal after a few thousand years."

"True, but I don't know . . ." He yawned. "I keep thinking about Seth—about his personality."

"Oh dear . . ."

A tired smile appeared. "Whether you want to admit it or not, you carry some of Apollo's traits. So logically, Seth would carry some from his own lineage."

There were worse things than being compared to Apollo. "Seth is arrogant and smug. That really doesn't narrow down the list." At Aiden's tired nod of agreement, I squeezed his hands. "Go to sleep. We'll figure this out in the morning."

Aiden insisted he wasn't that tired, but it didn't take more than a few moments before his breathing became deep and steady. I stayed in his arms, eyes glued to the entrance. I was still tired, and the headache had kicked back up the moment I'd awakened, spreading from my temples, but it was manageable.

Mulling over what Aiden had said, I had to give the idea there was something personal behind this some cred. But the only problem with that was the fact that all the gods probably had a damn good reason to cause discord. Apollo had even said once before that, after thousands of years of being together, they had nothing better to do than tick each other off.

We needed to figure out who it was behind this, but what could we do? Taking out a god was unheard of. Even the Titans had been entombed, not killed. The loss of any god carried cosmic consequences. The world wouldn't stop spinning, but all the gods would be weakened if one fell. It was probably the only thing that kept them from outright killing one another, but . . .

One massive problem at a time . . .

Seth and Lucian were our biggest problem. Hopefully, we'd find Solaris and she held the answer to stopping him. Part of me hadn't given up on the tiniest sliver of hope that somehow Seth could be saved—that he could be fixed. I sincerely believed that, without Lucian's and the aether's influence, he wouldn't have done the things he had.

But who was I to say that absolved him of his sins? If a drug addict killed someone while under the influence, he was still guilty. Seth had done what he had done and it felt like there was no going back from that.

Sorrow was like slush in my blood, dirty and messy, because it felt misplaced. As if I felt bad for a killer . . .

Pushing thoughts of Seth aside, I stroked the length of Aiden's fingers and wondered if I'd ever hear Aiden play the guitar again. I hoped so. Maybe even get him to sing, because he had a nice voice.

I wasn't sure how much time passed, but it couldn't have been more than an hour. The sky peeking through the holes in the roof of the cavern was still a deep blue and my headache . . . had steadily increased. Now it throbbed behind my eyes.

There was no fooling myself. I knew what it meant. Seth was on the other end of the bond and he was trying to reach me. The venom of panic gave me a sharp bite. Now was so not the time for him to pull this kind of crap. A freaking army of spiders could descend on us while I was with him. Worse yet, we could be discovered by Hades.

Carefully wriggling free of Aiden's embrace, I pushed to my feet and went to the pool, scooping the jasmine-scented water up and splashing it over my face. It had seemed to help before, but I had a feeling I was beyond help now.

I sat down, concentrating on my breathing. I could feel the cord now. It still slumbered, but the hum was louder, more powerful. Placing my head in my hands, I squeezed my eyes shut and waited. Part of me already knew there was no stopping this.

Seth was incredibly strong and hellishly determined when he wanted to be.

So I waited for pain to come, but it never did. Instead, the hum of the cord became louder and stronger, until it felt like my entire body vibrated. Then out of the white noise filling my head, a whisper grew until I could make out the words and recognize the voice.

Nice to see . . . or hear you again, Alex.

Seth.

My eyes snapped open and, unlike last time, I wasn't mentally transported somewhere by Hermes. The spring was still in front of me. I could hear Aiden's deep breaths and feel the slight chill in the air of the cavern.

I know you can hear me, Alex. I can feel it.

I groaned. *I'm really starting to get annoyed with this.*

Through the bond, I could feel his smugness. It was like before, when we'd been connected. His emotions flowed through to me and vice versa. I bet, if I closed my eyes, I could see him as clearly as he stood in front of me, but we weren't connected.

Deep down you love it, he said.

Uh, no. Tucking my damp hair back, I let out a low breath. *I don't understand how you're able to do this. We're not connected.*

After our last little social call, it's easier to tap into the connection. Whenever you're feeling really worn down or emotional, I can reach you. I guess it would be the same if you were in pain. There was a pause, and I swore I felt a flicker of concern. *Are you in pain?*

I rolled my eyes. Good news was that Apollo must've had a little talk with Hermes. *No, but you're a pain in my ass. Does that count?*

Seth's laugh still had that weird, warm feeling. *At least this way you can't hit me.*

Hitting Seth still felt like a viable option. *I don't have time for this right now.*

Curiosity filtered through the connection. *What is it that you're doing right now, Alex?*

What are YOU doing right now, Seth?

There was that laugh again. It was a nice laugh. It didn't have the same effect as Aiden's, but it was rich and deep and it reminded me of Seth.

Pre-killing-rampage Seth, that is.

You tell first.

Yeah, that's not going to happen. Glancing over my shoulder, I saw Aiden stir a little. Then I closed my eyes and focused on the connection. I figured I might as well glean some information from this.

A split second later, Seth took form in my thoughts. For some reason, he only had half his clothes on. I wasn't sure if that was me doing that or if he really was shirtless. Either way, it was way too much golden skin exposed. Treading lightly, I tested out the connection and the emotions it fed to me. I didn't know if I could somehow get sucked into him this way, so I proceeded with a great deal of caution.

The only thing I felt was . . . calmness, which was really—

A sudden cold chill snaked down my spine, and then Seth said, *Whatever you're looking for, you're not going to find it.*

What do you think I'm looking for?

With you, one can never be too sure.

Oh, that's the pot calling the kettle black.

Amusement flowed through the connection as Seth said, *Or it's the pot calling the pot a pot.*

I made a face. *What?*

Seth laughed. *Ah, I've sort of missed this, Alex.*

Opening my eyes, I resisted the irrational urge to admit that I too missed the banter, the out-snarking battle that neither of us won. It was weird—the dynamics of my relationships with Seth and Aiden.

Aiden complemented me; he was the yin to my yang, the "*now, now*" to my smartass. But Seth and I were too much alike, and in a way, we really were the same person. Together for too long, we probably would murder each other.

But yeah, there was a part of me that missed this—missed him.

Why haven't you started yelling at me yet? he asked.

I choked out a laugh. *Only you would ask that question. What? Do you want me to yell at you? I doubt that it would do any good. It's not going to change you.*

But that's never stopped you from doing anything before. Even if you knew the outcome and it was pointless, you'd still do it.

Like now? Staying away from you is pointless?

The smugness was back, settling over me like a second skin. *Very pointless*, he said.

Frustrated now, I closed my eyes and sighed. *Maybe you don't know me as well as you think you do. I know you don't care about anyone but yourself, but I really need to go.*

Pricks of irritation overshadowed the warmth of amusement and arrogance. *I want to talk.*

Immediately wary, my hands opened and closed. *What do you want to talk about?*

How wrong you are.

It was a good thing Hermes hadn't showed up, because my hand itched to connect with his face. *Oh, gods . . . Seth, I can't do this—*

I care about you, he said, surprising me.

I shook my head, wanting to deny it, because stripping my ability to make my own decisions was a hell of a way of showing how he cared, but it was the truth. But I remembered that night in Telly's house, that moment I'd seen the indecision in his eyes, the vulnerability. He hadn't wanted to hurt me then, but I believed that what he *needed* overwhelmed what he *wanted.*

I know, I said, because, deep down, I knew he did care.

Even more shocking, there was a sudden opening in the connection. Not that I could read any of Seth's thoughts, but there was a vulnerability that hadn't been there before. *It wouldn't have been bad between us, even if you never connected with me. It wouldn't have been terrible.*

My chest felt heavy and it ached, because there was also some truth to that.

But it never would've been enough, he added, and in a weird way, he felt closer now, like he was right beside me. *I'm man enough to admit that. Even if I fought for you fairly—and trust me, Aiden has nothing on me when I'm determined—in the end, whatever you felt for me would've been leftovers. I would've been a leftover. You would've never really been mine. I've always known that.*

I squeezed my hands until my joints ached. *Then why did you want to be with me—in the Catskills, you asked me to give it a try. Or was that a huge part of your master plan?*

Master plan? Seth laughed, but it was humorless. *Why wouldn't I have asked? I'm attracted to you, Alex. Doesn't take much to figure that out. And there's more. I've been drawn to you, ever since I first saw you. It's just the way it is for our kind.*

A distant, almost sad feeling crept through the connection. *That pull between us—I don't think you've ever understood, or even felt it, as much as I do. But anyway, like I said, I do care about you, too.*

There was a physical thing between us, partly due to the Apollyon bond and our own attraction to each other. I was grown-up enough to admit that it was still there, but it was watered down in comparison to how I felt for Aiden. But some things didn't change.

I care about you. The words were whispered and sounded broken to me.

For a moment, we said nothing. It was like a stalemate, a really weird, awkward and sad one.

Please don't do this, Seth.

He sighed. *Alex . . .*

I can help you.

The pricks of irritation soured my stomach now. *I don't need help.*

You do. I took a deep breath. *You're like an addict—the aether, whatever love and approval you're seeking from Lucian. You need help.*

I knew the moment I'd spoken that I'd said the wrong thing. Irritation flipped to anger and it was like standing too close to a fire. *I don't need your help, Alex. What I need is for you to understand that you can't escape Fate. That everything will be different—it will be better—if you just let Lucian do what needs to be done.*

Seth—

And I need you to understand, Alex, if you can, that maybe—just maybe—Lucian actually cares for me, that I'm worth that, and he wants the best for me—for us. Do you think you can do that?

My throat worked on the lump that had formed there. *You are worth someone caring about you, but—*

But what? His voice snapped fire, daring me to say what he knew I was going to say.

I drew in a stuttered breath. *But I can't do what you're asking. You are worth it—worth so much—but not Lucian. He's using you. And it'll be too late—*

It's not too late. In the end, no matter what, I will have everything that I want.

And then he pushed back and broke the connection.

24

When I opened my eyes again, Aiden was still asleep, and although the cord hummed softly in my stomach, Seth was gone for now. I climbed to my feet and quickly scanned the cave. Everything was the same—not exactly the Hilton Hotel, but safe.

Swallowing down the lump that felt like a permanent fixture in my throat, I shuffled over to Aiden and sat beside him, pulling my knees to my chest. Gods, I didn't know what was worse—if Seth was completely gone and there was no hope for him, or if there were a part of him still in there somewhere. Either way, wondering about it was hopeless. Right now I was on a mission to discover a way to destroy Seth. So did it matter? In the end, I couldn't allow him to transfer power from me. Too many lives rested on stopping him.

Aiden must've been the proud owner of an internal clock, because when the sky started to turn orange beyond the irregular holes in the roof of the cavern, he stretched like a jungle cat coming awake from an afternoon nap.

He sat up fluidly and leaned over, placing his hands on either side of my bent knees. Heat rolled off his bare chest. He pressed his lips to the sensitive space beneath my ear and murmured, "Good morning."

"Good morning."

"I'm guessing we weren't overrun by spiders?" Aiden popped to his feet and stretched again, raising his arms, his back bowing.

"No."

He sent me a look over his shoulder and then bent down, grabbing his shirt off the bag. "You hanging in there?"

I nodded.

As we ate a quick breakfast of gerbil food and got ready to head back out into the tunnel, I debated on what to tell Aiden. I couldn't hide the fact that I'd had some sort of interaction with Seth again, but I wasn't sure how to put what I was feeling into words that anyone could understand.

When he handed me the musty-smelling cloak, I finally said something. "I saw Seth last night."

Aiden stilled, hands clenching his own cloak. "Okay."

I focused on his shoulder. "I know I should've said something earlier."

"Yes. You should have."

A flush stained my cheeks. "I didn't really see him. Not like last time. He talked to me through the connection. He doesn't know what we're doing. He asked, but I didn't say anything."

"Of course." He slipped on the cloak with quick, stiff movements. "What did he want?"

I shifted my weight uncomfortably. "I think he just wanted . . . to talk."

"To talk?" Disbelief colored his tone.

"Yeah, he . . . I think there's a part of him still there. You know, a part of him that's confused, but he really believes that Lucian cares for him." I trailed off, shaking my head. "It doesn't matter. You ready?"

Aiden studied me a moment, then nodded. With our hoods in place, we left the little slice of peace behind and ventured out into the dark, narrow tunnels, traveling them in silence. Since I couldn't see Aiden's face or his eyes, I wasn't sure what he was thinking, but I was sure it had something to do with Seth. It was what I was thinking about as we navigated the darkness, with only our footsteps echoing in the silence.

I wished that I had seen what was happening to Seth before

it had become too late, noticed how the aether and akasha had been affecting him. Most of all, I wished I had seen how badly he needed someone—someone who accepted him, even loved him. Instead I had been so wrapped up in my own problems I hadn't seen what everything had been doing to him.

What I'd been doing to him.

In a way, I had seriously failed Seth.

After two hours of non-stop walking in the dark, a small speck of orange light shone ahead, and the closer we got, the larger the spot became until we could see the world outside the cavern.

"Finally," Aiden muttered.

He stopped at the rough, irregular opening and peered out over the sloping hill that led into a thick mist that blanketed the orange sky. "The Vale of Mourning," Aiden said. "We're close to the Plain of Judgment."

"Hopefully Apollo got word to Caleb." I stepped out. The drab grass crunched under my boots. "It shouldn't take long."

And it didn't, taking only a half an hour to get down the hill and to enter the mist, which gave way like stirred smoke, revealing the Vale.

The place was as depressing as it sounded.

Bare trees dotted the landscape. Their branches curled down at the ends, as if weighted by the suffering that seeped into the air. Slabs of gray rock rose from the dull grass and a small creek, its water dark and moody, parted the plain.

People were everywhere.

Some were by the creek, lying listlessly on their sides. Their fingers trailed into the water, their bodies shuddering over and over again with deep, heavy sighs. Others were perched upon rocks, sobbing openly, hands clutched to their chests. A few sat at the bases of trees, tucked into balls as they cried out.

The Vale of Mourning was a cesspool of heartbreak and suffering—the final resting place of those who'd died unhappily in love.

I couldn't get past these people fast enough. Although no one approached us, as they seemed too lost in their misery to even notice us, the lump that had been in my throat all morning grew rapidly. Depression was the air that was breathed here. Sorrow filled the river. Grief rooted the dead trees in place.

Even Aiden's steps seemed heavier, as if we were walking through the rain-soaked Asphodel Field.

"I don't want to be here," I said finally, drifting closer to him.

Aiden reached out, finding my hand under my cloak. "I know. We're almost through."

A man turned his tear-streaked face to the sky, letting out a hoarse cry. Near him, a woman collapsed onto the ground, sobbing and spitting hysterical, unintelligible words that no one was listening to. That was probably the suckiest part about the Vale. All these souls were here because of unhappy love, but no one cared. They were alone in their misery, as they probably had been in life.

But we weren't a part of the Vale, so we traveled on, able to do what these poor souls had been unable to do in life and death. We moved on, past the wants and needs that never had come to fruition, beyond love that had been lost, or never had been theirs to hold.

Some of the weight lifted along with the mist, and before us was a cobblestone road that honestly came out of nowhere as the skies cleared to the odd burnt orange. But we weren't alone. Hundreds, if not thousands, of souls traveled the same path as us. All kinds of people—young and old, pure and half—traveled toward their Judgment. Picking out the Sentinels and Guards was easy, even though their uniforms weren't covered in gore like they had been when I'd been in limbo. These souls all had been buried.

Aiden and I stuck out.

Very few of the souls traveling wore cloaks of any kind, since obviously that wasn't the fashion trend above ground. If anyone had passed away in a cloak, I'd be curious as to how and why. Most were in street clothing. Some even had ball caps on, and maybe we should've stashed away some of those. Someone was even rocking a cowboy hat.

Anyway, this wasn't good.

Hades' guards were posted along the road, atop their black warhorses. They kept the travelers in order and the path moving. It was probably an endless, boring job.

We moved toward the center of the group, hoping to get lost in the masses of tall Sentinels. Some of them passed cursory glances at us, but no one spoke to us. At the sound of a low nicker and approaching hoofs, my heart tripped up as I placed my hand on the dagger under my cloak. I felt Aiden move to do the same thing.

But the large warhorse blew past us, the guard riding low over the back. People darted out of the way; if they hadn't, they'd have been trampled under the powerful hooves.

Unease blossomed in the pit of my stomach, but it wasn't like we could turn back now.

Nearing the Plain of Judgment, it was hard not to notice the low reddish glow spreading across the horizon, and the further we traveled, the larger the . . . the *fire* grew.

Tartarus.

Whoa, I so didn't want to be anywhere near that place. And I really hoped that we wouldn't get caught and tossed into Tartarus.

My heart was throwing itself against my ribs by the time we entered the open Plain of Judgment. The mass of people crowding the crossroads was enormous and guards were everywhere, positioned just in case someone doomed for Tartarus tried to make a run for it.

Aiden stayed close to my side. "You don't happen to see Caleb?"

I laughed dryly as I scanned over the people. The crowd was

so thick I had no idea how I could see anyone in the throng. And I had a hard time not staring at the palace, which seemed way too close.

More of a medieval fortress than a home, Hades' palace rose like the mountains we'd traveled through, casting a dark shadow across the Plain of Judgment. Four turrets reached into the orangey sky, one from each corner of the stronghold.

Although I hoped Elysian Fields offered better scenery, I couldn't imagine waking every morning and looking out one of the many windows to see . . . all of this.

Focusing on the important stuff, I joined Aiden in the search to find the familiar blond head. There were a lot of blonds, but none of them were Caleb.

"What if word hasn't gotten to him?" I asked Aiden, afraid to say Apollo's name down here.

"He has to know," he assured me, scanning the rapidly increasing pile of people. "Gods, how many people do they process here in a day?"

Thousands, it appeared.

Proceeding forward, I realized I was pretty useless in the search for Caleb. Being so short, all I could see were backs of heads. My unease grew unchecked. The longer we were here, the more dangerous it was. I thought back to the guard who had raced ahead. My mouth went dry. We needed to find Caleb and we needed—

A heavy hand landed on my shoulder.

Sucking in a sharp breath, my fingers twitched around the handle of the dagger as I spun around, ready to use the blade if need be.

"Geez, don't stab me. I think we've had enough of that going on between the two of us."

I stumbled back as the familiar voice sunk in. He wore a baseball cap pulled low and a hoodie tucked over it, but wisps of blond hair poked around the edges. A wild grin shone from underneath the shadow of the cap.

"Caleb." My voice sounded hoarse.

Seconds away from tackling him to the ground, I was stopped when Aiden gripped my shoulder. "I know you want to," he said in a low voice, "but it would draw attention."

"Yeah, it would." Caleb nodded. "So let's keep the hugging and crying to a minimum."

I was already on the verge of crying, so thank the gods the hood hid that. Stepping away from Aiden, I stopped in front of Caleb. "I am so glad to see you again."

"And I'm happy to see you . . ." He lifted his hand, as if he would touch me, but stopped. "It's also good to see you back to normal."

I winced. "Yeah, about that . . . sorry?"

Caleb chuckled. "It's all good in the hood. Come, we've got to do this quickly." He gestured toward the road leading to Hades' palace. "I'm surprised you guys even made it this far without getting caught. The whole Underworld is in a tizzy over what's been going on topside."

"I imagine that's why they're so busy down here," Aiden commented.

"Yep." Caleb shoved his hands deep into the pockets of his jeans. "A lot of Sentinels and pures coming through here. Sort of blows, you know?"

"Yeah, it blows real bad. So why would we—?"

Without warning, the ground trembled violently and a great, terrible roar cracked overhead, shaking me to the bone.

I turned, as did everyone else, toward Tartarus. The smell of sulfur grew until it was thick and choking. Fear exploded in my gut. Aiden was beside me in an instant, his hand pressing into my back. "What's happening?" I asked.

"You'll see," Caleb responded.

I shot him a look, but then a ball of fire flew straight into the air over Tartarus, twisting and churning as embers flew in every direction. The fire shifted, morphing as it continued to stream into the sky.

The funnel of fire stilled for a moment.

On each side, the fire grew, spreading into giant wings that seemed to reach all corners of the Underworld. In the center, a dragon's head appeared. The mouth opened, emitting another bloodcurdling scream, and then it swooped down. The impact shook the ground as the fiery tail whipped through the air.

Then it quieted.

"Holy Hades," I mumbled.

"It's like the welcome party for those sentenced to Tartarus," Caleb explained. "Happens every time a group arrives in there. You get used to it after a while."

"What the hell . . ." I muttered. There was no way I'd grow used to seeing *that.*

"Come on, we've got to go." Caleb slid in front of us. "It could take years to find Solaris, but I know just the thing that—"

Four black stallions parted the crowd, their riders tall and imposing, garbed in leather. *Swords—freaking swords*—were leveled out from their sides. They surrounded us in seconds, herding the three of us until our backs pressed against one another.

Aiden reached for his dagger and ended up with the business end of a sword pointed at his throat. The look on the guard's face screamed he was neither afraid nor above using it.

"Crap," I muttered.

We were so screwed.

25

The guard's arm didn't tremble. "Move, and you will not move again."

Aiden froze, and I don't think I breathed. I was pretty sure Caleb wasn't breathing either, but then again, he didn't need to breathe, being that he was dead. But that didn't mean he would go without punishment. We were caught. *He* was caught, and all I could think of was the dragon we'd seen. Guilt tore through me like a wildfire.

The guard eyeballed Aiden. "Raise your hands."

"You told me not to move, so I'm not sure how I can raise my hands," was Aiden's dry response.

I bit back a laugh that wouldn't have been appreciated.

Not amused, the guard slipped the sword inside Aiden's hood. The sword tipped up, easing the material back. The guard smiled when Aiden's face was revealed and a thin trickle of blood seeped down his cheek.

Hot and fiery rage burned, and I wanted nothing more than to knock the ass off his horse, but the sword was too close to the skin of Aiden's neck.

"Raise your hands," the guard seethed.

A smirk crossed his lips as he slowly raised his hands. "Is this good enough?"

"The three of you are to come with us," another guard announced as he sheathed his sword. "If you do not obey, we have been given permission to use any method needed. Please be assured that a death in the Underworld is the same as topside."

The guards turned pale eyes beyond me to Caleb. "And there are things worse than death here, boy. You should've have thought about that."

Caleb said nothing, but we had to do something. We couldn't let them take us wherever they planned to take us. Problem was, only Caleb knew how to get Aiden and me out of the Underworld, and it wasn't like we could really ask him that right now. And I wasn't leaving Caleb to face this alone.

So yeah, like I said, we were screwed.

A guard on foot came between the two horses and headed straight for me. Aiden moved only a fraction of an inch, and the tip of the sword pricked his skin.

"We're back to the not moving part again." The guard smirked. "Is that good for you?"

Aiden glared at the guard and heat poured off him. The guard's smile tipped up in response.

The one in front of me grabbed a fistful of my hood and wrenched it back. His ice-blue eyes narrowed. "It's them."

My heart dropped to my toes. He said it like someone had been expecting us, and that was so not good. I tried to keep the panic out of my face, but it must have been evident, because the guard laughed as he turned back.

"Disarm them all," he said. "And then we must go."

The disarming part took seconds. Our cloaks were removed, daggers stripped away. Aiden's backpack was taken hostage. I threw Aiden a glance, but he stared ahead, his jaw set in a rigid line. Crap on a cracker, this was bad. Caleb seemed resigned, though, his shoulders slumped, as if he knew what punishment was coming.

Watching the backs of the guards, I wondered how quickly I could take them all out so the three of us could make a run for it. But that would probably require akasha, and where would Caleb hide down here? Where would we go? And to come this far, only to lose it all? I couldn't even come to grips with it. A cold knot of fear sat heavy in my stomach.

With dread raking deeper and deeper with each step, we could do nothing else but follow the guards to Hades' palace.

"I'm sorry," I whispered to Caleb.

He shrugged. "Like old times, though."

"Yeah, but this is different. There's a dragon made of fire that will—"

"No talking." The guard who liked to play with his sword rode up beside us. "Or I will make it that none of you can talk again."

Like my father? Sweet, hot rage exploded. My mouth opened, but Aiden's warning glare closed it. We were herded toward the palace in silence. Two guards on horses in front of us, two behind us, and one on the ground made it impossible to do a damn thing.

And then the gates to the palace were swinging open and we were ushered in across a sparse courtyard. Everything was happening so fast. My heart pounded; sweat dotted my brow. I felt naked without the damn cloak, and there was a freaking hellhound sleeping on its back by the entrance, its meaty paws kicking in the air as it dreamt of chasing souls or whatever hellhounds dreamt of.

Guards dismounted from their horses and strode toward the entrance, pulling open the palace doors. The guys on either side of me seemed to be handling all of this better than me, or they were just better at pretending not to be one step from spazzing out, but Caleb probably wasn't blown away by Hades' palace like I was.

After all, he played Wii with the gods here.

But Hades' palace was . . . opulent.

Gold and titanium plated everything—the walls, ceiling, furniture, and even the floor. Hades' symbols were everywhere. The bull and the two-prong spears were engraved into the floors, stitched into the elegant tapestries. Black velvet chaise lounges filled the great hall, but it was the covered thrones occupying the dais that caught and held my attention. They were truly fit for a king and queen—but it was also what was near them.

Slumbering beside them were smaller hellhounds—maybe puppy hellhounds. Their multiple heads rested on their paws, and acid drool pooled under the lolled tongues.

The guards stopped and, without any words, dropped onto one knee and lowered their heads. A second later, the floor-to-ceiling gold and titanium doors next to the thrones swung open. Even though Hades was supposed to be in Olympus, I fully expected the god to come strolling through the doors, ready to toss the three of us into the fiery pits of Tartarus.

Weak in the knees, I forced myself to keep my eyes trained forward. Sentinels didn't feel fear . . . my rosy half-blood butt.

But as the figure drew nearer, I knew it wasn't Hades. It wasn't even a guy. It was a female—and it was a goddess.

She was beautiful—tall, damn near seven feet. Waves of curly red hair fell to an impossibly narrow waist. Her eyes were all white, cheekbones high, lips plump, and nose pert.

And she was practically naked.

Her white gown was gauzy and completely see-through. I got a good idea of her bra size . . . if she'd been wearing one, which she wasn't. Underwear must be optional down here.

Aiden was staring. So was Caleb, although he looked like he was quite used to all this . . . woman on display. Hell, even I was staring.

She crossed the great hall, her long legs parting the chiffon of her skirt, playing peekaboo. Dear gods, I felt my cheeks start to burn, but I still couldn't look away. As she neared, her all-white eyes flared, and then dimmed. Two bright, emerald-colored eyes appeared.

Caleb relaxed beside me, a slow smile creeping across his handsome face—the face I'd missed so much. "Hello, Persephone."

My eyes widened on the beautiful goddess. So this was the

infamous Persephone. Even though I was Team Boy, I could see why Hades had become so enamored with her, going as far as to pluck her away and bring her down to the Underworld.

The first guard, not the one who'd cut Aiden, lifted his head. "We apprehended them as you wished."

"Apprehended" was so not a warm and fuzzy word.

"You three look surprised." Persephone's lush lips were tilted with mischief. "These are my personal guards and they've been keeping an eye out for you. I've been expecting you."

"How?" I asked, stunned.

Persephone smiled. "Caleb and I play Super Mario Kart every day at one, and when he cancelled on me I knew something was up."

I looked at Caleb slowly.

He shrugged. "It's not my fault she's observant."

"And very bored when my husband is in Olympus. Caleb keeps me company."

I so hoped it was the platonic type of company, because Hades wasn't known for his forgiving nature.

"Guards, you may leave us now." When they hesitated, she laughed. "I am fine. Please leave and do not speak of this to anyone."

One by one, they filed out of the room, sword guy eyeing Aiden like he wanted to slice his other cheek. Aiden held his stare as a smirk crossed his lips.

Men. Sigh.

Once the palace doors closed behind them, Persephone clapped her hands together. "I asked a few questions of a little nymph who had come into the Underworld just a few days ago—one of Apollo's nymphs. And it doesn't take a weather scientist to figure out it had something to do with his lineage."

"It's rocket scientist," Caleb corrected as he tugged down his hood and pulled off his cap.

She frowned. "Anyway, I figured it had something to do with

you . . . and I had a choice. Call my husband and he'd come rushing home, but then he'd be in a tizzy, and he's such a pain like that. Or I could just find out what you guys needed. I'm sure it will prove very interesting."

Aiden shifted beside me, clearly caught as off-guard as I was. I glanced at Caleb and whispered, "Can we trust her?"

Caleb nodded. "She's pretty cool, and actually this makes my job so much easier."

The goddess raised a delicate eyebrow. "Do tell?"

"I need to see the Calling Waters."

Calling Waters? I had never heard of such a thing, and from the look on Aiden's face, neither had he.

"And why would you need to use the Calling Waters?" she asked, folding slender arms under her breasts, like she needed help drawing attention to them. "If you would like to see someone, Caleb, you only have to ask."

"I know." He dropped an arm over my shoulders, and the gaping hole that had been there since he'd died filled. "But it's not for me. It's for them. They need to use it."

Persephone was quiet for a long moment. "Who do they wish to call upon?"

"Solaris," I answered. The Calling Waters suddenly made sense—call a soul to you. "We need to talk to Solaris."

"Because of what is happening topside with the First?" she asked.

I nodded.

Her bright gaze slid to Caleb. "And what did you plan to do? Sneak them in here to use it?"

"That was the plan."

The goddess shook her head. "If my husband were home and you were to do something so unwise, I would not be able to stay his hand."

A shiver danced down my spine. The last thing I wanted was for Caleb to get into eternal-damnation-type trouble.

"I know," Caleb replied, squeezing my shoulders. "But they are worth the risk, and Solaris could possibly hold information to stop the First. And that's what Hades wants, right? That's what the gods want?"

"Most of them," she murmured, her gaze slipping back to me, and then to Aiden. "But not all, it appears."

Something struck me. "Do you know who the god is—the one who's helping Seth and Lucian?"

She picked a glossy red curl and twirled it around one elegant finger. "If I knew such a thing, then that god would be taken care of. But I am rarely on Olympus and have little interest in the politics of who pissed off whom enough to end the world as we know it this time around."

Aiden cleared his throat. "This happens quite a bit, then?"

Persephone smiled, and when she smiled, even I lost my breath. "More than you will ever know. The world has been on the brink of total devastation several times over for one reason or another. But now . . . it is like when we faced the Titans. It has gone beyond a few pretty words used to gloss over a perceived insult." She let out a little sigh. "But anyway, I have very little to do, and if this Solaris can be of some help to you, then she will be of some help to my husband. Follow me."

As she turned gracefully on her heel, I was too shocked to move at first. Persephone helping us was not something I'd planned on.

Aiden smiled. "This is good."

"Way good." I turned to Caleb. "You rock."

"I know." He pulled me in for a quick, tight hug. "Missed you."

Holding him close, I swallowed the happy tears. "I missed you, too."

Caleb kissed the top of my head, and then pulled away. "Come on. Let's get this show on the road."

The three of us followed behind the goddess. Poor Aiden was

trying to look everywhere but at her, but underneath it all, he was a guy. Strangely, I wasn't jealous—probably more amused than anything else, because he was trying his hardest to keep his eyes north.

Slipping my hand around his, I squeezed. When his gaze flicked to mine, I grinned and he gave me a lopsided smile of apology.

As we headed down a long, dark hallway covered with black velvet tapestries, Caleb watched Aiden and me, a strange look on his face.

"What?" I asked.

He shook his head. "You guys are really doing this—the relationship, out in the open and all?"

Aiden's hand wrapped more firmly around mine. "I think right now the world has bigger problems than a pure and a half being in love."

My heart did a happy dance at the last part. Just hearing him say that—the L-word—could chase away all the dark shadows and expectations.

Persephone's throaty chuckle drifted back to us. "Isn't that the truth? Besides, they are not the first, nor the last."

Caleb's sky-blue eyes settled on Aiden. "And you're not going to try to hide the relationship once everything settles down?"

The challenge in his tone had me smiling.

"Not going to happen," Aiden told him. "It won't be easy, but we'll find a way."

"Good." Caleb's eyes hardened. "Because if you do her wrong, I will haunt your ass until you die."

I burst into laughter and so did Aiden, even though we both knew Caleb was being serious. Letting go of Aiden's hand, I wrapped my arm around Caleb. "That won't be necessary."

The goddess stopped in front of a bronze door. With a wave of her hand, it sprang open. Good thing she was helping us out, because I had no idea how Caleb would've pulled that off.

At the rush of cold air, we stepped into the circular chamber. There were so many weapons on the wall – battleaxes, spears, swords, and pikes. There were morbid items too, like the heads of long-forgotten animals slaughtered in the hunt and an entire section dedicated to cut-off ponytails.

I cleared my throat. "Nice . . . room."

"It's Hades' war room." Awe filled Aiden's tone. "Damn."

"The weapons are my husband's, but . . ." Persephone slid a dismissive glance around the war room. "These are mostly Ares' trophies, not my beloved's. Hades does have a tendency to swing a little on the morbid side, but the hair . . ." She gestured at the sheared ponytails tacked onto the wall. "Those belong to Ares. He likes to cut off the hair of those he's conquered and then string them up for all to see. It disturbs most of the other gods, so he keeps them here."

Caleb's brows rose. "Nice decorative touch, I guess."

There was something eerily familiar about the hair. Not the whole cutting it off and hanging it on walls, because, thank the gods, that was strange to me. But there was something that poked at my memory.

"You know Ares," Persephone said, drawing us further into the war room. "To him, everything is about war and its spoils. Peace practically emasculates him. He believes one should never turn one's back on war . . ." She trailed off and gave a dainty shrug. "He should be thrilled now, with everything on the brink."

"He's probably a happy camper," Caleb said, sliding a WTF glance my way.

I shrugged, but that weird sensation was there, nagging at me. Did Persephone mean never turn their back on *Ares*, a.k.a. "Mr. War," or just on war itself?

"Here we are." She stopped in front of a marble pedestal. Demonic faces were etched into the marble of the basin and ruby-red water filled it. "All you have to do is stand before it and call for the soul you wish to speak to—any soul—and they will be summoned here."

"Any soul?" My breath caught as an image of my mother filled my head.

"Yes, but I can only allow you to use it once. So choose wisely." Persephone giggled. "I feel like I'm in *Indian James and the Lost Ark.*"

Aiden cast his gaze to the floor, jaw flexing to hide his grin.

Caleb rolled his eyes. "*It's Indiana Jones and the Last Crusade.*"

"Oh." She shrugged. "Same thing."

My gaze dipped to the basin. My mom's name was on the tip of my tongue, and I knew without looking at Aiden that he was thinking about his parents. Either of us would probably give anything to see them, especially after how wrong the spirits had been at the portal.

Persephone's gaze turned knowing. "Ah, the chance to see a loved one is a hard one to pass over."

"You would know," Aiden said quietly.

Her smile slowly faded. "I would. Perhaps some find me selfish for the decisions I have made and the impact they have had."

Recalling the myth of Persephone, I shook my head. "No. You were smart. You made sure that both could have you—Hades *and* your mom."

If she felt smug for how it all turned out in the end, the whole splitting of time and the seasons, she didn't show it—surprising, since the gods weren't a humble bunch of folks.

Turning back to the basin, she clasped her hands in front of her. "It is time to make your choice, and then you must leave."

I looked at Aiden, who nodded. There was a hint of sadness in his eyes, reflecting what I knew shone in mine. Caleb placed his hand on my shoulder. As much as I wanted to see my mom, as much as I wanted to gift Aiden with the chance to see his parents, neither of us could be that selfish.

Stepping up to the basin, I stared into the still red water that reminded me of blood. Actually, it was thick like blood, and there was a faint metallic scent. Ew.

A second passed, and then I said, "Solaris."

Nothing happened at first, and then the water rippled as if I had blown a soft breath upon it. Part of me expected her face to appear in the basin, but the water settled again. Then there was a sudden fissure of energy that crawled up the walls and rolled over the floors. Tiny hairs on my body rose and a shudder worked its way across me. There was a soft gasp of surprise and I turned.

Solaris had arrived.

26

When I'd stepped into the Underworld, I really hadn't known what to expect. The same could be said for Solaris. I'd really had no clue, and still I was blown away.

Solaris stood directly in front of Caleb and she looked a lot better than I'd thought she would. For some reason, I'd expected that she and the First would be serving it up in Tartarus, but her white gown was pristine and intact. Silvery-blonde hair, long and wispy, settled over thin shoulders. She was tall and willowy and her eyes were like mine—a bright amber color. Her delicate, porcelain features reminded me of a frail, exotic flower, which I hadn't been expecting. Maybe I was rocking one hell of an ego or something, but I'd thought she'd look like me.

She was the complete opposite of me.

Solaris looked around the room, her pale brows rising as she took in where she was. Surprise and a little bit of fear flitted across her face, but when her eyes landed on me, a keen understanding seeped into those ashen eyes. A sense of familiarity washed over me, mirrored in her expression.

Striding forward, Solaris stopped a mere foot from me, her head tilted inquisitively. When she spoke, her voice was soft. "You are the Apollyon."

There wasn't much time for me to figure out how she knew what I was. "I'm one of them."

Another flicker of surprise shot across her face, quickly followed by sorrow. "So there are two again?"

I nodded.

She glanced over her shoulder. "And neither of these are he. I can tell. One of them is dead. One of them is a pure-blood."

I ignored Caleb's offended look. "No. The First isn't here."

Solaris faced me, brows knitted. "You have Awakened. I can see the marks of the Apollyon."

"You can?" I glanced down, surprised to find that my visible skin was all marked up. I hadn't even felt them.

"How can you be Awakened and not be with the First? You are not dead."

Yet. "It's complicated. That's why we've come to talk to you."

"Oh." The sorrow deepened and her lashes swept down. "He is like mine?"

Everyone in the room, even Persephone, was fixated on Solaris, but she seemed wholly unaware of them now. I took a breath and fought the sudden tightening in my throat. The grief rolling off Solaris was palpable.

"Yes." My voice sounded hoarse. "He's like yours."

Twisting away, she wrapped her arms around herself. "Then there is nothing that I can do for you."

I stared at her. "But we haven't asked anything."

"If he has lost himself to the aether, to the call of akasha, there is nothing to be done." Her chin tipped down, causing her hair to slip forward, shielding her face. "And there is nothing to be done for you. I tried . . . but the power transferred."

"Wait." I stepped toward, pushing down on the frustration roaring inside me. "I haven't transferred my power to him. He's only the Apollyon. Not the God Killer."

Solaris stiffened. "That's not possible."

"It is. I haven't been near him since I Awakened. There is something about the aether and akasha with him, but he's still just the Apollyon." I paused, drawing in a long breath. "I need to know how to stop the transfer."

She remained quiet.

"And I think—*I know*—that you know how to do it."

Her head swung toward me. "There is no way. I blocked that knowledge so no other Apollyon could learn it."

"Well . . . I saw something when I Awakened. You turned to him, tried to stop him. You knew how, but the Order found you first."

Solaris laughed a dry, brittle laugh. "Is that what history tells you?"

I glanced at the goddess, figuring she'd know, but she looked as confused as I felt. "But I saw it—"

"Did you? The Awakening is what the previous Apollyons wish for you to see. At the moment of your death, when it does come, you will implant your memories. Some of them may be as you wished to see them, but not how they truly existed."

Well . . . daimon butt. Did Seth know that? "What happened, then?"

Her lashes swept down again. "When I first met him, he wasn't like he was in the end. He was a beautiful, kind man who just happened to be the Apollyon." A small, sad smile pulled at her lips. "We really didn't understand any of it. We were the first to exist in the same generation. He didn't even understand why he came to find me. It was like he was drawn and I didn't understand what was happening when I Awakened. The pain . . . I thought I was dying."

I winced, unable to imagine going through that without Aiden and without any knowledge of what was happening.

"But when we met, it was like it was destined. For many months, we got . . . we got to know each other. I do not think even the gods knew what could happen." A distant look crept into her eyes, not quite overshadowing a pain that still hadn't healed. "He seemed to grow more powerful the longer we were around each other, able to harness akasha with little effort, and he would not grow tired. But he was more unstable. Never toward me, but I knew . . . I knew that it was because of me. There was a situation . . ."

My stomach sank as my gaze flickered to Aiden.

"A large group of daimons had attacked one of the Covenants and during the battle, he . . . pulled from me. The power he displayed was unimaginable. The Council grew concerned and then . . . then I met the oracle."

Ah, the oracle strikes again.

"She told me what would happen. That he would pull all of my power from me and he would attack the Council. I didn't believe her, because that would be insane." Solaris laughed softly. "But she was insistent that I stop him. That if I could not find it in my heart to kill what I loved most, then I must take the power."

My breath caught, and the walls seemed to do a Tilt-a-Whirl.

"I never thought he would act, but the Council moved against us. They wanted us separated, and neither of us, in our naïve selfishness, could bear such a thought. We left the safety of the Council and we went out on our own." Solaris shook her head. "They followed, sending their most skilled Sentinels. When they didn't succeed, the Order of Thanatos came."

She swallowed thickly. "He threatened the Council then, and I knew what the oracle had said was all coming true. She had given me the means to stop him, but it was too late."

I bit my lip. "What did he do?"

Her eyes met mine. "He would've never done it if the allure of the power—the draw of supreme power—hadn't overtaken him. But it did. Before I could stop him, he drew from me. There was a moment, immediately after he took my power, when he was not yet able to channel it. Like an Achilles heel, so to speak, and the Order attacked. The rest . . . the rest is history."

I didn't know what to say. Sorrow rode the back of my throat. It was obvious that Solaris had loved her First, so much so that not once did she speak his actual name. I couldn't bring myself to ask just to quench my own curiosity, because I knew speaking it would only bring her more pain.

"I'm sorry." It was all I could say.

Solaris nodded. "What is your First doing?"

I told her everything—the destruction, the impending war, and the hope that somehow we could stop history from repeating itself. If she was surprised, she didn't show it. Solaris simply walked up to me.

"I blocked it from him and from the other Apollyons," Solaris said again. "I'm not sure how you even saw it. Perhaps it was Fate?"

Gods, for once Fate wasn't trying to force me to take one for the team. Nice change. "Perhaps."

"It's simpler than you think." Solaris reached out, placing her cold hand over my right one. "You must follow the order of the marks as they appeared on you. The original." Solaris squeezed my right hand, "Θάρρος." *Courage.*

Then she cupped her hand around my left. "Iψεύς." *Strength.*

Letting go of my hand, she placed hers below my ribcage, over my navel. "απόλυτη ηξουψία." *Absolute Power*. Then finally, she reached up and cupped the nape of my neck. "αήττητο." *Invincibility.*

The air went out of my lungs and Solaris nodded. "You will need to press your flesh to his and call upon each mark by its true name."

"Wait," Aiden said. "Isn't that how he would transfer her power to him?"

I already knew, so when Solaris stepped away and turned to Aiden, I could barely look at him. "Yes," she said. "She will have to do it before he does."

Aiden opened his mouth, but there were no words. We had learned how to transfer power and that was something, but it would also be damn near impossible.

"Is that all?" she asked. "I wish to leave."

Persephone cleared her throat. "I believe so."

For an instant, Solaris' eyes met mine and I thought I'd be seeing her again. *And sooner than I probably expect.* I didn't know where that thought came from—if it was rooted in any real possibility or just paranoia.

"Are you sure this is what you want to do?" she asked, voice low enough for only me to hear. "For the power of the God Killer will transfer to you. And though you may feel strong and you may think you can control it, it can warp you, too."

Looking terribly sad, as if she knew this great secret, she sighed. "And for whatever purpose the gods seek to use you for, once they do, will you be left standing in the end? As the oracle warned me, there cannot be two of our kind in any generation."

And then she was gone, but her parting words lingered deep, wrapping their way over my heart and soul. Her words weren't a warning, but more of a statement of fact. I glanced down at my left hand and I felt as if my fate had been sealed long before I even knew what I was.

I let out a shaky breath.

"Well, that was depressing." Caleb ran a hand through his hair. "If I wasn't dead already, I'd feel a bit suicidal."

"No doubt," Persephone murmured. "But dead people—no offense—tend to be on the depressing side of things."

Caleb shrugged. "No offense taken."

Each time that I'd seen Caleb, he hadn't seemed depressed. As if he read my mind that moment, he smiled and I remembered what he'd said when I'd been in limbo. "You told me there was still hope for him."

Caleb swaggered over to me, seeming so alive it was painful to see. Wrapping his arms around me, he held me tight. "There's always hope. Maybe not the kind of hope you're thinking about, but there *is* hope."

I didn't understand at first, so I snuggled closer, knowing our time was quickly coming to an end. As I inhaled the fresh scent of Caleb, I realized I needed to know something that would probably slice me into tiny ribbons.

Pulling away, I turned to Persephone. "Where is her First?"

A whole minute passed before she answered. "He is in Tartarus."

I pressed my fingers to my mouth before the lump came all the way up. It wasn't so much the Fate of the First, but what it signified. If I succeeded and was able to kill Seth, his Fate would be the same. And so would mine.

I was like Velcro on Caleb for the next fifteen minutes or so, while Aiden busied himself studying the weapons and Persephone filed her nails or whatever. While we sat on the floor of the war room, our knees pressing together, Caleb told me about some of the stuff he was doing down here to pass time and I told him how much Olivia had wanted to see him. We didn't talk about what would happen next. I was pretty sure that Caleb was aware of all the crazy stuff going on and neither of us wanted to tarnish these precious minutes.

"Did you tell her what I asked you to?" he asked.

I nodded. "She cried, but I think they were happy tears."

Caleb's smile was broad. "I miss her, but can you do me another favor?"

"Anything." And I meant it.

"Don't tell Olivia that you saw me."

I frowned. "Why? She would—"

"I want her to move on." Caleb grasped my hands and stood, pulling me to my feet. "I need her to move on, and I think hearing about me is stopping her. I want her to live and I don't want to be shadowing every step she takes."

Gods, I hated the idea of lying to Olivia, but I understood what Caleb was saying. Olivia would never move on, knowing that, in a way, Caleb was conscious and as alive as he could be in the Underworld. It was like he was there, not reachable, but still *there*. Knowing that, how could she really move on?

So I agreed. I promised to tell everyone that it had been only

Persephone who had found us. Even if Apollo knew the truth, it wouldn't matter as long as Olivia didn't. In a way, this was his gift to her.

"Thank you," Caleb said, and hugged me once more. Part of me wanted to stay in Caleb's arms, because he'd always had this grounding effect on me. Caleb was my rational side. He was more than that; other than my mother, he was the first person I'd ever truly loved.

Caleb would always be my best friend.

"It's time," Persephone said quietly, and when I pulled away and looked at her, there was sympathy in her gaze. A god who could empathize was an abnormality.

Aiden returned to my side, swinging the backpack onto his shoulders before handing me back the weapons that the guards had stripped off me, as well as my yucky cloak. Persephone drifted toward the center of the war room and waved her hand. A black void appeared, completely opaque. "This gate will take you back to the one you came through."

"Thank you," I said to Persephone.

She nodded gracefully.

As I said goodbye and looked over my shoulder one last time, my chest squeezed as I met Caleb's blue, blue eyes. I knew then that death could stop a lot of things, but it could never cut the bond of friendship.

Caleb smiled, and I returned it with a watery one of my own, and then I turned back to the void waiting for us. Threading my fingers through Aiden's, we stepped back through the gate, armed with the knowledge we needed, but bearing the burden of needing to accomplish the impossible.

27

The Hummer was where we'd left it, and according to the clock on the dashboard, only three hours had passed—three hours in the mortal realm, forty-eight hours in the Underworld, and a lifetime for Aiden and me.

I offered to drive back, but Aiden insisted that he was fine and I knew he wanted me to sleep. I knew I should—to avoid Seth using the connection—but it didn't seem fair. Aiden had to be exhausted.

But it was a battle I wasn't winning anytime soon, so I snuggled into the passenger seat and tried to get some sleep. The only problem was that my brain would not shut down. Ever since I'd stood in the war room, something had nagged at me. What Persephone had said, the sheared ponytails on the wall—all of it seemed familiar, but I couldn't place how or why. And it was more than that. Solaris' parting words were unsettling and they poked around in my head.

What I could never figure out was why Apollo had kept me alive once Seth had gone all crazy-pants on the Council. Or why Artemis had stopped Hades from taking me into the Underworld. The gods—or at least all of them except one—feared the transfer of power, because when that happened there'd be no stopping Seth. Taking me out of the picture before I'd Awakened, or putting me out of commission afterward, made sense.

Keeping me alive didn't.

But I remembered what Artemis had said in that convenience store as she'd faced down Hades. Prophecies could change, and it didn't take a leap of logic to know that, if I became the God Killer, the prophecy *would* change.

Unease blossomed in my chest. Had Apollo and the others known that this was possible? Then I felt dumb for even questioning that. The oracles belonged to Apollo, and even though he didn't know all of their visions, the portion of what the oracle had told Solaris could've been shared with Apollo. Which made sense since Apollo had been oh-so supportive of me going down to see Solaris.

Part of me was naïve enough to hope that wasn't the case, because that meant Apollo had some explaining to do. The other part was more analytical about it, more reasonable. Apollo had said before that they needed to stop the god who was obviously working with Lucian. And how else would they stop him?

They needed the God Killer.

The real kicker of this whole crappy situation was that Lucian controlled Seth, and this god—whoever it was—controlled Lucian, and therefore he/she controlled Seth and all of those who were following Lucian. So if Seth succeeded and transferred my power to him, this god would then control the God Killer. Risky, because Seth could always turn on him, but in the end, once the god had Seth do what he wanted, I was sure he'd be creative enough to somehow keep him under control. Possibly that meant keeping a member of the Order stowed away, safe and sound.

My muscles tightened in reflex as I worked this out. None of it looked good. And Seth was being manipulated from every which direction and he had no idea. Hell, he refused to even think that was the case.

As the miles between Kansas and Illinois disappeared, I couldn't shake what Solaris has said about the gods using me, and what it would mean. Neither could I let go of the feeling that, by learning how to transfer the power to me, I had sealed my own fate.

The sudden weight of Aiden's hand on my knee drew my attention to him. His eyes were on the dark highway. "You're not sleeping."

I smiled as I placed my hand over his. "How did you know?"

"I just do." He sent me a brief grin. "What are you thinking about?"

Everything was on the tip of my tongue—my suspicions, my concerns about what Solaris had said, and what I now knew Apollo was hiding—but when Aiden glanced at me again, I found I couldn't tell him.

He hadn't heard what Solaris had said, and I didn't want to burden him with this on top of everything else. If my suspicions were correct, if everything was leading to one thing . . .

Taking a deep breath, I focused on the white lines parting the darkness. "I was just thinking about how I'm supposed to get close enough to Seth to transfer his power to me. Seems impossible, right?"

"I don't like it, Alex. I'm going to be honest; I think it's insane. To me, it's like sneaking up on a cobra. It's not going to work."

"I know, but what choice do we have? Besides, we don't just have to figure out how to get close enough to him. There're all the Sentinels and Guards who are backing him."

Aiden squeezed my hand. "We're going to need an army."

Slowly, I looked at him. "And where are we going to dig up one of them?"

"Good question." He barked out a short laugh. "What we need to find out is exactly how many Lucian has backing him—"

"I can always ask Dionysus to do some scouting," Apollo's voice boomed from the backseat.

Shrieking, I sprang forward, knocking my knees off the dashboard. Aiden's hand jerked on the steering wheel, swerving the Hummer into the left lane, which was thankfully empty.

Aiden cursed under his breath. "You need a freaking bell."

I twisted around in the seat, ready to knock the grin off the god's face. I was already pretty pissed off at him without him giving us a heart attack. "You could've caused an accident!"

Apollo leaned forward, resting his arms on the back of our seats. "But I didn't. Aiden has the reflexes of a hellhound."

Making a face, I shook my head. "How did you just . . . pop in here?"

He gave me a very un-god-like *duh* look. "These wards make your power invisible to the gods; they don't keep us out. You carry my bloodline. I can find you when I want."

"Well, that's not creepy."

Aiden glanced in the rearview mirror. "You want to know what we found out?" When Apollo nodded, a scowl appeared on Aiden's face. "And you couldn't have waited until we got back to Apple River?"

"Let's see . . ." Apollo tapped a finger off his chin. "The whole world is on the verge of a god apocalypse. Should I wait another six hours?"

"Six hours isn't going to change anything," Aiden replied, eyes turning a steely gray.

"I hope not." Apollo turned his gaze to me. "What did you learn?"

I debated telling him that I hadn't learned a damn thing, but that was pointless. "I learned how to transfer the power to me."

Apollo showed no reaction, and I really think I hated him right then. "And do you think you can do it?"

I glanced at Aiden. "There's the tiny problem of getting to Seth."

"Like I said, I can have Dionysus do some scouting. See what they have going for them," he replied.

"We still don't have an army." I flipped in my seat, facing the front and feeling all kinds of bitchtastic.

"Actually . . ."

I refused to turn around and take the bait. "What?"

When he didn't answer, Aiden growled deep in his throat. "What, Apollo?"

"About an hour after you guys left, one of the Sentinels who had been using Solos' cabin before you not-so-nicely kicked them out showed up. He brought news."

Aiden had gone completely motionless, and I wondered how he could still manage to drive like that. "And you trust this Sentinel?"

The god laughed darkly. "Let's just say I made sure he was playing on our team."

Curious, I started to ask how, but Apollo grinned at me. "Use your imagination," he said, and my imagination went to some really weird places.

"Anyway," he continued. "Most of the pures are fleeing the Covenants and their communities, heading to the University in South Dakota. So are their Guards. Makes sense—the location of the University is pretty remote and almost certainly cannot be breached. The Sentinels who haven't fallen in with Lucian have left their duties and are en route to the University."

"What about the daimons?" I asked.

"What about them? They will go where the pures are, and the pures will be well-protected. Then there are the daimons that Lucian is feeding the pures to. Nothing we can do about that." Apollo sat back, eyeing the roof of the Hummer like he'd never seen one before. He tapped the internal light once and it flicked on, then he turned it off. Shiny things must be distracting for gods, too. He did it again, brows furrowed.

"Apollo," I snapped.

His gaze settled on me. "There is a good chance that Lucian and the First will overtake the New York Council, so Council members and Sentinels are being secreted out of the Covenant."

My heart tipped over. "My—"

"I don't know if your father is among the ones who have already arrived at the University or is en route or alive. I'm sorry."

My shoulders slumped. "So what are they doing? Moving the base of operation to there?"

"Yes. So there will be hundreds, if not thousands, of Sentinels and Guards there. Those who have seen their friends and other Sentinels killed by those who have sided with Lucian. Those who want nothing more than to get a piece of him."

Aiden nodded slowly. "An army—our army."

"Marcus and Solos are already making plans to travel to the University. The sooner you all get there, the better."

I could get behind this plan. And yeah, there was a bit of a selfish reason behind it. Any chance that my father might be there was enough for me.

"It would be safer there for Deacon and the others," Aiden said. "It would be best."

Now I felt like a douche for only thinking of what I could gain. "How early can we leave?"

"As soon as possible," Apollo responded. "Once at the University, we can appeal to those who wish to put an end to this. Then we could move against Lucian—"

"And the god who's pulling the strings?" I threw in, unable to help myself. "We'll want to move against him or her, right?"

Apollo's vibrant blue eyes met mine and he held my gaze. "Yes. We will."

Right then I wanted to call him out, but the only thing stopping me was Aiden . . . and that part of me, the tiny part that Laadan had claimed was growing, becoming more mature. *She* sort of understood.

"But I need to check in with Dionysus." Apollo was still looking at me, and I knew I'd be seeing him real soon. "Check you guys later."

And then he was gone.

Aiden slid me a sidelong glance. "Sometimes I really hate him."

"You and me both," I muttered.

* * *

We arrived back at Apple River just as the sky overhead was turning from black to a dark blue. The cabin was dark as we climbed out of the Hummer and the distant call of birds was the only sound.

Aiden stretched, bowing his back as he worked out the kinks. He stopped, catching me watching him from the other side of the vehicle. "Come here."

He was probably the only person in the world who could demand that of me and I'd listen. All too obediently, I headed around the front of the Hummer and stopped in front of him. "What?" I asked, stifling a yawn.

Aiden cupped my cheeks and tilted my head back. "You didn't sleep at all."

"Neither did you."

A tired grin appeared. "I was driving."

I placed my hands on his wrists. Our eyes locked. "I can't believe we went to the Underworld and came back out."

"Me, neither." His thumbs traced along the curve of my cheekbones. "You were perfect."

"Except for the spiders . . ."

His head dipped and his nose brushed mine. "I wasn't talking about the spiders."

"You weren't?"

Aiden laughed and his breath was warm and tantalizing. "No. I was thinking about what came after the spiders."

"Oh . . . oh!" I sucked in a sharp breath and my legs suddenly felt weak. "*That*."

"Yes." His lips brushed mine. "That."

I started to smile, because that really had been perfect, but then Aiden kissed me and I melted into him. There was strength in that kiss, along with love and a taste of what a future would be like with him. I loved—*loved*—that in the midst of everything, we could still have moments like this. Where it was just us and there weren't any walls between us. The kiss deepened, his tongue slipping past my lips, and my fingers dug into his wrists. A low, sultry growl came from Aiden, and I wanted—

"You two should really get a room," Apollo said from out of nowhere. "My poor eyes . . ."

I groaned. Even in his true identity, he still had impeccable timing.

"Gods," Aiden spat. He pulled back, casting Apollo a disgusted look over my head. "Do you get off on sneaking up on us?"

"You probably don't want to know what I get off on."

I made a face. "Ew."

Aiden kissed my forehead as his hands slipped off my cheeks. Dropping an arm around my shoulders, he pulled me into the shelter of his body and I went, resting my cheek against his chest. "Did you already talk to Dionysus?"

Apollo leaned against the bumper. "Yes. He's on it as we speak."

"How can we trust that Dionysus isn't the god behind this?" I smothered another yawn. "And that he won't lie to us?"

"Dionysus cares little for war, and he doesn't have the motivation to engineer something like this."

"How long until he lets us know?" Aiden asked.

"We should hear from him by the end of the day." Apollo's gaze flickered to the deep blue sky. "It's almost morning. You two should rest."

Aiden glanced down at me. "Let's head in."

I pulled away, glancing at Apollo. "I'll be in in a few seconds. I want to talk to Apollo."

He hesitated, sending me a questioning look. I hated keeping him in the dark about this, but there was no other way, because if Aiden knew, he would stop it, and then the world would go to crap.

"It's okay." I smiled. "I'll be right in."

Aiden looked at Apollo and let out a low breath. "Okay. I'll go . . . wake up Deacon or something."

"I'm sure he'll appreciate that," I said.

A brief smile appeared. "True."

At the sound of the front door shutting behind Aiden, I looked at Apollo and felt the mask I'd been wearing slip away.

Our gazes met and Apollo sighed. "Alexandria . . ."

"I knew there was something you'd been keeping from me. That there was a bigger reason to why you all would want to keep me alive when it would be so much easier to just kill me. It would fix the problem with Seth, so I just didn't get why you'd risk it."

He looked at a loss to what to say. Good—I'd struck a god speechless. Score one for me. I was going to go for point two. "You need the God Killer."

A long moment passed. "We need to stop this from happening again."

"You need me to kill the god responsible." Anger grew inside me, but so did hurt, and that hurt had been festering since we'd left the Underworld. I didn't know why. Apollo might be related to me by blood, but he was a god and they'd missed out on the whole empathy train, sort of like a bunch of sociopaths, but it still hurt something fierce.

It cut deep.

Because in the end, I was the lion *and* the lamb; I would slaughter and then be slaughtered. Apollo didn't say it, but I saw it in what he wouldn't say.

"We cannot risk this kind of destruction again, Alexandria. Thousands of innocent people have died, and there *will* be more. And even if we stop the First, this will happen again." He placed his hand on my shoulder and it was heavy. "We cannot kill one another. We need the only thing that can kill us. We need the God Killer—we need you."

I stared at him, dumbfounded. "You don't want me to kill Seth, then."

He snorted. "On most days I do, but you must take his power, and he has to be alive for that. I need you to be able to defeat him and transfer his power to you."

My hands balled into fists and it took everything in me not to grab hold of those golden locks and rip them out. "You've been lying to me this entire time."

"No I haven't." He didn't even blink.

"Bull! You told me before I Awakened that you wanted me to kill Seth! You know, over grape soda and Spider-man cake?"

"I *wanted* you to kill Seth, but it's not what I *need*."

My mouth dropped open. "That's not even semantics!"

"And I didn't know for sure then that there was a way to transfer his power to you," he argued calmly. "I had my suspicions. So did my sister, but we couldn't be sure. Either way, he cannot be allowed to take your power. If you cannot defeat him and take his power, then you must kill him."

Apollo made it all sound so simple, like he was asking me to go to the store and pick up Crunchy Cheetos and if they didn't have them in stock, to get Cheetos Puffs. Insane.

"I don't want it to end like you fear, but there is only so much I can do to stay the hands of others."

"Yeah, because after I take out this god—if we figure out who it is—there's a good chance the gods will turn on me, because I will be a threat. And I bet they have an Order member just lying around, right? Even if I don't do anything, they will act as judge and jury on a crime I haven't committed?"

There was that damn pause again and then he said, "Everyone dies, but in the end it comes down to what you are willing to die *for*, Alexandria."

Gods, there was a part of me—a huge part of me—that wanted to kick Apollo in the balls, but I got it. As messed up as it was, I got it. And maybe that was why I wasn't flipping out on him. The loss of one life, maybe two, was worth the safety of billions. I could see that and if I was totally impartial about this—say, they weren't talking about *me*—then I'd probably even support it.

But it was me.

It would be me.

That was a lot to swallow. It was something that I couldn't really even begin to process. I felt too selfish, but I also knew what had to be done.

Gods, I was so not old enough or mature enough to be making these kinds of decisions.

It grew so quiet between us that the gentle winds stirring the branches seemed too loud. If I didn't have my freaky god-sensing abilities right now, I'd have thought he'd left. But he was still there, waiting.

"And there's no other way?" I asked.

He didn't respond, and I took his silence as a no.

Heart heavy, I lifted my head. "What will happen if I die?"

Apollo didn't answer immediately. "You will have a warrior's death. There is pride in that and you will want for nothing."

Except to live, but I figured that was a moot point. "Will you make sure that . . . that Aiden will be okay?"

The god's eyes met mine and he nodded.

Throat burning and tightening, I focused on the dark gravel. "He . . . he had to see his parents afterward, Apollo. I don't want him to see me, okay? Can you make sure he doesn't?"

"If that is what you wish."

I pressed my lips together, relieved a little that Aiden would be spared that horror—maybe not the bulk of it, but some of it. "And will you make sure Marcus and the rest of them are okay?"

"Yes."

"Okay." I swallowed, but I still felt like I was choking. "I want to be left alone for a while."

"Alex—"

I looked up then, meeting his gaze. "Please leave."

He looked like he was going to say something, but then he nodded and simply vanished. I don't know how long I stood there, but eventually I shuffled over to the porch and sat down on the steps.

The night air was still cool and it stung my hot cheeks. Tears burned my eyes, but I refused to let them fall. Crying served nothing. It wouldn't change what would happen. If I somehow managed to get to Seth, transfer his power to me before he took mine, and destroy the mystery god, I'd still be put down like a rabid animal. Possibly even Seth would be, as well, although he'd no longer be a threat. Maybe without me around to influence him, he'd get better. He'd just be the Apollyon then, like it was supposed to be—only one of us and all that jazz.

I rubbed my eyes until they ached.

What day was it? Sometime in April? Less than a month from now, I was supposed to be graduating from the Covenant. That was so obviously not going to happen. So much had changed, and so much would never be the same. I wondered if my Fate had changed, too, or if this had always been a part of it and no one had thought to clue me in.

An idea occurred to me. It was insane, but I thought about letting the wonky connection with Seth happen. The ache was in my temples. Maybe I could tell him what I knew. Maybe there was a part of him that still cared enough.

I shook my head and lowered my hands.

Seth would probably just use it as another reason for me to jump ship.

Taking several deep breaths, I pushed thoughts of Seth out of my head and, for some reason, I thought about my father. Features roughened by a hard life fell into place. Broad cheekbones and a strong chin spoke of a warrior's face. We really didn't look too much alike, but it was his eyes . . . they were mine.

I tried not to think about my dad. Perhaps that was wrong, but it was hard sitting here knowing that he was in the Catskills. And it was even harder acknowledging that there might be a good chance we'd never meet face-to-face, aware of what we were to each other.

Squeezing my knees together, I thought about the sacrifice he was making—had made—for so many years. Deep down I knew he probably wanted to be here with me, but he had a job to do. Through and through, my father was a Sentinel.

I respected him for that.

I don't know how long I sat there, but it couldn't have been that long before the door behind me eased open. Boards creaked as the footsteps drew near.

Aiden sat beside me, still in his Sentinel uniform. He stared straight ahead and said nothing. I looked at him. The dark waves were messy, going in every which direction. A slight shadow was forming on his jaw.

"Didn't wake up Deacon?" I asked.

"Nah, if I did then I'd probably never get to bed. He'll need entertainment or something and you know how that goes." Aiden tilted his head toward me. "When did Apollo leave?"

"A little while ago."

Aiden was quiet for a moment. "Is there anything I should know?"

My heart skipped a beat. "No."

His eyes met mine and I couldn't tell if he believed me, but he extended his arm. I scooted over, fitting myself against the side of his body as he locked his arms around me. He rested his cheek against my hair and I felt his breath.

Minutes passed, and then he said, "We're in this together, Alex. Don't ever forget that. We're in this together to the end."

28

By the time Apollo reappeared later that night, I hadn't really come to terms with everything. I mean, how could I? Going through all of this, facing only gods-knew-what, knowing there was a ninety-nine percent chance I'd die in the end really didn't help with the whole motivation factor. So I decided to do the only thing I could do.

Forget about the end result.

Probably not the wisest method, but it was the only way I could do this and keep sane, because right now I didn't know how to change any of it.

Apollo didn't return alone. When he popped into the living room, he brought along Dionysus. It was the first time I'd seen the god. He looked like a frat boy in his Hawaiian shirt and cargo shorts.

Dionysus dropped onto the couch in a lazy, arrogant sprawl. His heavy-lidded gaze moved over the females in the room, sizing them up like one looks at a menu. When his freaky eyes landed on me, I arched a brow.

He grinned. "So this is the Apollyon?"

"That would be me."

"For some reason, I expected you to be taller."

What the hell? Folding my arms, I shot him a bland look. "I don't know why people keep saying that."

Aiden leaned against the desk I sat on. "You *are* pretty short."

My height wasn't our biggest problem. Thankfully Marcus reined the conversation in, bringing it back to more important things. "Do you have news of Lucian?"

The god stretched, folding his arms behind his head. "Well, I got as close as I could. Something's different this time around."

Apollo frowned. I didn't like it when gods frowned—usually it meant something really, really bad. "What do you mean?"

"I could only get *so* close. Something barred me from getting among them, even barred my nymphs." He wiggled his toes. "No ward can do that. Only another god."

"I don't understand," I said. "How could another god block you?"

"A powerful one can, little Apollyon." Dionysus winked one all-white eye. "It would be like hitting an invisible wall. The First and the pure-blood are well protected."

"Hermes?" Marcus said, rubbing his jaw thoughtfully.

Dionysus snorted. "Hermes couldn't pull something like that off."

"Who could?" Solos asked, gaze shrewd.

"One of the core," Dionysus answered with a smirk.

"What do you mean?" Luke leaned forward in his chair, dropping his arms over his knees. "'One of the core'?"

The god spared him a brief glance. "There's a social . . . or political structure to things in Olympus—a ranking by power."

Across the room, Laadan cleared her throat. Beside her, Olivia remained quiet. She hadn't spoken since asking about Caleb earlier. I had kept his promise, as much as it sucked.

"Can you give us a little more detail?" Laadan asked politely. "I believe this is something that we are unaware of."

"Not really," Apollo answered. "You modeled your Councils after Olympus, with each Council having a leader, so to speak. Olympus is the same."

My curiosity swelled. "So who is the core?"

Dionysus might not have had pupils, but I was pretty sure that, when his head swung back to me, he was staring at my chest. And I was also sure that Aiden believed so, too, considering the way he stiffened.

"Zeus and Hera, followed by the ever-popular Apollo and his sister Artemis, then Ares and Athena," Dionysus answered. "Last but not least, Hades and Poseidon. They are the most powerful gods and the only ones who could pull that off."

"Well it's not Hades. He wanted to take me to the Underworld. And I doubt it was Poseidon since he went all water-god on Deity Island."

Aiden slid Apollo a look.

The sun god's eyes narrowed. "Yeah, like it's me."

"Could really be any of them," Dionysus said, and then yawned loudly. "They'd have to be fooling everyone, so they could've fooled even us." He shrugged as if none of this was a big deal. "It is what it is."

"Did you sense anything?" Apollo's hands closed at his sides when Dionysus shook his head. "Did you see *anything* that might tell us who the god was? Anything?"

"Really wasn't looking for that. You told me to see how many that idiot pure-blood had with him, and I did."

A muscle popped in Apollo's jaw and he all but growled, "So what did you see?"

"Nothing good."

"Details," Apollo said, exhaling through his nose. "Details."

I wondered if Dionysus was drunk or high. My gaze caught Deacon's on the other end of the couch, and I could tell he was thinking the same thing. Even Lea, who was sitting on the arm beside Deacon, was giving Dionysus a *what the hell* look.

"He has damn near close to a thousand half-blood Sentinels and Guards, maybe more. Plus, he's surrounded by some sort of inner circle—other pures. And it gets even better." He paused, and I knew it was for dramatic effect. "There were mortals with him."

My mouth dropped open. "*What?*"

"Soldiers," Dionysus replied. "Mortal soldiers—like the 'Be all that you can be' kind of soldiers. There were probably about five hundred of them."

I almost fell off the desk.

"How is that possible?" Lea demanded. Then she squeezed her eyes shut, features pinched. "He's using a compulsion."

"No." Marcus shook his head as he turned to Apollo. "No pure-blood could control that many mortals. Not even if he had a hundred pures surrounding him."

"It's the god." Apollo looked disgusted.

My stomach heaved at the thought. Using mortals like that was wrong on so many levels. They'd never survive a fight against a Sentinel or Guard, no matter how many guns they had. We were simply so much faster and better trained. Mortals would be cannon fodder and nothing more. It was revolting.

Anger filled the room, so thick I could practically taste it.

"I don't get it." Deacon ran a hand over his head, clasping the back of his neck. "How is the mortal world not paying attention to something like that?"

"One of the mortals must be high up in the army, someone who can make that kind of call and give some sort of reason." Apollo's lips thinned. "At least that's what I'd do."

"And they could've called some sort of state of emergency," Marcus added. "No part of the U.S. has gone completely unscathed, and I'm beginning to wonder if this god even cares about exposure."

Aiden gripped the edge of the desk. "I think it's obvious that the risk of exposure isn't important. Hell, maybe it's even planned."

All eyes turned on him.

"Think about it. Why else would a god be orchestrating all of this? Or going along with what Lucian wants?" Aiden asked. "To take out the gods and then what—rule Olympus? Or rule Olympus *and* the mortal realm?"

A shiver raced across my shoulders. My wildest imagination couldn't even fathom what it would be like if the world knew that gods did exist—and on top of that, if the world ended up being ruled by one.

"We can't let that happen," I said.

Apollo's eyes met mine. "No. We can't."

I averted my gaze, because right now I didn't want to think about what stopping this god meant. I cleared my throat. "I wonder if Lucian and Seth even know."

"Does it matter?" Lea asked, snotty as ever.

My lips quirked at her tone. "I guess it doesn't, but you have to wonder who's using who. And what will happen to them in the end if the god is successful. Does he plan to keep them around or get rid of them? Do they even have a clue?"

Most of the people in the room couldn't care less—that much was apparent—but Marcus strode over to where I sat and leaned against the desk on the other side of me. "I doubt they know. In a way, no matter what they have been responsible for, it is tragic."

"It will be tragic if they succeed." Dionysus stood and stretched his arms over his head. "Well, I'm out."

Apollo nodded and Dionysus bowed to the room, sweeping his arms out to the sides with a flourish. And then he was gone.

I shook my head. "Okay. Who else thinks he was high as a kite?"

Hands went up across the room and I grinned.

"So, we're leaving tomorrow morning for the University?" Olivia asked as she pulled on a springy curl. "Don't you think that, if this god is so conniving and smart, he's figured out that Alex will be going there? I mean, even if he's using Lucian and Seth for his ultimate evil plans, he's still going to need Alex, right? Because he's probably controlling Seth, or wants to."

Everyone grew quiet and I felt like a little ant under a magnifying glass.

I glanced at Apollo, but he was staring at the globe on the desk.

"Making any move is going to be as dangerous as sitting here," Marcus said finally. "But in South Dakota, we will be safer."

"Alex will be safer there, too," Luke murmured, staring at his hands.

I opened my mouth, but Lea spoke. "Well, I think our job is to make sure that Seth and this god don't get to Alex."

My mouth really dropped open.

She smiled smartly at me. "Can't have you going all psycho-Alex again and ending the world as we know it."

"She has a point." Deacon grinned.

I narrowed my eyes. "Wait. Guys, I don't want—"

"What?" Aiden nudged me with his elbow. "You don't want us having your back?"

"That's not what this is." I stared at Apollo, but damn, that globe *fascinated him.* "If there's going to be a god gunning for my butt—"

"It is a nice butt," Aiden murmured as he studied the toes of his boots. A small grin was on his face.

I stared at him a moment. "*Plus* Seth is out looking for me, this . . . this is going to be really dangerous. I don't want you guys risking your lives for me."

Lea snorted. "Damn, Alex, your ego is out of control. You know me. I'd sooner throw you in front of a daimon any other day, but if keeping you away from them means saving millions of lives, then I'm on your team. So this is bigger than you."

"I *know* this is bigger than me." My cheeks burned, and Deacon's idiot grin wasn't helping. "And I know you'd toss me in front of a daimon, but I don't want to see any of you get hurt."

"Everyone here knows the risks, Alex." Marcus' voice was stern, reminding me of the days back in the Covenant when he'd spent the majority of his time yelling at me. "No one is being forced to do this."

"And none of us would do anything else." Olivia offered a tentative smile. "All of us have lost people because of what's happening. We all have reasons to make sure this stops and doesn't happen again."

"Even me," Deacon said. "I haven't gotten my regular twelve hours of sleep since all of this went down, and that is damn tragic."

Aiden rolled his eyes.

"Everyone is ready to fight." Laadan crossed the room, smiling as she stood next to Marcus. "This isn't just your battle."

"It was never just your battle," Solos corrected.

"In other words," Marcus said, his jade-colored eyes meeting mine, "you're not in this alone. You never were."

"And you're not going to be," Aiden finished quietly.

Wow. I think I sort of loved everyone in this room right now, even Lea. Tears burned my eyes, and I tipped my head forward so no one could see. The thing was that, ever since I realized how all of this could end—probably would end—I'd never felt more alone. But sitting here, hearing them . . .

"Group hug time?" Deacon suggested.

"Shut up," I said, but I laughed.

Aiden slid an arm around my shoulders and tipped me toward him. Right in front of the entire room full of halfs, pures, and a god, he kissed my temple. "You're just going to have to accept that this isn't going to just be you. It's going to be all of us."

I lifted my head and looked at all of them, at a loss as to what to say.

Luke smiled. "I know. We're awesome."

I laughed again.

"And we were born to do this," Olivia said, shrugging. "We'd be doing this in a month or so, anyway. We're ready."

Lea slid Olivia a grin that said she was more than ready. "Bring it."

29

I'd only gotten a few hours of sleep when the sun broke through the blinds the next morning. Listening to everyone tell me they were ready to face whatever was thrown our way . . . even hours later, I still couldn't find the right words for how much it meant. But an unseen weight also had settled on my shoulders and it'd grown overnight, pressing me straight down through the mattress. I couldn't stop any of them—and I wouldn't, just like they wouldn't stop me—but a thousand things raced through my head.

And the main thoughts centered on any of them losing their lives in this. So many had already perished, and no matter how Positive Polly I tried to be, I knew deep in my core that something terrible, something violent, waited in the future. Death had come long before they'd pledged to see this through, and it was on the other side of the door, or in another state, waiting patiently, because nothing was as unwavering as Death. It probably had the most time in the world.

Even though I knew what awaited them—awaited us all—in the Underworld, I couldn't bear the idea of seeing any of them fall. If I could, I'd seal them all up in the cage downstairs, even Aiden. No doubt that wouldn't go over well, but I knew that, between what Apollo needed of me, what Solaris had warned, and how far gone Seth seemed to be, this would end in disaster.

When Aiden shifted beside me and dropped an arm over my waist, I grimaced. "Sorry."

He snuggled closer. "About what?"

"I kept waking you up." I pressed back against him, looking over my shoulder. Two silvery eyes peered from behind a mess of dark hair. "I know I did."

"Not that much." Aiden rose up on one arm. His body was relaxed, but concern radiated in his gaze. "How much did you sleep?"

I thought about lying, but I shook my head, and then wriggled onto my back. "We're leaving in a few hours."

Aiden nodded as his eyes searched mine.

Twisting my fingers together, I tried to smile. "How long will we be on the road?"

"We're looking at about ten hours."

Yikes. "Deacon's riding with us?"

"Yes. So are Luke and Marcus. Solos is taking the girls."

Something stirred restlessly in the pit of my stomach. I didn't want to name it. "You think that's okay?"

Aiden placed his hand over mine, stilling them. "Olivia and Lea are very good. You know that."

They were. Especially Lea—she was like She-Ra. And Solos and Marcus had gone out earlier, picking up two throwaway cell phones to help us keep in communication.

"And you know Solos will never let anything happen to them. Neither will Laadan." As he spoke, he eased my hands apart and threaded his fingers through mine. "We have six hundred miles of no man's land to get through. We're going to be okay."

That thing in my stomach tipped over. "I'm not afraid."

"I didn't say that you were."

My eyes narrowed.

Aiden cracked a grin. "But you are."

"I'm—"

"Do I need to find a sensory deprivation chamber again?" When my cheeks flushed at the memory, his grin spread into a full smile. Deep dimples appeared and, instead of my stomach tumbling, my heart did. "It's okay, Alex."

"What is?" My voice sounded terribly fragile, and normally I would've hated that, especially considering I was this big bad Apollyon, but with Aiden, I didn't need to pretend. Sometimes I forgot that, though.

"To be afraid, Alex, it's okay. What we're facing is some scary . . . shit."

I smiled then. "You cussed."

"I did."

My smile quickly faded though, because we *were* facing some scary shit. Crap that Aiden didn't even know the half of. "Are you scared?"

For a moment, he didn't answer. All that could be heard were the slow, steady ticking of the ancient wall clock and the distant chirping of the birds outside the rustic log walls. "Yes."

Hearing him admit that was both relieving and frightening. "You're never afraid."

Aiden shook his head, his smile slipping into a wry one. "You know that's not true. There're a lot of things that terrify me, Alex."

I met his eyes. "Tell me."

Stretching out beside me, he tugged me over so my cheek was pressed against his chest. "I'm afraid that Deacon is going to get hurt . . . or worse. I'm afraid that we will lose more people." There was a pause and his heart picked up under my cheek. "I'm terrified of what you're going to face—what you have to do and how it's going to affect you."

My breath caught around a denial as I curled my fingers into the sheet tangled around his hips. "I'll be okay." Those words were bitter on my tongue.

His chest rose sharply. "I don't want you to be okay."

I lifted my head so I could see his eyes. They were a dark gray and shadowed. He tried for a smile, but like mine earlier, it looked pained.

"I want you to be more than okay." Aiden cupped my cheek gently. "I don't want you to have nightmares for the rest of your life, and see Seth's face instead of your mother's. I don't want *this* to haunt you."

Suddenly, everything felt too real and I was too close. Sitting up, I put some space between us, but I still felt hot and suffocated. "I know what has to be done."

And I also knew what that likely meant for me.

He followed, capturing the newly gained distance. His face, those beautiful lips were only inches from mine. "I know, Alex. I also know that you're going to do it, because I cannot even think for one second that you will fail. You can't. You *won't*."

At the pain and determination in his voice, I pressed my lips together. Failing and succeeding kind of ended the same.

"Look at me," he ordered.

I hadn't realized I'd looked away, but I felt his hand on my cheek. He guided my chin up until our eyes locked and I couldn't move.

"But I also know that killing Seth isn't going to be easy, and I don't mean on a physical level. I know deep down you care for him. Maybe a part of you even loves him."

Horrified of what he must think, because he'd nailed it right on the head, I shook my head. "Aiden—"

"I understand." The small grin that played on his lips was real. "I know it's not the same as what you feel for me, but it doesn't make it any less strong or important."

"He . . ." I didn't know what to say. Aiden was right. Part of me still loved Seth, and it wasn't in the way I felt for Aiden, but it wasn't any less real or powerful. Even after all that Seth had done, I couldn't forget all that he had done *before* that. It had been the same with my mom, but in the end, I had taken her life like it had been fated all along.

You'll kill the ones you love . . .

Aiden's forehead pressed against mine. "Seth was there for you when you needed someone. You guys share this bond that . . . that is more than him connecting with you. We broke the connection, but there's something else underneath that. He's a part of you."

I drew in a surprised breath. "He's . . . he's done such terrible things."

"He has." Aiden pressed a kiss to my temple. "But he has done some good things, and I know you can't forget how he used to be. I know none of this will be easy for you."

Killing Seth would break a piece of me, and no matter how long I walked this earth afterward, it couldn't be repaired. He was a part of me—a part that was a bit insane—but still. It would change me in a way I couldn't fathom. Just as facing down my mom had. But this time was different.

Apollo didn't want me to kill Seth; he wanted me to strip him of his power. Knowing Seth, he'd probably prefer death. And if Seth figured out what I was up to, he'd come after me. So I would have to stop him—kill him. Killing Seth would be the only way I walked out of this alive.

"Alex?" Aiden whispered. "Talk to me, *agapi mou*."

"Don't be afraid." My voice was hoarse. "I'll be . . . okay."

His hand slipped to the nape of my neck, and he held on as if he could keep me there for ever. "You'll tell me that you'll be okay. And you'll act like you're okay, but . . ."

I squeezed my eyes shut. Aiden would know better. Seconds passed in silence. The truth was on the tip of my tongue, burning me from the inside out. I wanted to tell him what could happen—I really needed to—but putting that on him wasn't fair. Time stretched out, but it wasn't enough.

"'You will kill the ones you love.'" My laugh was dry and brittle. "I hate that damn oracle."

Aiden's fingers splayed across my cheek. "If I could change this, I would. I'd do anything to save you from this."

"I know." I tipped my head a little to the side and kissed him softly. "But Fate is a bitch."

"Or a bastard," he said lightly.

I laughed, because whenever Aiden cussed, I couldn't help it. It sounded wrong rolling off his tongue, but still elegant, somehow. Like a British person cussing. Anyway, I just couldn't talk about this anymore. I didn't even want to think about it, but I'd need a brain scrub to fix that.

Leaning forward, I looped my arms around his neck and all but climbed into his lap. "Can we talk about something else?"

Aiden looked like he was going to argue, but he nodded.

Staring into his eyes, I thought back to the days when he used to pop in and watch me train. That made me smile. "I used to think you were the source of my failure."

"What?" He arched a brow as he wrapped his arms around my waist.

"I could never get things right when you were around, especially when you used to watch me in class." I shrugged. "I wanted to be perfect in your eyes. I wanted you to be proud of me."

"I am."

I beamed at him, smiling for real for the first time since this conversation began. "But you're kind of like my source of strength, even when I couldn't concentrate because of you."

Aiden tilted his head to the side, causing his lips to graze my cheek. "We had the same problem then."

"Doubtful."

"You have no idea how hard it was." Aiden sighed against my lips. "To train you—to be so close when all I wanted . . ."

There was a flutter in my chest. "What did you want?"

He leaned in, his warm breath becoming my world. "How about I show you?"

Oh, I so liked where this was heading. So much better than the doom and gloom crap that wanted to pull me under, bringing Aiden along with me. "I'm down with that."

Laughing softly, he erased that miniscule distance and I let out a little sigh. If he kissed me like that every couple of hours, it would keep the darkness at bay. It would obliterate everything I feared and would probably come to regret. My world would be close to perfect.

There was a knock, and we drew apart an instant before the door swung open and Deacon's mop of a head popped in. Aiden groaned, but his eyes lightened by several shades.

"Good morning!" Too much cheer rang in his voice for this time of the morning.

My cheeks burned as I mumbled, "Morning."

Before either of us could say another word, Deacon darted from the door and launched himself onto the bed, soaring through the air like a human projectile. I jerked to the side with a split-second to spare. He landed with his legs on his brother and the upper part of his body between us.

Deacon threw his arms behind his head, folding them as he tipped his head back and grinned at us. "It's like a puppy pile."

"A puppy pile?" Aiden arched a brow. "You are so weird."

"Whatever." Deacon's gray eyes flicked to me. "Was I interrupting anything?"

Aiden rolled his eyes and I fought a grin. "Not at all, brother."

"Good, because you guys better get your butts in gear. We're leaving in an hour." Deacon crossed his ankles, letting out a contented sigh. "Time to hit the road."

I tucked my hair back, wondering how much coffee he'd had to be up this early and this hyper. "You're so unnaturally wound up."

"I'm excited," he replied. "I'm looking at this road trip like a real life game of Oregon Trail."

My brows rose. "Are you going to catch typhoid fever?"

"Actually, I was thinking about breaking a leg or drowning."

"There's always starving to death." My lips split into a grin. "Or you could get kidnapped by Indians."

Deacon's eyes widened dramatically. "They'd want me for my glorious blond locks."

"It's about time someone cut your hair." Aiden mussed the already unruly curls and then threw the covers back. "I'm taking a shower."

The look Aiden sent me said he hadn't planned on doing it alone, and my stomach did all kinds of crazy twists and turns. It didn't help that he strode across the room in all his bare-chested glory. The heat that zinged through my veins was hard to deny, but Deacon apparently wasn't going anywhere.

I waited until Aiden closed the door and I heard the hiss of the shower before I glanced down at his younger brother. "What?"

His lips tipped up on one side. "We need to chat."

Having no clue what was going to come out of his mouth, but positive it would be entertaining, I wriggled down and stretched out beside him. "Okay. About what?"

"You need to stay alive."

Okay, so not what I was expecting. "I'm not planning to off myself, Deacon."

"No, but you have that look of someone who is facing down death, practically even expects it." Deacon paused and his gaze went to the bare rafters in the ceiling. "I know what that looks like. I saw it in the mirror for a long time."

My mouth opened, but I couldn't find any words.

He laughed dryly. "I hated living after seeing what'd happened to my parents and those other people. If it hadn't been for Aiden, I wouldn't have survived. I shouldn't have survived. Neither should he." He gave a lopsided shrug. "I guess I had a mad case of survivor's guilt or something lame like that. Every time I drank or got high, I secretly hoped that I would overdo it, you know?"

As his words sank in, my chest ached. I reached over, placing my hand on his arm. "Deacon . . ."

"Ah, I'm okay now. I think I am, at least. But you know why I never really went there?" Deacon turned his head toward me and I knew what he meant. "I wasn't scared of death, but I was scared of what me dying would do to him."

Deacon nodded at the bathroom door and my gaze followed his. I couldn't see Aiden and I knew he couldn't hear us, but my heart was pounding like I'd just run up a thousand steps.

"He wouldn't get past losing you," I said, swallowing hard. "He's so strong, but . . ."

"It would kill him. I know. Losing you would kill him."

A chill washed over me, like I'd stepped into a freezer. Sitting up swiftly, I tugged my hair over one shoulder. "Why are you telling me this?"

"You've had that same look ever since you came back from the Underworld." There was a pause, and he looked at me with all the seriousness no one ever gave him credit for, and in that moment he reminded me so much of Aiden. "Whatever you do, don't break my brother's heart. You are his world. And if you leave it, it will destroy him."

30

Our Hummer was the party car—the cool one. Or at least that's what I believed. Between Luke and Deacon, the ten-hour drive to the wilds of South Dakota wasn't turning out to be that bad. Poor Marcus looked like he wanted to duct tape the two boys' mouths shut after two hours of their non-stop rundown of the last season of *Supernatural*. I wasn't complaining. Then, Luke moved on to this new show about thrones and dragons, which he tried to explain to Aiden. Seeing as Aiden was a fan of old black-and-white TV shows, Luke wasn't getting very far.

Marcus looked like he had a headache, which mirrored how I felt. It had nothing to do with the boys' chatter or the ridiculous—but hilarious—car games they insisted on playing. And I was pretty sure that, if Deacon leaned between the seats and punched Aiden on the arm one more time he saw a Beetle, Aiden was going to the pull the car over and strangle him.

I was also sure Marcus would hold Deacon down. The man had to have a wicked bruise on his leg from the last punch Deacon had delivered.

But after the fourth hour, restlessness set in. Minutes from turning into the kid the parent threatens to turn the car around on, I tried to get some rest. It wasn't like the scenery was much to look at. Lots of fields. Then lots of hills. Then lots of trees. Boredom itched at my skin as I stared at the wards, drawn in Titan blood throughout the car, that kept the gods from sensing me. But the fact that I was stuck in the vehicle for the foreseeable future wasn't the worst part. The steadily increasing throbbing in my temples sent a nervous rush through my system.

Seth was there, pecking away, waiting for that moment he could pop in and have a chat. Part of me almost welcomed it, because it would be something to do, but that was so stupid. Talking with Seth wouldn't help anything. He was on one side of the fence and I was clear on the other side.

I didn't want to think at all.

Twisting in the seat, my eyes met my uncle's. I smiled as he nodded at Deacon. The pure had finally passed out, with his cheek plastered against the window. Beside him, Luke was staring out the window, jaw locked down tight.

Not wanting to wake the talkative beast, I said nothing and turned back around. My booted foot slid over the sickle blade resting on the floor. We were just as stocked and well-armed as we'd been when we drove to Kansas.

I settled in the seat, carefully stretching out my legs when I really wanted to flail about. Out of the corner of my eye, I caught Aiden's amused grin. I made a face at him and he laughed softly.

Time slowed down to a crawl. Every time I looked at the clock on the dashboard I would've sworn two hours had gone by, but it was only twenty minutes later. When we hit the halfway point, Solos called Aiden. They needed to get gas.

Aiden wasn't thrilled about it. "We're too close to Minneapolis."

In other words, we were too close to a heavily populated area. Nearly every major city in the U.S. had communities of pures on the outskirts. Where there were pures, there were daimons. And that also meant there would be Sentinels and Guards—those who might be working with Lucian.

But we didn't have any choice. Both vehicles were running low on gas, and it was either stop now or run out of gas in the middle of nowhere and get eaten by wild coyotes and bears.

We pulled into a decent-sized travel area and I immediately reached for the door handle.

"I prefer you'd stay in the car," Aiden said, unbuckling.

I frowned. "Why? I have the talisman."

"I know." He shot me a look. "But knowing our luck, someone will recognize you."

"But I have to use the bathroom."

"Hold it," Luke said, opening the car door. "I'll get you something to snack on, and some water—lots of water."

I glared at him. "That's so wrong."

Everyone but me rushed from the Hummer and I flung myself back against the seat, folding my arms. I got that we didn't need another god smackdown in the middle of the gas station, but damn . . .

Aiden headed toward the other Hummer while Marcus pumped gas. Here I was, the freaking Apollyon, and I couldn't even go inside to get a bag of beef jerky by myself. Geez.

A few moments later, Aiden came around to my side of the car. I debated leaving the window up, but I rolled it down. He leaned in, resting on his forearms.

"Hey," he said, grinning.

I knew I was pouting, but I couldn't feel my butt.

"Olivia and Lea are checking out the bathroom. Looks like it's outside and around the back."

"Oh, thank the gods." I slumped in my seat.

His grin spread on one side. "I'll make sure Luke gets you something other than water."

"You're the best." I popped forward and kissed him quickly. "I mean it."

On his way past us, Marcus' eyes narrowed. "I feel like I'm going to need to separate you two."

Aiden's cheeks flushed as he pulled back and cleared his throat.

Marcus stopped beside him, folding his arms. "Especially the sleeping arrangements. And I'm not naïve enough to—"

"Whoa!" I cut in. "Not a topic that I'm willing to delve into."

Marcus gave me a bland look. "You are my niece and I'm your guardian."

"I'm eighteen."

"And you're still too—"

"Olivia! Bathroom break!" I threw open the door, nearly knocking Marcus over. Shooting my uncle a quick grin, I darted around him.

Aiden grabbed my arm. "Be careful."

"Of course. Other than dying of fumes and wanting to hurl, it's just a public restroom."

He still looked like he wanted to escort me in there, but Marcus was also eyeing Aiden like he wanted to punch him again. Aiden let go and I joined the girls at the sidewalk.

"What's going on over there?" Olivia asked.

I looked over my shoulder. Marcus's mouth was flying a mile a minute, and Aiden stood there, stiff and silent. I grimaced. "You don't even want to know."

"Probably has to do with the fact that you and Aiden are having sex," Lea announced, crossing her arms.

My jaw dropped.

"Nice." Olivia swatted her on the arm. "Way to just throw that out there."

Lea shrugged. "Hey, it is what it is. He's a hottie. I'd be doing it with him every five seconds."

"Okay. Thanks for sharing."

Olivia eyed the other half. "Speaking of having sex like a horned-up rabbit, have you heard from Jackson? He wasn't at the Covenant when . . ." She looked around and lowered her voice. "He wasn't there when Poseidon went nuts."

"No. My cell died and I don't have a charger." Her eyes narrowed on the overcast sky. "I don't know what he might be doing. We weren't really as close as you guys think. At least, we didn't talk a lot."

Olivia snorted.

"I don't think he's with Seth and Lucian," I said as we started around the corner of the cement building.

"Why?" Olivia tucked a tight curl back.

"Remember when Jackson got his face rearranged?" We'd stopped outside the bathroom door, and I could already smell the funk. The girls nodded. "I'm pretty sure Seth did that to him."

"Holy crap," Olivia murmured as she slid the key into the door. "Because of what Jackson did to you in class?"

I nodded. Jackson had taken sparring too far, planting his boot in my face—I had a tiny scar to prove it—and I was sure that Instructor Romvi had goaded him into it. As we headed into the bathroom and I looked for a somewhat decent stall, I wondered if Romvi was still alive.

Romvi had disappeared after Linard had delivered Head Minister's Telly's ultimatum, and Seth had had members of the Order hunted down, as they were the only real threat to us. As terrible as it sounded, if he had met his end, I wouldn't be too torn up. Romvi'd had it out for me from day one.

The trip to the bathroom turned out to be uneventful, since I didn't consider the risk of catching hand, foot, and mouth disease to be an event.

Back in the Hummer, with my lap full of Skittles and other assorted goodies, I was surprised by the fact Medusa hadn't appeared in the toilet and tried to eat me. Perhaps this trip wouldn't be so bad.

I glanced behind me, past where Deacon and Luke were sharing nachos. Marcus's arms were spread along the back of the last seat. His gaze was focused on the back of Aiden's head like he could somehow bore holes through it.

Okay. Perhaps this trip wouldn't be so bad for *me*. Aiden on the other hand . . .

Flipping to the front, I caught Aiden's gaze and offered a sympathetic smile. "Skittles?"

"Please."

I dumped some into his open palm, then picked out the green ones.

Aiden grinned at me. "You know I don't like the green ones?"

Shrugging, I popped them in my mouth. "The few times I've seen you eat them, you leave the green ones behind."

Deacon popped his head between our seats. "That's true love right there."

"That it is." Aiden's gaze flicked to the road.

I flushed like a little schoolgirl and focused on the remaining pieces of candy until Deacon drifted back into his seat. I handed all the red ones to Aiden.

A couple of hours after we'd hit the traffic apocalypse outside of Sioux Falls, the open skies had darkened and night was only minutes away. Knots formed in my stomach as I thought of the distance between me and the University evaporating. We were still about four hours away, but that was nothing after being in the car this long.

The University was nestled deep in the Black Hills of South Dakota. Not near Mount Rushmore, but in the part known as the Northern Hills. It was a heavily protected wilderness, only reachable in vehicles such as the one we were in. People had to know what they were looking for to even see the entrance to the school.

I'd never seen the University in person, but I knew it looked like something straight out of Greece. Like all the Covenants, the mortals believed the school to be a part of an elite, invitation-only education system. Even though I was sort of excited to see the school, my nerves hummed for a different reason.

My father could be there—or he could be on his way there.

Hope soared in my chest and I felt giddy for a few seconds. I didn't know what I'd do if I saw him—probably something along the lines of pouncing and tackling the man, and I so hoped I wouldn't bawl like a baby and embarrass myself.

I knew I shouldn't get my hopes up. My father might not be there. He might never show up there. He could be dead.

My stomach tumbled, and for a moment I thought I was going to hurl.

The thing was—and what I kept trying to tell myself was—I didn't know. And there was no reason to get worked up either way. And I had more important things to concentrate on, like how in the hell I was going to convince a bunch of Sentinels and Guards to risk death by warring against Seth and a god.

Aiden's cell went off, and the look on his face as he listened wasn't good.

"What?" I asked, feeling my stomach drop again. I wondered if I had an ulcer . . . or if that was even possible.

"Got it," he said into the phone, and then snapped it shut. "We're being followed."

I spun in my seat, just like Marcus and Luke did. The headlights from Solos' Hummer were right behind us. I squinted. Several car lengths behind there was another set of headlights. I wasn't an expert on those things, but it looked an awful lot like another Hummer.

Sentinels and Guards loved to drive Hummers. The bigger the better and all that jazz—probably making up for something else. Mortals drove Hummers too, but every instinct was telling me it was Covenant-issued and not a friendly.

Crap.

"How long?" I asked.

"Since we passed Sioux Falls," Aiden replied, eyes flicking to the rearview mirror.

"There's an exit coming up—take it. We need to get off the main highway." Marcus cussed as he leaned back, pulling out a Glock. "Good news is that the road will be clear of mortals. Bad news is that the roads will be clear."

There would be no one around for either side to worry about exposure, if they even cared about that anymore.

"Tell Solos to follow," Marcus said, "and to get close to us."

As Aiden relayed the message to Solos, I kept my eyes glued to the stretch of highway behind us as we hit the ramp and flew down the dark, back road. Then I saw what Aiden hadn't said, and what Marcus must've realized once Solos had moved into the other lane.

It wasn't one Hummer; it was two, and I was sure both were packed.

Double crap.

Luke was straining to get a better look. "We can't let them report back, guys. If they haven't already. We're too close to the university."

"So you really think they're his—Lucian's?" Deacon asked, gripping the back of my seat.

Aiden nodded. "Everything's cool, though. We've got this."

The strength in his words—the determination to get everyone through this—was so like him. No matter what, he held it together. He might falter a step or two, but he weathered the blows and he never gave up. Not on me. Not on his brother. And never on life. Gods, no wonder I loved this man.

As I stared at him and saw the steely resolve in the lines of his striking face, I realized something. Actually, it was like being hit by a seven-ton truck.

I needed to put my big-girl panties on—like, for real.

Deacon had been right. A part of me had accepted that my death would be inevitable since I'd left the Underworld, that in the end Fate would find a way to win. Me—I'd felt this way—believed it. *Me?* The girl who pretty much said F.U. to everything, especially Fate.

Holy crap . . .

Sort of stunned, I faced the front of the vehicle. I was better than this—better than wallowing in my own pity. And I was a hell of a lot better than letting Fate control me. I wasn't weak. I'd never been a quitter before. I was born to be the ultimate warrior.

So if anyone could walk out of this situation unscathed, it should be *me*.

It *would be* me.

Because I was a fighter. Because I didn't quit. Because I was strong.

As the front end of Solos' Hummer reached the midway part of ours, there was a distinct popping sound and their car suddenly jerked to the left.

"Holy crap," Deacon gasped. "They're shooting at them—"

Our back window exploded. Glass shattered and rained through the car. I spun in my seat, finding that Luke had Deacon plastered against the seat. I didn't see my uncle.

"Marcus?"

"I'm okay," he called out.

"Alex, get down." Aiden kept a tight grip on the steering wheel with one hand as he reached for me, grabbing my arm and yanking me down.

Marcus popped up and returned fire in a quick succession. Tires squealed; the Hummer next to us jerked again, and then flew ahead in a roar. I couldn't believe they were actually shooting at us. And then it struck me. They didn't care about anyone else in the vehicle. They knew I'd survive the crash one way or another.

They were going to keep shooting until they made us crash.

Another pop, and the window beside Aiden blew out. Shards of glass flew sideways, pelting Aiden and me. He winced, and I was so over this.

"Stop the car," I said.

"What?" Aiden's hand pressed down on my back as he sped up, putting some distance between us and the vehicle full of psychopaths.

I struggled up. "Stop the car!"

He glanced at me, and gods knew what he saw in my eyes, but he cursed under his breath and veered onto the shoulder.

The other vehicles shot past us, the sound of their tires squealing on the pavement.

Before Aiden could stop me, I threw the door open. Another curse exploded from him and I heard Marcus yell out, "What the hell?"

I slipped out of the Hummer, keeping low. There was one dagger attached to my thigh, but that wasn't what I needed.

Aiden slid out the passenger side, eyes narrowed on me. He had a gun in one hand. "What are you doing?"

"Good question." Luke shoved Deacon onto the embankment. "Stopping doesn't seem like the smart thing to do."

"I can't believe they are actually shooting at us. *Us?*" Deacon started to stand up. "What is wrong—?"

"Stay down!" Aiden twisted forward, pointing at Luke. "Keep him alive or—"

"I know." Luke yanked Deacon down and behind him. "Nothing will happen to him."

Up ahead, Solos had pulled over and they all spilled out of the car, keeping to the passenger side. I breathed a sigh of relief and then edged toward the front of the Hummer.

"Alex!" Aiden followed in a crouch. "What are—?"

The two vehicles had turned around and were nearly on us. There was really no time to think about what I was doing. Using the speed that all halfs have, and the extra oomph of the Apollyon, I darted around the bumper and into the lane.

Aiden let out a ripe curse.

I was bathed in headlights as I threw up my hand, summoning the element of air. It was like unlocking a door inside me. Power rushed from the inside then spread out, slipping over my skin. Air barreled down the highway, blowing past me, faster and stronger than what a pure could wield. Hurricane-force winds slammed into the first Hummer.

It went up on two wheels, tires spinning in the air as the headlights pierced the night sky. The Hummer hovered there a second, and then flipped over the second vehicle. Through the air it tipped over and over—something was flung from one of the windows, perhaps a person.

Seatbelts save lives.

The first Hummer landed on its roof. Metal crunched and groaned, then gave way. The one behind it spun to the right to avoid a direct collision. Amber-colored sparks flew.

The doors on the second opened and I counted six Sentinels garbed in black. They were halfs, playing on the wrong side of the field.

One charged forward, and I flung him into the thick elms that crowded the roadway with a flick of my wrist. There was a sickening crunch upon impact that said that tool would be out of commission for a while.

A second brandished two Covenant daggers as he headed straight for me. "Come with us and we'll let your friends live."

I tipped my head to the side and smiled. "Well, isn't that clichéd as hell? How about this—turn away and I might *let you* live."

Apparently the Sentinel didn't understand English, because he lurched at me. I stepped to the side, reaching up and catching his arm. I swung it down as I brought my knee up, making contact just above the elbow. Bones snapped and the Sentinel yelped. Swinging behind him, I caught his other arm and twisted. His back bowed and the dagger fell to the pavement.

Marcus appeared in front of us. Without blinking an eye, he shoved a dagger into the chest of the Sentinel I'd dropped. The man didn't even make a sound.

I let go, and his body fell to the street.

My eyes met my uncle's. A second later he had the Glock raised and aimed. I was so close I saw the tiny spark as the trigger pulled. Gasping, I spun around.

The bullet smacked between the eyes of a female Sentinel.

"Geez," I said, stumbling back.

"They know they can't kill you." Marcus grabbed my arm and shoved me back toward the Hummer. "But I do believe they wish to take you in, no matter what your condition is."

"I'm starting to see that."

Solos and Aiden were working on two Sentinels. Looking behind me, I saw that Olivia and Lea had two more cornered. My attention swung back to the crumpled Hummer.

There were halfs in that car, and as expected, they weren't down for the count. Another six piled out. Feeling the rush of adrenaline coiling tight around the cord, I shot forward with Marcus right behind me.

I reached a Sentinel, gripping the dagger in my right hand. He dove at me, but I ducked under his arm, faster than the half-blood's eyes could track. Swinging around, I caught him in the back with my boot and he went down on one knee. Something inside me turned off as I gripped his hair and yanked his head back. These weren't Sentinels. They were enemies, like daimons. I couldn't think of it any other way. I brought the dagger down in a clean and quick kill.

Hearing pounding footsteps behind me, I whirled and jerked to the side, narrowly missing a meaty fist to the face. Springing into the air, I spun and delivered a nasty I-hope-someone-sees-this spin kick.

The Sentinel hit the ground, clutching what was most likely a broken jaw. Flipping the dagger over, I started forward. Man, I sort of missed fighting with Apollo. We'd be keeping count—

Hands grabbed my shoulders and yanked me back. I hit the pavement and slid. Pain burst along my spine and I stared up, stunned.

A dark-skinned Sentinel stared down at me. "You could make this—" His words were choked off. Something wet and warm sprayed into the air. His body went in one direction and his head went in the other.

I rolled onto my knees, clamping my mouth shut against the urge to hurl.

Olivia stepped back, her gaze flicking from me to the dagger. "That . . . that was nothing like what they teach you in class."

Pushing to my feet, I shook my head. Was this the first time Olivia had fought? For her first kill to be another Sentinel . . . I didn't know what to say. And we didn't have time for a therapy session.

Broken Jaw was standing. He spun around, his dagger arced low. I felt the hiss of the sharp blade along my stomach. Material split, but that was as close as he got.

Aiden appeared behind him and gripped the sides of his head. There was a quick twist, another sound that would creep back in and replay over and over again later, and then the Sentinel dropped.

Aiden's eyes met mine and they were the color of steel. "Even though that display of power was hot as hell, try not to run out in traffic anymore."

I started to respond, but a shadow slipped up behind him. My heart stopped. "Aiden!"

Before I could even raise a hand, he spun around like the wind, letting go of the dagger. It smacked into the chest of the white-garbed Guard sneaking up on him. Darting forward, he pulled the blade free before the Guard collapsed, and then threw it again, taking out the other Guard who'd cornered Solos.

Damn. Aiden was a badass ninja.

Only a couple of minutes had passed and we'd been lucky so far, but approaching headlights warned that we were out of luck.

"Olivia, get Lea and go around to the other side of the car."

Her gaze dipped to the fallen Sentinel once more and then she nodded, taking off. She grabbed Lea's arm and pulled her toward where Luke and Deacon started to emerge from the embankment.

A sedan stopped behind the crumpled Hummer. Sheathing

the dagger, I jogged up to the car just as the driver's window rolled down. A middle-aged mortal surveyed the scene with growing horror.

"Oh, my God," he said, holding a cell phone. "I can call for help—is that a body?"

I knelt down, forcing the mortal to look me in the eye. "There's nothing to see here. You will see nothing as you drive past. You will go home and . . . kiss your wife or whatever."

The mortal blinked slowly and then nodded. "I'm not married."

Whoops. "Uh, do you have a girlfriend?"

He nodded, eyes trained on mine.

"Okay . . . then go kiss her and tell her . . . that you love her?" Gods, I sucked at compulsions. "Anyway, go. There's nothing going on here. Move along."

As the car drove past, I turned to find Solos gaping at me. "What?" I demanded.

"Did you just Jedi mind-trick him?"

A small grin pulled at my lips. "I've always wanted to say that."

"Dear gods," he mumbled, turning back.

Shrugging, I followed him and passed Aiden. He was stopping at each body, placing two fingers on the still forms. I watched as sparks flew from his fingers and traveled over the bodies with an unnatural quickness. Violet-hued flames covered the fallen, and within seconds nothing remained but ashes. The air was thick with the scent of juniper, blood, and burnt flesh and metal.

South Dakota had never smelled more gross.

When Aiden headed toward the two Hummers, I turned and saw a body near the rear of our car. Swallowing down the bitter taste building in my throat, I went to the Sentinel and knelt. As weak as it sounds, I couldn't look at his face as I placed my hand on the motionless shoulder. It too became nothing but ashes.

Heart heavy, I stood. "Sorry."

Aiden reappeared, taking my hand. "Are you okay?"

I nodded. "You?"

"Yes." His gaze moved to the pile of ashes and his hand tightened. "We need to get going."

On the other side of the Hummer, two Sentinels were on their knees before Solos in the dirt and gravel. I recognized one of them as the guy I'd flung into the tree. Both were bruised and bloodied.

"Who is the god behind this?" Solos demanded.

One lifted his head and spat a mouthful of blood. Tree Guy laughed.

"Did I say something funny?" Solos knelt before them. "I didn't think so. I'll ask one more time. Who is the god behind this?"

"Kill us now, because we aren't going to talk." Tree Guy lifted his head and his gaze settled on me. "You guys can't win in this. They are going to change the world, and if you stand in their way, they will destroy you."

I stepped forward. "By 'they' you mean Seth, Lucian, and this god? You do realize that not a single one of them gives a flying monkey's ass about halfs, right?"

Tree Guy laughed again, the sound broken and chipped. "And you do realize that you can't escape him, Apollyon?"

Anger flared. "I think I'm doing a pretty good job at staying away from Seth, jerk-face."

The other Sentinel arched a brow. "Do you think we're talking about the First?" He laughed. "You have no idea what you've stepped in, little girl. This is bigger than you and the First, bigger than a simple Council seat."

A shiver shot straight down my spine and I took an involuntary step back. "What is?"

Neither of the men answered. They said nothing as Solos questioned them about Lucian's plans. Marcus stepped in then, but when he used compulsion on them, they remained silent.

"They're not going to talk," Marcus said, hands clenched at their sides. "Either it's a stronger compulsion than a pure can do, or it's blind loyalty. Either way, we are wasting precious time and risking too much."

"We can't let them go," Aiden said quietly.

My heart sank a little in spite of the fact that, if given the chance, these two men would slit the throats of those standing next to me. They were young, maybe a few years older than me—too young to be out here, about to die. But Aiden was right; we couldn't let them go.

Marcus quickly rounded up Deacon and the others, taking them back behind the damaged Hummer Solos had been driving. It was still drivable, but would draw attention if we had the thing out during the day.

Placing my hand on Aiden's arm, I twisted toward him. "I can—"

"No." He used that voice that I'd come to loathe and respect—the *no argument* tone. "You will not do this."

Laadan, who'd stayed out of the fight with Deacon, turned away.

I wanted to, because an execution was the last thing I wanted to see, but as Aiden broke free of my side and headed toward them, I forced myself to stand still. If he had to do this, then I had to witness it. It was the most I could do, and the least.

Aiden moved lightning fast. The kills were clean and quick. They hadn't felt it. Their bodies slumped forward, separated from their heads.

No matter how quick and painless Aiden had made it, I knew that he would feel this in the dark corners of his soul for a long time to come.

31

Back on the highway, I tried not to let the chilly wind blowing in my face get on my nerves. Things could be worse. People I care about could have ended up dead. They could've been like those unfortunate souls we'd put down like rabid dogs.

Right now, we all had it pretty good, with the exception of that creeptastic warning the Sentinel had given us—or me.

Glancing at Aiden for like the hundredth time since we'd gotten back into the car, I chewed on my lower lip.

"Penny for your thoughts?" he said, not taking his eyes off the road.

I took a deep breath. "So, we know that the god is a 'he', and apparently I don't know what I'm stepping in."

"Do any of us know what we're stepping in?" Luke commented dryly.

"I don't think we do," I said, staring at the dark stretch of highway. "Was it just me, or did it sound like they were loyal to the god, and not Lucian or Seth?"

"That's the way it sounded to me," Aiden said.

"Unless even their loyalty came from a compulsion." Marcus sounded bone-weary. "But it doesn't matter. Loyalty is just as bad as a compulsion. The end result is the same."

I nodded. "I wonder if Lucian or Seth know. I mean, I know it doesn't matter, but Seth and Lucian both have egos the size of a god's. If they think they have complete control over their army or whatever, but they really don't? That isn't going to be pretty."

"Who knows how much they really know?" Aiden gripped

the steering wheel so tightly that his knuckles bleached. "This god could be promising Lucian the head of the Council or gods know what else. And Seth, well he . . . he will have everything he wants."

Hot and uncomfortable knots twisted my insides. Seth had said the same thing, but what he wanted—love and acceptance—he'd never get this way. It would be a caricature of the real thing. One day he might realize that, and it would be too late . . . for all of us.

And gods, he did deserve better than this. I knew I shouldn't think that, but I did.

Letting out a low breath, I tipped my head toward the passenger window and watched the blur of dark trees. Most of South Dakota was prairie land, but the Black Hills were something else entirely. Trees clustered together, so thick that no one could see what rested beyond. Somewhere up ahead, the University was spread across one of the largest mountain meadows.

"Do you think Apollo is telling you guys everything that he and the other gods know?" Deacon's voice broke the silence.

I snorted. "I think Apollo tells us what he thinks we need to know when he wants to."

"Gods are such douche bags," Deacon muttered, sitting back.

Marcus actually laughed, and I thought the world was coming to an end. "They are arrogant," he said. "That's the problem. With arrogance comes great blindness."

It was kind of funny hearing that, because I thought of three blind mice, but it was true. All of the parties involved were pretty arrogant. Gods knew I had a healthy dose of it myself.

"None of them think anyone will truly step up against them, not even one of their own." Marcus sighed. "Their arrogance led to this."

Everyone fell quiet after that, lost in their own thoughts. I was doing a mental rundown of all the gods, trying to figure out who won for Most Arrogant. Seriously, it could be any of the male gods: Hades, Poseidon, Zeus, Ares, and even Apollo. It might not even be one of the core, but a lesser deity tired of being pushed around. It was like looking for an especially drunk guy at a party full of drunk guys—impossible. Good news was that we at least knew it was a "he," unless the Sentinel was messing with us.

Closing my eyes, I breathed out slowly and winced. My temples throbbed something fierce. It was like having a toothache in my entire face and I had no idea how long I'd last before it was time to have another chat with Seth.

I stared. "Holy . . ."

"Crap," Deacon whispered over my shoulder.

Silence fell, thick and heavy as we all sat in the car and stared. I knew the same thing was happening behind us in the other Hummer. None of us knew what to say.

Horror engulfed me. This . . . none of this had been expected.

About an hour earlier, Aiden had found the narrow lane that looked like a fire access road, but was really the five-mile long entrance to the University. We'd made it up the rocky road about a half a mile when the scenery had changed from clusters of juniper trees to . . . a scene straight out of *Red Dawn*.

The headlights from our cars cast light on a gruesome scene. Burnt-out Hummers crowded the sides of the road, resting against equally charred trees and scorched ground. There were so many—half a dozen crispy car skeletons. I couldn't tell if there were bodies in them, not from this distance.

I swallowed. "Aiden . . ."

He placed a hand on my arm. "It could've been Sentinels trying to infiltrate the University."

Blinking rapidly, I shook my head. I had a bad, bad feeling about this. Call it a spidey-sense or whatever, but this wasn't good.

"Can we, like, call ahead?" Deacon said in a hushed voice. "I mean, they're expecting us, right?"

"They are." Aiden glanced back at his younger brother. "It's okay. I promise. Nothing is going to happen."

"I can't get a damn signal at all." Marcus glared at his cell phone like he could wish it into Tartarus. "Nothing at all." He glanced up, eyes hard as gems. "Any of you?"

Aiden checked his phone. "Nope."

I wet my lips as my gaze fell back to the scorched vehicles. My heart pounded and my head ached. "There must be a lot of firebug pures in there . . ."

"No doubt," Aiden muttered, both brows rising.

Solos appeared on Aiden's side of the car, running a hand through the dark strands of hair that had escaped his ponytail. In the shadows, his scar was less visible. "You think the Covenant did this?" He gestured at the vehicles. "Their version of torch security?"

"It's possible," Aiden replied, but I wasn't sure he believed it.

"I can't get hold of them, so I'm assuming you can't, either, right?" When Aiden nodded, Solos folded his hands behind his head and stretched so that his back bowed. "I guess we can make it through."

"We can from what I can see." Aiden sat back, thrumming his fingers off the wheel. "We'll have to go slow."

As I watched the two Sentinels, I knew in my core that Aiden and Solos didn't want to do this. We were blind to what lay ahead. It could be a murderous band of grizzly bears, or a legion of Sentinels waiting to make S'mores out of us. We just didn't know.

Solos sighed and dropped his arms. "Well, I guess we do this."

"We really don't have any other option." Aiden shifted the gears back into drive. "Let's do this."

With a curt nod, Solos loped back to his vehicle. I squirmed in my seat as the Hummer lurched forward. Easing around the torched cars wasn't an easy feat. It was like driving a boat through a china shop. Thank the gods that Aiden was driving because I would've plowed through the wreckage on the first narrow turn.

More burnt-out cars lay by the side of the road every so many feet, and with each one we passed, the scorch marks looked fresher, the acrid smell thicker . . . as if each time someone had tried to reach the University, they'd made it a little farther than the group before them. And farther up, deep orange flames crawled across the hood of a Hummer, licking at the smoke-filled air.

Oh, this was so not good.

"How will they know we're friends?" Deacon asked, thinking along the same lines as me. He leaned between the seats, face pale. "Aiden, we should stop—"

Aiden suddenly did stop, but not because of what Deacon was saying. Debris was strewed across the access road, choking the lane. As far as I could see were scattered skeletons of cars. Many of them still smoldered, glowing hellish red in the pre-dawn dark. The apocalyptical landscape was something straight out of nightmares.

"Gods," Aiden muttered darkly.

My stomach twisted into knots as I undid my seatbelt. "This isn't good."

No one said anything for several moments, and then Marcus spoke, "We're going to have to walk it from here."

"How many miles?" I asked.

"We're about three miles out." Aiden killed the engine, leaving the headlights on.

All of us climbed out of the Hummer, casting anxious looks at all the burnt-out cars surrounding us, feeling like we'd been driving around with a giant bullseye on us.

Quickly, we weaponed-up with daggers, sickle blades, and

Glocks. As I strapped a gun on, I looked over my shoulder and saw that the crew with Solos was doing the same thing.

We looked like we were preparing for war as we came together between the two Hummers. In a way, we were—we had been this whole time. We were at war.

A chill suddenly snaked its way under my skin. We stood in a circle, the nine of us, silent with the exception of titanium clips clicking into place, daggers snapping onto our sides. We were nine. But somehow—in a way I couldn't explain but knew to be the truth—I knew we weren't going to return as nine. At that cold realization, I looked at the faces of those around me. Some had been virtual strangers, others enemies until recently, and a few I'd considered friends from day one.

And then there was Aiden.

I took a breath, wishing I could forget the fatalistic feeling taking up residence around my heart. But the somber faces of those around me pretty much told me that I wasn't the only one who was thinking the same thing at that moment.

As a unit, the nine of us turned. Ghastly, flickering flames lit the road ahead. The weight of the daggers and guns was sobering and grounding. We had no idea what waited ahead of us, other than the big, fat unknown, and most likely a big, fat kick in the face. The gravity of that was killing me—killing *us*.

I squared my shoulders. "Release the Kraken!"

Several sets of eyes settled on me.

"What?" I gave a lopsided shrug. "I've always wanted to yell that since I saw that movie. Seemed like the perfect moment."

Aiden laughed.

"See! That's why I love him," I told the group. "He laughs at the stupid crap that comes out of my mouth."

In response, Aiden leaned over and pressed his lips against my temple. "Keep talking about loving me," he murmured, "and we're going to scar some of these guys for life."

I flushed beet red.

Someone cleared their throat. Another groaned, but I was grinning as I lifted my gaze back to the road. Jokes aside, everyone was waiting for one person to take the first step, so I did. And then we all did.

Our eyes adapted to the darkness, but I stayed beside Aiden, who stuck close to Deacon and Luke, as we carefully made our way around the shells of vehicles. I didn't look inside them, absolutely refused to, because there was a certain stench in the air . . .

The night was eerily silent with the exception of our footsteps. In South Dakota, I expected to hear the chilling call of the mountain lion, the scurry of tiny creatures, and the squawking of birds that could probably snatch up a baby, but there was nothing.

Dead silence.

The creeped-out vibe didn't go away after we started making quick progress, covering well over two miles. The destroyed cars littering the roadway didn't help. There were so many of them.

"Gods," Lea whispered, stopping beside one of the charbroiled piles. "Oh, my gods . . ."

I told myself not to look at what so obviously horrified her, but I rarely listened to that little voice of common sense. I turned and almost lost the Skittles.

Behind the charred wheel of a Hummer was a body . . . or what was left of one. Burnt, blackened fingers still clutched the steering wheel. Nothing else about the body was distinguishable. It could've been a male, female, or a hydra. And it wasn't alone. Charred remains were in the passenger seat . . . and in the rear seats.

Someone sucked in a sharp breath. "The plates are crispy, but these are New York tags."

"Gods," someone else said.

People were moving backward, checking the plates on cars that'd received less damage, but I already knew in my heart. These weren't Lucian's Sentinels coming to fight. These were people—innocent pures and halfs—seeking sanctuary.

In the furthest seat of the Hummer, some of the clothing remained, just bits and pieces of singed material, but the color was a deep forest-green. Council robes, I realized slowly.

Mother-freaking Council robes.

It dawned on me suddenly that it was a really good thing that we'd gotten out of those damn Hummers, because these people—they'd been trapped. And this whole road was nothing but a graveyard.

"We need to get out of here," Aiden ordered, and my heart dropped. "We need to go now."

Lea whirled around. "But where are we going to go? This has—"

A ball of fiery light split the darkness ahead, casting an eerie glow over the debris and the burnt, twisted ground. It flew past the car I stood by, smacking into a small juniper tree, enveloping it in flames and thick, bitter smoke.

I jumped. "Holy . . ."

Everything happened so fast. Balls of fire seemed to come from the heavens, raining down on us. Everyone scattered, splitting into smaller groups as we moved off the road and into the uneven terrain. A hand found mine—*Aiden*—and I was running with him and his brother. Luke was behind us. In seconds, I lost sight of everyone else.

32

We were running, *running* away.

Fire still fell, splattering off the earth, shaking the ground. It was chaos as we scrambled over the small hills, hitting the ground each time the sky lit up and another volley of fire filled the air.

And where in the hell was popping-in-when-you-least-expect-it-Apollo when we needed him? Sure, he could poof in when I was about to get some kissy-face time with Aiden, but oh no, when we actually *needed* him, he was nowhere to be found.

I started to push up, but Aiden held on. "I have to find Marcus! And Olivia! Laadan—"

"No." His grip tightened. "You're not running out in the middle of this!"

On the ground beside me, Luke moaned. "I think . . . my arm is on fire."

"*What*?" I rolled toward him, grabbing at the back of his shirt, aware of Deacon trying to scramble past his brother. Flipping him onto his back, I winced as another blast hit far too close. "Gods . . ."

His right arm was an unnatural, bright shade of red from the elbow to the wrist. Patches had already begun to bubble. He offered a wobbly smile. "Well, I've been wanting a tan."

I stared at him, and then Deacon shot around us, grasping the front of Luke's shirt. Before the bronze-haired half could utter a word, Deacon planted one on him. I fell back on my side, breathing heavily.

Then Deacon lifted his head, eyes wide. "Don't ever scare me like that again. Okay?"

Luke nodded slowly.

"What is it with the St. Delphi brothers and their attraction to halfs?" Solos grunted, hitting the hill near us. Laadan was with him, her hair falling loose from her neat chignon, pants dirtied and singed. "Don't get me wrong," he went on. "Being a half and all, I totally support equal love, equal rights, down with the Breed Order and blah, blah, blah."

"We just have good taste," Aiden replied, as he glanced over his shoulder at the half-blood Sentinel. "Unlike some . . ."

Solos snorted.

"Do you know where Marcus and the girls are?" I asked, eyeing the calm-for-now sky. "Did you see them?"

He nodded. "They're on the other side of the road, down in a ditch. They're okay." Solos glanced over at Laadan. "She saved my rosy red butt, you know? A ball of fire was heading straight for my head, and she just lobbed it away with air."

Laadan shook her head. "It was nothing."

"It was something—"

A deep shout shattered the air, like a chorus of battle cries. A sound I'd never heard before. It wasn't human; it wasn't animal, but a twisted and revolting mixture of both. Suddenly it became all too obvious what was coming.

Hephaestus' automatons.

It didn't make sense. They were supposed to be *protecting* the Covenants. Had they deemed us a threat? Well, obviously, since they were trying to turn us into crispy critters. But those people in the cars . . . No way would they attack first and ask questions later. It defeated the whole purpose of having them here and moving Council members to the University unless . . .

I looked at Aiden. "The god . . . is it Hephaestus?"

Aiden opened his mouth, but the ground trembled under the weight of the approaching storm. Over the rise of the hill, no more than a few yards away, tall and imposing shadows marched out from behind the stand of trees. When they stepped under the slice of moonlight, I sucked in a shrill breath.

Holy daimon butt . . .

Their thick-as-tree-trunk thighs and large hoofs were made of titanium. Dark, matted hair covered their broad chests and muscular arms. Each head was that of a bull—two horns and a long flat snout that sloped into a mouth full of strong teeth and jaws.

"Dear gods," I heard Laadan whisper.

There were over a dozen of them forming an unbreakable line between us and the University, and I doubted they were acting as sentries like they were supposed to be.

One of the larger automatons opened its mouth and snorted loudly.

"I bet his breath stinks," I muttered.

Deacon nodded. "No doubt."

Then it opened its mouth once more and a stream of fire shot forth. A ball formed, heading straight for the ditch on the other side of the road. The girls scattered over the hill.

The first gunshot came from Solos, directed at the monstrosities. Then Marcus was on his feet and so was Aiden, their guns blazing. Titanium bullets ripped through the air, smacking into the automatons but doing little to stop them.

Fire streamed toward our group and we broke apart. My hand was on the trigger, systemically squeezing at anything that looked like a whacked-out version of a minotaur. And they returned fire with . . . uh, fire.

Flames spread across the ground and I darted around the blaze. The automatons raced toward us, spitting fire, then fighting.

The first one reached Marcus, hitting him with the broadside of its beefy arm. Marcus flew back several feet, landing in a groaning heap. Another was before me and I dipped under its flying arm. Springing up, I leveled the gun at the back of the automaton's head and let loose. Silvery-colored blood and gore splattered the low bushes as the automaton dropped and then turned to dust.

Well, that was one way to kill them. Sort of like zombies . . .

I swung around, realizing the daggers were absolutely useless and the Glocks were only helpful if we were able to sneak up behind one. Heart pounding, I hit the ground as another fireball shot straight at me. Crap. This was bad—beyond bad. This was a nightmare come to life. Horrified to the core, I froze for an instant on the dry, burnt ground. Tiny stones prodded my stomach and thighs. Oddly, I felt every one as if it were the prick of a hot knife.

Everything slowed down and the air halted in my lungs.

Marcus was back on his feet and he fought back-to-back with Lea, darting forward with their sickle blades, lopping off an automaton's arms. But the thing kept coming at them. Solos was trying to keep Laadan out of the line of fire. Soot covered Aiden's flushed cheeks as he delivered a blast of fire at the creatures. Deacon actually had a gun in his hand as he stayed near Luke. Olivia was cornered in some trees.

In a rush, I recalled the premonition I'd had earlier. They were going to die, all of them. Like those well-done bodies in the cars, they would be charbroiled and that would be the end of them.

Something snapped inside me—something primitive and absolute. Power rushed through me and my skin tingled with the appearance of the marks. The shadowy battlefield was suddenly tinted with shades of amber. I welcomed the almost-foreign surge of energy, even though it was like poison in my veins. My brain clicked off and I was no longer Alex.

I was the *Apollyon. I* was the beginning and the end.

Loose strands of hair began to rise above my head, and I'd swear that for a moment time really did stop as I rose to my feet.

The sickle blade and dagger fell from my fingers, and then I curled my hands into fists.

Oh, it was on like Donkey Kong.

I flew over the barren land toward Olivia as she tried to fend the thing off. I dipped under the automaton, springing up between it and Olivia, slamming my foot into its hairy stomach. It went down on one knee, rattling the nearby trees.

Absolute power—unforgiving and hard, pure as it was deadly—coursed over my skin. I reared back, summoning the fifth and final element. Intense blue light erupted from my palm.

Akasha ripped from me, arcing through the air like cloud-to-cloud lightning, homing in on its target and striking true. The sky crackled and heated. One second, the automaton was on its knee, and the next it was nothing but a pile of shimmery dust.

"Good gods," came Olivia's hoarse whisper.

Another automaton took the fallen one's place, swinging out with a metal hand that clinked and clicked. Fire sparked from its open mouth. I spun, catching the broad side of its arm and twisting. The hoarse shout of pain was lost in the clash of metal, the thunder of bullets finding another automaton.

It raised its bull face and snapped at me with massive jaws.

"*Please.*" I placed my hand on the massive forehead.

Blue light coursed over the head and down the body, lighting up the metallic skull and bone structure. For a moment, it was like a pretty X-ray or a jellyfish—a really disturbing jellyfish—and then cobalt light radiated from its eyes and open mouth. It *imploded*—caved in on itself, turning to nothing but dust.

And then the crap really hit the fan.

The automatons—every last one of the freaky bull things—turned on me. They moved quickly, metal legs rattling and clinking. Fire spewed from their mouths like the poor man's version of a dragon. They came from all directions, Apollyon-seeking missiles with "Kill Alex" stamped all over them.

Fire came from them, blinding and intense. Nothing existed outside the flames. No sound. No sight. My world was red and orange . . .

And my world was tinted in amber.

Alex? His voice came through the thrumming connection.

I ignored him and the way his consciousness slid in alongside mine.

What are you up to?

Still I ignored the pull of the First. Instinct on a deep, ancient level I wasn't familiar with had taken over. The marks of the Apollyon flowed across my skin as I lifted my hands. The fire stopped inches from me, forming a fiery circle. Heat fell back on me but did not burn. I blew out a soft, steady breath and the fire flickered once, twice, and then faded out.

The automatons drew up short, puffing and snorting loudly.

My arms rose to my sides, my finger splayed out, and the air hummed with power and anticipation. Blue light crackled over my fingertips, waiting . . . wanting . . .

One of the automatons, the biggest of those remaining, charged. At the sound of the dark roar, akasha pulled tight and constricted just like the bond between Seth and me.

I let it go.

The blast of power rushed from me, rolling like storm-tossed waves. The surge smacked into the automaton nearest me. Blue light flared from the creature's eye sockets and open jaws. A second later, it imploded. The swell crashed into four more, taking them out before the outpouring of akasha eased off.

As the shimmering dust settled onto the dry soil, exhaustion swept through me. The bond to Seth still felt open, even though the world was shaded in deep blue and black again. Being that this was my first time using akasha like a fly-swatter, I wasn't prepared for the exhaustion that followed. My legs trembled under my weight as I struggled to hold myself up. I reached for my daggers and realized, like a total tool, I'd thrown them somewhere over yonder in a fit of an "I am so awesome" and "who needs daggers when I have akasha fingers of power?" ego trip.

Luckily, others still held their weapons, and the automatons were distracted with me. Marcus took out one with a point-blank shot to the back of the skull. Aiden wielded his sickle blade like an executioner, lopping off the head of another.

One of the automatons reached for me and I darted—er, stumbled—to the side and plopped down on my rear. And once I was down on my butt, I really didn't want to get up. I was like a toddler, all tuckered out. Pathetic—I needed to learn to pace myself.

The automaton uttered a guttural growl.

I crab-walked backward, putting very little distance between us. Just when I was pretty sure I was about to end up with a deep tan, Lea came out of freaking nowhere, shoved the sharp end of her Covenant dagger through the back of the automaton's neck, and then wrenched her arm to the side.

My eyes widened as the shimmery dust fell near the toes of my boots. "Wow."

Lea cocked her head to the side as she frowned at the gore dripping from the blade. "Well, that was gross."

"Yeah," I said slowly, looking around. I counted eight and then Lea. Nine. All of us were still standing. Bruised and exhausted, but we were still fighting. I let out a weak laugh. "Gods."

The sound of metal crunching, along with the wet, fleshy give of bone and muscle, continued as the rest of the automatons were taken out in less explosive displays.

Lea reached down and wiggled her fingers. "You gonna sit there the rest of the night or get up? Because I'm sure as hell not carrying your ass. You probably weigh a ton."

Grinning weakly, I lifted my hand just as a dark shadow appeared behind Lea. My heart leapt into my throat as fear balled in my chest. The extreme burst of emotion had Seth in a tizzy, and I could tell he was paying close attention even though he was put out from me ignoring him.

"Lea!" I shouted out as my fingers brushed hers.

She turned halfway, sucking in a breath.

Finding a reservoir of energy, I shot to my feet but—*oh, gods*—it was too late. I summoned akasha, but it was like tapping a dry well. There was nothing left, but I was the Apollyon and there should have been something that I could do—there had to be, but before I could use the air element to move Lea out of the way, it had happened.

The automaton grasped the sides of her head and twisted. The crack of bone was deafening, as loud as thunder. Her fingers spasmed and the dagger slipped from them. The sound . . . it whipped through me, stealing my breath and twisting my insides into raw painful knots. The sound . . . it would stay with me for ever.

Lea was on the ground before me, a boneless, motionless heap of nothing more than flesh. My brain couldn't reconcile what'd just happened. Like with Caleb, denial rose and it was so strong, so potent that I *refused* to believe it.

Someone came up behind the automaton and there was an explosion of shimmery dust, but I didn't know who it was and I didn't care. At that moment, automatons could rain down on us and I wouldn't care.

There had been nine of us . . .

My heart stuttered and then sped up way too fast. The world whirled around me, a kaleidoscope of muted shades with flashes of intense amber. Someone was calling my name, the deep, near-frantic voice mixing with the low hum of Seth's.

I wanted them to shut up—both of them, because this wasn't real. It couldn't be—and then in a moment of painful and stark reality, I couldn't understand how I could be so surprised. As if I hadn't expected death. As if death couldn't touch us. How could I be so surprised? Every one of them had set out knowing that this was dangerous, that any moment could be their last. And a few miles ago I had known death was coming, so much so I could taste the sorrow on the tip of my tongue.

I dropped to my knees, hands shaking as I placed them on Lea's shoulder and gently rolled her onto her back. From the odd angle of how her head lay, to the pale color bleeding under her tan skin, to the way her eyes . . .

My fingers trembled as I brushed the coppery strands off her cool forehead. Gods, how could the body cool that fast? It didn't seem possible or right. It definitely wasn't fair.

Lea's beautiful amethyst eyes—eyes I had envied as a kid—were fixed on the dark sky. There was no shine to them, no inner light. There was nothing.

Lea was gone, like Caleb and Mom, like all those people back in those cars. She was . . . I couldn't finish the sentence. That one little word couldn't be taken back.

I jerked my hands away, folding them under my chin. Others were nearing us. Someone was crying softly. Voices rose, uttering denials, and then there was silence. My breath caught again.

Someone knelt on the other side of Lea. A Covenant dagger was carefully placed on the ground and soft words were uttered in ancient Greek. A prayer for a warrior's death—a hymn delivered during burial.

I lifted my gaze and my eyes locked with dark, tumultuous gray ones. Aiden's face was so pale; the horror etched into his features mirrored my own. His eyes were dry, but anger and sadness burned from within them. He shook his head. My lashes felt damp.

I couldn't sit here. I just couldn't.

Pushing to my feet, I stumbled past Marcus and Olivia. I went past Luke and Deacon, beyond where Laadan and Solos stood. I kept walking, having no idea where I was going or what I was going to do.

Alex?

My hands curled at the sound of Seth's voice. Red-hot anger roared through me like a train derailed. He hadn't snapped Lea's neck like it was nothing more than a twig, but his hands were bloody, weren't they? *I don't want to talk to you right now.*

There was silence—for now.

Stomach churning, tears coursed down my cheeks. Part of me was still in shock, as stupid as that was. The nine of us had been *alive*. We all had been still standing. I had laughed. And then Lea was gone. Just like that, with no real warning.

Gods, Lea and I had been far from best-friends-forever, but we'd come so far. I'd respected her, probably longer than I'd realized, and the same went for her. There was so much between us that needed to be addressed—to be repaired—but there would be no more time. And even though we'd spent the better part of whatever time we'd been together hating on one another, she'd come to my aid and she'd stood her ground.

Realizing that cut so deep it matched the pain of Caleb's loss.

"Alex," Aiden said from behind me.

I shook my head. "I can't . . . I can't do this right now." My voice cracked. "I need a few minutes."

He hesitated, and then I felt his hand on my shoulder. I pulled free and walked ahead, dragging in deep breaths even though they didn't seem to be pulling enough air into my lungs. I couldn't afford to lose it like I had after Caleb's death. I couldn't disconnect from this or self-destruct. I had to deal, but . . .

Godsdammit. I bent over, placing my hands on my knees. The urge to vomit was strong, but there was nothing coming up.

Had I apologized to her about what a douchebag I'd been to her when we were kids? I didn't think so. I squeezed my eyes shut and saw her body lying on the ground back there.

Alex? There was a pause and the bond pulled taut. *What's happening?*

I sat down—probably fell down—for the second time that

night. Keeping my eyes closed, I kept the shields up but followed the bond to Seth. I didn't know how to feel about that. Maybe it was all the anger taking up too much room to feel anything else. *Is this what you wanted?* I asked.

Seth didn't respond immediately. *I'm not sure what you mean. I can feel your emotions. Something has happened.*

Shut up! I'm not sure what did it—the almost-sincere quality to his voice, or the fact that he had taken Lea's sister and my mom had taken her family and, because of what Seth and I were, she had lost her life. I broke wide open in an instant. *Shut up! Just shut up! Are you happy, Seth? Is that what you wanted from this?*

Tears tracked down my cheeks, fast and furious. My arms shook—my entire body trembled to keep the shields up. I couldn't let them down, not when Seth was inside my head like this. He'd know where I was and there'd be more death.

I threw my head back and there were no words, just sorrow, guilt, and rage. They poured from me in a scream that made no sound outside my body.

Stop, he said, and there was a pressure around me, almost like Seth was wrapping his arms around me, holding me still. *You need to calm down because you're bursting a lot of my brain cells. Take a couple of deep breaths. Just calm down. Okay?*

Several moments passed, and I breathed heavily through them. I sat there, eyes closed, seeing nothing and feeling nothing. None of this seemed real.

Who's dead? Seth asked, and I could tell by his tone that he expected the worst.

Lea. Even the voice inside my head sounded numb. *She's dead, like her whole family*.

Seth said nothing. Maybe he knew the significance. After all, when we'd been connected before, he'd seen a lot of my past, and he probably could guess that I had no idea how to deal with this. Perhaps he was even thinking the same thing I had—that our connection had taken everything from Lea, including her life. I doubted that, even if he was thinking that, it would make any difference. Seth would continue doing what he was doing. And so would I. He didn't say anything as I pulled my legs to my chest and balled up, desperately not wanting to feel the biting loss again. And he said nothing as the odd pressure inside me increased.

We were enemies to the core, more so now than ever, but my loss was his. When I suffered, he suffered. It was the way we were built, and even the death that he had indirectly caused couldn't breach that or shatter what lay between us.

Nothing could.

33

I don't know how long I sat there, but when I opened my eyes again, the sky was still dark and Seth's presence was gone. At some point, I'd felt him ease away. I thought he had whispered something before the connection faded, but I had to be hearing things, because it couldn't be right.

I'd thought I'd heard him say he was sorry.

Obviously I was losing my mind. Seth rarely apologized, and given his needs for power and acceptance that had driven him toward this endgame, I doubted he felt remorse.

Taking a deep breath, I almost choked on the bitter remnants of smoke. I knew what I needed to do—pick myself up and get moving. Sitting out here in the open, waiting for more automatons to come along, wasn't safe.

I stood and turned, brushing the dirt off my tactical pants. The group was still around Lea's body. Olivia was sitting beside the fallen half-blood, her head in her hands. Deacon and Luke flanked her, the half cradling his injured arm.

Wiping my hands across my cheeks, I stopped beside Aiden.

Olivia looked up, her eyes shiny in the moonlight. "She didn't feel it, right?"

I shook my head. "No. I don't think so."

She nodded, and then picked up Lea's blade, holding it close as she stood. "What do we . . . what do we do from here?"

It was Solos who spoke. "We need to move quickly. There's no telling if more will come along, and we're sitting ducks out here."

"Do you still think the University is a safe place?" Marcus asked, rubbing his chin. The palm of his hand came back red. I realized then he was bleeding.

I started toward Marcus, but he waved me off. "I'm okay. It's just a scratch," he said gruffly. "How do we know that the University is still standing? The automatons could've torched it and . . ."

And all those people. My head swam as I glanced down at Lea. Someone had closed her eyes. Mine burned.

"We have to find out." Aiden thrust a hand through his hair. "We're about a mile from the campus."

Luke shook his head. "There could be more of them. Hell, there could be a dozen or more over the next damn hill and we'd be walking into that blind."

"Or there could be nothing but open land and the damn University," Aiden countered, his jaw set hard. "As far as we know, these automatons may've been here to stop anyone from reaching the campus . . . or to stop people from leaving."

"Or the campus could be gone." Deacon backed up, running his hands down his sides.

Solos stepped forward, clapping a hand on Deacon's shoulder. "I cannot believe the whole campus is gone."

"With all those automatons, anything is possible." Luke straightened his injured arm as he stared in the general direction of where I assumed the campus was. "But we have to see. We've come this—"

"Wait!" Olivia's voice rose above the guys'. "I wasn't asking about going to the University or not. I was talking about what we were going to do with Lea."

Silence fell again and I turned to Aiden. "We can't leave her here."

Pain flickered in those deep gray eyes. He reached out, extending his hand, and I went, pressing myself against his side. My fingers dug into his singed shirt, finding tiny burnt holes in the material. "We can't," I whispered.

His arm tightened around me. "I know."

"We can't . . . take her with us," Solos said. "We have no idea what we'll be facing."

Olivia went off like a nuclear bomb, holding that dagger like she was considering impaling it between Solos' eyes. "We can't leave her here like this. That's so wrong I don't even need to explain."

Sympathy shone in Solos' scarred face. "I know, but we—"

"We bury our dead—our warriors." Olivia's lower lip trembled. "We don't just leave them here to rot."

Laadan placed a pale hand on Olivia's arm, but Olivia was beyond consoling. "I don't care what we have to face or what is waiting for us! We can't just leave her here." Her gaze swung to me. "We need to bury her."

"With what?" Solos asked gently. "We don't have shovels and this ground is rock hard."

Olivia sucked in a sharp breath and turned. Her slim shoulders shook as Luke wrapped his good arm around her.

"Aiden, we have to do something," Deacon pleaded. "I don't know what, but something."

Pulling away from Aiden, I glanced down at my hands. I wasn't sure how much juice I had left in me, or even if I could use the earth element to create . . . to create a grave, but I would try. There was no way we could leave Lea out here.

"I don't know if this will work." I tucked my hair back, having no idea what'd happened to my ponytail.

Aiden's brows slammed down as concern flared. "Are you sure you're up to it?"

I nodded. "Where do you think we should do it, Olivia?"

It took her a couple of seconds to pull away from Luke and process what I was asking. She looked around and seemed to recognize that there really wasn't a suitable place. She headed off and I followed her. We stopped near two juniper trees that had remained unscathed from the fire and battle, their sweet scent so at odds with the lingering acidic and metallic smells.

"This should work," she said, clearing her throat. "It's not much, but the trees . . . she'd like the trees."

I looked at her.

Olivia slowly turned to me and she let out a choked, hoarse laugh. "Okay. Lea really wasn't big on nature or trees."

"No." I smiled and it *hurt*. "She's probably thinking *what the hell* right now."

She blinked. "You think?"

"Yeah, I mean, when I was down there waiting, I couldn't tell what was going on up here, but maybe it's different for her." I thought of the oracle I had met, and then the old woman. "It seemed different for everyone, but I know she's not in pain."

Olivia nodded slowly. "That's the thing about death, I've realized. They're gone to us, but not really, you know? There *is* life after death, just a different kind of life." There was a pause. "I wish we'd become friends before all of this crap. Lea . . . she was pretty cool if you got past the bitchiness."

I rubbed my temple, feeling an incredible empty place in my chest. "I wish I hadn't been such a bitch to her."

"What?"

Shaking my head, I lowered my gaze. "It's a long story."

Olivia looked like she wanted to push it, but didn't. "She'll see her family again."

"Yeah, she wanted that." My eyes were starting to burn again and I knew, if I let the tears fall once more, they wouldn't stop and I'd be utterly useless. "Okay. I can do this."

Taking a deep breath, I got down on my knees and placed my hands on the dirt. I closed my eyes, wiggling my fingers into the leaf litter until I found the topsoil. I'd made the ground move before, when I'd fought Aiden, so I imagined I could do this.

I pictured the soil loosening and giving way under my fingertips. The ground trembled slightly and my confidence bloomed.

I created an image of the ground cracking open, deep—deep enough for a decent burial. In my head, the soil was darker—a rich brown—the deeper I went. Inhaling, I caught the damp, earthy scent of disturbed soil.

When I opened my eyes, the ground really was split open. Mounds of fresh dirt lay on either side of the circular six-foot hole. Seeing that it was deep enough, I sat back and wiped my shaking hands along my thighs. I felt dry inside and a little brittle. And I was definitely not going to stand anytime soon.

Everyone started doing their own part. Someone found a blanket in one of our backpacks and Lea was wrapped in it. When her body was lowered into the grave, Marcus helped me up. He handed me a bottle of water, along with the daggers I'd dropped.

"Thanks," I murmured, gulping the water down before sheathing the daggers. And then something struck me. "Wait. Does anyone have any coins?"

Aiden patted his pockets, as did the rest of the guys. They came up empty and my stomach sank. "Burying her doesn't really make a difference," I said. "That's for us. But she needs passage for Charon or she'll be stuck there."

"We can bring back coins," Solos suggested.

"No." Panic bubbled. "We have to have something. Trust me, she needs the coins now."

Laadan stepped forward, reaching behind her neck. "I have this," she said, unclasping a necklace and pulling it from underneath her shirt. "The embellishments are gold coins, ancient ones. They will be worth more than enough."

My muscles relaxed, full of relief. "Thank you."

She smiled as she handed the necklace to Marcus, who then snapped off two of the gold coins. Parting the blanket, he placed them in Lea's hands.

I took a breath, trying to ease the burning and the ever-increasing knot in my throat. Aiden came to my side, wrapping his arms around my shoulders. I turned into him, resting my cheek against his chest. The steady rise and fall of his breathing soothed my frayed edges.

Solos had found two thick branches, and shoved them into the ground above the disturbed earth after Laadan and Marcus had used air to push the dirt back into the grave. Deacon and Luke had gathered up a few rocks, which they placed around the branches. It wasn't much of a tombstone, but it would have to do for now.

We stood around Lea's makeshift grave as Laadan murmured a prayer in the old language. I didn't realize I was crying until I felt Aiden's thumb brushing the tears away. I couldn't help but wonder how many more times we would be doing this before it was over—and who would brush Aiden's tears away if it were my grave they ended up standing over.

The sun had begun to rise by the time we reached the outer wall of the University campus, casting a sliver of orangey light that stretched across the mountain meadow. We'd spent the last mile of the trip in solemn silence. There was no conversation, no joking or laughter. Talking seemed inappropriate after the loss we'd all suffered. I knew I wasn't alone in convincing myself that Lea was, or would be, in a much better place—a place where the fighting could no longer reach her, where the future was no longer precarious, and where she was reunited with her loved ones.

It helped a little.

But when the outer stone wall came into view, we pretty much knew things were going to suck daimon butt.

Entire sections of the marble-encased outer structure were either gone completely or in the process of crumbling down. It looked like someone had brought in a wrecking ball and played yo-yo with it.

"Gods," Marcus muttered. "This could be a problem."

I arched a brow at my uncle. "Really?"

The eeriest part of it all was the hundreds of trees just inside the outer wall. They were all tipped over at the trunks, the limbs reaching the ground, roots exposed and ash-white, like they had succumbed to a powerful wind.

"I've never seen anything like this," Laadan said, her head moving slowly from side to side. "It's like a great unseen hand forced them all to the ground."

I walked up to one, placing my hand on it. I half-expected the tree to fall over, but it was stable. "So weird." I turned to Aiden. "Any idea what could've done this?"

"No clue." He frowned at the rising sun. "But hopefully we'll get an answer to this. We need to move on."

We continued on, the eight of us weary and desperately hoping that the University was safe and in one piece. It almost seemed like too much to ask for.

The second wall looked better. Damage showed in places, but the gate was still standing and locked. Kind of good news, I guessed. But how in the hell were we supposed to get over a twenty-foot wall?

I folded my aching arms. "Before anyone gets any ideas, I am so not knocking a hole through this."

Aiden sent a wry grin over his shoulder as he joined Marcus and Solos approaching the titanium gates. The sharp spikes along the top caught my eye, and my imagination placed decapitated heads on the things.

I shuddered.

Luke dropped an arm over my shoulders. "You hanging in there?"

"Of course."

His brows rose. "You've been running like the little Apollyon Energizer Bunny."

I almost laughed. "Hopefully, we'll all get to recharge soon. How's your arm?"

"Not as bad as I initially thought." Luke squeezed my shoulders and let go. "I think Deacon's getting blisters on his feet."

At the sound of his name, Deacon scowled over his shoulder. "My feet *are* covered in blisters."

"Your poor precious feet," Luke teased.

From the gate, Solos raised his hand, silencing us. My heart sped up as I grabbed the daggers strapped to my thighs. Luke moved Laadan and Deacon behind us as I inched forward.

"What's going on?" I asked in a low voice.

Dawn had yet to crack the darkness beyond the gate, and all I could see were the shadows of more twisted trees.

Marcus cleared his throat. "Hello!" he called out, and his voice echoed on for what seemed like for ever. "We . . . we come in peace."

I rolled my eyes and muttered, "Wow."

My uncle shot me a dark look and then continued. "I am Marcus Andros, the Dean of the Deity Island Covenant. I have Sentinels with me and the—"

The sound of guns being locked into place was a rat-a-tat-tat that shut Marcus up and probably stopped everyone's hearts. Not a single shadow had moved beyond the gate.

"Turn around and lower your weapons now," came a dark voice from behind us.

Oh, crap on a cracker.

My eyes flicked up, meeting Aiden's for a brief second, and then, because I really didn't want to be pumped full of titanium, I turned and hoped I hadn't tapped that well of power inside me completely dry.

Two Sentinels stood behind Deacon and Laadan, guns pressed against their pale cheeks. But there were more than two Sentinels. Over a dozen surrounded us, forming a half-circle. They all held Glocks and looked more than ready to use them.

We were surrounded.

34

"Lower your weapons," the Sentinel said again. He was tall and older, maybe in his forties, and apparently was used to being listened to.

Gods, it was truly possible for a crappy situation to get even crappier.

Aiden was the first to lower his daggers, placing them on the ground beside his feet. Then he rose slowly, lifting his hands. I knew he carried more weapons on him, and I hoped the other men didn't realize that. Following suit, I got rid of my daggers, but left the gun shoved in the back of my waistband just in case.

The Sentinel in charge stalked forward, keeping his gun leveled on Solos, which I thought was kind of funny. Out of the four of us, he really should've had that gun pointed on me.

Then I realized he didn't know who I was. Part of me relaxed, because if they were playing for Team Evil, I was sure they would have had pictures of my face plastered across their bedroom walls.

Marcus prepared to speak again, but the Sentinel's eyes narrowed in warning. "I heard where you said you were from and that you mean no harm, but please tell me how we're supposed to believe that."

Good question. I glanced at my uncle, brows raised.

"We were a part of the group that escaped Deity Island," Marcus said.

"Well, obviously," replied the Sentinel.

I sort of liked this dude, gun pointed in our faces

notwithstanding. A muscle flexed in Marcus's jaw. "We are not working with Lucian or the First. I am not sure how to prove that to your standards, but we have traveled far to come here and have lost one of our own, courtesy of the automatons guarding this place. We are not your enemy here. We want the same thing, to stop Lucian and the First. Sentinel Mathias was on his way here. He should've arrived with news of our travels."

"If this Sentinel was set to reach here within the last twenty-four hours, then he's among the poor souls beyond the wall." The leader's gaze drifted over us. "No one has made it past them for over a day, which makes me curious how your group has."

I hadn't met the Sentinel who'd arrived while Aiden and I had been in the Underworld, but it sucked to hear that he was now among the dead.

"They turned on you then?" Aiden asked calmly. "They weren't guarding the campus?"

At first I didn't think the half-blood was going to answer, but he did. "The automatons were guarding the campus up until about a day ago, and then they started firing upon those seeking sanctuary here. We tried to stop them, and we ended up losing half of the first wall and many lives. So again, I am curious to how a group consisting of teenagers and two untrained pure-bloods could've made it past them."

"I'm the Apollyon," I said, squaring my shoulders. "That might have something to do with it."

Every damn gun went straight to me, and I wondered if that'd been the best thing to say. Out of the corner of my eye, I saw Aiden start to move toward me.

"It's okay," I added quickly, keeping my hands out in front of me. "I'm the good Apollyon, as in the one who *doesn't* want to take out the Council and kill the gods."

The Sentinel in charge didn't look relieved or awed. Instead, he appeared ticked off and like he really wanted to put a bullet between my eyes. Which wasn't good, because I was pretty sure Aiden was already calculating the time it would take for him to pull his gun and take out this Sentinel.

Bullets were about to fly—just as the sun started to crest, too, and wouldn't that really gore up a beautiful sunrise?

"Half of the Sentinels and Guards who have sided with the First are looking for you, and you came here?" Anger flashed in the Sentinel's eyes. "Do you have a death wish?"

Good thing I hadn't mentioned that Seth and I were still sort of connected. "Actually, I don't have a death wish. And you can shoot me if it makes you feel better, but it's not going to kill me."

He looked like he was seconds from finding out.

I took a deep breath, trying to keep a grip on my temper. "Look, I get your unwillingness to house me. I understand that, but you need me—you need *us*—because we took out those automatons and we can protect you. Not to mention I'm the only one who can stop any of this. So if you throw us out to the wolves, you're sealing your own fates."

The Sentinel stiffened but said nothing.

"And you have to realize this isn't about a pure-blood's thirst for power. This is bigger than that. Only a god could've turned those automatons. Not Lucian, and not the First. And that god is going to wipe out anyone who stands in his way."

I gave my best smile, the one that usually got me out of trouble or ticked off those on the receiving end of it. "And that god isn't the only one you're going to have to worry about. There's another one who goes by the name Apollo—yeah, *that* Apollo—and he's going to be pretty pissed if you turn us away. See, we're kind of related and he sort of likes me."

Someone swore under his breath.

My smile tipped higher. "Just one more thing—you hurt any of my friends, you're going to seriously regret doing so. Get my drift? So let's all play nice and become best friends for ever."

"I think we should let them in," one of the Sentinels said.

"Sounds like a smart idea." Dark humor laced Aiden's tone. "You might want to get your gun off my brother's face while you're at it."

No one moved for a second, and I seriously hoped this guy didn't call my bluff. I wasn't sure I could do much in terms of the Apollyon thing, but luckily he raised a hand and the guns disappeared.

I let out a relieved breath.

"I hope I don't regret this," the Sentinel said, slipping his gun back into his holster. Then he extended a hand, much to my surprise. "My name is Dominic Hyperion."

My brows rose as I took his hand. He had a firm shake.

"Hyperion?" said Marcus. "Interesting last name."

Dominic grinned wryly. "I guess someone had a sense of humor, taking the surname of a Titan."

"I guess so," I murmured, relieved to see my friends no longer had guns pointed at their heads.

Stalking past me, Dominic stopped at the gate. "So you guys really took out the automatons?"

"Unless they send more, you should be free of them," Solos answered.

"That is good." The half paused. "You say you lost one?"

Olivia cleared her throat. "Yes. She was only eighteen, training to be a Sentinel. Her name was Lea."

Dominic's chin tipped down. "I am sorry for what you all have lost. The gods know we can sympathize with what you're feeling." With that said, he turned back to the gate. "Please follow me."

"So you really can stop the First?" another Sentinel asked. He was younger than Dominic, around Aiden's age. A certain gleam filled his eyes when I nodded. "Well, I'm sure there're a lot of people beyond these gates who'll be happy to hear that."

"Do tell?" asked Aiden, who was suddenly by my side. He placed an arm over my shoulders, and I sent him a curious look.

The Sentinel's eyes about popped out of his face as they landed on Aiden's overly possessive arm. "You're a—and you are a—"

Oh, dear.

Aiden smiled, his eyes a dark gray. "We're what?"

"No. No. It's just . . ." The Sentinel looked back at equally flabbergasted halfs. No one came to his aid. "It's nothing. Never mind. Bigger problems, eh?"

"Yeah, *bigger* problems . . ." There was a clear, cold warning in Aiden's voice as he steered me around.

The gate was opening as Aiden's arm slid off my shoulder, drifting across my back, leaving a wave of shivers in its wake. Dominic went through first, followed by Marcus and then Solos.

I stopped, twisting back to the bug-eyed Sentinel. "You said others would be happy to hear that I knew how to . . . stop the First? Who would that be?"

Dear gods, the guy looked at Aiden first before answering. "Before the automatons went crazy, a handful of groups made it in from other locations, including the Catskills."

My heart stopped. "Council members and Sentinels?"

When he nodded, I was close to doing the Muppet arm-thing. I hadn't let myself consider that my father could have been one of those burnt corpses lining the road, but knowing that some had made it to the University safely sparked hope deep in my chest. It didn't ease the tight pain of Lea's loss, but it was something to go on.

It was something, and that was better than nothing.

As dawn crept across the lush meadow, throwing light over the tiny blue wildflowers, we reached our destination. The University campus was large, spreading between two mountain peaks like its own little town in a hammock. I imagined it was like any other college in size and atmosphere, but that was where the similarities ended.

Early-morning light reflected off the large sandstone buildings modeled after the ancient coliseums. Courtyards were filled with what seemed like every flower and tree known to man, scenting the air. Statues of the Muses guarded one academic building, while sculptures of the Olympian Twelve lined the road. Dorms that looked like mini-skyscrapers rose in the background, housing potentially thousands of students.

It was so like Deity Island, but on a much larger scale, that there was a pang in my chest.

In the center of the campus was what I assumed was their Council building, and that was where we were heading. Muscles in my legs ached, and visions of beds were dancing in my head, but I forced myself to keep going instead of sitting down in the middle of the road and going to sleep.

Busts of the Olympian Twelve were carved into the marble and sandstone structure. It was circular, like an indoor amphitheater, and a cold shiver rolled down my spine. I don't know what it was about the Council buildings that always freaked me out, but they did.

As we climbed up the steps, I saw the statue of Themis and almost laughed. Her scales were balanced, but in whose favor?

There seemed to be no one else moving around as we entered the brightly lit lobby. Students were probably still asleep, if they were even continuing with classes. Hell, I didn't even know what day it was. It might've been the weekend for all I knew.

Dominic led us around another cluster of statues, and by then I was so getting tired of seeing them and, of course, we headed up a never-ending flight of stairs. Not even the damn University could throw some money at an elevator.

It was when we were heading down a wide hallway, and I saw the Guards standing before double doors sheathed in titanium, that I knew where we were heading.

"The dean's office," I said.

Dominic nodded at the Guards, and then they moved as a

unit, opening the heavy doors. My first glimpse of the office really struck home. It was nearly identical to Marcus's. Lush. Spacious. Tons of expensive-looking leather furniture, including a big old desk that probably made someone feel powerful and all kinds of special. There was even an aquarium built into the wall behind the desk, with vibrant fish zooming back and forth.

I glanced at Marcus and saw that his face was impressively blank. Months ago I would've believed that Marcus just didn't feel anything, but now I knew better. Seeing this office had to bring forth memories both good and a buttload of bad, and I sincerely felt for him.

A door opened to our left, and a tall man with ice-blond hair and startling blue eyes entered the room. He was dressed like Marcus used to—a poster child for Golf Club of the Month. Behind him, a smaller figure entered and my mouth dropped open.

"Diana," Marcus gasped, and then shot forward.

A wide, beautiful smile spread across the Minister's face. I'd met her while I'd been at the Covenant in the Catskills, and she had been the only Minister to stand against Telly by voting against me being placed into servitude.

So, yeah, I liked the woman.

Marcus clasped her hands in his and it seemed like he wished to do more—maybe pull her into his arms, hug her . . . kiss her like a man who'd never expected to see her again.

"I am so . . . thankful to see that you've made it here safely." Marcus's voice was gruff and heavy with unspoken emotion. He so had a thing for this woman. "So very thankful."

Pink stained the woman's cheeks. "As I am to see you here."

The Dean cleared his throat. "I was unaware that you were familiar with my sister, Dean Andros."

Sister? Oh . . . *oh*, awkward.

Marcus let go of Diana's hands and faced the man. "We are . . . friends, Dean Elders. She's a lovely woman, but as much as I'd like to list her glowing attributes, that is not why we are here."

My brows inched up my forehead.

The Dean's lips twitched as if he wished to smile. "I am also grateful to see that you have made it here safely. Not many have recently."

"That is what we have heard and seen." Marcus clasped his hands behind his back, throwing me headfirst into memories of him in an office very similar to this, where he'd been about to lay into me for something stupid that I'd done.

He made a quick round of introductions. The Dean seemed measurably surprised when Marcus announced Aiden's name. His head cocked to the side. "I have heard that name before—a pure-blood who used a compulsion against another pure to protect a half-blood?"

Crap. With everything going on, we'd forgotten that Aiden was Public Enemy Number Two.

My fingers inched toward my daggers, but Aiden spoke, his voice even and calm. "That would be me. And make no mistake, if you're looking for remorse or guilt, I have none. I'd do it again."

The Dean smiled then. "Ease yourself, Sentinel. At this moment, I could care less what you have done. It is not an issue . . . now. As I am sure most of the members of the Council would agree."

The way he tacked on *now* did not make me all happy face.

"Thank you for your hospitality," Marcus said, obviously trying to diffuse the building tension. "Hopefully we will be able to repay you in some measure."

My uncle was such a diplomat.

The Dean of the University nodded. "Please start by explaining how you made it past the automatons."

Between Marcus and Dominic, they filled the Dean and Diana in, for the most part, on how we made it here in one piece. The conversation quickly turned, though, when Dominic announced that I could stop the First.

I shifted restlessly, surprised to be so uncomfortable with all the eyes on me. Usually I loved being the center of attention. I had no idea when that had changed.

"I can stop Seth," I said finally. "It won't be easy, but I know how."

"And how can you?" the Dean asked. "From what our history teaches us, the First has complete control over the Second, and if you two are around each other, he can transfer your power to his, therefore becoming the God Killer."

Folding my arms, I met Dean Elders' curious stare. "Well, obviously the First doesn't have complete control over me. And there is a way for me to reverse the transfer, stopping him from becoming the God Killer. And if he's not the God Killer, then Lucian has no real weapon protecting him."

Diana leaned against the oak desk, her brows pinched. "But you would have to be near him to do this, correct?"

I nodded. "Yes. We came here hoping there would be others who would be willing to . . . to fight for this. There's no way that just the eight of us can breach the army that Lucian has surrounding him, so that I can reach Seth. We need our own army."

Dean Elders looked at Dominic, who shrugged. "We have many Sentinels and Guards here, plus half-bloods who are receiving advanced training. And we also wish for the same outcome. This needs to be stopped before more innocent people are lost, so you may recruit whomever wishes to join you."

Well, that was surprisingly easy.

"There will be some, maybe even many," the Dean continued, "but none will be forced to join the cause, Apollyon."

I found that funny considering how an entire race of halfs had been forced into either servitude or a certain early death, but somewhere along the line, I'd learned to keep my mouth shut. Kind of.

"Understood," I said. "As a half-blood, I would never force people into something that would risk their lives."

The Dean's brows rose. "Point taken." He gazed over the rest of my group. "I imagine you all wish to meet with the Sentinels and Guards here as soon as possible, but all of you look like you could use showers, food, and clean beds. While you rest, Sentinel Hyperion and I will have time to set something up for you."

"Okay," I said, wondering when whether or not I agreed had started to matter. I wanted to talk to the Sentinels now, but I knew if I did, so would Aiden and most of the others. We all needed to rest; we were barely standing. "That will be fine."

"There are many rooms available for your rest," the Dean said. "Sentinel Hyperion will show you to them."

Unable to hold back the question any longer, I turned to Diana. "The Sentinels who have arrived from the Catskills . . . do you know any of their names?"

"Some I am familiar with," she said.

Then it struck me. My father probably wouldn't be known as a Sentinel, at least not any longer. "What about the servants?"

I couldn't tell by Diana's pained expression if she knew what I was getting at or if she was aware that my father had been a servant at the Catskills. "Things were in a state of chaos when we left there. Some servants were brought here, and those who no longer appeared to be under the influence of the Elixir escaped into the woods. Some remained behind. The servants could be anywhere."

"Oh," I whispered. They could be anywhere—my father could be anywhere. I felt Laadan's hand on my back and I drew in a sharp breath. "What was the state of the Covenant when you left?"

A dark shadow crossed Diana's face. "The walls had not been breached, but it was only a matter of time. Lucian and the First wish to take the Catskills. It does not matter that the bulk of the Council no longer resides there. It is the seat of power, and whoever sits upon the throne rules our society. It is the law."

It was an incredibly stupid law that didn't mean a damn thing to me.

"May I ask a question?" Diana countered. When I nodded, she went on. "If you were to succeed in transferring the power to you, what would happen?"

At the unexpected question, I blinked. "What would happen to Seth? He would still be alive. I guess he'd still be the Apollyon, but weaker. The tables would turn. The prophecies . . ." I shook my head. "The prophesies would change."

"And what would it do to you?"

I could feel the eyes on me again, mainly Aiden's. "I would become the God Killer."

Her brows knitted in confusion. "Please do not take offense at this, but isn't the God Killer the last thing the gods want?"

"I imagine so, with the exception of the god who is working with Lucian. That god obviously wants the God Killer for his own reasons. Speaking of which, it must be Hephaestus, considering he created the automatons." I threw that out, hoping the topic would change. "I don't know why he'd do this, though. I mean, he helped keep me away from the First, right?"

Aiden nodded. "He did."

"It doesn't make sense, but when do the gods ever make sense?" I forced out a laugh. "I guess he was tired of being known as the gimpy one."

"But what about the other gods?" she persisted. "They cannot be pleased with the idea."

Seeing no way around this other than ignoring her question, I sighed. "It is what Apollo wants. And it is what the gods want."

Aiden turned completely toward me, as did half the room. I felt like slinking under the desk. "After I become the God Killer, they want me to take out the god responsible." I looked up, my gaze settling on a marble bust of Zeus. "The Olympians want me to kill one of their own."

35

That little ditty went over like the Titanic. Everyone was pretty stunned. There were a couple of ripe curses from Aiden and Marcus, and some surprised gasps from the rest of the peanut gallery.

I got the whole "Holy crap-a-roo" thing going on. The gods had fought on and off for millennia, but had never seriously wanted one another dead, not since the Titans fell. But things were different now. This god, surprisingly one whom no one would've expected, had gone too far. Although many mortals had died, the gods were most likely more concerned with the fact that Hephaestus hoped to use the God Killer against them.

So, yeah, things were different now.

Once the shock died down, Dominic led us to the first dorm and showed us inside. They were nothing like the ones in Deity Island. These rooms were suites—two bedrooms joined by a shared living room and bathroom.

We were left to figure out the sleeping arrangements ourselves. Before Marcus could go all parental on us again, Aiden claimed one of the suites for the two of us, practically dragging me inside. Before he'd even shut the door, he leaned down so that our faces were only inches apart. I knew he was mad—the steely, thundercloud-colored eyes, the rigid line of his jaw, and his stiff movements pretty much gave him away. That and the fact he hadn't so much as looked in my direction since we'd left the Dean's office. "Take the shower first, and then we need to talk," he said, his voice low, leaving no room for argument. He disappeared into his room before I could even agree.

Olivia's lips pursed. "Someone's not a happy camper."

"Can I bunk with you?" I was only half-joking.

She leaned against the door of the suite across from mine, smiling slightly. The tight curls drooped around her face. Shadows bloomed under her eyes. "My room is your room, but seriously, you do need to talk to him. It's obvious he didn't know about what you'd been asked to do. None of us did."

I scrubbed my grimy cheek. "I . . . I wasn't even sure I was supposed to say anything."

"Does that matter?"

"I guess not. I just didn't want anyone to worry."

"I get that. I'm sure he does too, but there are some things you shouldn't keep from those who love you." Olivia turned, opening her door. "Talk to him."

Not like I had a choice when it came to talking to him. "Thanks."

She nodded and then slipped into her room. Letting out a loud and largely obnoxious sigh, I went into my room. My gaze immediately went to the full-size bed and I groaned.

"Shower first. Epic bitch-out session second, sincere apology third, and then sleep."

Freshly showered, I was thrilled to find someone had dug up a pair of jeans and a clean shirt that fit me. Most likely Aiden had done so while I was hogging all the hot water. It was so like him, even when he was mad at me. Alone for a few moments, I sat on the bed and crossed my legs. The bedroom walls were a nice shade of buttercup, while the door and window frames were trimmed with titanium, as were the headboard and the small end table. On the far wall, a picture of Artemis hunting with her bow and arrows was framed in titanium as well.

It was like these people expected daimons to pop out from under their beds.

But studying the décor wasn't the whole point of me sitting on the bed like a Buddha knock-off. Ever since Seth's appearance after Lea's death, he had been oddly quiet. As if he was gone, actually. The cord was still there, but his unmistakable presence was absent. Like before I'd Awakened, when my head and body had been my own.

Closing my eyes, I concentrated on the cord. It was there, humming softly and barely discernible.

But there was no Seth.

I screwed my face up in concentration. This wacky long-distance internal phone call crap should be able to work both ways. Maybe I was crazy to be the one initiating contact, but a quiet Seth made for a really nervous Alex. It wasn't like him. He was up to something. He had to be.

Seth? I called his name again . . . and again. At some point, I heard the low hiss of the shower and then it turned off. The muted sound of a door closing followed minutes later. That was how long I sat there, looking like an epic fail at meditation.

The door to the living area opened, and Aiden came in carrying a plate of fruit and roasted turkey slices. "I bring gifts in the form of food—what are you doing?"

"Nothing." I flushed as I patted the spot beside me. "I'm starving. Thank you." And I was also surprised that he was bringing me food.

Aiden sat beside me, placing the plate between us. He smelled of clean soap and spice. Moving a few slices out of the way, he found a thick piece of dark meat.

"Aiden—"

"Eat first."

I frowned at him, but he held the turkey way too close and my mouth watered. Taking it from him, we spent the next several minutes gorging on the meat and fruit. As I chased a ripe strawberry across the plate, he leaned over and tucked a damp strand of hair back behind my ear. I looked up and our eyes locked. All the air fled my lungs. Aiden was probably ready to throttle me, but that look in his silvery eyes . . .wow, simply wow.

Aiden leaned back, observing me, studying the blush I knew was spreading like a fever across my cheeks. "Before this goes any further, what you did with the automatons was nothing short of amazing. I haven't had a chance to tell you, but I wanted you to know."

I blinked. "Really?"

"Yes. That kind of power—it was epic and graceful. It was pretty amazing."

My gaze fell to the empty plate. "If I hadn't worn myself out, I could've saved Lea."

His fingers found my chin, tipping it up. "Don't blame yourself for what happened to her. Her death was not your fault. And if you hadn't used your power, all of us would've died."

I nodded. Those words weren't as easy to swallow as they were to say.

"Done?" Aiden gestured at the plate. He placed it on the table when I nodded again. There was a stretch of silence where he just looked at me until I squirmed. He sighed. "How could you not tell me, Alex?"

"I didn't want you to worry," I said lamely.

His eyes narrowed. "That's bullshit, Alex."

I jumped, eyes going wide.

"We're in this . . . this screwed-up situation together, right? Both of us would do anything for each other, am I correct?" He didn't give me a chance to answer. He was really on a roll. "We love each other. And call me stupid or old-fashioned, but I think all of that means we don't keep secrets from one another, especially potentially dangerous secrets that the other party really should know about."

My cheeks were burning for a whole different reason now.

Everything he said was true. Keeping him in the dark had sprouted from the best of intentions, but he was right.

"I'm sorry and I mean it. I should've told you when I figured it out."

His brows lowered. "When did you figure it out? Wait. While we were in the Underworld, right? You were different when we came back."

Damn. He was good. "It was when I was talking with Solaris. Things sort of clicked, and then I confronted Apollo. He confirmed that the gods wanted me to become the God Killer so that I could stop the god responsible."

Aiden cursed under his breath. "Sometimes I want to hit that bastard."

"Join the club."

He was silent for a couple of moments. "They expect you to fight Seth and have the power transferred to you. Then they expect you to fight this god?"

I nodded.

"I don't like this—I don't want you to do this." Anger burned in his gaze. "This is too dangerous—every part of it. Besides the fact that Seth could transfer the power from you, no god is going to go down easy. It's insane."

It was, but when had anything in my life been completely sane? I wriggled closer to him. "But it has to be done, Aiden. Even if we manage to stop Lucian and Seth, this god will try something again. Look at all the people who have died."

"I don't—" He cut himself off.

"You don't what?"

He looked up, features rigid. "I was going to say that I don't care. Not when you could die doing this. I don't care."

I had no idea what to say to that, and I knew that it took a lot for Aiden to admit that. Hell, it would take a lot for anyone to admit that. But it was the truth, and sometimes the truth wasn't pretty or ethical or fair. It just was.

Aiden tipped his head back and sighed. "What if I asked you not to do this?"

My mouth opened in surprise, but no words came out.

He shook his head. "I know I can't ask you that. I know it's incredibly selfish. Don't answer it, okay?"

Tears moved up the back of my throat so quickly I didn't think I'd be able to hold them back. By some miracle I did. I knew I needed to tell him that there was a good chance I wouldn't survive this in the end. It wasn't like I was giving up, because Deacon had sort of given me the kick in the rear that I needed, but it didn't change the possibility.

Aiden made a sound in the back of his throat and he reached for me. I went, climbing into his lap. As his arms circled me, squeezing me so tight against him that I could feel his heartbeat, I couldn't tell him that now. I didn't think I could ever tell him.

And that was the thing about truths and secrets. Sometimes the truth didn't need to be known. The lie was healthier than the truth and, while some secrets could set people free, other secrets could destroy them.

I didn't feel good about it as I closed my eyes. Guilt settled in my stomach like a handful of sharp stones, but this secret wasn't meant to be shared.

Finally, Aiden's grip loosened and his hands moved from my shoulders. He held me back, his gaze searching my face. "Have you been having any headaches recently?"

Grateful for the change in topic, I shook my head. "Not since . . . Lea died. Seth was there afterward, but he's gone. I mean, I can still feel the cord, but it's weird. It's like he's taken a vacation."

Aiden arched a brow. "He's up to something."

A small grin pulled my lips. "Exactly what I was thinking."

"Great minds think alike." With one hand, he smoothed his thumb over my lower lip. "You have to be exhausted."

I shrugged. "So do you."

"We should get some rest." His hand fell back to my shoulder.

"Marcus isn't going to be happy with you sleeping in here."

"I know." He leaned back against the headboard, his eyes hooded. "We're probably going to have to cut the whole sleeping together thing back."

I pouted.

Aiden chuckled. "I said sleeping together, Alex. What I have in mind doesn't involve sleeping."

"Oh." Warmth spread through me like I was back in the steaming shower. "*Oh.*"

A slow grin tugged at his lips as his hands spread down my arms to my hips. That dizzying warmth stole into the marrow of my bones. "Little slow on the uptake, huh?"

I laughed and it felt . . . okay to laugh. Bending forward, I pressed my forehead to his. "Sorry. My mind isn't in the gutter, like some people I could name."

"So you say." His hands tightened. "We'll just have to see about that."

Aiden moved so quickly that one second I was in his lap, and the next I was on my back and he was hovering above me. He lowered his head so that his lips brushed mine softly. That one all-too-quick touch nearly undid me.

"I love you," he said, and those were the last words spoken for quite some time.

36

Aiden hadn't left the bed, so I guess cutting back on the whole sleeping arrangement thing wasn't going to start today. Not that I was complaining. After . . . well, not sleeping and then sleeping for several hours, and some more of the "not sleeping" thing, we were summoned by a knock on the door.

We exchanged a quick look. "Uh, should I be answering the door, since this is my room?"

Aiden nodded and I started to rise, but he caught my arm. "You might want to put some clothes on first."

"Oh. Ha." I giggled as I started searching for my clothes. "Good call."

"Uh-huh."

Hopping around the room, I shoved my legs into the jeans. "Be right there!"

I was sure Aiden got an entertaining eyeful, and my face was blood-red by the time I reached the door. Opening it wide enough for me to slip through, I saw Dominic.

"Hey," I said, hoping I didn't have a mad case of naughty-in-bed hair.

His expression remained bland. "I'm sorry that I've woken you, but we have new arrivals. One of them, I do believe, was an Instructor at Deity Island."

"Really? Wow. Where are they?"

"Currently with the Dean," he replied. "Your uncle is already aware. I stopped by Sentinel St. Delphi's room, but . . ."

"Oh. Yeah, um . . ." I was pretty sure I matched a fire truck. "He's a heavy sleeper."

"I'm sure he is." Dominic stepped back. "If you wish to join your uncle, I'll be waiting outside. You should have time to get ready. Your uncle is a . . . heavy sleeper, also."

Whaaaa . . . and then it hit me. Ew. Ew. Ew.

Hurrying back into the room, I closed the door, and then leaned on it. "Dear gods, that was awkward. You heard?"

Aiden stood beside the bed, buttoning his pants. My eyes got hung up on his fingers and then that stomach. "Yes. He didn't say who it was?"

I wasn't thirsty, but my mouth sure was dry. "No. Just that it was an Instructor. Do you think we should check it out?"

"Sure." Muscles popped as he reached over his head, pulling a shirt on. "I think it'll be good to see a familiar face."

I thought it would be good for him to take off that shirt, but what did I know? After running a brush through my mass of hair, I grabbed a slender dagger, slipped it into my back pocket, and tugged my shirt down over the handle.

Daggers. Never leave home without them.

It was late evening and the air seemed unseasonably chilly when we joined Dominic and my uncle. Then again, we were pretty high up in the mountains, but I was pretty positive it was the beginning of May and made a mental note to find a calendar pronto.

"I wonder who it is," I said, feeling a little high-strung. A bad case of the hyperactivity disorder was probably about to occur.

"I do not know," Marcus said.

I increased my step to stay in line with the long-legged freaks. "Do you know of any Instructors who had escaped?"

"Many were not at the campus when Poseidon attacked."

"That's right. They were away on break." I shoved my hands into my jean pockets. "So it really could be anyone."

Marcus glanced down at me, a single brow arched. "It really could be."

I pulled my hands out of my pockets. "Why didn't Diana come?"

My uncle shot me a look and I grinned.

"Anyway, I hope it's someone I know." I started to shove my hands back into my pockets, but Aiden grabbed my wrist.

He frowned. "What is your deal?"

"What do you mean?"

"You're acting like a little spaz right now."

I pulled my hand free. "I don't know. I'm just hyper."

"Oh, great," Marcus muttered.

Shooting him a look, I tried to keep my jittery movements to a minimum. It wasn't hyperactivity. More like nervousness, but I didn't have any reason to be nervous. Well, besides the obvious, but this was different. The marks of the Apollyon were bleeding though my skin, moving sluggishly into glyphs.

The stairs weren't as killer this time around. As always, two Guards were posted at the end of the hall, outside the Dean's doors. They stepped aside as they opened the door and in we went. Curiosity had begun to outweigh the edginess somewhere on the stairs.

My gaze drifted over the room, finding Dean Elders first, and then to the far side of the room, to the oval-shaped window and the figure who stood in the light, his back to us.

Aiden and I hung back as Marcus strode to the desk. I wasn't sure if Dean Elders really wanted us here.

"Dean Andros," Dean Elders said, bowing slightly. "Thank you for joining us. Our newest arrival was most pleased to hear that some of his colleagues from the Deity Island Covenant had reached our campus."

The man by the window turned slowly, and I recognized the thinning dark hair, olive skin tone, and near obsidian-colored eyes. My mouth dropped all the way to the floor.

"You have got to be freaking kidding me," I said.

Instructor Romvi smiled tightly. "I am happy to see you too, Miss Andros."

Well, I guess I knew my suspicious about some Order members escaping Seth and the Sentinels were correct. One of them was now standing in front of me.

Aiden and Marcus both moved toward me, drawing their daggers. The poor Dean of the University looked like he was about to have a coronary.

"Guards!" he yelled, moving behind his desk as if that could somehow protect him in case the poo was about to hit the fan.

The doors behind us flew open and the two stepped in, eyes darting around the room. Dominic held his dagger out too. "What the hell is going on?"

All of this wasn't necessary. I was no longer the student in class. I was the Apollyon and fully charged. Let Romvi try something. I'd seriously look forward to throwing his monkey ass out the window.

"He is a member of the Order of Thanatos, which tried to kill Alex." Fury rolled off Aiden, and I expected something to catch fire. "He is not what we'd consider a friendly acquaintance."

Instructor Romvi clasped his hands in front of him. "As I remember, I was not the one who carried out the deed, which was successful, might I add."

Oh, that was the wrong thing to say.

Aiden's stance said he was about to break all kinds of bad. "That is correct, but you are a member of the Order and you—"

"Have the ability to kill the Apollyon?" interrupted Romvi. "Yes. I do. But I am many things. Stupid is not one of them. It appears Miss Andros has many gods on her side, and the Order's only real mission is to serve the gods."

"And that meant killing me?" I said, folding my arms.

His eyes met mine. "It did at the time."

"And not anymore? We're supposed to believe that?"

Romvi cocked his head to the side. "We are on the same side, Miss Andros."

That nervous, too-much-caffeine feeling was back, tying my stomach up in knots. The runes were really going crazy now. "And what side is that, Romvi?"

"The only side there is to stand on," he replied. "In war, there is only one side to truly stand on, and that is on the side that wins. And make no mistake, Miss Andros, we are at war."

"You never seemed like the philosophical type," Aiden said.

Romvi's smile didn't slip. "I'm sure I didn't seem like much to you, St. Delphi."

Aiden replied, but I wasn't listening. I was getting a weird feeling again, the one I had had while standing in the war room in Hades' palace. That odd, nagging feeling, like there was something I should remember, that I should see. It was much stronger now.

"In times like these, we must let go of mutual dislike." Romvi still hadn't moved closer, but I felt . . . choked by his presence. "We must work together."

"We are always at war," I murmured, feeling very, very odd.

Romvi arched a cool brow. "You remember my teachings. That pleases me."

I thought of the strangest thing then. When Romvi and I had sparred once, what had he told me? I should cut my hair. Something to do with vanity, but I recalled that war room all too well and what Persephone had said.

He likes to cut off the hair of those he's conquered and then string them up for all to see.

I slowly unfolded my arms. My heart sped up. Romvi was watching me curiously, as if he was waiting for something. Memories of what Persephone had said pieced themselves together rapidly. *To him, everything is about war and its spoils . . .* What had she said about him? Without war, there was nothing.

"One should never turn their back on war," I said, moving my hand behind me. "I also remember you saying that."

And I also remember Persephone saying that about . . .

Romvi's gaze dropped. "No. One should never turn his back on war. I believe that is why we are where we are today. The fools have turned their backs on it, even though war always exists."

Suddenly, the weird, edgy feeling and the marks made sense. It wasn't nervousness or hyperactivity. No, not at all. And the automatons. There was one other god who could wield control over them—they were creatures created *to fight*. There were the mortal armies that were backing Lucian. That made sense now.

Son of a daimon donkey.

Moving lightning quick, I pulled the Covenant dagger from my back pocket. With speed and perfect precision, I threw the blade across the room.

The pointy end embedded itself deep in Romvi's chest before he could take his next breath.

"What the hell?" Marcus exploded, whirling on me. "What is wrong—?"

Aiden turned wide eyes on me. "Alex . . .? Holy crap . . ."

The Dean of the University started toward Romvi, but drew up short. And Marcus and Aiden quieted down, because Romvi was still standing.

And he was laughing.

Marcus took a step back. "What the . . .?"

The Guards and Dominic exchanged looks, and then moved toward the Dean, surrounding him and edging him toward the door.

Romvi's laughter faded. "I was beginning to think you weren't that clever, Miss Andros."

Then a blue shimmery cast surrounded Romvi's body, swirling around him until we couldn't see the man behind the eerie, godlike glow. Then it receded, revealing what stood behind it.

Ares was impressive.

Well over seven feet tall, he neared Godzilla-size with his

height and bulk. He had more muscles than a pro wrestler, like Apollo on steroids.

He wore leather pants and a tunic that was punctured by the Covenant dagger still in his chest. Snake-like bands covered his biceps, but as he lifted an arm, I realized they weren't bands at all.

They were bronze snakes, pulsing and slithering around his arms.

"Holy crap," I whispered.

Reaching up, Ares wrapped a meaty hand around the handle of the hilt and pulled the dagger free. It turned to dust in his hands. "That wasn't very nice, Miss Andros. The gods and the Council fear the First, but who's the one lobbing daggers at a god?"

To say I wasn't scared would be a bald-faced lie. Ares was the god of war and discord. Armies trembled at his feet and nations fell under his wrath. His children were gods of terror and misery. There wasn't a single thing about him that didn't send a spike of fear straight through me or any other living, breathing creature.

This must be the god who was a part of Seth's bloodline, the one who'd been working behind the scenes with Lucian.

We were so screwed.

At least now I could understand how Romvi could kick my ass day, night, and on Sundays. It struck me then. I'd been sparring with *Ares*. Dear gods . . .

His cold, apathetic gaze drifted over us. "Silence? No one is going to cower before me? Beg for mercy, like thousands have before you? How disappointing. But there will be time for that in the future."

"How?" Marcus choked out.

"How what?" Ares' dark brows rose. "How have I been right under your noses this entire time? The same way apparently Apollo was, I assume. I avoided him whenever he was around, and therefore he never sensed me. The Golden Boy had his suspicions, I am sure, but . . . well, he just isn't that smart, is he?"

"What do you want?" I was proud that my voice didn't shake.

Ares brushed the dust off his hand. "Oh, you know. Just . . . everything. And to get everything, I need you to connect with the First."

Aware that Marcus and Aiden were moving in behind me, I tipped my chin up. "That's not going to happen."

He sighed. "I was really hoping I wouldn't have to tack on the cliché 'or else' at the end of that, but I see that I do. You can make this very easy, very painless. You know what I am, what I am capable of. Apollyon or not, you cannot even begin to hope to defeat me. I am the god of war. Connect with the First or else."

I held my ground. "Or else what? You're going to stand there and glare me to death? You can't kill me. And you can't force me to connect with the First."

The smile that etched over his lips sent an icy shockwave through me. "You are right *and* wrong. I may not be able to kill you, but I can bend you to my will and I can make you wish for death. And I can kill all those you love."

Ares threw out his arm, and several things happened within a matter of seconds. The Guard closest to him was flung across the room and through the window I'd wanted to toss Romvi/Ares out of. The second Guard moved toward him and Ares closed his fist. The Guard crumpled to the floor, blood streaming from his nose, mouth, and ears. Dominic was next. He was thrown back, his body contorting and twisting in air. Bones snapped through skin. He was nothing but a mangled mess when he hit the floor. Then, Ares turned on the Dean of the University.

Ares turned his wrist and the man's head twisted to the side. The crack of bone echoed through the room.

Aiden started around me and true terror stole my breath. In

a flash of horror, I saw him taking the place of Dominic, as would Marcus. Ares *would* kill them. Everything was happening too fast, but there was no way I could allow this.

I did the only thing I could do.

Throwing my arm toward the door, I summoned the element of air and I used it against Aiden and Marcus. The gust of wind was so strong there was nothing they could do but submit to it.

There was a second when my eyes met Aiden's, before he was pushed through the door along with Marcus, when I saw the stark horror in his silver eyes. When I knew there was a good chance he'd never forgive me for this.

The heavy doors swung shut and locked from the inside.

"Aren't you a killjoy," Ares said, chuckling softly. "I was really looking forward to ripping the heart out of St. Delphi in front of you. But there's always later."

I turned around slowly, my breath catching in my throat.

Ares winked. "Now it's just you and me."

"Well, that's not freaky or anything."

"Ah, that's so like you. To joke when you're afraid." His large boots thumped as he took a step forward. "Or what do they call it? You're *'snarky'?*"

My chest rose sharply as fists pounded on the door behind me. The thick titanium muted their voices. "That's what some people say."

"Hmm . . ." Ares tilted his head to the side, brows raised. "You know what I think about this snarky thing you have going on? It's a poor attempt to mask how affected you are by things. What?" He grinned. "You look so surprised. Do you think I don't know you? That I haven't watched you just as long as Apollo has? See, I'm just smarter than him. After all, I am a great strategist."

"The god of war has been stalking me? Wow, I feel all kinds of special. Usually the other gods are known for such creep things, but you? Wow."

He laughed again, the sound deep but flat. "You are amusing. Very pretty, too. I see why Seth is quite fond of you."

"I'm guessing, since you're here, Seth won't be too far behind."

Ares just smiled, and the fists on the door continued.

"How did you find me, by the way?" I asked, buying time—time for what, I wasn't sure.

"Oh, I have comrades everywhere, little girl. Ways to get around stupid talismans." One more step and he was only two feet away from me. "You're shaking," he whispered.

I was?

"You went to the Underworld recently. Pray tell, what for?"

My throat felt like it was closing up. "Well, I guess you don't have comrades *everywhere* if you don't know."

Ares smirked. "Charming. You will tell me what you were doing there, or this will end with you not being able to talk. It's your choice."

I refused to back up even though every instinct screamed that I do so. "I thought I was going to end this begging for death. How can I do that when I can't talk?"

He laughed again. "You are so simple, little girl. There are other ways to beg for death than with words."

"Are there?" My voice cracked a little and I winced.

His all-white eyes gleamed. "I've seen it all in battle. There is the way the body curls into itself when it wants death. There is the silent scream for release. There are the eyes, and they speak even when the tongue no longer works. And then there is the soul that rots so poorly when death is wanted but withheld that it carries a certain stench."

Ice shot through my veins, turning my blood to slush. At that moment I knew, no matter how much I fought, this . . . this was going to suck.

"So unless you want to experience these things firsthand, you will tell me why you were in the Underworld, and then you will submit."

I swallowed, wincing as fists hit the door behind me again. "I'm not big on the whole submission thing."

"You may want to rethink that." He sounded civil as he suggested it. "Look at this rationally, little girl. All that I ask is that you connect with Seth. Allow him to do what he was made to. That is all. He will take care of you. You know that. How is that so bad?"

"He will strip me of who I am."

"So what? You'll be happy and alive. You will want for nothing." He tipped his chin down almost playfully. "I'll even let the ones you love live. It's a win/win situation."

"Except for the gods you want taken out, and the thousands, if not millions, of people who will die."

He shrugged. "Consequences of war."

"Sickening," I said.

"It is the truth."

My stomach churned. "Why . . . why are you doing this?"

"Why not?" He tapped a long finger off my chin. "For too long the Olympians have sat on their thrones doing nothing. Letting the entire world be overrun with the children of demigods and mortals while we are sequestered on Mount Olympus. The world should be ours."

I shook my head. "The world belongs to humankind."

"The world belongs to the gods!" he roared, eyes crackling. "To me and any other god who sees the truth. That is who the world belongs to."

My fingers curled helplessly. "Why don't you just take me to Seth? Why try to convince me?"

"Well, I can't really just pop you there, now can I?"

"You didn't think this through, did you?" I forced out a laugh. "You could just knock me out and stuff me in a car. Why go through this?"

His brows slammed down and a muscle ticked in his jaw.

"There's something. You *can't* force me to go with you." My pulse sped up. "Can you?"

The god was seething. "You are the Apollyon. Therefore I cannot force you, but keep in mind, little girl, I can and will hurt you."

"This 'little girl' is having a hard time believing that." Courage fed my bravado, which usually was never a good combination. "Unless you're like every villain who wants to give a long, unnecessarily boring speech, I'd figured you were a more-action-and-less-words kind of god."

Ares' lips parted. "You have no idea. The rules that protect the Apollyon are like all things in nature—balanced. While you cannot be forced with compulsion or by hand, you can be persuaded by certain other means."

"You suck as a salesman, so you aren't persuading crap."

He let out a low, deep growl. "Submit, or so be it."

I met the eerie all-white eyes. "Go to hell."

For a moment, he almost looked disappointed, like the kind of disapproval parents feel when their kid is too stupid to figure something out, but then he smiled broadly. "I don't think Seth will like this, but oh, well."

"What do—?"

Ares shot forth, in my face in half a second. All thoughts of Seth fled, and instinct kicked in. I summoned forth akasha, knowing it wouldn't kill but hoping it would send him back to Olympus with his tail between his legs, but that wasn't what happened.

He caught my arm by the wrist and squeezed with what was probably the slightest pressure, but the spike of pain caused me to lose my concentration. "You will not like my persuasion, little girl."

Then he pushed, and I hit the door with enough force to knock the air out of me. Unfortunately, his Dr. Evil speech hadn't been all pomp. But if he could hurt me, I could take it. I wasn't submitting. Too much was at stake. Too many lives. I could deal with this, and all I could hope was that he forgot about Aiden and Marcus when he was through, or they got with the program and got the hell out of Dodge.

I can deal with this.

Pushing off the wall, I spun to the right and extended my arm, but where his chest had been was empty space, and I stumbled into it.

"Missed me."

I whirled around, finding him behind me. Dropping down, I swept my leg at his . . . but hit nothing but air.

"You can keep this up if you want."

Looking up, he was leaning against the door, arms crossed. Now I was starting to get pissed off. Launching to my feet, I gained momentum and pushed into the air, twisting into the perfect butterfly kick that—

Arms snagged me out of the air from behind and I let out a surprised gasp.

He held me like I was nothing more than a sack of rice. "I am the god of war, little girl. There is no move that you know, no method of battle or maneuver that I do not."

Crap.

"I will always be one step ahead. I will always out-think you. You cannot fight me."

Throwing my head back, I hit his broad, hard shoulder. Then I swung my legs, but Ares dropped me. Stumbling to my feet, I saw he wasn't in front of me.

Double crap.

Whirling around, I kicked out into nothing. I spun back and suddenly—*dear gods*—his hand was on my throat, lifting me off the ground as I kicked and clawed at his hand, too panicked and distracted to try to summon akasha again.

"You will wish for death by the time I am through." His fingers dug in deep, cutting off my air supply. "You will beg for it in all the ways I listed. You had your choice. You had your fun. Game over."

For a terrifying second, I thought he'd crush my windpipe, and I told myself again that I could deal with this. But then I was suddenly flying backward through the air. I crashed through the aquarium. Sharp glass sliced through my back as water and fish poured out around me.

I hit the floor on my side. Vibrantly striped pink-and-blue fish flopped on the marble floors. Sucking in a sharp inhale against the pain, I put my hand down and pushed up. I grunted as glass sliced open my palm. Blood mixed with water.

I can deal with this.

I stood up, breathing raggedly as I lifted my head.

Ares stood in front of me. Without a single word, his backhand hit the side of my face. Starbursts flooded my vision like a dozen firecrackers going off at once. I smacked into the leather chair behind the desk. Blood pooled in my mouth as I caught myself on the edge of the desk. Something had split. My cheek? Entire face? I had no idea. And over the pounding pain, I could hear them at the door.

I can deal with this.

Grabbing the keyboard, I ripped it free and swung around, aiming for his head. Ares caught the keyboard, yanked it free and then snapped it in two like it was a twig.

I stumbled back, reaching blindly for something. Daggers and swords hung from the wall, but he was on me before I could go for them.

Ares picked me up like I was nothing more than a helpless kitten. Before I could wriggle free, before I could taste the raw fear building in the back of my throat, he flipped me over, slamming my back into the corner of the upturned desk.

There was a crack I *heard* and felt. Sharp pain came in a flash of light, and then every nerve ending fired at once. My senses overloaded as I slipped to the ground, eyes fixed on the ceiling.

Something had come unhinged inside me. I could feel it. A searing hurt roared through me like a gunshot blast. I was wet and warm on the inside and if I hadn't been the Apollyon—if I had been only a half-blood or a mortal—I knew whatever Ares had done would've been fatal.

But I wouldn't die and I couldn't move. Something bad was broken. The tips of my fingers were numb, and I couldn't feel my toes, but I felt *everything* else. And I figured that, if anyone knew the right place to snap the spine to immobilize someone but ensure they could still feel everything, it would be Ares.

I can deal with this—oh gods, I can deal with this.

He loomed over me, smiling, eyes all-white. "This can all end now, little one. Just say the words."

My throat worked, and my tongue felt way too heavy. It took everything to get the words out. "Fuck . . . you . . ."

The smile slipped from his face and then he moved lightning fast. Pain . . . it was everywhere. Another bone cracked—maybe my leg, or a kneecap, but I couldn't be sure. My mouth opened to scream, but a wet, warm whimper came out instead.

I . . . I can deal with this. I had to . . . I had to.

When he snapped my other leg and then each rib, one at a time, the pain became my world. There was no escaping it—no breathing around it or hiding. Consciousness was slipping away from me and I fought the fog, because when he was done with me, if he'd ever be done with me, he would move on to Aiden and Marcus, to the whole University. He was the god of war and he would lay waste to everything.

But that pain . . . it rotted me from the inside. It reached down into the tiny part where I was still a person, where I was still Alex, and the pain took over. I couldn't take it. I couldn't deal with it. My shields crashed down and the cord roared, but the growing hum was overshadowed by the terrible pain, and the growing hopelessness dug in deep with razor-sharp claws and pulled away my entire sense of being.

I wasn't as strong as I thought I was, or maybe I'd just hit my limit, because I wanted out—I wanted to *die*. There was no pride in this. There was no purpose. My soul fragmented and I broke wide open.

Ares grabbed hold of my broken arm, dragging me to the center of the room, over broken glass and dead fish and the blood of those who'd already died in here. That fresh burst of pain seemed like nothing in comparison to everything else, but out of the corner of my eye, I saw Ares pick up a dagger.

He knelt over me, lips curled back. There was a blade in his hand, and this was about to get much, much worse. "Say the words."

I was shattered and I was weak. He had won, and I wanted to die, but I couldn't, and there was no way—I screamed as the first strike of the blade sank deep.

With another sharp slice, my vision flashed amber momentarily and then reverted, but something . . .something was different. A foreign sensation wiggled around the broken bones and severed muscles. It wasn't from me, but it was a part of me. It was cold and it felt like steel and it was fury, dark and endless.

It wasn't from me, because what little part of me that was left had curled up in a ball and was waiting and praying for this to be over. It had given up, cowering away from more pain like an abused dog. It wanted this to be over. It wanted to taste the peacefulness of death.

But that fury built and, as Ares bent over me holding the red-tipped dagger, I knew that the anger was filtering through the connection between me and the First.

It was Seth.

Was he angry that I hadn't gone with Ares? Or was it because I was so weak that I wished for death? Or was it something else, something deeper than which side we stood on, because Seth . . . Seth had to feel this now. He had to know, and that last little shred of my being refused to believe that he would condone this. I suffered, and so he suffered.

The god laughed coldly. "I wonder, if you cut the head off the

Apollyon, does it grow back? Guess we could find out, huh? You'd like that."

Part of me died right then, maybe not a physical death, but on some mental, some emotional level I was good as dead. When all of this was over, I wouldn't be the same.

Wood and metal splintered, and I knew the door had finally been breached. As the god brought the dagger down, a body crashed into him. The blade impaled the floor harmlessly beside my neck. Before I could take my next painful breath, the three of them moved above me, engaging in a sick, macabre dance of sorts. Ares. Aiden. Marcus. They moved too fast for me to track. The three of them were too close together.

Light exploded, casting the room in white light as bright as the sun. The presence of another god filled the room, and I was blinded. I tried to take my next breath and wheezed. Wet warmth spread along the left side of my body, pooling across the floor like red rain. My blood? Someone else's? Gods . . . gods didn't bleed like us.

There was an inhuman roar and Ares spun around, his attention on whatever was behind me. In an instant, the god of war threw out his arms. A shockwave rolled through the destroyed room. Shattered wood and broken furniture flew into the air, along with prone, lifeless bodies . . . and Marcus and Aiden.

Red rain seemed to pour from the ceiling now.

My name was called, but it sounded so far away. I struggled to sit up, to see Aiden and Marcus, to know that they were okay, but I couldn't move and I couldn't breathe. Hands landed on me, but my skin felt detached. There was screaming in the background, and I wanted them to shut up—*to just shut up.* My entire body felt slippery as I was lifted, my head flopping loosely to the side.

Where were they—where were Aiden and Marcus?

The mounting horror took over the pain and it mixed with Seth's rage. The marks spread across my skin and the cord hummed violently. There were voices, so many voices, and one came through so clear, and I didn't know if it was spoken out loud or in my thoughts.

"Let go, Alex."

Then there was nothing.

37

There was nothing, and then the pain came back, starting with the cracked bones in my toes and then crawling up my shattered calves and knees, licking over my pulverized pelvis in waves of white-hot, fiery pain. When the fire reached my head, I tried to scream, but my jaw wouldn't unhinge. The scream tore through me still, silent but full of rage that tasted of the blood that pooled in my mouth.

Death . . . oh gods, I begged for death over and over in my mind. A relentless, steady stream to whatever god was listening to take this away, because the pain was splitting the seams of my sanity.

But the pain didn't lessen. It burned. It remained. It continued to rot me from the inside until I willed my eyes open.

My vision didn't focus as first. What I saw was a hazy blur of blue, but when my sight cleared, I didn't understand what I was seeing.

Maybe I'd already gone insane.

I was staring at a sky—the brightest blue I'd ever seen. Like the deepest ocean water, untouched and pure. No sky was that color. And I'd been in the Dean's office, where Ares . . . where he . . .

I couldn't think of that. I couldn't think of anything.

The air smelled of jasmine, like . . . like the pool in the Underworld, when I'd been with Aiden.

Aiden . . .

Oh gods, I didn't know what'd happened to him, if Ares had

hurt him or Marcus. I didn't know where I was, or how I had gotten here. All I knew was pain. It was in every fiber of muscle, every splintered bone and burst vessel, but that . . . that wasn't true. There was one thing that I did know.

The cord—the connection between Seth and me—it was gone.

There was no humming. No rage. No outside presence mingling with mine. Oh gods, I was nothing now but pain.

"Alexandria."

I didn't realize my eyes were closed again until I forced them to reopen at the sound of the vaguely familiar voice. At first, I didn't see him, or anything other than that beautiful, unreal sky.

A shadow fell over me and then a form appeared, blocking out the sky. Seconds later, the man pieced together. Tall and broad and a head full of honey-colored hair, the man had the face of an angel.

Oh for the love of gods, I couldn't catch a freaking break.

Thanatos.

The god's lips tipped up a little on one side, as if he knew what I was thinking, and I wondered then if I was actually dead, if someone had lied about the whole Apollyon-death thing, because I was staring at the god of peaceful death.

Then again, my death, if that was what this really was, had been anything but peaceful. Had he come to answer my prayers? To take this pain away?

Easing down, Thanatos tipped his head to the side as he leaned over me. "Can you hear me?"

I tried to open my mouth but couldn't.

"Blink if you can," he said with surprising gentleness.

I blinked.

"We may have been foes in the past, but I am not here to harm you now. I'm watching over you until Apollo can return with his son, Asclepius."

Apollo? His son? Confusion swamped me and I dragged in a

deeper breath I immediately regretted. Pain arced across my chest.

Thanatos moved to place his hand on my forehead, but stopped short. "It's okay. You're in Olympus."

Olympus? How in the world was *that* okay?

"Well, just outside of Olympus, if you want to get technical." He glanced over his shoulder, sighing softly. "What you did by standing up to Ares? Not many would—no mortal, demigod and surely not even the Apollyon. You could've submitted to him. You would've saved yourself so much pain."

Thanatos leaned in close, focusing on me with white eyes that held no pupils or irises. "You held your ground, and I can respect that. I can also admire that."

Maybe, if it didn't feel like my body had been shattered into a million pieces, I could really appreciate that statement. The jasmine-scented air stirred, and two more shadows fell over the spot where I lay . . . in the grass, I realized dumbly. My entire back felt wet and I wasn't hopeful enough to think that it was dew instead of my own blood . . . or someone else's. No. It couldn't be someone else's, because that would mean that Aiden or Marcus . . .

Apollo came into focus, and instead of showing off those creepy god peepers, he stared down at me with eyes that matched the sky over his shoulder. A small, almost-sad smile tugged at his lips, which I found so strange since it was rare that Apollo showed any real emotion.

"There was no way I could heal you in the mortal realm. The damage is too extensive," he said, and for the first time, he cut right to the chase. "I had to bring you here, as close to Olympus as possible. All the aether surrounding my home will help Asclepius."

I wanted to ask about Aiden and Marcus, but when I finally managed to open my mouth, only the smallest whimper leaked out.

"Don't try to talk," Apollo said. He leaned back, making room for another god. "My son is going to heal you." A wry grin twisted his lips. "And I know if you could, you'd say something like 'how many kids do you have?' and my answer would be 'many'."

Yeah, I was kind of curious, and I also wondered if it meant that Asclepius was related to me, but what I really wanted to know was what had happened to Aiden and Marcus.

Asclepius took the place of Thanatos. This god barely resembled Apollo. A full beard covered his face, making it difficult to gauge his age, but the fine lines spreading out from the corners of his white eyes made him look much older than his father. My eyes moved to Apollo, and I was comforted to find that he was still there. He hadn't left me with Thanatos and a stranger.

Finally, Apollo took pity on me. "The last I saw of Aiden and Marcus, they were fine. But I haven't been back since I brought you here."

I closed my eyes and swallowed hard. It wasn't a hundred percent confirmation that they were okay, but it was something that I could hold onto.

"Do you know the story of my son?" Apollo asked.

When I did nothing, Asclepius laughed. "He loves to tell this story."

"His mortal mother died during childbirth, and while she was on the funeral pyre, I cut him from the womb." As Apollo spoke, his son eyed my numerous injuries with a mixed look of disgust and challenge. "I gave him to the centaur Chiron, who raised him in the art of medicine. Of course, having my genes, he already had a knack for healing."

Of course.

"But my sister had asked Asclepius to bring Hippolytus back to life, and between Hades being pissed off about that, and Aphrodite's whining, Zeus killed my son with a thunderbolt." A muscle popped out in Apollo's jaw. "So I killed Cyclopes, ensuring that Zeus would have no more thunderbolts."

Oookay . . .

"I ended up banned from Olympus for a year," Apollo continued blithely, "but in the end, Zeus resurrected my son to ensure there would be no future feuds with me." He paused. "You're wondering what the moral of this story is? I *always* find a way to take care of my own."

Before I could process what that meant, his son placed his hands on my chest. Under normal circumstances, I wouldn't have been thrilled with the idea of being felt up, but incredible warmth swept through me. From the tips of my aching toes to the top of my fractured skull, dizzying, wonderful warmth invaded every pore.

The god closed his eyes. "This may sting."

What? No, I wanted to scream, because I couldn't take anymore, but then the warmth blistered my skin and I *did* scream.

Fire raged through me, spreading out of control and searing every cell. My broken body reared off the ground.

Asclepius' face blurred into a severe frown. "There's something else here . . . ."

For the second time in however many minutes, I was pulled into the void, lost in a black sea of nothingness.

When I opened my eyes, my vision was clear and I'd been moved into a circular chamber with marble walls. Birds shrilled in a soft, lyrical verse from somewhere outside the room. A table sat in the middle of a raised dais. Resting atop the table was a pitcher full of honey-colored liquid. Heavy, scented air flowed through a small opening in the wall, stirring the white canopy hanging from the posts at the foot of the bed I rested in.

A bed? Obviously it was a step up from lying in grass, but confusion pinged at me. I pushed up onto my elbows and winced as an ache rolled through my entire body.

I'd been healed, but . . .

Memories pieced back together, of Thanatos, Apollo and his son.

Holy crap, I was in—or near—Olympus.

Never in my life had I thought I'd breathe the aether-enriched air of the gods, but here I was. A low hum of excitement trilled in my veins. I wanted to race off the bed and investigate. Olympus was rumored to be the most beautiful place in existence, even more so than the Elysian Fields. Creatures of myths roamed freely here, and plants that no longer flourished in the mortal realm grew to staggering heights in Olympus. This was a once-in-a-life . . .

The excitement gave way to unrest. I wasn't here for sightseeing. It wasn't like I was on vacation and Apollo would pop in and give me a tour along with keepsake mouse ears. This wasn't Disney World, and I was here because Ares . . .

In the back of my mind, and in the center of my very being, there was a dark and ugly thing that had been born and taken root, a distinct coldness that no amount of warm air could quell. My thoughts swung to Ares and my heart turned heavy. Raw terror formed in the back of my throat, tasting like bile.

But, oh gods, it wasn't just Ares, or the thought of facing him again. It was the pain that had festered and rotted me, the pain that had shattered me into pieces and caused me to beg for release—for death. Even though I had never spoken the words aloud, I knew that Ares had felt it. It had been in my eyes; my very soul had been laid bare.

Ares knew.

Seth knew.

Shame and something dark rose inside me, twisting and choking like a vile weed.

I'd begged for death.

Me. Alex. The all-powerful Apollyon. The girl who got knocked down only to jump back up and ask for more. I'd been training to be a Sentinel, a warrior bred to disregard fear. I'd known pain before this, both physically and mentally. I'd even come to expect it.

But Ares had broken me wide open.

A raw vulnerability inched through me. Feeling sick, I tugged the soft blanket up to my chest. Gods, I felt . . . I felt like a poser in my own skin. What would Aiden think if he found out? He would never have begged or given up like I had—oh gods, what if Aiden really wasn't okay? What if Apollo had lied?

I started to throw the blanket off, but stopped. Indecision smacked into me. What was I doing? Where was I going to go to demand answers? My hand tightened around the blanket until I thought I was going to undo Asclepius' hard work.

I couldn't move.

I was frozen by . . . by what? Fear. Distress. Shame. Confusion. Anxiety. A hundred or so emotions whirled through me like an F-5 tornado. My breath sawed in and out painfully. Pressure blossomed out of nowhere, clamping down on my still-tender chest. This was worse than how I'd felt after Gatlinburg, magnified by a million.

I couldn't breathe.

Images of the fight in the Dean's office flipped through my head like a twisted photo album. The maneuvers that always had been too late. The kicks and punches that'd never landed. Being picked up and thrown like I was nothing more than a sack of rice. The breaking of my spine and every bone thereafter and then the knife . . .

The sound of Aiden and Marcus banging on the doors, desperately trying to get in, haunted me. So many memories of Ares owning my ass kept on coming in a continuous onslaught of how-not-impressive-I-really-was. How could I've thought I could stand against Ares—the god of war? How could any of us?

And I'd begged for death.

I couldn't breathe.

The pressure constricted my chest again and I let go of the blanket, pressing my hand to my clammy skin. I stumbled out of the bed, falling on the chilled granite knees-first, and then I pressed my forehead to it. The cool floor seemed to help, like the night I'd been slipped the Brew.

I don't know how long I stayed like that—minutes or hours—but the floor had this wonderful grounding ability. A bone-deep exhaustion set in, the kind a warrior felt at the end of the final battle, when he was ready to turn in his sword and fade into eternity.

Somewhere in the room, a door opened, scraping against marble. I didn't lift my head or try to sit up, and I knew how I looked to whomever was in the room—like a dog cowering in the corner. That was me.

"Lexie?"

My heart stopped.

"Lexie? Oh my gods, baby."

I was frozen again, too afraid to look and discover that the voice didn't really belong to my mom, that it was some kind of messed-up illusion. A different kind of pressure fisted in my chest. Fragile hope swelled.

Warm arms surrounded me in a gentle, painfully familiar embrace. Inhaling a ragged breath, I caught her scent—*her scent*. Vanilla.

Lifting my head, I peered through the strands of hair and lost my breath, along with any ability to form a coherent thought.

"Mom?"

She smiled, sliding her hands up to my cheeks. It was her—the oval face and complexion slightly darker than mine, lips spread in a wide smile and eyes colored the brightest green. She looked like she had the last time I'd seen her in Miami, the night before the daimon attack that had changed her into an aether-addicted monster, before I had killed her.

That fist squeezed down until I couldn't breathe, couldn't think, and couldn't see anything other than her.

"Baby, it's me, it's really me." Her voice was as I remembered—soft and melodious. "I'm here."

I stared at her until her beautiful face began to swim. Part of me couldn't allow myself to accept this—*this gift*—because, if it wasn't real, it would be too cruel. The spirits guarding the gates to the Underworld had almost fooled me.

But her hands were warm and her eyes were full of tears. It smelled like her and sounded like her. Even the dark hair fell in waves past her shoulders the way it had before.

Then she came to her knees and leaned forward, pressing her forehead against mine. Her voice was tight with tears. "Do you remember what I said to you that night?"

I struggled to get the words out. "That you loved me?"

"Yes." Her smile was watery. "I told you that, with or without purpose, you were a very special girl."

Oh gods . . .

"And you told me that, as your mother I was obligated to tell you that." She laughed and it seemed to catch in her throat. "Even I didn't know how special you truly were."

It was her—really her.

Clamoring forward, I threw my arms around her, nearly knocking her backward. With a soft laugh, she enveloped me in a strong hug—the hug I'd been missing and needing for so long. Mom gave the best hugs ever.

She squeezed me tight, and I clung to her while she smoothed my hair back with one hand. Tears burned the back of my throat and welled in my eyes. Emotion poured into my chest until it felt like my heart would explode. I'd been waiting for this moment for what felt like for ever, and I never wanted to let her go.

"How is this possible?" My voice was hoarse and muffled. "I don't understand."

"Apollo thought it would be good for you after what

happened." She pulled back a little. Tears glistened in her eyes, and I hated that. "He called in a favor with Hades."

Apollo must have a lot of favors at his disposal.

"I've missed you so much." She placed her hand to my cheek and smiled. "And I wish I could've been there for you when you lost Caleb and faced the Council. I wish for that more than anything else."

A red-hot lump filled my throat. "I know. Mom, I'm . . . I'm so sorry. I—"

"No, baby, don't you dare apologize for anything that happened to me. None of it was your fault."

But it *was* my fault. Sure, I didn't turn her into a daimon, but we'd left the safety of Deity Island because of what I would become. She sacrificed everything—her *life*—for me, and I'd still connected to Seth when I had Awakened, spurring horrific, catastrophic events across the globe as the gods retaliated. How was that not my fault?

"Listen to me," she said, clasping both sides of my face now and forcing my gaze up. "What happened to me in Miami wasn't your fault, Lexie. And you did the right thing in Gatlinburg. You gave me peace."

By killing her—my mother.

She pressed her lips together, and then took a shaky breath. "You can't hold on to that kind of guilt. It doesn't belong to you. And what happened after you Awakened wasn't something you could control. You broke the connection in the end. That is what matters."

Her words were so sincere that I was *almost* convinced, but I didn't want to spend this time with her talking about all the terrible things that had happened. After everything that had happened, I just wanted her to hold me.

Pushing down the guilt was like taking off a pair of too-tight pants. I could breathe now, but the marks were left behind on my skin. "Are you happy?" I asked, scooting closer.

Mom gathered me close again, resting her chin atop my head, and I closed my eyes, almost able to pretend that we were home and that a heart actually beat under my cheek. "I miss you, and there are other things I miss, but I am happy." Pausing, she tucked my hair back. "There is peace, Lexie. The kind that erases a lot of the negative stuff and makes it easier to deal."

I was sort of envious of that kind of peace.

"I watch over you when I can," she said, pressing a kiss on the crown of my head. "It's not something they suggest for us to do, but when I can, I check in. You want to tell me about this pure-blood?"

My eyes popped open, and heat flooded my face. "*Mom.*"

She laughed softly. "He cares for you so much, Lexie."

"I know." My heart squeezed as I lifted my head. "I love him."

Her eyes lit up. "You have no idea how happy that makes me to know that you've found love among all of this . . ."

Tragedy, I finished silently. Wrapping my hands around her slim wrists, my gaze fell to the window. Thin branches swayed in the breeze. Bright pink flowers were open, their teardrop-shaped petals moist with dew. I stared at them for an obscenely long time before I spoke.

"Sometimes I wonder if it's right, you know—if I should feel happiness and love when everyone is suffering."

"But *you* have suffered, too." She guided my gaze back to hers. "Everybody, no matter what is happening around them, deserves the kind of love that man feels for you, especially you."

Flushing again, I wondered just how much Mom had seen. Awkwardville, dead ahead.

"And that kind of love is more important than anything right now, Lexie. It's going to keep you sane. It's always going to remind you of who you really are."

I took a deep breath, but it got caught. "So many people have died, Mom."

"And people will, baby, and there'll be nothing you can do about it." She pressed her lips to my forehead. "You can't save everyone. You're not meant to."

I wasn't sure how to feel about that. Was being the Apollyon all about death and destruction instead of saving lives?

"Can you stand?" she asked.

Nodding, I pushed to my feet and winced as pain splintered down my legs. Concern pinched my mom's features, but I waved it off. "I'm fine."

She stood, keeping a hand on my arm. "You should sit. Apollo said that it would take a little while for . . . you to feel normal."

Feeling normal wasn't possible, probably never again, but I sat on the edge of the bed and watched my mom glide toward the raised dais and the table. She didn't walk—never had. My mom had this innate grace I always wished I'd been born with. Instead, I stomped around like a cow most of the time.

She picked up the pitcher and a glass that had been behind it. "He wants you to drink this."

My brows rose in suspicion. If I'd learned anything over the last eighteen years, drinking or eating something from the gods warranted a hefty amount of misgiving. "What is it?"

Mom poured the contents into an ancient-looking glass cup and headed back to the bed. Sitting down, she handed it over. "It's a healing nectar that Apollo's son concocted to aid what he had done. You can't stay here the amount of time that it will take you to heal completely, but this will help. Even for you, there's too much aether in the air. It will suffocate you."

Suffocation sounded sucktastic, but I stared at the chalice warily.

"It's okay, Lexie. I understand your hesitation, but this isn't to trick you."

With a great deal of trepidation, I took the glass and sniffed it. The aroma was a mix of honey and something weedy. Because I knew this was my mom, and I could feel that truth deep inside me, I drank from the glass. I was relieved when I discovered it tasted sweet and not like butt.

"Drink it slowly," Mom cautioned. "It's going to make you sleepy."

"It is?" I frowned down at the chalice.

"When you wake up, you'll be back in the mortal world."

A cold wind filled my chest. "This isn't a dream, is it?"

"No." Mom smiled as she reached out, catching that piece of hair that always fell forward and tucking it back. "This isn't a dream."

Letting out a stuttered breath, I took another sip. There was so much I wanted to say. Many times since she'd died, I'd fantasized about seeing her again and had created this massive list of things I wanted to say to her, starting off with a whole slew of apologies for sneaking out, cussing, fighting, and being a general round-the-clock nuisance. And then I'd move on to how great of a mom she'd been. Now, it was funny and strange. When I opened my mouth, emotion choked out that list, erasing it completely. The words I spoke were, "I miss you so much."

"I miss you too, but I am with you as much as I can be." She watched me drink the healing nectar. "I want you to promise me something."

"Anything," I said, and I meant it.

A small smile appeared. "No matter what happens, and no matter what you have to do, I want you to absolve yourself of guilt."

I stared at her. "I—"

"No, Lexie. You need to let the guilt go, and you need to let what Ares did go."

Lowering the glass, I looked away and gave a little shake of my head. Let go of how badly Ares had broken me, how I had begged for death? Impossible. "Did you . . . did you see it?"

"No." She placed her hand on mine and squeezed. "But Apollo told me."

The laugh that came out of me sounded incredibly bitter. "Of course he did. And where was Apollo when I was getting my ass handed to me, by the way?"

A pained look crossed her face, and I immediately regretted saying that. "I'm sorry," I whispered. "He was probably off doing important god stuff." Or chasing nymphs.

"It's okay." Her hand swept across my cheek, and I was surprised to find that my face no longer ached. "Apollo is very concerned about you. So am I."

"I'm okay." The lie rang false in my own ears.

She tilted her head to the side and sighed. "I didn't want this life for you. I wanted to spare you this darkness."

"I know." Looking at her, I soaked up her features. Gods, my mom was beautiful. It was more than good godly DNA. It was what was inside that bled through—her goodness, love, and everything I aspired to be. In my eyes, she shone. And her life had ended way too early. She deserved so much more, and I wished I could give that to her. But I couldn't, so I gave her the only thing that I could.

"I promise," I told her. "I promise to let it go."

Her lips curved up at the corners. "I want to kill Ares for what he did to you."

I choked on my drink. I don't think I'd ever heard my mom say she wanted to kill anyone, except after she'd turned into a daimon. Then, she'd wanted to kill everyone. A different kind of ache filled my chest. Not wanting to think about that, I swatted those thoughts away.

Smothering a yawn that came out of nowhere, I finished what was left of the sweet drink. Mom took the cup from me and stood, replacing it on the table. By the time she'd turned around, I was lying flat on my back.

"Damn," I murmured. "That stuff . . . it's strong."

Hurrying to the bedside, she sat beside me. "It is. I wish we had more time, baby."

"Can't we?" I tried to lift my arm, but it felt cemented down. Panic clawed at my chest. I wasn't ready to let her go. It wasn't fair. I *needed* her now more than I'd ever needed her. There was something inside me and it scared me. "There's so . . . many things I still have to tell you, that I want to ask."

With a smile that wrenched at my chest, she cupped my cheek. "There'll be time later."

"But I'm not ready. I don't want to leave you. Please . . ." Strange. I forgot what I was saying. Apparently I'd drunk the ADD nectar.

As my lids became too heavy to keep open, I heard her say, "I'm so proud of you, Lexie. Always remember that I'm proud of you and that I love you." There was a pause and then her sweet voice said, seconds before I slipped away, "Don't give up hope, baby. Paradise is waiting for you in the end."

ACKNOWLEDGEMENTS

It takes a village to write a book—thank you to the awesome team at Spencer Hill Press: Kate Kaynak, Rich Storrs, Marie Romero, Traci Inzitari, Anna Masrud, and Rebecca Mancini. Without you guys, Alex would just be a sparkle in my eyes. Thank you to Kevan Lyon for being the best agent.

A big thank you to my friends and family for putting up with my crazy writing deadlines, which means I pretty much don't do anything other than write. Thank you to Cindy Husher and Stacey Morgan for talking me off the writing ledge many times over. To Molly McAdams for giving me an awesome sauce blurb and a huge thanks to my beta/crit team for telling me it sucks . . . when it sucks.

None of this would be possible without the readers. Thank you for reading and enjoying the Covenant Series. I know a lot of authors say this, but I have the best readers ever. You guys rock.

In the *Covenant* series:

Half-Blood

Pure

Deity

Apollyon

Sentinel

Daimon: the prequel to *Half-Blood*

Elixir: a *Covenant* novella

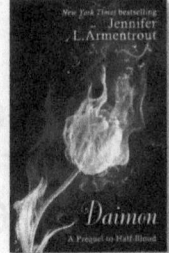

Available now in eBook and paperback